Cache

By

Donald Smith

Published by New Generation Publishing in 2021

First Edition

ISBN   978-1-80031-146-6

www.newgeneration-publishing.com

 New Generation Publishing

PROLOGUE

SOUTH AFRICA 1994

Maghiel Hendrick Grobelaar chuckled to himself as the movement of the train again made him slurp his celebratory Moet & Chandon. He could hardly believe his luck had held. A sixty-four year old Afrikaner slowly becoming a bit less agile in life's race had comprehensively done it!

It was a daring, high risk, plot. If things had in the slightest way gone wrong, he and his two accomplices would have ended up in jail with a massive sentence. Just before the exotic, world renowned, Blue Train pulled out of Cape Town station a couple of hours ago he had contacted them both with the good news.

"The dog has found a home."

They too could now breathe more easily.

In the darkness of that night they had delivered to him far more product than in his wildest dreams he would have thought possible, and his carefully laid plans had to be instantly revamped.

The theft had been necessary. It was something he had been desperate to do. White power should have kept control of the country no matter what. But forces greater than he had ordained that change must come. In a few weeks' time the movement to another regime would be complete. To him that meant disaster. White domination of the country for all time was writ large in his genes.

The new universal franchise inevitably meant black government, and that broke all the rules. His people, and all his beliefs, were being torn asunder. His job at the top of the Mines ministry was going and, together with thousands of others, he would be ignominiously replaced. Life for most whites would become intolerable.

For long past he had been working closely with another like-minded Dutchman. Johannes Kokot was a senior executive in the Mint, the place where they transformed valuable metals into coinage. Part of Maghiel's government remit was to enable the smooth running of this wealth producing organisation and Kokot was his main contact there. Over the years the two had become very close. A couple of months ago he had brought things to a head. They spoke frequently in Afrikaans.

"Our jobs are going, my friend."

"No doubt of that. If you ask me we will be lucky to get away with our lives, Mandela or no Mandela."

Kokot was scared too!

Grobelaar's rasping voice rose a whole octave.

"We must do something!"

"What? The die is cast. Our own leader has succumbed. We can reverse nothing. That nasty priest is now really in full flow----"

"No, no, Johannes, I mean something for *ourselves*. We all know we are being thrown to the hyenas. I've had my cocky successor already discussing my job with me! It was patronising and bloody awful. We must *make some money*."

Kokot looked despairingly at him.

"Maghiel, I agree with you - but how?" He had often fretted about his inability to put together enough to get his family back to the Hague where they all held dual nationality.

"By taking some of what is ours by right. We developed this country. The Boers worked it up from bush to fantastic agricultural land. Just look at the wines and foods. The wealth built the towns and, of course, alongside all of this came the---er---mining."

Kokot knew instantly what was coming.

"No, no, my friend. Not the Mint! Everything is metered, checked, weighed, re-checked and monitored every step of the way. We couldn't possibly lay hands on anything from there."

"But there are times when *you* are in control."

"That is only on my shift and it happens rarely. Responsibility is split between three of us. Everything is double checked at sorting, striking and weighing the gold and the copper. Then this is measured against coinage output. Even after that my work is fully scrutinised by some red neck."

Grobelaar's voice became low pitched and hoarse, seemingly forcing itself up with difficulty from his substantial gut in strongly South African accented English to give his words some emphasis.

"What if *sommething happenned* to this red neck guy for a couple of days?"

Johannes frowned thoughtfully. "Then I take full control. That is my contract."

"So how many krugers could you get minted in that time?"

"What the *hell* are you suggesting, Maghiel?"

"Just tell me!"

"Two days? Perhaps a thousand or more. I would have to arrange for correct blanks to arrive in place at the right time. That's always a problem with the refinery suppliers-----" He stopped and contemplated his hands, his mind trying to make some pattern to these wild ideas.

"Are there any of *us* working on those raw material supplies?"

"There is only one I would trust. Name is Van der Merwe. A funny man but underneath that he is as tough as nails. We deal directly with each other."

Maghiel Grobelaar came to the point in a flash. His friend was now quickly catching on. Urgency had to be the way. It was now or never.

"Johannes. Talk persuasively to himm. He too must know the *futillitty* of our situation. You have this one *opportunnitty* - truly heaven *sinnt* - to ease all of our families lives for the future years."

Kokot looked glum. This idea could not possibly be viable. His friend was ignoring the strict secret security measures which routinely remained in place. They would swing relentlessly into action at the first sign of irregularity. But Maghiel warmed to his plan and the voice now became staccato.

"Your contact delivers as many gold blanks as he *cann* arrange over a *shortt* period. You mint them and bring to me in an undercover way. I will hide the krugers so securely that they cannot be found. When the coast is clear we will share the proceeds. *It's that simple!"*

Johannes stared at him wide eyed.

"But - the paperwork. The new computer controls. Those cold-blooded accountants! The constant spot-checking--"

Maghiel broke in.

"It has to be done at a time when you have full charge. The problems should not then arise."

"Yes, but there are many other surveillance systems---"

"Dammit man, you have to organise it between the two of you. Kill any *stattisstic* before it gets into the system. Flash meaningless bits of paper around if necessary. *Precippittate* a riot by hiring a mob at a precise time when you have large stocks and total *responsibilitty*. Cut the cameras that are all around. Send people home for their own safety. Divert the maximum *quantitties* in to your already prepared vehicle, loaded carefully by yourself or your visitor Van der Merwe. Take full control and *treesh* the place. Then blame the rioters. But remember - timing is everything."

"It cannot work! There are ruthless really tough armed guards everywhere."

"A couple of bloody grenades and they'll run!"

"Mmm."

Kokot was thoughtful again and said nothing for a full minute. The whole idea worried him stiff. But so did black African control and the inevitable retribution which would follow.

"So, you think I could make accounts just stop?"

"Correct. Just keep all *conttrol* to yourself. Issue the instructions. Get the work through as normal. Then ensure all records for that period are either set *alaaght* or otherwise destroyed. You can arrange that?"

"Well, er, yes." He wrinkled his sun kissed forehead. "It's possible - maybe. But what about the other senior staff involved? People in the valuable metal business don't mess about, Maghiel."

"Exactly. But they will never expect a *substantial amant* to disappear. Van der Merwe himself should have no problem since any loss will have occurred, not at the refinery, but only in the Mint. Six weeks down the line if we hear nothing we can assume we're home and *draay*."

"They will know exactly what is missing. This is *gold*, man, assayed like nothing else!"

"Ok. If a truly *large* amount is missing, assumed taken by rioters, then they dare not say anything. The *integrittee* of the Mint, indeed of the whole mining industry, is at stake. They could *never* admit their *shorttcomings* to the world! My bloody department would order you not to!"

"Maghiel, what then would happen to the krugerrands?" His tone had become hushed.

"You deliver to me. I hide them somewhere very safely until we are sure any searching has *abaatted*. My secure place is already very carefully planned. Later we share the take. One third each." Grobelaar slid a small calculator from his pocket and pushed the buttons. "A total of something probably over two thousand krugers will keep us from starving for life." His eyes did an acquisitive swivel. "That *does* become really interesting."

He shoved the figures across for his colleague to read.

There was a very long silence, both men sizing up the pros and cons. Then Kokot spoke very quietly. Maghiel had touched a deeply sensitive nerve.

"OK Grobelaar. I *will* contact my friend. We wouldn't have to spike English's tea. I know for a fact that he is off in about five weeks' time for a fortnight's holiday. I am to cover for him! But I'm still pretty sure this whole thing will never get off the ground!"

Van der Merwe had proved receptive to the scheme. In fact, he positively jumped at it and became its mover and shaker. His extreme Calvinist tradition reflected Dutch Reformed teachings. For him there was no question. The whites should rule and the disastrous arrival of full-blown democracy had to be wrong. The whole scenario must lead inevitably to chaos. His was a simple, straightforward philosophy. The black man should keep to his place. The Good Book said so.

He chose his time well, increasing delivery schedules during that fortnight which coincided with Kokot's control of the Mint. There was a surge in the intake of gold. Krugerrand stocks rose fast. Then followed the worst localised riots on record, the Mint itself for a short time being penetrated and most important data destroyed.

Slick organisation and timing ensured that at exactly the right moment the heavily laden chariot was spirited away.

Maghiel had moved to the dining coach and was slowly demolishing a celebratory bottle of Bockenhoutskloof red with his high protein meal. He aimed to sleep soundly as they passed through the Karoo. Incredibly Van der Merwe, whom he still had not met, together with Kokot, had exceeded his highest expectations. In all something near to *three thousand* krugerrands were delivered in to his keeping. It was certainly one of the biggest thefts of gold ever known in Johannesburg's colourful history.

Maghiel was jubilant. For him it was not so much the money, though that was important, but their race, in some small way, was taking back its own. The plan had succeeded against all odds. Maybe, just maybe, at some time in the future, the Afrikaner would resume his rightful position and take back control of his country. But, for now, a small success would have to do.

The pudding arrived with a flourish from the waiter. This gratuity would be substantial. Grobelaar, still in celebratory mode, had chosen a huge meringue covered in chocolate with a thick cream centre. He would finish with cheese and a couple of Irish coffees before retiring, happy in the knowledge that tomorrow he would arrive back in Pretoria where his wife would listen with apparent interest about another of his short visits south to discuss the proposed new Ministry of Mines office in Cape Town.

Maghiel Grobelaar suffered a severe heart attack in the early hours. He was alone in his torment. He sped his way to oblivion reflecting on the extreme irony of the situation.

They found him in the morning with a weak smile still impressed on his cold features.

ONE

TWENTY-FIVE YEARS LATER

People noisily pushing and shoving in the crowded street were suddenly electrified by the sound of shots being fired. Piet Geldenhuys joined the masses who were struggling to get behind the protecting walls of the Sandton Sun. Inside the hotel harassed staff were trying desperately to control a suddenly challenging situation.

"This way. Large bar area up those steps. Please do not push!" The maître d' was used to being in control.

"Cold Castle please - and another for my friend here?"

Piet didn't know him from Adam but in this melee the man's chances of catching the barman's eye were remote.

"Yes please! I think we're here for some time."

They negotiated their drinks through the growing density of bodies sat on the floor, backs against the wall. The man introduced himself as Elias Mubanga and thanked his new found friend for the libation.

"What the devil is going on out there Elias? I'm Piet Geldenhuys by the way."

Hi Pete." They shook hands. "Worse than hell itself! Militant trades unions protesting as usual against living standards came up against a bunch of old Boers demanding a secure whites-only homeland and singing Sarie Marais and all the old Transvaal songs. The infuriated police are shooting in the air to calm things down!"

"And I thought they had all these things sorted." Piet cast an eye over Elias's smart suit. "You work for the government?"

"I did. They fired me yesterday. Saving money and all that. What about you?"

"I'm a sort of agent for a Brit company. Often over there."

"Married?"

"Divorced. All my fault. Away too often." Piet did not seem all that upset.

"That makes two of us. She walked out five weeks ago." Elias looked very dejected. "Lost job, no wife, age fifty-five and we never had children."

Piet smiled weakly. "Same sort of thing for me. The Yanks are taking over my employers and I am pretty sure I'm for the chop."

Elias studied the almost handsome face beneath an unruly mop of black hair. It just could be possible.

Well you're twenty years younger than me. Take my advice. Find yourself a *good* woman and another job *quickly*!"

"That's easier said than done----"

Piet stopped abruptly as automatic gunfire raked across the massive hotel door. Everyone except Elias froze.

"They're now firing *at* the Boers. It will work but there will be some dead bodies. Breaks things up in no time." Elias seemed curiously calm.

Piet was inquisitive. "You've been in on this sort of thing before?"

"A couple of years ago we all had to do part-time training in security. You learn all about how it goes. I tell you it won't be the Union guys they are shooting at!"

Mubanga bought the next round, spilling considerable amounts on his return journey.

"Thanks Elias. Nothing to do here but drown our sorrows. Have you sorted out things at home after she left?"

"Yeah. Stuff all over the place. But at least I have the flat. She went happily off with some muscle man ten years younger. Terrible shame. I could have been----"

Crump!

He was interrupted by what sounded like a bomb exploding outside. Another huge surge forced open the door and many more very scared people fell in, one bleeding profusely from what looked like a shoulder wound.

"Where on earth do we go if those police come looking?" Piet was getting more than a little worried.

"Under the bar. Thick enough to be bullet proof I should think. But they won't shoot up private property like this." Elias still seemed unperturbed.

"So they will kill people but protect property?"

"No, not people. Just militant Afrikaners."

After a huge effort those inside managed to ram the hotel door shut again, this time locking and fully bolting it.

"How long before we get out of here then?"

"Half an hour. Now they have started shooting at one or two troublemakers things will steadily begin to ease up."

After a lengthy pause he gave Piet a very straight look.

"Do you often go over to London?"

"About three times a year."

"You know how to get around there well then?"

Heavens yes. Good place when you can find your way about. I have a range of friends, which helps."

A gentle murmur was rising all around. People were trying to feel a little less anxious. Elias bent over closer, his white eyes flashing like diamonds in his black face.

"And you know Holland, no doubt?"

"Well, I suppose so. All I have there is one relative whom I've never seen. My grandfather was Dutch, grandmother Scottish."

Piet was beginning to sense something unusual in the man - fear maybe - but of what? He was fishing for something.

"Are you from Jo'burg or somewhere else?"

Elias smiled. "Born near Pretoria. Worked here in Jo'burg all my life. I had a brother who died of malaria aged thirty-six. The other one disappeared somewhere three years ago. I spent six years doing menial office jobs while we struggled under apartheid. Promoted steadily after that---but I've lost it all right now. Not the right guy for the recent style of things."

"Where did you actually work?"

"Ministry of Mines. I rose from the lowly keeper of the files to the one who created them in the last few years. How's that for progress?"

"Great stuff! Ever go down a mine?"

"Only once. I did not like it one bit and learned that I suffered badly from claustrophobia!"

There was a sudden shout from the slim, wiry individual whom the hotel manager had positioned at a high window overlooking the scene outside.

"Police dispersing. Everyone going home!"

His audience below clapped in appreciation. Sanity and, with it, safety were returning. Maitre d' raised his hand.

"Ladies and gentlemen. We will shortly open all the doors. Please go out slowly to avoid any further injury. The Sandton Sun has been pleased to be of service. Please come again!"

Applause erupted all around.

Elias looked suggestively at Piet. "One for the road?"

"Just what I was thinking. Nothing really to rush away for."

They stood up, stretched their legs and made for the nearest two comfortable vacated seats. Elias raised his hand. Two more beers were on the way.

"So you are shortly to be jobless too?"

"Yes, I think so."

"Anything else in mind?" Elias looked carefully around the emptying bar. Only a few people were staying on and none was within hearing distance.

"Not really."

Piet studied his beer. He was now sure this man was trying to get something out of him. Feeling his way. Unsure of how far to go. He had seen it once before. In that case it was a friend thinking of suicide but asking for help without saying much. Piet had worked that one out just in time to help the man save himself.

"Do you believe in honour amongst thieves?"

"Depends."

"Ok if you found something of value which years ago was lost by someone else would you keep it?"

Piet shook his head. "Probably not. Unless it belonged to the tax people."

They both laughed.

Elias said it very quietly. "Or a government?"

Piet breathed out very slowly and thought fast. Something was taking shape.

"Has this anything to do with mining?"

"Maybe."

"And you may be in need of help?"

"I will need somebody's help."

"What sort of *value* are we talking about - roughly?"

"Perhaps several million dollars."

Piet stiffened. He certainly did not believe that. He had been around too long, even at the tender age of thirty-three, to take that figure seriously. But he felt a surge of inquisitiveness. Even twenty thousand----. Blow it he had nothing to lose.

"Right Elias. I'll help all I can, but obviously you will have to spill a few more beans."

"The funny thing is, Pete, you tick all the boxes. I rarely meet people like you. Experienced yet young, overseas connected, soon to be unemployed and therefore hungry. And we get on. Here is my personal card." He rested it down on the table.

"Do you have one?"

Piet handed over his company card which contained his address, phone and email. Elias perused it carefully before pocketing.

"I must go. I may be in touch."

They rose, shook hands and Elias quickly departed leaving behind a half filled beer glass and a very puzzled Piet Geldenhuys.

The next few days were frantic. Piet's sister, Suzanna, had given birth in Pietermaritzberg. He did a quick visit. It was a boy to be called Harry, a name much approved of by his father who was "British" and from the Cape. They wanted Piet to stay over for a week but one night was all he could manage.

He then visited three employment agencies. He was surprised to find they all liked his past experience in the wine industry, particularly when considered together with the detailed marketing research he had carried out during the past four years for the highly rated company AandA of London. One of the agencies had already fixed two employment interviews for him to attend.

Back home - a small apartment adjacent to Pretoria's Freedom Park - Piet spent the day completing the compilation of his latest, and probably last, survey. This time London had asked detailed questions about shoes. He had visited fourteen specialist outlets where he discussed shoe design styles with many interested parties from a variety of backgrounds - racial, wealth, class, creed and sex, and had now processed the details in the form London required. All had just been emailed to David Johnston when his mobile vibrated against his chest.

"Good evening Piet. It's Elias. Sorry it is so late. Any chance of your coming round here for a chat?"

Piet recognized his voice instantly. He had felt sure he would hear nothing from the man again. On reflection their meeting had seemed to Piet to be like ships passing in the night.

"Bit difficult, Elias. I have some job appointment interviews coming up."

"Just a short time. What about tonight?"

"Do you *really* want me Elias?"

"Yes. You must come."

Piet pulled the card from his wallet.

"Ok, just off the Jo'burg super highway. I'll be with you in a couple of hours."

"Thanks Piet. The beer will be good."

Piet pocketed his mobile, re-walleted the card and smiled to himself. This whole thing really was a madness. Nothing could possibly come from this man's fantasizing. The situation was crazy and would lead nowhere. Maybe he should return the call and cancel. That he did not do so landed him in a situation way beyond anything he could possibly ever have imagined.

Piet arrived on time. He had no problem in finding the small ground floor flat. The lawned garden led to a solid looking entrance. Two small surveillance cameras peered protectively down at the front door. Elias appeared immediately, shook him vigorously by the hand, bolted the door behind them, and led through to a large lounge.

"Beer, or something else?"

"I'll settle for what we had before!"

"Excellent."

Elias ushered him to a seat at the substantial table and opened a couple of cans. He sat facing Piet and had beside him a large open case full of what looked like paper cuttings and documents. He clearly had no wish to mess about and came straight to the point.

"In the Sandton Sun you asked me if I worked for the government. I did. Right from the early days I worked in the Mines ministry. Menial task, but I was young and needed the money. You can guess what it was like for us then. There were three of us minions looking after the boss man's every need."

"The top man?"

"Yes. Very top. Man called Grobelaar. My responsibility was the filing system. I did that job for years. I became indispensable. Knew where everything was and never caused any trouble. But, but, but--- I never let on that I spoke Afrikaans. Many Africans speak it but few really fluently." He gazed slowly around the room. "Ask me why that was important."

"Why was that important?"

"Because one day I overheard my boss pushing one of his friends into bringing about a theft."

"Where from?"

"The Mint. That internationally famous place that churns out incredible amounts of wealth!"

"I know it well. Not far from home. Impossible to get anything out of there. You heard all this just before apartheid came to its end?" Piet was aware of other similar situations occurring as the white man lost his authority.

"Exactly. This man came often and I was sometimes able to listen in, albeit with great difficulty. They planned to lay hands on a whole lot of krugerrands. My boss took the train to Cape Town a day after rioters broke in to the Mint. It may be that he had quite a bit of luggage, but I don't know about that."

"Good heavens. Maybe they got something out and he hid it all down there!"

"That would be one's first thoughts though I've never been able to follow through satisfactorily. He died of a heart attack on the return journey and had clearly not informed his associate of the hiding place, as the man called in and bullied me for all his papers soon afterwards. I am sure he was looking for clues as to the gold's whereabouts. But he took nothing away on the first visit."

"But then you did?" Piet was eyeing what was before him on the table and catching on fast.

"Yes. I guessed what they were up to. I took all papers of significance – files, diaries, small scribbles, desk drawer notes, all of that, and substituted meaningless and inaccurate bits and pieces."

"Very smart!" Piet chuckled.

"Well I wasn't the filing clerk for nothing! The very next day, on the pretext of it being a Mines priority matter, the same man, whose name was Kokot, came back accompanied by a man I had never seen before called Van der Merwe. They took what they thought were all my deceased boss's papers."

Piet smiled. "So, you have all the genuine paperwork, any bit of which could point to a fortune, and they took away a load of rubbish."

"Precisely. But I became a bit scared, rightly as events have shown. For years these two men did not give up searching. Luckily for me, and quite reasonably, they would have felt that junior staff like us would know nothing."

He paused for a moment, letting me catch up. "I was promoted to be an executive in the department some eight years ago. It was then I learned that some of the long-standing personnel who stayed on had been visited over the years at home and pilloried about what they knew of Grobelaar's movements in the few days before he died."

Piet felt himself becoming inexorably snared in Elias's trap and recalled their conversation in the hotel.

"This whole thing must be of considerable value."

"You're there in one. Three months ago, Grobelaar's closest retired office colleague was tortured - poor guy knew nothing - and was then left in a state of permanent agony. He died shortly afterwards. The police do not know who did it - but I do!"

"Those two are still are looking - getting desperate, you might say. Time is running out?"

"Yep, exactly right. Until that death I felt nothing. There couldn't be much in it or the Government would have made a big noise at the time. But those killers and the sum of their activities really concentrated my mind. No Mint in the world would own up to any large loss - well it never happens, they are too well monitored. But if something major *did* occur *they would never be able to admit it.*"

He glanced back at the table.

"I have kept this case together with two other similar ones sealed up and buried in the garden, virtually forgotten, all these years. That murder and my age has brought me up sharp and to another level of thinking. Maybe, I say to myself, now is the time to lay hands on some money!" He looked at my glass and pulled two replacement Castles from the adjacent fridge. "I dug up and opened everything. All three cases were in pretty good condition. And after weeks of work on it I think I know *exactly* what and *exactly* where!"

TWO

The two men stared at each other for some time, saying nothing. Eventually Elias broke the silence.

"There will be a lot of effort required to recover the krugerrands and then gradually to exchange them for cash. I feel you are the man to work with me on both matters."

"Elias, why on earth me? Do I look that harmless? I might turn on you and take the lot!"

"Two reasons, Piet. One, I've looked you up everywhere. What you told me about yourself was totally true. Two, you are exactly right for me, particularly with all that overseas knowledge. And I judge you to be a gentleman, not at all a crook."

"Ok Elias, I love that sort of compliment! So how many krugers are involved?"

"I'll tell you in a minute. But first we need to agree on the take. If everything we do goes well, I suggest your share is one third."

Piet did a quick think. He really had nothing to lose.

"I would call that generous."

They shook hands. Elias was in a hurry. He moved on quickly and pushed a 1994 diary across the table.

"See 28 March."

Piet looked carefully. "It says C.T. Presumably short for Cape Town. Bit of a scrawl."

"The press at the time reported a disturbance at the Mint on 26 March but there were no further reports after that and there is no other reference anywhere. Whole thing went stony dead."

"Played down by all to the point of boredom. Governments do that all the time you know."

"I agree. Now look at this. Took a whole week before I came across it. And a further week for me to understand the significance." Elias extricated a rough invoice from one of the heaps of paper and pushed it across.

Piet studied it. The company was called "Roadlayers" and the amount 450 rand. He read aloud. "For sundry repairs to outside road Min of Mines 26/27 Mar 1994."

"I went to great lengths to check back in the 1994 accounts. This bill was neither presented nor paid by our officials. Grobelaar must himself have settled in cash. Paid on the spot! Just why would he do that?"

"Ye-es."

"I have examined all around the area. There is just one small road repair and it is very nicely finished off. Almost certainly unnecessary and illegally done. I am convinced the heist was stashed there at night by Grobelaar and simply filled in the following morning under his supervision. The dates are remarkably close."

"That could very much be chance Elias."

"Yes, I agree." His voice went low, almost to a whisper. "Look back at the diary, bottom of that weekly page 24 to 28 March."

Piet looked. "There's nothing there."

"Turn over."

Pete saw it and caught on immediately. At the very bottom of the page was a tiny encircled word "R'layers."

"He knew them! This little note was probably to remind himself of their name. Elias you are brilliant!"

The dark features creased into a wide smile.

"Right. Now you wanted to know quantities. I did a rough calculation keeping to the low side. I estimated possible depth of hole in road. The space would accommodate up to two thousand kruger mint "jewellery" boxes. They can be packed two hundred to a parcel. My guess is ten parcels would easily fit in to that hole. There would be many more if not boxed."

"How much is a kruger in, say, sterling?

"Work on seven to eight hundred pounds. It varies a lot."

Piet went very silent. He would make a half a million pounds or even more dollars. But money like that never came that easily.

"Elias, I do not understand the trip to Cape Town?"

"It was a decoy. You see the date of the train trip was 28th, one day after the hole had been sealed. The whole thing was a charade. It would have foxed any investigation which may have taken place. Or maybe Grobelaar intended double crossing Kokot and Van der Merwe. Either way nobody would think of digging up part of a road to have a look!"

THREE

It was three a.m.

A large portable floodlight was set up with a small road warning barrier. Elias's extremely well paid "no questions asked" pneumatic drill operator began to work flat out on the square patch of road. The night was dark and it was raining and blowing hard. Late night party people were by now safely tucked up in bed at this hour. There was no traffic.

It took five minutes of deafening shock waves before the man had opened it up. He then withdrew to prepare the replacement tarmac. Piet and Elias armed with a pickaxe and shovel made a deep hole quickly. It was hard work but the potential reward made them notice neither the blisters nor the wet.

Earth and stones were thrown up on each side and the deeper it got the more the anticipation grew. Any time now there should be large boxes or other strong packages showing up. Piet hit something which sounded metallic. He dug more carefully and found it was an under-road pipe. On and on. Toil and travail. It had to be soon.

Ten minutes later doubt began to enter their heads. They dug frantically, like mad men, pure earth now, down, down much deeper than they had planned.

"There's nothing there! Nothing!"

Elias screamed the words into the night, unable to believe it. To his mind this was simply impossible. Impossible because he had been so careful. There simply *had* to be something. They inspected the earth base and the sides of the hole, digging away yet more of the sediment.

"Elias---we - were - wrong!"

Piet said it slowly, trying hard to be as gentle as he could. His knew what this project meant to his friend. He also knew in his boots that fortunes never came easily. He had said this to himself so many times but had nonetheless been willingly sucked in by Elias's enthusiasm.

"Well, where are the bloody things hidden?"

On and off Elias had invested many months in this project. The disappointment was unbearable. He stood looking disconsolately down the hole, oblivious to the water streaming down his face. His detective work had been rubbished in a matter of minutes.

Piet forced himself back to the reality of the moment. "We've got to get out of here Elias. We're actually committing quite a crime. We mustn't get caught now." He started refilling the hole.

Elias staggered off to fetch his man back. Barrier and lighting were removed with rehearsed speed and thrown into their waiting car. Pneumatic drill man completed the road repair job quickly, cleaned up the area, and made off to his own escape route. The whole exercise had taken them less than an hour. The result was not what they had anticipated but at least in the morning road users would notice nothing.

Piet drove a completely broken Elias home, tried unsuccessfully to console him, and then made his way back to Pretoria. Neither of them felt up to conducting an inquest.

FOUR

LONDON

It felt like the end of the world.

I had arrived back from a two-day trip to Frankfurt. The lift took me rapidly up to the twenty-third floor. As I entered our open plan offices I knew at once. There was no pleasant, or even rude, greeting to welcome me back. Simply a sea of glum faces speaking volumes about the chill winds of redundancy. I hung up my coat, lowered my briefcase to the floor and sank down at my desk all in one movement.

"So, it's happened Jonny?" He was my deputy.

"Yeah, 'fraid so, David. It's as we thought. We are all to be looked at over the next month. They reckon most of us marketing people will go."

We were a British great. Armstrong and Acherson had just celebrated one hundred years of constant growth. Foods, beverages, household cleaning agents and the whole gamut of consumer products gave the company huge prestige in business circles. If you wanted toothpaste or cat food it was not a problem. Pharmaceuticals and cake mixes were internationally known. We did it all! Hundreds of branded products were made and sold by well over two hundred thousand employees and agents working in our company operations around the planet.

In recent years the track record had been so good that our Uncle Sam competitors in the form of Global Trading Inc. could not keep their hands off. That company had assembled massive dollar reserves and borrowings with which to tempt our loyal shareholders, and, at the same time, satiate their own corporate lust.

Five years ago, AandA had enticed me away from my Japanese employers as they needed my specialised field of expertise. My small new department, together with its wide range of overseas agents, fed carefully programmed computers with enormous amounts of information. The distillation of this enabled even the meanest of AandA companies in the farthest distant land to predict its people's buying habits more accurately than any of our competitors. Sales worldwide continued their constant increase.

"The boss wants to see you upstairs."

Elizabeth, our industrial psychologist, had just come back down. She was looking very shocked.

"What, right now?" I needed time to settle and mull things over.

"Yes, he says it's urgent."

John Wilberforce, a good man who had been with the company some twenty-eight years, stood admiring the Vauxhall Thames far below. He waved me to a seat.

"Good trip?"

"Yes sir. There are strange things happening in Germany. Mind you, they think there are peculiar ideas doing the rounds here too!"

He turned away. He wasn't interested!

"You're fully aware of the ramifications of this takeover?"

"Yes, they told me as I arrived in. I'm not surprised. The Yanks have been feeling around for some time now. Does my department have a future?"

"Days rather than weeks. New York and Connecticut are working frantically on *eradicating duplication*. They are being unpleasantly forthright."

"What are my chances?"

"Better than most. Man called Eisenbauer was asking after you. Does your sort of sleuthing work for them. Could you continue to operate under him?"

"No. He's good, but not that good. Impossible. I've met him at the odd seminar. Bloody loud-mouthed too."

"Well, start looking. You have a superb track record. And you'd better make sure your overseas people are fully briefed on what is going on. It's all been a bit of a shock."

He went suddenly limp. For him, approaching retirement age, this must mark a particularly unsatisfying end to a brilliant career.

I muttered it quietly, "They're not as good as us you know."

"Nowhere near, I would say. But that is why they are paying over the odds to get us. Your division is a special target. They are desperate to understand how we get our results. They may well want to hang on to you for a while."

He turned to look out across London again and I made for the door, my mind building to a mild frenzy. I was the best micro-marketing analyst in the business. I would *not* go back to the Japs. Few other British companies could fully utilise my skills. The Germans? Maybe, but I ought to speak the language. And I did not wish to live in the Big Apple. Go independent? Not enough resources.

At thirty I was alone, probably soon jobless, and unattached. Sally, with whom things had been going well, had broken it off months ago. She said that my boffin image, workaholism and constant travelling was massively upsetting her. I believed it. Then followed a couple of parking fines and a bad speeding conviction. The car was written off in a crash. In my tiny new flat, three storeys up in Charles the Second Street, two computers fouled up and had to be replaced. My routines, like getting into bed on time, ceased. I drank too much and what little cooking I did was hell. Worst of all, despite the angry departure, I missed her.

The only relief from depression came with work. Intense computer programming research enabled me to forget for a time. I could get lost in the mind-bending stuff we were doing. Recently I thought I might just be beginning to beat it.

But now this!

I *must* be positive! Talk with, and help, staff. Inform all overseas contacts of the changes about to happen. Feel out employment agencies, peruse journals and newspapers. And, above all else, keep Eisenbauer away from all on-going research I had not yet put within the company domain.

FIVE

Elizabeth Nye was well-heeled whichever way you looked at it. The family mansion had looked down at the river for two hundred years and her father, in today's more unsettled times, had somehow kept things going. Posh schooling, high academic achievement in psychology and human resource management, wide experience in Anglia Ruskin and Oxford, and then practice in Harley Street, all contributed to her pedigree.

She had been there for three years when I booked in for an appointment. It took quite a time for her to realise that *I* was interviewing *her* for a job with *our* company. My research on her had been thorough. Initially she was furious with me, incensed at being misled in such a way. I thought she had mellowed when I tried combining what I thought was humour with excitement about the scope of what we were asking. International travel. Psychological analysis applied to half the human race in order to guide the product design of a big number of items. Enterprise in a massive way.

But she threw me out. Like an idiot I persisted by phone, emails and, even that strangest of things, a handwritten letter. Eventually, despite herself, she joined AandA as a strategist in the psychology of marketing. Father, who was a high court judge, had made clear to her his view that she had taken leave of her senses by linking with a bunch of artisan manufacturers.

She was good at it as I had sensed she would be. Her analyses, put together with massive detail provided by our worldwide army of agents and fed through our specialist computer programmes, added again to AandA market share. As time went by she had become synonymous with success. Her cerebral input allied to our programming skills brought about systems unequalled anywhere in the annals of company marketing history.

But it wasn't just that. She possessed a knack of unravelling the impossible when all else was failing. She was a born optimist who somehow made her line of thinking win through against impossible odds. Call it persistence. Call it luck. Or maybe even something genetic. Whatever it was I had at that time no inkling of how crucial she would be to us as future events unfolded.

SIX

As I was entering the lift my mobile vibrated.

"Jonny here. Yank called Jack Eisenbauer is demanding to see you down here."

"Thanks. With you in one minute."

A couple of staff from Accounts joined me to descend.

"Hi David. Floor twenty-three?"

I made a quick decision.

"No. Stop her at twenty-four please."

Once there I sped across to our IT room to which only Jonny and I had access. I grabbed my latest research disks, computer sticks and the all-important small red notebook from the safe, and pocketed them. My eyes scoured the room. There was no other "top end" stuff lying around. I returned everything to normal, pulled the door locked shut and ran down three curving flights of stairs to my office. Eisenbauer was pacing around like a caged tiger.

He was well over six feet tall, with black sleek hair which was lacquered across his head. Handsome in a low-grade fashion magazine style. And piercing blue eyes with a demanding nature to go with them. My five foot ten, mousey brown hair and modest facial arrangement was simply no match.

"Hello Jack, good to see you."

It wasn't.

"Hi there Dave. It's been a long time since those meetings we attended."

The accent was that of Jack Kennedy "going to the moon." His grip was vice-like. He slid possessively down into the visitor chair facing my desk.

"Just thought I'd call in. Circumstances, you know."

Unsurprisingly there was to be no small talk.

"Yes, well, it's all yours now."

He glanced around and judged nobody was quite within hearing.

"It could be yours too."

"You want to offer me a job?"

"I have Board authority to offer you six months before any decision is made."

They wanted to milk me. Then throw me out.

I played poker.

"Sounds great, Jack. I was told two months."

He lowered his voice, oozing confidentiality.

"That's for most of the others. You're the brains behind the good moves. We need you."

"How long do you want for a decision?"

I guessed the answer.

He didn't disappoint.

"Three days."

No way could I get another job in *that* sort of time.

"Make it a week?"

"No sorry but the Board said-----"

I cut him short.

"OK Jack. Three days it is. Good of you to think of me in this way."

The toneless sarcasm was wasted on him.

"Now, any chance of having a look at your IT set up?"

That really did not take long in coming. Involuntarily my arm slid across the slight protrusion in my breast pocket.

"Well we don't usually open shop for anybody outside the company, and then even only on a need-to-know basis."

That would be what he expected.

"Come on Dave. You know I have to move in now the purchase is complete."

"I haven't been instructed to that effect."

He wouldn't stay nice for long!

"Well we might look at things together. You know I *could* get the OK to inspect right now." He pulled out an expensive looking mobile.

I was right!

"OK Jack. My deputy will show you around. He has full knowledge of the set up. Bad timing, but our man in Madrid will be visiting me shortly."

I gave no time for reply and walked quickly across to Jonny's desk to hand him the key.

"Jack would like a look around the den. There's *nothing* he can't be shown."

He nodded his understanding. I introduced them although they had already half met. Jonny took over.

"Come upstairs with me Jack. I'll explain all that's there."

They went speedily off.

I sat and started moving the now pointless paperwork around my desk. I had known Jack Eisenbauer Jr for years. He was good but I was better. Even if they offered me a long-term contract there was no way I could work under him.

My phone buzzed.

My first difficult closing down session was due to begin with Raoul Gonzales, hot over from Spain.

SEVEN

"Caught you at last, David Johnston!"

The following morning I was drowning my sorrows alone in our twenty-fifth floor auto coffee shop. At a touch our Italian company machine had just frothed out a cappuccino.

"I came in here to think, Elizabeth. We all have a lot of it to do." I smiled at her. "What sort of coffee?"

"I'll join you with the same if I may."

We sank back in to two very comfortable chairs - more company products - and caught the glint of the distant London Eye moving imperceptibly in the weak sunshine.

"Sorry to interrupt you but this won't take long."

"Take as long as you like. I'm not too busy just now!"

"It's about Eisenbauer."

I frowned. "What about him?"

"He's offered me a job. He had me in for a chat in the directors suite on the thirtieth floor. I must say I liked that sumptuous rosewood table and the works of art hanging around the walls. I'd not been up in there before. He doesn't think you and Jonny will be staying that long. And I guess most others in the department?"

"Correct."

"What do you think about the man, David? You know him better than most."

"You are exceptionally good. You know much more than he does about our methods and he's very aware of that. Your expertise would be pretty useful to him."

"He offered ten per cent more money and said the product range would increase. They want quite a few of their products to go through our marketing machine."

"Keen to hang on to you. There's a lot they don't know about us and how we do things."

I gulped down my coffee in an attempt to disguise my raw feelings about everything. The turn in events was difficult to stomach now that it had actually happened.

"What would you do? He did talk quite smoothly about a couple of marketing people from the States coming in shortly and fitting seamlessly into our system."

She looked at me almost pleadingly.

I cursed myself for messing up her Harley Street career.

"Keep Eisenbauer waiting! He will not be the easiest man to work for. Feel out all relevant employment agencies. Study press job adverts. Check through your old psychology mates. I think you could keep your options open for some time. He won't lose interest in you. And don't worry about the ethics of it all. The Yank in business can be brutal. I'm not sure about how "seamless" the arrival of their people will be."

"What will you be doing?" She sounded faintly motherly.

"First, finishing off here. Wishing a fond farewell to all our overseas colleagues. Then I think I may take a holiday - I have a few bucks in the bank. After that the great search."

She sat silently studying me for a couple of minutes. Then her pretty features hardened.

"Ok David. What do you *truly* think of Eisenbauer."

"I can only go by what I have heard from others in the past few years. It seems he is not above some pretty nasty activity to further his career interests. With him anything goes. Mind you this sort of low-level activity does exist in a wide range of human activity - he just seems to be better at it than most. He is an unprincipled bastard, not to be trusted. If you do work for him always watch your back."

We finished our coffees and wandered slowly out to the lift together.

"You know I could have told you all of that, just by meeting the man for a short time. Feminine intuition. He was oozing hypocrisy from the very start of our meeting. It's difficult to know exactly what to do. If I do stay awhile it can only be for the short term."

I felt totally inadequate when it came to giving her any advice. I had landed her in this situation. She seemed a very unhappy lady and I could now do damn all to help.

EIGHT

That night I could not sleep. I had gone to bed early to try to blot out the day's horrors but they all came flooding back.

After my chat with Elizabeth I had gathered together all eleven in the department. They of course knew that Eisenbauer was already milking them, trying to get to grips with our ways of working. We sat round in a circle and chatted. Most already sensed they would soon be on their way and had fallen into the anxious state of probable joblessness. It was written large across their faces. I told them how sorry I was that we were breaking up - but incredibly they wouldn't let me develop the subject. We were a team. Mates. As a group we had been unstoppable. *They* would not let *me* be miserable. It was all too emotional for words.

One would have thought some anger might have been directed at me. In these sorts of situation irrational thinking often takes over. Somebody has to be responsible for *me* losing *my* job. Governments get blamed for high inflation. Top entrepreneurs can suddenly find themselves aggressively attacked by their employees, often for things for which they are not responsible. And departmental heads can be held to account for something like this which was completely beyond their control.

But there was none of that.

I was pulled up sharply from my thoughts as suddenly my ring tone started quacking. I shoved away my pillow and pressed on the light. Who on earth --- at this time of night? I slid from the bed, moved across and extracted the phone from my shirt pocket.

"David Johnston."

"Hi Dave. It's Piet Geldenhuys."

"Good heavens! Good to hear you Piet. Where are you?"

"Came into Heathrow. *Any* chance of seeing you before bed time?"

"It's just on midnight!"

"I know. Problems though. I need to speak."

"I'm sure you are aware? The Yanks have done it to us."

He quite possibly didn't. Whenever I'd stayed with him in South Africa he had rarely looked at television or read any newspapers.

"It's not that. I need just half an hour. *Please*."

There was an urgent tone to his voice. I knew I had nothing ahead except an agonizing and sleepless night going over and over the events that had visited our company.

"OK. Remember the address?"

He had only once been to my new flat.

Well--ar--actually I am already just on the corner of the Haymarket. Took a taxi on arrival. I could be there in ten minutes."

That simply wasn't like Piet. Turning up unannounced. He really did have something on his mind.

"Right. You know the way up. Don't wake the neighbours."

"Thanks, Dave. You're a brick."

He clicked off.

I had little time to slide into pants and shirt and make the place somewhat less bachelor-like. Not that it really mattered. His was a similar sort of male existence. I had just removed a huge mound of clothing when he entered through the flat's opened door. All of six minutes I would say.

"Hello there Piet."

We shook hands warmly. He was breathing heavily. Handsome face, dark hair, tall with a permanent African sun tan. He hadn't changed much since I last stayed at his Pretoria home some six months previously.

"Sorry to barge in like this." He dropped a small bag down in the corner of the room and hung up his coat.

"Beer, tea or coffee?"

"Tea please. The plane substantially alcoholed me."

I wandered out and plugged in the kettle.

"I'm getting the message there's something pretty urgent? You're not usually this active, particularly at this time of night."

He made a face, thinking, wrongly, that I disapproved.

"It's a long, extraordinary story."

"Leading where?"

"Maybe nowhere. Complete conundrum just now. But in view of events I think probably somewhere."

He lowered himself slowly into a seat and pulled out a small pocket book. The kettle called and I made the tea. I carried in the mugs and a pack of biscuits in case he was hungry.

"Sorry about the timing but, you know, sometimes in life things happen. I want to deal with it all and I need your help. But I'm afraid it has to remain private."

That was easy for me. He wasn't just our business partner. He was my close friend. When Sally marched out on me he had, calling on his own experience, helped to drag me back from that desperate pit of despair known only to those who have been there. For that I owed him an awful lot.

"No problem at all Piet. I'll never say a word without your say-so. And I'll help you all I can of course."

My tea remained untouched and forgotten as I sat back and listened to his increasingly extraordinary story.

NINE

"I ordered the usual salads and a South African white."

Piet had remembered the drill from his last London visit. And he had managed a table with a view. I sat down opposite him and gazed out at the lightning fizzing across the river.

"Excellent. A pity you couldn't do something about this country's weather, like bringing over some of that South African sunshine! On a day like this I really do envy you people down there."

He grunted, shook his head, and cleared his throat.

"Now where did we get to?" He was keen to get on. Small talk was obviously out.

I searched the depths of my mind for what I remembered from last night. "You and Elias had failed to find anything by digging up the road. You collapsed with exhaustion on to the couch at two in the morning muttering that you hoped I understood the urgency of the situation and that you would see me in Barnaby's for lunch. I crawled into bed and actually slept soundly for once!"

"Yes, well, sorry if I was a bit of a bore. Difficult to be coherent about a situation like this." He shook his head as if to codify his thoughts.

"A question for you Dave."

"Go ahead."

"Just how good are you with all the research us backwoodsmen feed in to you?"

"We are the best."

His brow puckered. He was questioning my claim.

"How do you *know* that?"

"Simple. We get the best market results by far. Company profitability is higher than any competitor. You can check the statistics if you know where to look. Why do you think the Yanks have gone out of their way to grab us?"

"But all those market details I send in are nothing special."

"One hundred per cent wrong! You are asked for much more information than is normal. You may not appreciate it but all those questions are arranged in a way to try to prevent boredom on your part. We are looking for more off-centre, seemingly unrelated, stuff. Come off it Piet, despite our efforts at simplifying things you are always bloody complaining about the arduous nature of the work!"

He uttered a sort of sigh. "Ah yes, those ghastly forms. Ok then. *Exactly why are we so good?"*

"Precision, programming and processing. Done well it works." I was enjoying the meal and the excellent wine but I really was not in the mood for another last night session. "Piet, where is all this going?"

"You once said to me that you would soon be able to profile the person - the buyer if you like. With the right input you could forecast how they would act in most circumstances."

"I said that?"

"Two years ago in Pretoria. I was impressed."

"I went too far."

"You mean it's not true?"

"You're stepping over the boundary mark, Piet."

"Promise nothing will go farther than here. I have good reason for asking."

His persistence was something new for me when discussing my work. Eyes usually glaze over.

"Right. You are only the third person to hear what happens right at our cutting edge. We have developed ranges of software which can accept enormous amounts of information, process it, shake everything around and feed out results in forms suited to answer the questions we have asked. Usually it is about what people will buy today. With jigging we will soon look forward and forecast with, what I think will be great precision, decisions for our companies about what they should make for long into the future. Others do this but not to such a high degree."

"You are not there yet?"

"With a little tweaking we will be - or would have been."

There was a short silence. He was mulling over my words.

"Ok. You look forwards and anticipate market buying decisions. From there you will soon be able to anticipate the directions of a person's life?"

"Not quite. It would just be impossible to study every individual. Hell, there are millions of them. We can simply take existing methods a crucial step farther." I was on the verge of bringing about the conversation's wind down when two coffees miraculously arrived.

"But you could look at only one person if you wanted and if you had access to sufficient detail?"

"Well---yes, I suppose so. You wouldn't make much profit from that though!"

I sensed at last that we may now have arrived at the crunch point of what had dragged him all the way over from South Africa in such a hurry.

His steely eyes were fixed unswervingly on me.

"What about looking backwards?"

"Well you would already be aware of what had happened in their past. There would be no point! Silly question?"

"But *could* you do it?"

I found myself doing what I hate in others. Swirling the remaining coffee around the cup and staring at it, in my case in frustration. The going was getting harder to take.

"Yes, you could make an intelligent guess at actions people may have taken in relation to events which occurred, I suppose, but the inputs would have to be a re-run of history. How on earth would that be of any use?"

"You couldn't simply reverse everything?"

"No Piet, it very obviously is not like that."

He ploughed on unabashed.

"Is your very top level stuff now in the hands of the Americans?"

"No."

"You have it and they don't?"

"Yes, well the sensitive end of things is still being fine-tuned."

"I have a proposition for you."

"Piet I do not want to set up some bloody thing in South Africa for delving into people's ancestries. The whole world is at it and it would be horrendously boring. Frankly I cannot think of anything I would less like to do. Neither can I get involved in any of those damned lost diamond searches. Your country abounds in stories about that. People desperately scratching around underground, usually finding nothing, and sometimes taking massive risks and dying as a result."

"Mubanga is dead."

Those three words changed everything. I jerked upright, instantly recalling last night's story. He now had my unwavering attention.

"A week after the dig I received a call from the Charlotte Maxeke hospital in Jo'burg. They said he had not long to live. I drove there fast and found him with massive head and body wounds, just about able to speak.

He pulled out a small recording machine, placed it on the table, and pushed ON.

"----got around to me at last---I think the drill man was---reporting to them---everything, just everything. They---watching me some time. My flat was t-totally turned over. Smashed my head and face. Said I must have—papers. I said nothing. They k-kicked me to the ground. I said nothing. No nothing at all. Piet I know k-k-rugers somewhere. See paving st-t-ones fifteen sixteen---p-path to flat. Promise you will keep---looking."

"Of course, Elias. I promise."

"Beware-- those two-------d-desperate---will k-kill. But do it my f-friend. Take this."

Piet turned off and faced me, raw emotion showing.

"He passed me a small envelope he had been clutching and then suddenly let go, was no longer conscious, and died within half an hour. They knew of no relatives."

I sat back and stared at him.

"God, how awful. He was right! They *are* still looking!" I was glued to the seat, all my scheming for a quick departure forgotten. *Sometimes three small words can change the world.*

"Yes, and there's something else."

At that moment the waitress arrived.

"More coffees please and a couple of brandies." Piet did not even ask me.

"What?"

"He once told me he had a warning system in place."

"Where?"

"In the flat. Stuffed in a drawer with a few false Grobelaar papers was a sketch showing a basement wall in the Mines Ministry building with an arrow pointing very precisely at a section of it. The only writing was an exclamation mark. And---you know what? Last week my local radio reported on an explosion in Jo'burg."

"Elias's old offices?"

"I went around to check. It was in the basement."

"So they raided Elias's flat, beat the hell out of him, searched everywhere, came up with this clue, blew the wall in and found nothing?"

"Got it. He was betting on not being at home if they ever arrived. Blowing the wall would have warned him that they would soon be visiting him in person."

"Poor old Elias. Wrong place. Wrong time." I examined my newly-arrived brandy for a couple of minutes. This whole thing was turning into what might be a major exercise. I had to find out more.

"Your recording mentioned paving stones?"

"Yes. I pulled up stones fifteen and sixteen and found two sealed units. The third was under number seventeen. Together they contain literally thousands of Grobelaar's papers - office, private, diaries, calendars and an old wallet, though heaven knows how Elias obtained that!"

"Interesting reading?"

"Yes, but the *mass* of information is enormous. Somewhere there may be a clue as to where the loot is stashed - and that is the information that Kokot and Van der Merwe seem willing to kill for."

"But there may well not be."

"True, but unlikely. Think about it. He spent most of his working life in that office. He thought, he planned, he kept seeing Kokot and, according to Elias, he became incredibly active in the last few days before the heist. There have to be a range of clues, maybe going back some time. Things must be written down somewhere. Dates, times, places."

"So where are the papers now?"

"Just before I left I fedexed them to your place. The tracking says they will arrive tomorrow." He put on his brazen look. "It was the safest thing to do - and I thought you might be interested."

"What!! Bloody hell! You didn't even ask!!!"

"I honestly think you are the only man alive who could make this search work. Your analysis facilities could do it. We've been all over that. You sort of said so." He pulled out that small notebook.

"This is the third time that damned book has been produced and you've not looked at it once!"

He was not at all fazed and opened it with aplomb as if it were a valuable relic whose contents should be checked.

"Elias said he once heard Grobelaar extract from Kokot an estimate of at least a couple of thousand krugers being possible to produce in the time available. It was apparently a whisper in Afrikaans with a bit of English thrown in."

He paused, waiting, toying with me like a fish slowly approaching the hook at the end of his line.

I bit hard. "What's that worth in sterling?"

He studied the book.

"Two thousand krugers are today worth, give or take a bit, something over one and a half million but under two million pounds."

TEN

SWITZERLAND

At an earlier age Breck Haffenbeker had operated in
the intelligence section of the notorious East German
Ministerium fur Staatsicherheit, or Stasi. These highly
effective secret police infiltrated every aspect of daily
life, kept citizens in a state of permanent wariness, and
held copious files on them. All Stasi staff were hated
and feared. He had distinguished himself by setting up
a range of collaborator spies who operated throughout
the country and reported in on anything which
remotely challenged complete state supremacy and
control. Later, he was involved in penetrating West
Germany's military and intelligence services, thus
entering the unedifying upper echelons of the Stasi
spooks.

When the Berlin wall came down he fled to
Namibia where he had a range of connections. He was
soon sought out and recruited there by an international
organisation which officially no longer existed. It had
once sported the name "Diamond and Gold Resolution
Society," known inevitably as "Daggers," but its
activities became so illegal and often violent that it had
to go underground. Breck's atrocious record suited
their requirements like a glove.

Daggers was covertly funded by some of the large
internationally known precious metal companies and
dealers. No accounts were kept and often many of
those company board members were unaware of, or
were careful to avoid, any skulduggery which might be

going on behind the scenes to protect their company interests.

Now, nearly thirty years later at sixty-three years of age and still very much hands on, Haffenbeker had risen to the top of this small but effective organisation. He had made his headquarters here in Geneva, where he lived. The building comprised an unremarkable three bedroomed detached house, a large part of which served as the organisation's operations centre. At any time their business records and all other related paraphernalia could instantly be destroyed, though such evasive action had never yet been required. The disciplined care he and his colleagues deployed had for years kept them well below any Swiss police or international intelligence radar.

The most recent project which they had undertaken involved working with a Russian mining oligarch who had crossed disastrously with the Kremlin and who wished to escape his home country, taking as many of his assets with him as possible. Their expertise ensured all went well and the reward for work done exceeded one hundred thousand dollars plus all costs. But this one had been an unusually close call in St Petersburg where they had seasoned successors of the KGB, assisted ably by competitor GRU activists, snapping at their heels.

His reminiscing ceased as he saw a familiar figure some ten years his junior hurrying to his front door. Three days ago he had received from this man a coded message urgently requesting a meeting. Marita, his multi-lingual Spanish "Mata Hari" wife, had prepared the spare room. She could do both housewife and spy with equal expertise and was fully active in all that went on.

"Greetings Albert."

He shook hands warmly with his subordinate and took his case.

"Hello Breck. I'm a little late." He missed out all other formality. "I had to come quickly and unfortunately the first plane out of O. R. Tambo was held up. Extraordinary how this happens just when one is in a great hurry."

Breck, aware that something important must be coming up, motioned him to a seat and poured coffee from the flask Marita had prepared before going out for her weekly shop.

"So, what is this urgency all about? Something remunerative I would hope."

"Well, yes maybe. Do you remember M85, the file that has come up from time to time over the years? It was shelved, we thought for good, about five years ago. Maybe the word "Krugerrands" would help your recall?"

Breck's mind went through a few numbers. M85 meant nothing. They had a reference system which had changed a couple of times since he had been doing that job. Krugerrands, however, meant a lot. His mind moved inexorably from one memory to another and the penny quickly dropped.

"Yes, ages ago, that theft from the South African Mint. We were seen as more or less legal then. They tolerated us as we could sometimes be of use to them. The government approached us to ask for our help. This blatant theft was about the only matter at that time which we were never able to solve for them. We tried like hell and our investigations went on for a long time, but we kept coming up with duff information." He paused, memories returning fast. "I recall there was a strong indication that the top Mines government servant might have been implicated. But he died - I can't remember how - and then later it all fell flat."

"There has been movement. A man whom we know was somehow involved has been beaten up, left badly wounded and has subsequently died."

"What, all these years later?"

"Yes."

"And?"

"We are pretty sure the two guys who have been harassing a wide range of people over many years are implicated. Although we gave up on the case long ago I have been quietly monitoring their activities. They always fully covered their tracks. Until recently. A man who has worked for many years in the Mines ministry was beaten up in his home, we are pretty sure by these individuals, and he died. We immediately installed our own cctv on site viewing the dead man's house - our normal practice in cases like this as you know - and two days later we were watching pictures of an unknown man at night vigorously digging up the path. Eventually he pulled out some boxes - they looked like small, smart metallic suitcases sealed in some sort of polythene."

"The missing krugerrands?"

"No. Nowhere near heavy enough for the figure of two thousand plus that the Mint informed the government were stolen. Our records show they admitted to you at the time that they never actually knew the exact quantity as the robbery, although on a huge scale, was carried out too quickly and methodically for production to be thoroughly investigated and recorded."

"So?"

Years of experience prevented him from showing it but Haffenbeker was now falling over himself to know more. This project had legs, real long, strong marathon-winning ones! When involved with this matter at the time he had been devastated that they could not solve it. It had been a total failure. He was delighted that they were back in the running.

"We're not sure - but we think almost certainly the boxes contain the documents which we know a man called Kokot and his thug friend have been chasing all these years. We just managed to keep the two of them in our sights all that time in case they ever were to come up with anything." He glanced meaningfully at Haffenbecker. "These contents could be maps or other material maybe indicating where, with some precision, the loot was stashed. We just do not know."

"What are the police doing?"

"Simply investigating a murder. No idea of anything else."

"And the two killers?"

"Gone to ground. They are probably safe if they do nothing. I think it very unlikely the law will catch up with them, not after they have evaded it all this time."

"Damned good show! What is the resultant on this?" "Resultant" was a word coined by Haffenbeker to express the fee they would make for any project's successful conclusion.

"We would get ten per cent if the present South African government can recall and indeed honour the agreement made with us long ago, and we could come out of hiding and be returned to their good books. Probably not difficult given the circumstances. That would come out at up to a quarter of a million dollars we think. Of course, it's difficult to be precise."

Can you find the guy with the boxes?"

Breck could smell blood, his face now becoming slightly contorted. He was back into territory he knew well. The passing years had in no way mellowed his instincts for profitable action.

"The system registered his car number plate. His name is Piet Geldenhuys. We watched him for a short time. He flew to London."

ELEVEN

The following morning I left Piet anxiously tracking his parcels. Arriving in at my desk I immediately checked on the whereabouts of Eisenbauer. He was out for the day and unlikely to be back. I went straight up to the Den, removed some notes from my pocket that I had scribbled down last night, and positioned three chairs so that their occupants could speak comfortably together. Then I summoned Jonny and Elizabeth.

She arrived first. Her eyes swept around the small room taking everything in at one look. "Ooo, I've never been allowed in to this male preserve before. Promoted to the top in double quick time!"

Jonny breezed in and we all sat down. They were clearly turned on when I swore them to secrecy. Then I told them a condensed version of the whole Grobelaar story. They listened with increasing interest and looked very thoughtful when I mentioned the likely value of the heist. In all it took about half an hour to get the full story across. I didn't pull any punches and let them have the full details, warts and all.

"You want our help." Jonny didn't take long, and I suppose his conclusion was pretty obvious.

"First I wanted to dissect the whole thing with you. Then you can each decide for yourselves. I spent most of last night mulling over my personal situation. Career, conscience, anger, excitement, acquisitiveness, revenge, continuity of a murdered man's work. All of that and much more."

"Then you didn't sleep much." Elizabeth had been studying my care-worn face!

"I trust Piet and know him well. We have worked together for several years. I think I, or maybe we, can assist him with his problem. But, of course, there can be absolutely no guarantees of anything in a situation like this."

"I think you have missed out the most important matter." Jonny was showing his normal attention to detail and seemed quite wound up about something.

"What?"

"Danger! Those two guys. They sound extraordinarily nasty."

I realised safety should of course have been at the head of my list. "Sorry. Yes. Attention from Elias's murderers if they were ever to know of our involvement will be direct, possibly painful and even life-threatening. The history indicates that they stop at nothing to get answers as evidenced by their shocking track record."

"How much paperwork was in those cases?"

"All I know at present, Elizabeth, is that there are hundreds, maybe thousands, of documents, cuttings, small booklets and jottings of all descriptions. It seems Elias did a thorough job without anyone at the time realising what was happening. He was of course in charge of most office files and maybe was the only person to have access to Grobelaar's more personal paperwork. Piet took it upon himself to arrange for its arrival chez moi today."

"And the content of every single scrap of paper must be programmed in, scanned, classified and prioritised to the target - which is where he hid the loot. I'm bloody in!" Jonny had also got to know Piet during his fleeting visits to London and I knew the two of them got on well.

"Me too! I'm not so well up on your precision stuff but I jolly soon will be." Elizabeth, too, was quite obviously turned on by the project.

"OK, thanks. I thought you would want to help but the whole thing could end pretty abruptly - even nastily."

Elizabeth, striking a very laid-back pose, said quietly, "We're with you every inch of the way." Something in her attitude seemed to indicate this was a natural progression for her. It was her way. A problem in business when it came up would be turned by her into a near normal event and she would always deal with it accordingly. No panic. No rush. Just calmly follow through. She usually solved things in the end.

I had my expected responses from them. "Right then. There will only ever be the four of us in this. It will probably end in total failure. If it succeeds something up to half any net profit, I suggest, should go to Piet who brought in the whole story and we share out the rest equally."

"You should get more than us." Elizabeth, I knew, was pretty well off.

"If we ever find *anything* I am sure we can work things out amicably." I returned quickly to my plan. "Security. Let's put that at the top of the list. Very simple. Not a word to anyone, and I mean anyone. Large amounts of money sometimes do awful things to people - as we have already seen. If we keep shtum we are close to being safe, although nothing in this sort of thing can be absolute."

They nodded agreement.

"Now - the way of working. I have at home the hardware and software which might just do this job.

Difficult to make computers think but Jonny and I have systems capable of, believe it or not Elizabeth, a range of what might be called thought. All of it will have to be moved somewhere where we can work safely and without interruption for pretty lengthy periods of time."

"That's *the* horrendous question these days. Just where?" Jonny knew we needed space. He had frequently worked at home in my small flat with me on mind-bending ideas and would be aware exactly of the floor area required.

I wanted ideas, having tried to resolve the matter last night without success. "We have to decide quickly. We need to rent rooms somewhere which will not draw in anyone's attention."

"Expensive and few and far between in London." Jonny had himself been fighting with housing problems for months.

"You could install it all in my flat?"

"Thanks Elizabeth, but, like my place, as time goes by that may be a bit obvious and therefore potentially dangerous. You are linked to us and we to Piet. We want somewhere that is completely detached from any of us."

There was a long silence. London is a huge place but very crowded when you are seeking privacy and any form of real estate. We sat studying one another, waiting for the slightest spark of an idea to lighten up someone's features. There was a long silence while we all thought deeply. I knew what would be going through their minds. I had been there last night. It would not have surprised me if we finished up without a viable solution.

"What about hiring a caravan, perhaps in a holiday park somewhere? Some of those sites are near to

London but away from its swathes of humanity. And a modern caravan offers pretty good office space." Jonny looked hopeful.

"Too many miles away for quick access. It would have to be not too far from where we all live." I had already considered that one.

We were jerked out of the next long silence with a softish shriek. "Got it! Of course! The perfect hideaway!"

Elizabeth beamed at us.

"OK. Spill the beans." Scepticism and hope in Jonny's voice.

"Little Venice on a narrow boat. Huge space inside. Great security, I mean you can lock everything away very safely."

I didn't like pouring cold water on her excellent suggestion but I knew the area well. "They are all buddy-buddy. Would know all about us in no time. We wouldn't be able to keep them out. The people there are far too friendly, I fear. And, anyway, I believe the whole area is packed out. There's tremendous competition for residential space there and along the whole Thames."

"OK, so here's a better idea." She came down an octave to her reasoned discussion style. "I was there the other day. St Katharine Docks beside Tower Bridge. We get a suitable boat and book her in for, say, three months. Springtime should not be difficult. In the summer months finding space there will be a bit more tricky. People often go in for long periods. Some stay permanently. You can get power laid on and most facilities can be supplied. One could be warm and *secluded*. Nobody knows anybody, Dave. Well, only a very few long-term stayers who spend some considerably time aboard actually talk to each other. All the others are coming and going the whole time and no-one would ever guess, or even be interested, in what was going on inside anything moored up. I've been there! I've lived it. I know it! And I think it really would work."

I looked at Jonny. His face, too, had brightened a lot. Bingo!

I tried hard to think up any disadvantages with her idea. I was not a seafaring type but she could obviously look after that side of things.

"Go on Elizabeth."

She beamed. "We don't want anything special. Just seaworthy enough to negotiate Tower Bridge and all around there. Big and square but not *too* ugly to attract attention. Perhaps a souped-up retired hire boat. There are quite a few around. Lots of space. Cooking if you need it."

"Price?"

"Up to thirty thousand pounds would do it."

"Ten thousand each!" Jonny was adamant, although I guessed he had less immediate cash available than we two.

Elizabeth, sensing our warmth towards her idea - well there was no instant dismissal of it - instantly assumed full control. Boy, and was she capable of that! She knew boats. I was now seeing my newest member of staff in full flow. No time was allowed for further discussion. She just went straight in.

"I'll handle it all. Jonny, you can be my crew. I can train you up very quickly. In a few days' time, David, you can move everything in. Best just before dark. Definitely nobody around then in that place. We'll let you know."

TWELVE

Jessica Rees-Morgan, now Lady Banforth, but in a younger life Marguerite Villeneuve, strode purposefully out from King's Cross station, hailed a taxi, and gave the driver his destination. She had that day come in from her country home outside Cambridge where she would spend the occasional day with her globe-trotting elderly old-Etonian homosexual husband, Lord Banforth. Most of the time she was alone.

They had married five years ago on her twenty-eighth birthday. He wanted a token blonde and had assumed she was after the high life. What he did not know was that she needed a cover and occasional access to the country's movers and shakers. To her he was simply a pawn in the game. She had always treated the male of the species with controlled contempt, feelings which it paid her to keep well hidden. Even in this modern day and age there still existed an assumption of superiority on the part of most men. It was not confined to France. Her experiences in England had simply reinforced her views. But, pushed to the ultimate, most invariably showed themselves to be mere wimps. She had, of course, encountered a couple of exceptions, one of whom she was now about to meet.

As a young language graduate from the Sorbonne she had been carefully selected to join the small secret women's section of the Direction-Generale de la Securite Interieur just prior to its official formation in two thousand and eight. She learned to exhaustion about espionage and counter terrorism and a whole range of personal mannerisms aimed at extracting often delicate information from others. Her achievements were noted as outstanding (for a woman of course!)

It was some eight years later whilst working on a Paris project linked to uranium that she became involved in Niger. Whilst there she met a Daggers activist engaged from a different angle on the same project for another paymaster. She had enjoyed being manipulated, recruited and very neatly removed from her French employers by this Scarlet Pimpernel style set-up. She spoke fluent BBC English but bore absolutely no loyalty to that nation. She was precisely the sort of person Breck's people sought, and she fitted in wonderfully to their illegal organization.

To date she had been active in three projects, two of them involving months of shadowy work. All were concerned with "righting wrongs" in the Hatton Garden area of London, and each was brought to a successful conclusion. The thankful client mineral companies had, as always, been more than generous to her Daggers superiors and they, in turn, to her.

Today was quite different. Twenty-four hours ago she had been summoned urgently with a coded message. That in itself was unusual. Something major was afoot. Daggers normally liked to keep things simple. Rushing around simply risked drawing attention to their operations which was the last thing they wanted.

The taxi dropped her in Piccadilly. The place was buzzing with activity. Some were simply window gazing; others were business people desperate to get to places. Coffee shops and ordinary stores were heaving with activity. There was colour, movement and noise everywhere. This suited her. She could sink into obscurity. As she walked towards Green Park she was nonetheless checking and re-checking that nobody followed as well as frequently consulting her watch. At exactly midday after one final glance around she entered the Ritz hotel and felt a great sense of relief as Breck Haffenbacker rose from his seat in the foyer and came forward to meet her. He gave her a hug and they walked slowly to the lift. On arrival at the correct floor she followed him out and along to room 412. He ushered her in, closed the door and turned up the radio. By chance they were playing French military music which she felt was a good omen.

Standing immediately in front of her was a smallish, wiry, hungry looking man with greying hair and a most unattractive, unsuitable moustache. He was dressed in a sagging grey suit and his blue tie was badly knotted.

"Marguerite, this is Albert Jacobi, our man covering Africa, resident in Johannesburg. You haven't met before, although he has been with us for ever."

"How do you do." She shook hands and they sat down. She was immediately sensing in the man a sort of macho let's get on with it feeling, as if she was already holding things up. Life had taught her that some men, particularly the less effective ones, often felt women a drag on quick action. But she knew Haff - that was *her* chosen name for him - would not tolerate any nonsense of that kind, were it directed towards her. Rather, he would usually appreciate her input and always treated her ideas with respect. She was now in no doubt at all that something very positive was afoot. She knew Haff well and inwardly registered the energy he was exerting on this as yet still unknown project.

Watch your step, Marguerite, this could be very interesting.

"We have a situation." Haffenbacker went straight to the point. "Albert and his team are on the track of a krugerrand heist from the Johannesburg Mint which took place over twenty years ago. We were given instructions by the South African authorities after the theft to root out the perpetrators and bring them to justice. More to the point they wanted us to find the krugerrands. Until now we've had no success. To be honest we all but gave up after a couple more years of expensive investigation. Unusual, but I was in control there at the time and very much regretted that we had reached a complete dead end."

"Who stole it and how?" Her face was now total concentration.

Jacobi took over. So far this was a small triumph for him. He wanted to make it big. *Little man, top hat.*

"The name is Grobelaar. The man was head of the Mines department. He inconveniently died just after he had hidden it. Our only ongoing contact with the case was to continue to keep a limited watching brief on his two accomplices who clearly were not informed of the theft's hiding place. Over the years they have beaten up some and talked nicely to others to try to establish the gold's whereabouts. Months could go past without action and then suddenly they would investigate yet another individual who worked with, or was related to, Grobelaar. To date they would seem to have achieved no tangible result, well nothing that our guys have noticed."

"They've been at it all that time?" Marguerite sounded incredulous.

"Yes. It seems to be an all-consuming long-term project with them. But out of the blue a couple of weeks ago the desperation game really hotted up. The years were passing by. They had found nothing and were no doubt getting distraught. They had zeroed in on a man called Mubanga who was Grobelaar's office clerk for many years. Throughout we think they had assumed he was too low-level to know anything and so was left out of their investigation. He was attacked, tortured in the most gruesome way, and he eventually died. We discovered that a man called Piet Geldenhuys, who is somehow connected with Mubanga, dug up something at night from his garden. We followed it through and know that he is now in London."

"Any idea what that something was in the garden?"

"The pictures showed up some sealed cases."

"Containing?"

"He opened one. It seemed to be full of files and paperwork of all sorts, but our night time pictures were unclear. We thought about this a lot and studied the pictures closely. They are probably office records stolen by Mubanga at the time. He must have had an inkling of what was going on and squirreled away his boss's documents for future investigation."

"And maybe not, in which case all this is a waste of time." Marguerite's forthrightness was asserting itself. "Maybe we could---"

Haffenbacker broke in. He knew when to stand up to this assertive young woman.

"We think that's wrong. If you were planning to hide a fortune, and could tell no-one, you would note things, plan, mark a map, make clues of something you had to remember. Even keep a full-blown record -

somewhere privately of course. There has to be a pointer there I think."

"Albert, how do you know that man's name?"

"My guys left a cctv hidden at the site after Mubanga was taken to hospital because we knew of his association in the past with Grobelaar. Routine in this sort of case. It also recorded the car number plates but failed to get a picture of his face. We eventually tracked him to Pretoria where our people broke in to his place while he was away. The only filing cabinet there was securely locked. They left that untouched. No other bags or boxes were in evidence despite a thorough search throughout the whole home." He coughed and then pulled an envelope from his pocket and gave it to her. "Here are details of his flight Jo'burg/London and a few other notes. But nothing that gives direct detail about where he may now be or indeed what he is doing."

"Thanks, Albert, that may be useful!" She smiled for the first time since they had met. She now knew exactly what her instructions would be.

"What we would like you to do, Marguerite, is to establish where he went after landing at Heathrow. For some reason he came here to the UK. Above all *we need to look into those cases!*" Haffenbacker was appealing and demanding all at the same time. She could read him like a book. He was in great need of help.

"Yes, I can probably do that." She certainly had no doubt about her own competence with this sort of thing.

"And then follow through wherever it leads?"

Marguerite was now registering hugely intensified vibes coming out of these two. The atmosphere in the room was akin to pressure build before the breaking of a huge thunder storm. They were positively bristling and trying not to show it. There must be a considerable amount more to find out. The best way was straight in.

"Overall value of the heist is---?"

There was a long silence. She had reached the icing on the cake with one straight question. They looked blankly at each other. Eventually, with a giveaway shrug of the shoulders and a look at his senior colleague from Jacobi, out it came.

"Nearly two million, maybe more. The exact amount is unknown." Haffenbecker breathed it out slowly.

"Pounds, dollars, rands or something else?"

"Dollars, maybe pounds."

She now understood the urgency of the summons from Switzerland. They were dealing with a fortune. But she was in no way finished with her search for complete understanding.

"Surely whoever finds keeps?"

"Well, we are committed to the South African government who asked us in in the first place." Haffenbacker could not look her in the eye.

"That was twenty odd years ago, Haff! To them we no longer exist! The last thing we go near these days is a government! *You* said that, not me. They see us as crooks. Probably don't even know we exist right now. Have you had *any* contact in the last ten?"

The ensuing silence was accompanied by an embarrassed shuffle from Jacobi. He gave off all the signs of having been caught out and was behaving like a naughty schoolboy. She hoped he was better than this at the day job.

"Well, have you?"

"No."

Marguerite's mind was now racing. She was key to what was undoubtedly Haff's largest ever assignment and now she fully realised what the two of them had been hatching. Fierce training in France allied to her own innate cunning was now guiding her. How to get everything out in to the open? She must make things easier for them!

"The two accomplices names?"

"Van der Merwe and Kokot."

"They sound like very dangerous individuals."

Albert responded firmly for once. "They've gone to ground. The police are looking for Mubanga's *murderers*. I can assure you they won't be raising their heads any time soon."

She glanced slowly from one man to the other. "Haff, I really think we should find these krugerrands for ourselves. Nobody would know. Nobody would be hurt. The whole thing has been hanging around for years, more or less forgotten. Maybe you've thought of doing things for us Daggers for a change. No paymasters to please and all that formality---"

The two men looked at each other, poker faces slowly changing. She had to come in. They'd already discussed the possible, in Haffenbacker's view inevitable, outcome. There was no pulling the wool over this lady's eyes. And her appreciation of the situation was bang on.

"That could just be. What do you think Albert?"

"I would suggest---"

"I would like one quarter of a million dollars if we are successful." Marguerite now wanted no more prevarication. They needed her and the expertise she was able to bring to bear on the situation.

There was hardly the lull that one would expect. No pause for thought. Not even one of those male grunts. Haffenbacker, the Alpha male boss, came straight out with it.

"Right. Agreed."

Nobody, not even Jacobi, would ever find out that he was pleased the figure was no higher! He had achieved what he came to London for and was more than satisfied. Dealing with Marguerite was a tricky business at the best of times. He had sealed a good deal and he was not in a mood to let Albert prolong matters.

"Time for lunch. We can discuss the detail over a good meal." He turned off the radio, picked up his briefcase and they followed him from the room.

THIRTEEN

A dark, foggy and damp February evening is not normally the best time to offload heavy computer equipment, boxes and other paraphernalia from a car, carry it down some steps, then wheel it a couple of hundred yards and load into a boat.

It was three days since Elizabeth had found her ideal craft. She completed the paperwork and then quickly taught Jonny the rudiments of crewing for her. It was tough for him but he was up for it. Two rigorous sessions, each lasting about three hours, and he had learned enough to control ropes and fenders while leaving Elizabeth to do the rest. Additionally, they arranged the fixing of double security systems for main cabin entry. Then, yesterday morning, they had taken Marianne down river and through the lock into St Katharine's as the Thames rose.

She was a river hire boat, safe for tidal use but incapable of more than minimum speed, and the price had come in at just under twenty thousand pounds. When inside the haven they had moored her comfortably alongside a projecting jetty in their allocated slot. This was away from all contact with the main marina. Marianne was booked in for three months with an option to stay longer if necessary. On the port side was moored an unoccupied fifty-foot cabin cruiser and to starboard a neglected old river boat that looked as if she had not been boarded for months.

Elizabeth unlocked and slid back the door into the main cabin. She dropped off her small bag. Jonny, following, wheeled alongside the two large computers, lifted them up on to the boat deck, clambered aboard, and then carefully lowered them down inside the main cabin. Both then returned to unload the remaining items and carry them from car to boat. This whole exercise was completed in half an hour. Jonny then drove off to find a parking while Elizabeth set about fixing the substantial thick curtaining she had made and making the place as comfortable as possible.

Piet and I arrived half an hour later. Jonny welcomed us aboard, worthy able seaman that he had now become. Getting into the boat was not nearly as tricky as I had thought it might be.

"Incredible!"

I had only one word for what they had achieved. This upper cabin was exactly what we wanted.

"Magnificent!"

Piet had another, his eyes moving quickly around.

"Your three boxes are down below." Elizabeth knew how anxiously he had awaited the Fedex delivery. She and Jonny had taken special care of them - they were of course crucial to the whole arrangements we were making.

With curtains across and lights on we sat around in the cabin while Jonny prepared a hot chocolate drink on the boat's small gas cooker. *Crew's work, not the skipper's!*

"I think you ought to know that I resigned from AandA yesterday. It was quite amicable and I am now free to work on the project full time." Elizabeth smiled happily. There were obviously no regrets on her part.

"Excellent. I cannot believe it was *that* simple though. What did Eisenbauer have to say?" Something way down inside me relaxed.

"Just that he was 'real bloody sorry.' No exhortation to stay or anything like that. That surprised me when I recalled previous conversations which I had with him. I think he realised it was not going to work, no matter what."

Jonny passed around the mugs. He appeared to have done a good job and must have been taught all about the galley during his short period of instruction. I wondered wickedly if his cooking was up to much.

"I'm staying on. They wanted me to. Three-day week for two months. Longer term - nothing was said. However right now it helps them and keeps me financially ok. The rest of my time I will be here processing all this stuff - that is if you still want me!"

They had answered all the questions which I had been storing up. No preliminaries. No need now to clarify anything. Elizabeth totally without commitment, Jonny free much of the time and Piet and I intending to concentrate on nothing else. We were clear to proceed.

"Jonny, that's great. You can show Elizabeth how things work with the computers - she knows most of it anyway. Starting tomorrow if possible?" It was the weekend.

"Yes please!" She was keen to begin and cast a quick glance down in the box direction. "Do you think we could have a look now?"

I turned to Piet. He nodded and Jonny climbed down the three steps into the lower cabin and, with some difficulty, fetched up one case which he laid flat on the deck in front of us all. Piet punched in the code numbers and the case instantly flipped open. He then handed Elizabeth a small card.

"All three cases open with the same number. Keep this somewhere really safe on the boat and I guess we should all memorise it. Elias passed it to me as he was dying in hospital! It was his last effort towards finding the looted krugers. You know that guy was really something, not even spilling the beans when he was being horribly beaten up by those bastards."

We all looked as closely as we could at the contents as Piet pulled the lid fully open. He shut his eyes, thumbed around inside, pulled out a few of the items randomly and then told us what he had.

"Scribbles on a pad, small diary for 1993 and a schedule of visits for one month. Some of the stuff in there which I have seen is awful waste paper basket rubbish - but I suppose even that may contain some clue. There is a huge amount of material in here and the other cases, lots undated. I really have not yet studied much of it but what I have seen is really not very exciting. Checking through all of this on my own would take months. That is why I immediately thought of you, Dave, when I saw it all for the first time."

I took over, ignoring what I thought was his attempt at a joke. "This all has to be read and put into the system. Most, maybe all, will not immediately throw any light on what and where Grobelaar deposited the heist! But my guess is that something, or even a few things, maybe small scribbles somewhere, will jerk us right out of the boring day to day negativity we will experience. The system should, with luck, cache snippets of information which may seem to complement each other. But it is, of course, not infallible. It will also make mistakes and incorrect assumptions which is where we humans come in. The system sorts out some things and we try to do the rest."

Jonny's mind was running ahead, linking our late evening mind-blowing sessions with the here and now.

"Presumably we use our new T.A.S.K. system with variable inputs?"

"Yes Jonny. Spot on. That's what I felt as soon as I saw the problem. I suggest you and I fix the fine detailed programming here - say very first thing tomorrow morning. What do you think about six o'clock before anyone's around?"

He nodded. Elizabeth smiled. It was pretty clear she would be in on it too.

"We need a longer-term rota system. Two people should always be here when we work. Jonny and I are the experts. I suggest he works with Elizabeth on his days off and, say, Saturdays, and Piet and I get together the rest of the time. Piet, your most important task throughout will be to interpret any Afrikaans into English - there's quite a bit of it I imagine, probably a full-time job doing just that. Elizabeth can perhaps also double up as cook - food, drink etc. By the way, wonderful curtains!"

She beamed and grimaced all at the same time. A comely mother figure she was not! Jonny would certainly be doing his share of the donkey work.

"And I have to mention it again. Security is top priority. Remember people have been beaten, tortured and killed and there seems to be no limit to the effort those dreadful guys will use to achieve their ends. This boat is the safe house. Keep it that way. We must take care to come and go casually, as often as possible after dark. Make ourselves authentic by sometimes carrying boating stuff. Geographically we are a long way from South Africa but always exercise care. Piet, I think you are the only possible connection with all that has gone on out there?"

He looked thoughtful. "The only way I could be known was my short contact with Elias in the hospital. Almost certain that those who murdered him would not be anywhere near there. They'd be desperately keen to remain invisible. I saw nobody but two nurses and a doctor as well, of course, as a number of other patients and relatives who were milling around."

"Good. But vigilance everywhere please. And tell me if you have any suspicions, however far- fetched! Those two thugs Kokot and Van der Merwe will still stop at nothing!"

I was getting nervous again.

FOURTEEN

Early the following morning all four of us assembled on the boat. Jonny and I went below and installed, tested and opened up programmes which we had decided were appropriate to the requirements of the situation. That was done, unsurprisingly, in record time as we had been working on them for many months. In a short while Jonny shouted up at Piet for the information which he had previously asked him to obtain.

"Krugerrand details please."

Piet was fully prepared.

"Size in millimetres----Diameter 32.6 Thickness 2.74 Weight 34 grams. President Paul Kruger on one side and a springbok antelope on the other. If you want to know when the project began, they were first designed and minted in 1967."

"Great. Quantity we think we are looking for?"

"We think upwards of two thousand, but it could be lower."

"Anything else we should know?"

"There is a small amount of copper in with the gold - long ago they found it hardened the coin. The value goes up and down on a daily basis and there can therefore be sudden substantial movements in price. This depends on the world economy, the politics of aggression and all sorts of factors. Presently a krugerrand of this size is worth approximately eight hundred pounds sterling." Piet could think of no other snippets of information which might be relevant.

"Right, we have the detail. All set to go." Jonny nodded to me to start familiarising everyone with the process.

I moved over and took four non-Afrikaans items of information from the opened case. I slowly read out the content of each and fed in the detail - the date where possible, place, time, action and description. In all, processing those four items took about fifteen minutes but I knew it would quicken as we worked our way through it.

"This really is going to take ages!" Elizabeth had been studying her watch and mobile calculator assiduously. "If we have, say, two to three thousand items it will take weeks even if we go flat out just to upload everything. After all that, presumably, we have to analyse whatever details are found. We are then in for long periods of studying the results and reacting accordingly. No griping at all on my part but we ain't arf goin'a be workin' our bleedin' socks off!"

We all laughed. I watched a strange look had passed very briefly across her face when she was talking kruger quantities and for a brief second I sensed her heart wasn't quite in it. Maybe it was nothing. She was right. No doubt about that. I did my best to explain things as succinctly as possible.

"The main thrust of the analysis will be done electronically and those results will be straightforward logic with maybe some of what we would call thought thrown in. But human imagination, flair, assumption and brain power have not been replaced. Although this technology is better than most, if not all, it is where *it* finishes that *we* begin! With luck we should have pointers indicating directions where we should further investigate. Probably not much more than that." They all nodded, now deep in thought. "We should start immediately and work whatever times we have available, over and above our agreed rostering. In other words, we really try and push things along fast. Lights at night must not be visible outside the boat. Security has to be first and foremost always. Jonny and Elizabeth I suggest you start right away now. Leave the Afrikaans stuff for later. But as ever some things are more important than others so Piet and I are off to that coffee shop for breakfast. Any problems call us."

During the next few days we settled in to a concentrated routine which was flexible enough to maximise working hours. Elizabeth's dire predictions were not actually coming to pass. Piet particularly surpassed himself spending many hours turning Afrikaans into English in good time for the rest of us to process. Every visit was made carefully and often after dark. Each one of us in his own way had become both serious and really positive about what we were doing. Together we would solve Elias's problem if humanly possible and, maybe, make ourselves become a little wealthier in the process.

FIFTEEN

The following day Marguerite was still elated. Things were really moving. She was good - very good - at what she did. Haffenbacker was one of the few men worthy of her respect. And he believed in her. Her husband, unsurprisingly, was again away so she had the run of the estate to herself. She would find Geldenhuys and, by fair means or foul, make a quarter of a million!

The small pack she received from Albert had simply contained written confirmation of his air flight to London. No hotel booking. No contact names. A few copies of supermarket bills, a car service with itemised list and what seemed to be a personal note reminder saying "Lon - check AA dates."

It was this last clue where she decided to start. No-one at the Automobile Association in Basingstoke recognised his name. Buying, selling, customer service, legal and all other departments were adamant. Smaller establishments in London and Cardiff too produced the same negative results. Then she scoured the country's Alcoholics Anonymous centres. Helpful, but secretive they had to be. There was nobody in management bearing that name. And almost certainly the man was unlikely to come six thousand miles simply to deal with cravings of the kind with which they specialised.

He had travelled South African Airways to Heathrow. But where to from there? Her hunch was that he took a taxi from Terminal 2 in to London. Find the cab? Impossible, there were Pink Apple Cars, Uniform Transfers, traditional Black cabs and all sorts of others. It would have been dark, as he landed early evening. Probably went to a hotel--- she spent the day telephoning the most likely ones but had no joy. She called the very few London phone listed Geldenhuys names. Not a Piet among them and nobody had any advice to offer. No one suggested they could be a relative – even a distant one. They all seemed to be Brits!

Two days later, after a massive country-wide search her cool began to slip! The man seemed untraceable. With the name he had she should have come up with something. Her husband arrived back from his Helsinki business trip and the Estates manager straightway came nosing around in his obtrusive way. Home life was assuming its normal bloody awful course. Her frustration rose. This was ridiculous. She could usually find people. Her French training had been meticulous. Never give up. She could hear the indoctrination music rising in her mind now---"jamais, jamais, ja---mais"!!----ok, but where on earth next?

Taking tea with his lordship she was regaled with stories of icebreakers off Finland, permanent winter-long freezing conditions and gorgeous warm coffee shops where business was often done over a really hot cuppa. Whilst there he had purchased a whole new clothing outfit that she thought seemed more suited to a trek across Greenland rather than a visit to the smart boardrooms of Finnish business. His sartorial sense was sadly lacking, but that was of no interest to her. Gently, she led him away from Finland and on to another subject.

"What does AA mean to you Gerald?"

"Automobile Association of course. Why?"

"A crossword I was doing. That wouldn't fit."

"Architects Association, Armstrongs and Acherson, Ack Ack, Anti-Aircraft, Alcoholics Anonymous---can't think up any more on the spur of the moment, my dear? But one of those might fit."

"No, all too long. Ack Ack wouldn't be any good either."

He resumed his boring Helsinki business stories, punctuated by fairly regular gulps at his favourite Scottish tipple, and she sank back into her traditional form of hibernation.

"Armstrongs and Acherson!"

It was the following morning before Marguerite was free enough to make calls on her mobile. She had checked on the company. It was absolutely massive and had many interests in South Africa. She had missed it and was kicking herself. Paris would really have taken her to task. *You should have widened the net much sooner.*

"I wonder if I could speak with your South African representatives please?"

She was put through.

"Africa desk?"

"May I have the names of your people in London who deal with South Africa?"

"Overseas Director John Wilberforce. I'll put you through to his secretary."

There was a click.

"Clementine Payne, Overseas. How can I help?"

"Oh, thank you. My name is Christine Adler. I am off on a business tour of South Africa shortly and want to visit some of your establishments there. Do you have a person in the country with whom I can discuss things on arrival?"

"Umtata, James Groth. Based at Drack Camping. He co-ordinates all links between AandA companies in South Africa. You might give him a call on arrival. Full details are on line. May I have your company name please?"

"Yes, of course. World Wide Hydraulics." She recalled a name Gerald occasionally mentioned.

"Have a good trip."

"Thank you. Goodbye."

SIXTEEN

I spent Sunday with Piet.

We fed in a huge amount of information. Some of the bits of paper looked vaguely as if they could lead somewhere, the rest had to be rubbish. But I knew it all must be electronically assessed and categorised before us humans took a look at the end results. The method we had evolved had to be strictly adhered to and we did not deviate from the task in hand.

We worked well together despite huge differences in background, experiences and temperament. Maybe the tinge of danger in what we were doing cemented the bond between us. The system that we evolved working together enabled us to move much faster than originally anticipated. In all, during that one day, we dealt with at least one third of the first box's paperwork. Well up on Elizabeth's calculations!

After thinking through the situation Piet had elected to sleep and live on the boat. He borrowed bedding from me and brought in enough food to keep the wolf from the door. I avoided asking if he was uncomfortable in my place, or, more than likely, whether he had safety concerns about the boat and its contents. Either way it was an excellent move and he was able to put his translation skills to work out of hours.

Exhausted, I departed stealthily just after dark, leaving him still at it, and drove back to my bachelor flat at the back of Charles II Street. Once inside I raided the fridge for a beer, turned on the music and collapsed thankfully into a chair.

What on earth was I getting into? I doubted I would have given Piet's ideas the light of day had my work at AandA not fallen apart. Like the others I was attracted by his down to earth rendition of events. We were all freaked out by our employment situation and the power of the story drew us towards it like steel to a magnet.

Personally, I had nothing to lose. This sense of purpose was going some way to bringing me back from a meaningless hell. There was risk. Just now I was coming to appreciate the potential danger much more deeply than I had let them see. No point in frightening the troops. But when I seriously analysed what we knew of happenings over the years, I had to put caution at the head of the list. All that activity was proof, if any were needed, that large rewards were out there somewhere. Worth going after? Maybe. No! And yet---of course it was! I was fencing with the unknown.

Those two guys had invested years, money and huge effort in tracking down their deceased partner's every move. Lying, cheating, blowing things up, spying, torture and even murder, all seemed acceptable in their agenda. Understandable, I supposed, if you had set up the whole thing - the raw material, the manufacture, the enormous deceit that must have taken place all around, and the actual theft and delivery of the product. The risks they must have taken were enormous. After a time you would come to assume that what you had stolen really was yours! The more years that passed the stronger would be those feelings and the more the frustration would grow.

And we were now intimately involved!

We had found and decided to pursue the only possible way of solving what they had failed to do for all that time. This fact would put us right in their firing line if the slightest connection with us were ever made.

The one person in the world with whom I could have shared my innermost thoughts was no longer with me. She had a sharp instinct about things and was usually right. I missed Sally's ability to go for the jugular, to sort out fact from fiction, realism from fantasy, foolhardiness from common sense. Lord knows I needed all of that now!

The numb feeling of cold feet. Should we jack it all in? Despite my personal grief I none the less still felt I was too young to lie down and simply let life ebb away! I could find another job that would be almost certainly not so interesting or all-consuming as what I was leaving. And some time, somewhere, I might even recover some interest in the opposite sex.

The team never questioned the dubious relationship between my tweaking of future behaviour traits of the masses, as I had spent years doing, to feeling out the past likely actions of one man who stole and hid a lot of krugerrands. I had my answers ready but really the substance of my argument was paper thin. To work backwards to determine his movements and actions related to depositing stolen gold based on snippets of information from a mass of paperwork was---well, pretty difficult to sustain. They were aware of some difficulty but still wished to push ahead. We were all suffering from a sort of madness and I was very concerned about where this might lead us. We were not that far away from having the mind set of international criminologists. And therefore vulnerable.

Unheralded, the word "coward" was trying to force its way through from the back of my brain. I refused to let it. I was already committed to Piet and the other two. I bloody well had to go through with everything now! Dammit, I had become the prime mover, bringing in the other two, laying down the systems to be used and generally overseeing everything. It really was down to me!

I hooked out another beer. The die was cast but the picture it stamped out to me right now was one of impending disaster. It weighed on my mind and the words kept returning like bad pennies. *Security, security, security!* My friends must come to no harm. I tried to identify our possible vulnerabilities. They were everywhere. I had to be the eyes and ears. If it all went wrong, and somebody got hurt, I could never forgive myself. Forget the loot. Strange that for the time being the value of gold was just an afterthought.

Slowly, very slowly, calmness followed panic. My mind ceased racing around. See things as they are, not as they might be. I began really to analyse our situation seriously and in depth. Cool and steady. One step at a time. The only danger lay in failing to keep a grip.

Coward I was not!

SEVENTEEN

Marguerite sensed a breakthrough.

She studied every detail of the huge Armstrong/Global website. Even if Geldenhuys worked here he would still be tricky to locate. Above all she personally had to remain incognito. She noted the U.S. takeover. This could complicate investigations. All the signs were that the initial work had to be done in South Africa. She code-texted Haffenbacker.

> URGENT. LIKELY BUT NOT CERTAIN THAT SUBJECT WORKS FOR ARMSTRONGS AND ACHERSON SOUTH AFRICA WHICH MAY ALREADY BE CALLED GLOBAL INC. COUNTRY-WIDE GROUP COORDINATOR IS JAMES GROTH OF DRACK CAMPING, BASED UMTATA. CAN ALBERT'S PEOPLE ESTABLISH OUR SUBJECT'S WHEREABOUTS, JOB DESCRIPTION ETC? OBSERVE USUAL ANONYMITY. GREAT CARE. M.

The reply arrived in just fifteen minutes.

> WELL DONE. LET'S HOPE. ALBERT'S ON IT. THEY RECKON UP TO ONE WEEK TO ARRANGE. WILL KEEP CLOSE. H.

EIGHTEEN

The teamwork proved terrific.

My attempt at rostering was forgotten by everybody. We worked day and night with hardly a break, and the task was completed much more quickly than originally envisaged. The contents of all three boxes were perused, classified, the data fed in and then the paperwork physically re-filed in date order wherever that was possible.

I was summoned late on day five to hear self-appointed organiser Jonny's initial reactions to a stream of computer printouts. Feelings in the rocking boat were heavily charged and the thunderstorm lighting the sky and blowing torrential rain against the windows gave an appropriate atmospheric background to the occasion.

"This was never going to be easy. I think we all harboured doubts about anything of substance coming to light." He looked around as if to ensure we were paying attention. No problem there! "We have pointers. Bones upon which to put some flesh, if you like. The time has now come for us to start using some of this much heralded human input! Hercules - he pointed towards the larger opulent looking computer down below - has come up with twelve location possibilities. Nine of these Elizabeth and I have studied and turned down as extremely unlikely or impossible. You can go through and check all this stuff yourselves at any time. You may well come to different conclusions from us but I doubt it. But three of them could very reasonably point in the direction of the krugers present resting place. And, incidentally, one of our rejected ideas is a suggestion about that hole in the road! Proof that Hercules really is getting something right."

I could feel the angst. We had all had worked our socks off and feared failure. Night and day one or more of us had ferociously pushed the system. We were all tired. There was an extraordinary determination that I really had not contemplated. But I felt it was not sensible for us all to get too worked up at such an early stage. I winked at Jonny. "Drinks all round?"

"And I'll draw the curtains while you put on the light, Piet." Elizabeth caught on fast.

Jonny quickly made up the coffee and passed around the mugs. The aroma in that confined space revived a little conviviality.

I ventured a suggestion. "I would guess at least one of those three places will not be in South Africa." I was going on a few "links" I had noticed when processing the paperwork detail.

"Correct, Dave. Ok, here we go. Number one suggests Grobelaar's younger brother in Bloemfontein. We know where he lived at that time and my checks say he is still there. There are a couple of indicators that they met in Johannesburg hours before Maghiel took the train for Cape Town. Hans Grobelaar could have transported home that weight of product in his car. I have to say this seems at first glance to be very unlikely but it is possible."

"Surely he would have disposed of the krugers by now?" Piet could see an investigative job coming up fast. "And why then would Grobelaar shoot off to Cape Town?"

"Unlikely. The gold market knows everything. Four or five a year from one source probably would not attract interest. More would. And maybe the Cape Town trip at that time is most likely to have been a hoax."

Nobody moved a muscle. We were assembling genuine bits of history. After a long silence Elizabeth asked brightly, "What about melting them down?"

"Again, unlikely. But possible. A large percentage of the value is lost when you do that sort of thing."

"Any evidence Hans was ever visited by Kokot and Van?"

"Don't know. We may have to find out." Jonny wanted to get on. Knowing him well I knew irritation when I saw it. He was not waiting for more questions.

"Secondly, Maghiel was in the habit of taking plane trips to Mauritius, an island in the Indian Ocean to the north-east, heavily used by South Africans for business and holidays. He and his wife often stayed there. They frequently wined and dined some serious punters, particularly a director involved in the sugar industry called Patou. They purchased a villa a mile or so from Port Louis, which, after a lot of research, we have established has been inherited by Maghiel's cousin. Man going by the name of Luuk Finder. It's certainly a place to investigate. If the answer is here somewhere it could well have been hidden by Maghiel in some way and possibly nobody is aware of it. Another burial maybe?"

I wondered about this one. "Any more detail? That is all a bit thin. Is there anything even a little closer to the target?"

"Sorry, this is the nearest we get on this one. You can go through it all at your leisure." He pointed to a heap of paperwork now standing proudly sorted on the small bench and leaning against one side of the boat. Ominous stacks of it.

"And thirdly, a couple of flights to Oslo were made during the weeks preceding the heist. Tickets for foreign trips were usually purchased by the Ministry, but these were paid for personally by Grobelaar. It was only when Hercules cache- linked a variety of items to Norway that this whole story showed up."

Piet asked, "Any connection business-wise? Do the Norwegians have interests in South African mines or any other sphere of activity there?"

"At that time there was nothing special going on as far as I am aware."

A heavy squall seemingly coming from nowhere hit the boat hard. Piet just saved his sliding coffee mug and quickly swallowed down the contents. He had been looking thoughtful. An idea was in an embryonic state at the back of his mind.

"The Norwegian Embassy is in Pretoria. Maghiel probably had a fishing mate there - something like that?"

I couldn't hide my disappointment.

"Is that all? There's nothing of substance in *any* of this. All that data should have brought up *something* a bit more positive."

"But you yourself said the technology would only throw out ideas, point in certain directions, pick up coincidences. It has actually damn well done that. Dave, *you* were cautioning *me* against expecting too much. There will be substance when these ideas are considered together with the relevant physical notes, invoices, scribbles etc which we have so painstakingly assembled. It is not like selling AandA's awful bloody office furniture to Indonesia!" After all his hard work

I was not being helpful. Things were getting to him a bit.

"Yes, sorry. There is another level of research to go through. But Hercules should have done better. As I see it there are holes going right through all three possibilities. I agree any form of perfection to emerge right now is unlikely, but pointers with some meaning really are in short supply!"

Piet had his own ideas. This stage of our project had injected a mild form of madness into him.

"I would like to take Number One, Bloemfontein. I will read up everything and if it makes sense I will go there and investigate in depth. My country. I know the ropes." He sat back quietly giving me that look again. The challenge was well and truly on.

"I'm thinking a trip to Mauritius may be necessary. Can do that if you all agree." Elizabeth avoided looking at me. I was quite obviously being far too negative for her.

"Which leaves Pretoria /Oslo also to me." Piet now *had* to have action. "Pretoria is home and I can follow on from that by going to Oslo if necessary. I do have a contact in the South African Norwegian embassy. Jonny must stay in London here as he is still employed and you, Dave, will, I hope, be resident coordinator. Elizabeth and I will keep closely in touch with you throughout, won't we?"

It was hardly a question – much more a demand!

She nodded her agreement. "Who knows what will be thrown up! I suggest we email or phone in to you a short report of our activities as and when. You can then assess it all."

Jonny, backing these initiatives completely, simply muttered, "Affirmative. And I will work with David. I don't trust him left here on his own." He paused. Settled then?"

They were all studying me intently. I smiled. There was no point in doubting their desire to get things moving, and, who knows, they might just get somewhere.

"OK, let's go for it!"

"Champagne? I think the situation calls for it. I put a bottle in the fridge." Elizabeth always thought of everything.

NINETEEN

Three days later that Marguerite received a good response. Her mobile vibrated as His Lordship was leaving to be driven into London in the Rolls. He never arrived back before late evening, if at all. She routinely pecked him on the cheek and went rapidly up to her study. It was about time for something from Switzerland. And she was right. Quickly she decoded the message.

> ALMOST CERTAIN YOU ARE CORRECT. MORE DETAIL PROVING DIFFICULT BUT WILL BE COMING. SUGGEST AWAIT THIS BEFORE WE TAKE FURTHER ACTION. ESTIMATED MAX TIME NOW THREE DAYS. WELL DONE. H.

It *was* AandA/Global!

Marguerite heaved a sigh of relief. She was still perturbed at her failure to detect this company sooner. Her own plan of action, given this positive response from Haff, was already mapped out in her head and could now be implemented to the full.

She unlocked a drawer, extracted all the details she had so far accumulated, and spread them across the desk. Not much, but, amongst other things, she had downloaded the company's overseas structure which showed some detail of their South African operations. Not appearing anywhere amongst a whole raft of names was that of Geldenhuys. Nor was he shown in any of the many company website lists she had studied. The overseas division did not to know him. Switchboard had talked of the overseas director, John

Wilberforce, and she looked through all his global area managers and staff. But all had proved negative.

She again went through everything in great detail, hoping to have overlooked something which might give a clue. But the result was the same. She had missed nothing. After an abortive hour she packed it all up, put everything back into the drawer and carefully re-locked it.

Further action was necessary. If the man was active on company business he must surely appear somewhere in their records. Something here was not like any normal business set up. It required a big effort from her and she knew that a trip to those Millbank offices had now become essential. *Get on with it woman!* She unlocked and pulled open a small cupboard, grabbed a largish bag which had lain dormant for some time, checked that its contents were the correct ones, and quickly carried it across the landing to her bedroom.

Out came hair dye, special lipsticks, face powders, false eyelashes, perfumes and a wide range of disguise materials she had been drilled into using in the days of her French training. She sat down in front of her dressing table set to work quickly and effectively. Within the hour she was looking at a woman in her late sixties with greying hair, a lined face, a tooth problem, and who was shortly to acquire a small but pronounced limp. The appropriate clothing came next, finished to perfection with her oldest pair of shoes and a nondescript hat.

She carried out a final check on money, car keys, mobile and dark glasses before locking everything else back into its normal resting place. She left the room, tidied her study and went silently downstairs where she made her way outside. She locked the outer manor door, hurried through to the garage and, taking great care not to be seen, drove her modest Renault out of the estate and on to the London road.

TWENTY

Forty-eight hours later I was alone.

Piet and Elizabeth had flown off and Jonny was back at work. I took a morning walk to Victoria station and then the tube out to St Katharine's. Rush hour was at its height and we were packed in like sardines, but I did not mind. I was keen to get back to the problem. I was oblivious to the humdrum all around, my mind planning ahead on the day's activity. It was difficult keep myself away from Marianne. We were operating the technology to its known limits and had obtained some results. Strange ones which needed further examination. To me nothing that had emerged seemed very satisfactory and I wanted to saturate my mind all over again with both the IT results, Maghiel's documents, and any other papers which were around. We were not getting sufficient light shining deeply into the crevices of the problem.

A few people were strolling around the Haven's shopping arcade but otherwise the coast was clear and there was nobody at all in the mooring area. I dialled 1965 in to the boat owners' security gate, passed down the descent slope and across to Marianne. I took some time unlocking her and boarded. Nobody anywhere had shown any interest in me. Inside the main cabin I hung up my coat, pushed the heating button, switched on the lighting and started up the coffee. I pulled from my inner pocket copies of the latest notes left by Piet and Elizabeth and dropped these, together with Jonny's summaries, down on to the table. Then I went across and gently uncovered my beloved Hercules.

Piet had been incredibly enthusiastic, due, no doubt, to his closeness to Elias. Taking Bloemfontein and Oslo together made sense as both investigations were related to his home country, but it was a very extensive range of work and would take him some time. Elizabeth clearly liked the idea of Mauritius. I had caught a glint in her eye when she jumped at the possibility of a visit. I guessed she would find time to explore the place as well as carry out her investigations.

A tweak of a curtain and a peek outside showed all to be very quiet. I poured coffee into my mug, added a little sugar and sank back into the comfortable seat. A benign word, sketch, address, name, number or something lying around me simply *had* to offer a more positive indicator than anything so far found. I was very sceptical that our findings to date would lead anywhere. But in this I was most definitely alone.

Occasionally when working on an AandA marketing conundrum I had groped my way to a solution by doing the holistic, usually late at night. Sitting back and letting the mind roam across the whole spectrum of computer conclusion and human suggestion. And I now also had added to the mix assorted paperwork in date order, wherever anything was in fact dated.

Where would *I* have put a fortune of krugers? They would have to be easily retrievable yet hidden from the world. Probably in a fairly long-term place until the flak had died down.

Might I have embarked on a train journey to deliver them to my hiding place in or around Cape Town?

How would I have carried that weight and kept it safe? A large car or van would be one means of transport. But then the train could have been another - accompanied by Mr Grobelaar of course.

There was no evidence of a train freight charge, but that would be logical as Maghiel would probably have made sure to lose it. But the logistics here would have been difficult. The security investigative police could later have become aware of his journey and he would have known this. Maybe my colleagues were right and it really was a hoax trip and nothing else.

Mauritius as a venue? I thought that unlikely. Too distant. Difficult to ensure safe delivery and recover at a later date. And Bloemfontein? Would I inform a cousin of my criminal deeds? Possible, but unlikely. We would have to be extremely close. Rare for most cousins. The only other Hercules throw-up was Oslo and that seemed almost impossible, being totally without evidence of connection other than visits to the Norwegian embassy.

I began the long search, thumbing through Grobelaar's papers for late 1993 to January 1994. Hercules would have investigated and extracted for us anything in the slightest way relevant. But had we missed some off centre but crucial clue? Or did the questions which we put to the technology not range widely enough?

His diaries for this period were immaculate. His expense claims calculations straightforward and all of the letters he had received were interesting. I read an enormous amount and found absolutely nothing that seemed of direct relevance to the matter in hand. This reconfirmed to me the great care he had taken to conceal. That would be normal to a man who was hiding a fortune. My drink, which I now swallowed down, was already nearly cold.

I switched on and went through the Hercules items rejected by Jonny and Elizabeth. The printouts were nearly all understandably wide of the point - precise objectives are hard to programme in even to the great IT intelligence I had put together. Then I checked the waste paper basket contents which had been so meticulously kept by Mubanga. Thumbing through all that again I could find nothing. Simply *nothing* which seemed relevant to our cause.

Lunch time came and went. I munched a sandwich I had brought, washed down with something non-alcoholic from the boat's small fridge. Where? How? I needed to know! An inner anger was rising. Maghiel really had taken great care with everything. There would normally be *something*!

The afternoon slipped away as I thrashed around. Time passes incredibly fast at times of high concentration. Soon it was dark but I had noticed none of it. I was simply desperate to find what it was that both human and computer brains had missed. There was always a clue somewhere. I'm built like this - a sort of surreal weariness can set in as the hours pass - and failure makes me blame my own imperfections. I continued on and on getting madder and madder as I ploughed through everything yet again.

In the end fatigue inevitably won the day. I realised I could hardly move and it was midnight. I killed the gas, heat and light and staggered below. I fell on to Piet's bed, covering myself with the only blanket which was there. Sleep came immediately, successfully blotting out my feelings of abject failure.

I awoke to see the bright winter sun shining through a porthole. My watch told me I had slept through to eleven o'clock. I felt ghastly, hungry and cold, all at the same time. I straightened out Piet's bed and staggered up the steps to the main cabin. Things were a mess and I set to, putting all paperwork back in order and generally returning things to their former state. I looked out through a curtain. There were a few people strolling around the Dickens hostelry but generally it looked fairly quiet.

I smartened myself up a bit and stepped casually down from the boat, carefully locked up, and made my way across to the coffee shop where I picked up the neatly advertised croissant/cappuccino. At the top of the spiral staircase I could see only one other person sat there. I selected a seat which overlooked the majority of boats moored down below and tried to enjoy the view while I ate.

My mind kept returning to the same question. How would I have done it? I was half way to putting myself into Grobelaar's mind set, but the other half was as if I was still peering into a thick mist. The man had me going up a whole range of cul-de-sacs. So much so that I was ready to conclude that his actual intention really was to double-cross Kokot and Van der Merwe and disappear with everything, leaving no clue anywhere - a near-impossible task which he seemed to have accomplished in style. Had he not died he would have collected a fortune from somewhere many years ago.

As I was demolishing the remainder of my second croissant my mobile vibrated. It was a text from Elizabeth.

Booked in to Esplanade Hotel nr Pt Louis. Sand, Sea, Sun. Good swimming! Met Patou - long story - but almost certainly not implicated. Late sixties. Happily married. Still holds advisory position with govt. Visits to S.Afr. were in role as tourism publicity supremo.

Knows all heads of depts. and political big-wigs there as has carried out this role for years. And when here the more important visitors still go with him to The Caudan Chic. He is almost certainly off our list! Now checking on Luuk F. Luv Elizabeth.

I wasn't surprised. Jamie Patou had been singled out by Hercules as he was a constant connection both when visiting South Africa and when Maghiel went to Mauritius. But visits to the Caudan Chic were routine. Not anything special. This gave added value my strengthening conviction. It was probable that everything we were investigating was simply either a result of our own enthusiasm or of Maghiel's hocus pokus.

I glanced at my watch. It was time to go. I had arranged another handover meeting with Eisenbauer which was scheduled for two o'clock. I replied with a quick thanks to Elizabeth and left.

TWENTY-ONE

The ground floor of the newly-named Global Tower was bustling with activity. Reception was way over to the left where three harassed ladies were trying to sort the paperwork, change the names shown on hotel style pigeon holes to make them tally with the numerous new company departments now organising themselves throughout the huge building, and, additionally, open boxes, parcels and mail that had been delivered out of the blue. At the same time they had to deal with a large variety of visitors and their inevitable wide range of questions.

To the other side of the huge open area was the security officer, specially imported from Connecticut. Everybody called him George, nice and succinct, perhaps because his Italian parents had named him Alessandro. He was large in stature, heavily muscled and skilled in dealing with bad situations, or doubtful people. In a previous life he had been head bouncer in a high-powered casino in Las Vegas. He was not someone to be messed with! His major asset was his long-term loyalty to the company. Unknown to most of the staff he was on close terms with all the American directors, some of whom had used his skills to short cut the way to solve problems. He looked after the company and it in turn rewarded him handsomely. Like most large, tough men he had a streak of kindness in him which could be brought to the fore when someone was in real trouble.

Behind Reception, stairs led to the first floor and then all the way to the sometimes cloud-covered penthouse suite. Rarely had anybody walked all the way up. It had been done on arrival from Connecticut by a couple of young employees. They were timed and the challenge was now on for others. Four large, powerful lifts situated straight ahead worked constantly to keep people and goods flowing smoothly. They were at full stretch for most of the day.

This was the picture that confronted Marguerite as she hobbled slowly up the steps and into the building. She was pleased to see large numbers of preoccupied people, all of them far too busy to notice her. One look at Alessandro instantly decided her to keep clear. He was one of those who might well see through her disguise. She looked carefully around the whole place, then shuffled slowly over towards the Enquiries/Reception sign where she waited patiently to be noticed. It was not long before someone came in her direction. Age demanded precedence over most other things.

"My name's Ruth. May I help you?" She spoke with a slight attractive American twang.

Marguerite carefully acted her years. "Yes, please, my dear. A small matter I assure you. I will not take up much of your time as I can see you are very busy. I am looking for a list of the people who work with you in Johannesburg. I have a young relative there and he badly wants to join with your company's African organisation."

"I am very sorry. We have no lists here. Particularly right now. The two companies are amalgamating which complicates things." Her arm swept around, pointing to nothing in particular. "As you can see it's all a bit chaotic."

"Oh dear." The old lady looked totally crestfallen. The bottom had fallen right out of her world. "Is there *nothing* I can do to help my nephew?" *Keep pressing girl. If Paris could only see you now!*

Ruth was keen to get away. She had a lot on her mind but knew she had to do something. Her training emphasised that it was not company policy to ditch people, particularly the elderly and infirm. She had to hand an internal Staff List which she thumbed through carefully. Within a couple of minutes she had a name.

"All I can suggest, my dear, is that you phone in, ask for this gentleman's department and I am sure someone there will deal with your enquiry. Leave it for a few days if you can while things here calm down." She scribbled down the details on a company card and handed it over, hoping against hope that that would solve the matter.

"Thank you so much. I really am truly grateful." Marguerite inserted it carefully and slowly into her purse. When she looked back to be more effusive Ruth had gone. She turned slowly and hobbled towards the door. Twenty minutes later, back in the multi-storey park and safely in her car she pulled out the card. The main details read

> Jack Eisenbauer Jr
> Overseas Director
> Department Extension 245

TWENTY-TWO

Emails over the next forty-eight hours confirmed my worst fears. The first was from Piet.

Flew into Bran Fischer. Hans Grobelaar, retired butcher, is seventy-two. Married. Two sons emigrated to Australia years ago. I visited his home which is a corner cottage off Walton Street. Run down, painting required, brickwork needs repointing, glass pane broken in shed, garden a mess. Met his wife Marie who offered me tea (I told her I was doing a survey which offered a monetary reward. The mention of money seemed very welcome to her!)

She explained he was totally incapacitated - he was hurt badly eight years ago. She arrived home to find him in a coma. Two white men had entered the house, dislocated his arm amongst other injuries and kicked him senseless. She said it was all to do with his brother who worked in Jo'burg in the old government. They wanted to know the whereabouts of a large sum of money. Hans knew absolutely nothing and said so. The Police investigation was useless. And no compensation was to be had. She was certain this contributed to his present state of mind.

I asked a few questions about her views on kitchenware and gave her a 2000 Rand thank you.

Definitely not our man!!

The other was Elizabeth's second.

Luuk Finder inherited house on death of Maghiel. Wife, Henrietta, still there, lives frugally. He died six

years ago. Had had a rough time trying to answer questions from "two South Africans" a couple of years before he died. No relatives. No sign of any form of wealth. This is no place for us, I think. Coming home.
Elizabeth x

And one day later had come Piet's final offering.

Have just met Jan Shuter, the guy I vaguely know in the Royal Norwegian Embassy in Pretoria. He has only been there a couple of years but introduced an old hand who long ago had occasionally been in touch with the Consulate in Cape Town (their main representation in those days). He remembered the "Mines man"--he thought he was called "Grobson"--- who would talk about Norwegian investment in mining etc to the Consul but then invariably went fishing mainly for tuna with the part-time accountant, a Cape Town resident called de Villiers, with many years sea experience and who owned a boat. He sometimes helped out with accounts for a small local boatyard.
   I can see little or no connection with our project. 'Fraid the trail ends there. Flying back tomorrow. All damned disappointing. Your pessimism regrettably correct.
   Piet.

TWENTY-THREE

"Overseas Department. May I assist you?"

Another American accent. It was two days later and Marguerite was following up on her visit to Global.

"Good morning. I recently visited Ruth in your Reception and she suggested I call you for information on South Africa?" Her best old lady voice, low in pitch and unsteadily delivered.

"Yes, how can I help?" *Uncle Sam is here to assist.*

"I have a nephew there who would like to work with your company. He has recently qualified in Business Studies. I promised I would do my little bit to aid him in his search for a job. Do you have any names of local staff who might be able to help a young person like this?"

"One second." There was a rustle of paper. "The main office which coordinates this sort of thing is in Umtata, name James Groth. But each operating unit hires locally. I would contact him first and he should direct you."

That confirmed her earlier investigations. "And there are how many of those operating units?"

"I guess five. I will email them to you. But I must warn you many things will be changing in the next few months. They are all now subject to review."

Marguerite was ready and croaked out, "I'm so sorry my dear, I am elderly and not very computer literate. Never really took an interest and now it is too late. Can you possibly read me those names and I will write them down?"

"Of course."

She read slowly. "Port Elizabeth - kitchen goods - Andrew Giles. Durban - shoes etc –John Bamba. Rustenberg - Bedroom furnishings - Claude Falleur--- she slowly spelt this one. Carnarvon - Bathrooms - Max Nsaka and finally Mossel Bay - specialist foods and drinks - Julie Ponyata. If you ask someone to Google these for you all the information will come up."

Marguerite was recording everything. "Are there any others associated with you in South Africa?"

"All I have here are the names of three independents who travel a lot in the whole continent doing research work I think - names are Mapoma, Geldenhus and Arthur Jones, but they are not employed people and are probably by now no longer with the company anyway."

It was automatic for this highly trained spy to keep emotion from her voice no matter what. Internally she was bubbling.

"How do you spell that second one?"

"G-e-l-d-e-n-h-u-y-s. Strange name that."

"Thank you so much, my dear. I will follow up what you have told me. That gives me a lot to go on. Goodbye."

"Goodbye, and may I wish you every success."

As she lowered the phone Anthea Sachs suddenly realised that she had no name for the old lady. Not to worry. She had unwittingly broken the rules but nobody would ever find out.

Marguerite switched off her stolen mobile - she kept several spares - soaked it in the nearby basin, then crunched it underfoot and went quickly downstairs to throw away the pieces.

After that she texted Haffenbacher.

TWENTY-FOUR

SOUTH AFRICA

"Come out or we open fire!"

Five heavily armed members of South Africa's elite police Special Task Force, headed by Colonel Andreas Yapp, faced the small apartment block near to Johannesburg's Parktown. All residents had been quietly taken from the building early in the morning except two who now leapt fearfully from their beds knowing instantly that their cover had been blown and retribution was at hand.

"Out now. I will count to ten."

It was staccato megaphoned Afrikaans and very frightening. Yapp had risen to his position by exquisitely blending carrot with stick to achieve his required results. Only one in fifty of the applicants who apply to join the STF is accepted. Most could not show the aptitude and controlled brutality required for high-risk operations such as hostage rescue, dealing with illegal drugs factories and anti-terrorism. Relative to all that sort of thing this job was a piece of cake.

The two targets of the operation had sent their wives back to Holland years ago. Their lifelong mission was fraught with danger, but, throughout, every investigation undertaken had been carried out with extreme care. Someone, somewhere, had sussed them out. They emerged as they slept - in boxer shorts and vests with hands held high as the count reached Nine. Both were quaking. They had never before actually killed anybody and they knew the penalty. They lowered their arms and were instantly cuffed.

"What is this all about?"

The taller of the two hoped there may be a chance.

Yapp's deputy, Captain Heppskoof, stood down the other men who immediately entered the building to carry out a routine detailed search. That meant every conceivable item was checked, letters read, clothing pulled apart and all personal belongings closely inspected for evidence.

"Names?" Yapp ignored their question. Speed was of the essence.

"Johannes Kokot."

"Elan Van der Merwe."

"Occupations?" He addressed Kokot.

"Both retired."

"How long have you resided at this address?"

"Eight years."

Yapp had to be sure he had the right people.

"Where did you work in 1993, 1994?"

"The South African Mint. I was there for many years."

Yapp nodded at Van der Merwe.

"I was a driver for a couple of mining companies."

Yapp had his suspects! His heart leapt but his face reflected nothing. He beckoned them into the large police van which awaited and, together with Heppskoof, whose hand remained firmly holding the Heckler and Koch in his pocket, followed them in and slammed the door shut. He sat beside a small table on which he had a sheaf of notes.

The other three stood.

"I want to cut this short. An admission of guilt now may lower your sentences later. But I want that and I want it now. Do you know a man called Elias Mubanga?"

Both shook their heads firmly. They had absolutely no idea who he might be.

Yapp was a highly tuned practitioner of law enforcement in the world's most violent democracy. He dealt at the top end of criminality. He did not like lies. He hated courts, which stood for fair play, as he had spent his life putting away thugs who had committed such awful crimes they did not deserve a hearing. Time and space. He had none of it. These guys had to admit guilt now before he went on to the next job. That was how he worked. There was no other way. And that was how he had risen to the dizzy heights at the top of specialist policing.

"I will give you one more chance." He then began to exaggerate. "We know, and can prove, that you killed Mubanga. I want to confirm one thing. Why did you do it? Because if you come clean with me I can suggest some leniency to the court. But if you continue to deny your involvement, well I will have no choice but to become persuasive."

At this point Heppskoof pulled his pistol. They had set procedures for this sort of situation. The two of them had spent much time evolving a set of routines for dealing with the very worst kind of thugs. And these two undeniably fell into the bottom end of that category.

Slowly Kokot was recovering his equilibrium. They could expect no mercy, he knew that. He had seen this hideous sort of performance a couple of times. He understood with absolute clarity how these people worked. The only question left now to try to answer was the one about getting out alive.

"Why?" Yapp shouted.

"We didn't do it."

They could not admit to it. To do so would eventually reveal a multitude of beatings and mutilations they had inflicted over the years, let alone robbery in the Mint which in itself was probably a treasonable offence.

"Who on earth is Mubanga?" Van der Merwe too had realised that for them denial was possibly the lesser of two evils, though he also was fully aware of the disastrous situation they were in.

"I will tell you. He is a man who left your two names in a letter to his lawyer, *"----if I am harmed or murdered seek out Elan Van der Merwe and Johannes Kokot---"* So cut the crap. I am asking for the final time. Why did you kill him?" The words already spelt out a definition of guilt.

Silence. Both men were becoming increasingly terrified. There was nothing they could say. Their massive effort to remain incognito, successful for years, had now run its course. In fact, they had never intended a complete kill. It was simply bad luck he had died. But there was certainly no future in saying anything like that either. And claiming it in a court of law would get them absolutely nowhere.

Yapp nodded imperceptibly at his deputy. He was in no mood to spar in this way for much longer with these two.

"Why did you murder Mubanga?"

Hepskoof moved alongside Kokot. There was no immediate answer so he fired into the floor just beside the tall man's big toe.

"Why did you murder Mubanga? Please do not encourage me to hurt you. I will. You must know that."

The pressure was intensifying, progressing towards its inevitable conclusion. Kokot had to say something.

That shot had seriously unnerved him. Denial was no longer an option. He spoke quietly through pursed lips out, one final attempt to find some sort of favour with these bastards.

"He was a criminal who had robbed us. Please leave me alone!"

"Not good enough!"

The next shot went right through his small toe. Kokot screamed out in pain. Both STP men remained icy cold. They were long since immune to any feelings inflicted on their fellow beings. Dealing with crooks who kill people was second nature to them. This was their job and they did it well.

Yapp spoke across to Hepskoof, raising his voice so that he could be heard above Kokot's howls of agony.

"Perhaps if we turn our attentions to Van der Merwe here we might get to the truth. Most people do not usually need to kill a man simply in order to steal from him."

"Well?"

Hepskoof moved over beside the other frightened man who was traumatised by simply watching the blood seeping slowly from Kokot's slipper. But Merwe still felt he had to stick to their story. There simply was no other way. Admitting murder was something of which he was not capable - or so he thought!

"Yes, he stole all our---"

The next bullet ripped through his big toe. He screamed and shouted out in unimaginable agony. Everything changed in that instant. Indescribable pain. Unbearable pain. Anything to stop the pain. He would tell them *anything*!

But Hepskoof had turned his attentions away and moved back to Kokot.

"The next, big boy, will go through *your* big toe. Really, really painful! Just look at the state of your friend. You do not want that do you?"

Kokot was not a fool. This pain would be dished out in increasing amounts until they got what they wanted. He knew they were beaten. Probably dead within a month. The shots would continue until they did tell Yapp what he wanted to know - and certainly they would not finish up dead right here. Their two interrogators were too skilled in their trade to ease down on the pressure now. There was maybe a slim chance that on a good day it could still just be a life sentence. Above all he had to avoid the imminent mutilation of which these people were capable. They had broken him.

"I will---- tell you-- everything."

The words slithered out through teeth still chattering in agony. He could see that Van, too, had completely given up. It would all have to come out. They might just succeed in saving their lives but for that they would need a large slice of luck. Yapp would have all sorts of snippets of information so anything they watered down would be noticed and dealt with. He realised right now that he would have to tell their whole story. Eventually that might include everything they knew of the Daggers organisation who were their historical competitors in this affair. He reckoned they had been sometime involved in this matter. Somehow the idea that "we are not the only ones" might help in their defence.

Hepskoof, having uncuffed them both, withdrew and led Van der Merwe away for some primitive medical attention. Yapp pushed the recording button and beckoned Kokot to stagger over to his desk and lower himself carefully into the chair which was there.

Complete admission of guilt was about to begin.

TWENTY-FIVE

Two days later Jonny had arranged what he called the "debrief" for seven in the evening. It was a miserable meeting. We all agreed there was nothing else to be done. Maghiel had out-manoeuvred everyone. A very clever thief. The hiding place was likely to be for ever unknown. Our clandestine boat meetings were over. It was all a great shame and very sad.

"At the bottom of the sea somewhere?" Piet was feeling guilty for having brought us all into this in the first place.

"Could be a very large tree with a hollowed-out trunk almost anywhere in South Africa." Elizabeth felt that was an easier solution. "Seriously, it could be anywhere. It's almost like trying to work out someone's password when you know nothing and do not have even one single clue to go on. The possible combinations are infinite! Finding a needle in a haystack would lower the odds quite a lot."

"Or sticking a damned pin into one of those revolving world globes." Jonny needed to join the grief.

I felt it deeply too but tried to lessen the misery. "We have to be practical. We've failed. We must accept that. Now each of us must work out what to do to get back on to some sort of normality. First, we must dispense with the boat."

"No problem. It will sell. I'll do that - and maybe make a profit." Elizabeth knew how. She made a face. "At least I got to learn about Mauritius. You know it's a marvellous island. Wonderful for a holiday if you like the sea, sand and sun. One day I'd like to go back for a proper break."

I raised my eyebrows at that. She really had enjoyed the visit!

She noticed and quickly changed the subject, "Who's for a farewell brandy?"

Three hands went up as one, just a little too fast.

"Secondly, my computers."

"We'll shift those back to your place tomorrow." It was an off-work day for Jonny. "And I'll work with Elizabeth to do the best we can to pay us all back as much as possible of what we have put in."

He had assumed the role of administrator from the beginning but had left Elizabeth to do all the work. We were all minus in the cash stakes but at least we might get a good sale and recover part of our losses. We lapsed into silence. We had all been fired up with the project and the idea of the whole thing collapsing was miserable. There was no way out of this sad situation.

"You know after that gold was lifted some pretty high- powered brain must have been employed to find it. Both by the Mint, and, come to that, the State also. And they got nowhere. I was too bloody ambitious to think we even stood a chance. All pumped up by Elias and what happened to him. Hindsight now of course."

"You were actually right to pursue the whole thing, Piet. The problem remains unsolved. Somebody, somewhere one day will walk into a fortune! Just imagine Joe Bloggs buys a house somewhere and after a year or two he does a clear out of his loft and finds unlimited krugers stuck away in a corner."

I too was feeling deeply depressed and frustrated, all exacerbated by something I felt was important niggling away at the back of the brain which I could not bring forward into reality. The brandy helped allay the misery - well, a bit anyway. We drowned our sorrows and spent the next couple of hours trying to ease the soreness of the occasion. We learned a lot about Mauritius and the historic structures of Norway's representation in South Africa.

Then three of us for the last time, quietly and with great reluctance, left for home.

I awoke with a start.

Piet had given me too much brandy, but it wasn't that. The clock was showing three in the morning. About the time when I would sometimes puzzle out the next programming step with an A&A problem. This was the sort of madness which had upset Sally so much.

Those krugers.

They *had* to be somewhere! Everything in me was shouting out for some indicator. You simply could not have that huge amount of detail without the author of it mentioning *something* about one of the major heists in history which he had planned and successfully carried through to completion. That simply did not happen! He really could not have kept things so totally hidden.

And yet he had!

In those dark hours I could not hold back from another mind bending visit to everything we knew. My brain seemed to be spinning like a top. No thought of sleep. I had sensed the Piet and Elizabeth visits were long shots which were very unlikely to produce anything and I was right. This was what had driven me to examine for myself all Maghiel's scribbles, bills, diaries and documents, fine tooth combing everything. Mubanga had collected a massive range of paperwork and I had made sure to examine each piece in detail. Each piece! No exceptions!

As had Hercules!

Neither one of us had found anything untoward. And *that* was very strange. Usually our combined strengths would realise at least a part of what we sought. Throwing a little light on a problem often led in the longer run to a partial or complete solution. But this situation we had did not easily fit with either a specially programmed computer or a human brain.

A lorry growled by in the street below, its light passing slowly across my ceiling. Probably carrying out a night-time delivery. Day movement in this part of London would these days be almost impossible for him. I pulled the blanket over my exposed cold shoulder, slid down into the bed, turned over, adjusted the pillow yet again, and went back to sleep.

A couple of hours later I sat bolt upright.

There *was* something. Cling on to it! Do not forget! Piet's visit to his contact in the Norwegian set-up in South Africa. The Consul in Cape Town.

What about it?

Something didn't fit!

I had seen two luncheon bills smoothed out from the waste paper basket. On one Grobelaar had written something. I could not remember what. The restaurant location was close to the old Consulate address. The bills were paid *personally* by Maghiel. I shook my head.

Why would *he* pay? It was clearly not government business. The timing - I had to check. If the dates were anywhere near the time leading up to the heist there could be a link. A clue! Something to follow up. I jumped out of bed, flipped on the light, and threw my dressing gown over my shoulders.

Why was he there? Cape Town. That was where he had taken the train shortly after the Mint was raided. Coincidence? Who were the two people he had wined and dined? I recalled that one bill was a pretty substantial amount. I needed more information and some detailed conversation with the only person in the world who would understand and empathise. Someone who was as mad as me.

But at four in the morning?

I called Jonny.

The response was immediate. He spoke quietly.

"Hello Dave. A bit early, even for you."

"Any chance of a word?"

"Of course. A moment while I leave the bedroom."

I could just make out a low female groan in the background and felt a deep pang of guilt.

"Sorry to get you up at this time."

"Not at all. I couldn't sleep a wink. Mind doing a lot of cavorting around."

We both knew why.

"Jonny, I have a wiggle."

This was what at work we called a possibility that one was on to something. In our years together at the sharp end we had evolved this sort of abbreviated communication. A wiggle invariably had substance.

"Great. What?"

"Do you remember the date Maghiel wined and dined those guys in Cape Town?"

"Can't recall exactly. Why? Is that important?"

"Because he paid personally!"

"So?"

"It wasn't Mines business."

"And if the events occurred just before the heist he could have been fixing something. Suspicion slightly enhanced by the fact that it was to Cape Town that he took the train immediately after the fun and games."

Jonny was instantly in the loop.

"Exactly! There in one."

"But tenuous. We need the dates of those food bills he paid." He was getting fired up.

"Yes." I held my breath.

"Now?"

"If you can make it?"

"Too bloody true! See you on the boat - about half an hour."

I called Piet and warned him we were coming.

We arrived together. No small talk. Just quickly on board. Piet had the curtains across, lights on and paperwork all laid out. Jonny found the Wild Boar restaurant details in three minutes dead and scribbled a few details on a pad.

"Expensive meal for three seventeen days before the robbery. Very expensive meal for two seven days before. He was down there twice before and once, we know, immediately after the event took place! And these bills were crumpled up. He had thrown them away! How the hell did we miss that?"

He shook his fist at Hercules.

"Is there something written on one of them?" I was remembering.

"No?"

"On the back?"

"Yes! On the expensive one. A circle with "deV" beside it, PR a couple of figures above."

"De Villiers!" Piet had been quietly listening.

"Who's he?"

"The guy I talked about after visiting the Norwegian embassy!!"

Jonny went quiet for a while, mulling over what we had. I could see the thought processes running across his mind, slowly, then faster. There was the beginning of something here. Maybe.

"We must pursue this line."

His firm statement confirmed my feeling that we really might be on to something. Up to this moment I had been awaiting the put down from everybody.

"We certainly will, Jonny. Nothing positive as yet, but maybe suspicious. Tomorrow is Saturday. You maybe could both be here at eight for a think-in? But for now I suggest you both get a few more hours more sleep. I can't make eight. Early morning out-of-hours handover meeting with you know who." I had submitted my formal resignation to the Board and Eisenbower had fixed the date. "Can make it by eleven. Oh, and you'd better include Elizabeth or she will get nasty!"

"OK. Eleven it is for us all." Jonny looked hesitant.

"You coming now?" I had a feeling he might not.

"No, staying. The jungle drums have started a gentle beat. You've set me wiggling too. There's something *I* need to look at."

TWENTY-SIX

Haffenbacker's excitement shone through the comprehensive early morning message he had sent in reply to Marguerite.

> CONFIRM YOU ARE CORRECT. SUBJECT HAS BEEN SOUTH AFRICAN RESEARCHER FOR A&A FOR YEARS. BASED PRETORIA BUT TRAVELS SOUTH AFRICA AND TO UK ON OCCASION. THOUGHT TO BE ON HIS WAY OUT DUE AMERICAN TAKEOVER. IN LONDON NOW - REPORTS TO OVERSEAS DIRECTORATE BUT UNLIKELY TO APPEAR IN THEIR OFFICIAL STAFF LIST. I WILL BE WITH YOU TWO DAYS - WEDNESDAY ABOUT 1500 RITZ. CAN YOU LOCATE WHERE HE IS STAYING, IF STILL EMPLOYED THERE, AND, MAYBE, TO WHOM REPORTS (OR REPORTED) IN THE COMPANY? DO NOT BREAK COVER IN ANY WAY AS MAY GO TO EARTH. BIG QUESTION--IS HE WORKING ALONE ON PROJECT OR HAS HE ACCOMPLICES? SEE YOU SOON. HAFF.

That was about what she had expected. They were at last getting somewhere. The fact that he was returning was good. Most men would muscle in on her preserve as an ego boost, but not this one. He sensed real progress and would further the project jointly with her. Trouble was, as boss man, he would inevitably lead, and she couldn't countenance that - particularly as she had so far done most of the heavy lifting. Marguerite decided right now to move things quickly forward. She grabbed from her cupboard another acquired mobile and called AandA. The answer was immediate.

"Global."

"Extension 245 please."

"That is Mr Eisenbauer madam." She sounded protective.

"Yes, that's the name. It is rather urgent."

"I'll put you through."

Marguerite breathed in deeply - part of a routine taught by her French instructors. Surprisingly there was no intermediary. She had the boss.

"Eisenbauer!"

He sounded like a man in a hurry. The commanding American twang rang out loud and clear.

"Mail deliveries here Mr Eisenbauer. We have a parcel for a Mr Geldenhuys. We were put through to you." Her cockney accent wasn't bad, but she was a bit concerned that it could be better. She need not have worried.

"No longer with the company. Sorry."

"Oo." A short silence. "Please where should we send it?" She tried to sound little girl in a lot of trouble.

"Send it here care of David Johnston. He calls in occasionally and knows Geldenhuys."

Caution to the winds.

"It is urgent. Does Mr Johnston have a home address?"

"SW1 somewhere. You people should know. Geldenhuys is staying with him. If that fails then contact Reception. Do not come back here again!"

"Thank you so much sir. We will look him up."

Eisenbauer slammed down the phone and continued his tete a tete with the company vice-chairman.

Marguerite disposed of her mobile in the time-honoured way. She was elated but calm. Things were developing fast. She spent some time consulting lists of SW1 residents and surprisingly found only one

David Johnston. There were other similar but not identical names there but this one was almost certainly her man and lived in an apartment in Charles the Second Street - just off the Haymarket. She would try to find his face on some AandA staff internet pictures.

She made herself a Bloody Mary and sank back into her most comfortable chair. There would now be plenty of feed to give Haffenbacher and she was reasonably happy for him to assume some, but only some, responsibility for the next move.

A couple of celebratory drinks were in order.

TWENTY-SEVEN

I found Eisenbauer sat at my old desk. I had arrived bang on time.

He motioned me to sit.

I did.

Slowly.

"Sorry you are leaving us---"

He didn't look one bit upset.

"--- but I guess we are getting good with AandA products now, blending in alongside our own."

"That's great, Jack. Nothing too tricky I hope."

We eyed each other like two boxers in a prize fight.

His desk phone buzzed.

I looked around the open plan. I could see only two of our personnel there and raised a hand. The rest were complete strangers. The desks had all been rearranged to squeeze in a few more people. Pretty soon some the floor power points would need adjusting. Jack's desk top was empty. He clearly didn't work from it.

He put down the phone and continued our conversation.

"I was promoted last week. Top floor now. The new overseas director."

"Congratulations. You have the Wilberforce job then. Combining him and me?"

"Yes. I had hoped Elizabeth would fill in a bit but she has gone. Silly girl. She seemed well switched on and would have done well."

Conceited idiot!

"She missed out on a lot more money. Ever see her?"

I thought quickly, possible responses flashing through my mind. Then I lied like a trooper.

"Not really. Once or twice just before leaving here."

"Bet she was asking what you made of me?"

Big headed bastard.

"No, not at all. I think she's very much her own woman. Keeps her thoughts to herself."

"Really good looker. I would have thought----" He looked at me in a smugly suggestive way.

I quickly changed the subject.

"I hope you have arranged my pay-off package? Some things are a lot more important than others!" I tried a sort of very mild joke but he just didn't do them. There were no curves to his nature. Just straight lines going unerringly to the point.

"All done. Should now be in your bank. You're a rich man for a while."

"Thanks."

"OK if I call you if any queries? There may still be a few loose ends." He assumed the attitude of a ship's skipper throwing a rope to a man fast sinking in a very rough sea.

"Yes of course. You have my mobile?"

I knew he had.

"Yep. I'll maybe be in touch." He consulted his Rolex and stood up, gently smoothing his immaculate jacket.

"Got to go. Board meeting coming up in a couple of minutes."

The newly assumed self-importance of the man was sickening. He reached over and shook hands limply. Then moved fast away. I clearly wouldn't be needing to thank him for the coffee and biscuits. He stopped abruptly and held open the door, suddenly glancing back at me over his shoulder.

"Geldenhuys is staying with you isn't he?"

"Er----yes."

"Post office woman phoned trying to locate him for a delivery. I told them to find your address."

Then he was gone.

I arrived before eleven. The other three were there and had been deep in conversation.

"Morning Dave." Jonny gave no sign of having been up half the night.

"Morning all. What's the latest?"

Elizabeth passed across the usual coffee as I slumped into the boat's comfortable inboard seating. I sensed a slight reawakening of the old communal feeling. Tentative, but it was there. We were at it again.

"We think you've got something." Elizabeth looked warily hopeful. "We've been here since eight o'clock discussing and analysing what you pointed out. We cannot understand why he personally paid those bills, particularly the big one. How on earth did you come up with that from all these masses of files and papers? It was completely overlooked by your mate Hercules whom you say misses nothing - and yet, almost disastrously, he did miss out on this!"

"Middle of the night high tensioned brain activity. Jonny knows about these things. There was just, well, something. Hercules wouldn't perceive it that way. He never sleeps so I suppose is not open to these impulses."

Jonny smiled. "Humans still have some use. Call it intuition. Long time before the Hercules will have that!" He pushed one paper over for me to examine. It was the the expensive bill for two. Almost as my mind's eye had envisaged, but not quite.

"See the reverse side."

I turned over. There was a crudely drawn circle with PR in capitals inside it. "deV" was to the west side of the circle and 34 to the south. Up in the top right corner of the paper was jotted what looked like thirteen eighths (thirteen over eight). Well it looked most like a three but could just have been a scribbled anything if seen from other angles.

Piet started the ball rolling.

"A pretty sure guess would be de Villiers, his old fishing mate who took him out in his boat when he visited. They were close and almost certainly he took this man to an expensive dinner, probably to thank him for a wonderful day out on the water catching whatever they could."

"That's good enough to accept as a starter. All agreed?" Jonny checked that three hands were raised. "But now the hard bit. These two have had a good meal. They are on the coffee and, I see, large brandies, and Maghiel asks for the bill which he settles with his card. DeV says something which he notes down. He has no paper to hand so, quite logically, he turns over the bill to write on the reverse side."

"It must then have some meaning for him as he hangs on to it long after the meal." We all nodded positively at Elizabeth. The point was well made.

Jonny resumed. "Ok, so next we have a circle drawn around the letters PR with 34 scrawled beneath it. Anyone know what PR stands for?" Remember we are looking for any clue about hidden krugers. Something that has to be really relevant to that."

I tried to help. Being negative sometimes fires up the positive. "Well it can't be Public Relations. That's the last thing they want!"

Piet chipped in. "It's probable that it's in Afrikaans. A fair proportion of his jottings we know are in his mother tongue. And what is the significance of 34? Let me guess something straight off the cuff. The PR could be short for Prys in Afrikaans, Price in English, and the 34 could be the cost of something in Rand—might be three hundred and forty, three thousand four hundred or something much more.

"Then why the circle?" Elizabeth and I asked the obvious question almost together.

"Maybe meaningless. How often have you circled something just to emphasise what is inside it? We do it all the time."

I looked at Jonny, seemingly now lost in thought and solemnly contemplating his navel. "Any future in asking Hercules?"

"I have. Questioned him in several different ways. Nothing. Absolutely damn all!"

We lapsed into silence. It was freezing outside but our wonderful heating continued noiselessly running and controlling the internal temperature. I peered out through the curtain just behind me. Sleet was now driving hard across the marina and, understandably, there wasn't a soul in sight.

"Other Afrikaans words beginning with PR are Fun, Picture and Taste. Not that those words contribute to the cause in any way I think."

Piet was trying hard - and not really getting anywhere.

Elizabeth pushed me for all she was worth, some desperation now showing. "Dave, can you please seriously apply your magic again to *this* insoluble problem. How should we progress it? We are all truly, truly stuck."

"Holistic approach. Let your brain soak up the whole page and somehow eventually a penny will drop. Maybe won't solve anything but might clue in for another differently structured brain to unravel!"

She groaned. "Oh my god, another blinking psychologist. I had thought there was only one of us. Right. Just let's take in the picture. PR circled with 34 underneath. To me that must mean a diameter of 34 inches or millimetres. May be a medallion present for PR to wear around his neck for something achieved? Although in inches it might be a bit heavy!"

Piet helped out. "It will be metric. Down there feet and inches went out years ago. Not wishy washy as you lot here, having it both ways. The diameter is almost definitely 34 millimetres."

Jonny cleared his throat and summed up so far.

"Maghiel and de Villiers were talking after a good meal about how to hide a sizeable, extremely valuable, heist. To remind himself of some detail Maghiel draws a circle of 34 millimetres diameter which is somehow related to a person or thing either beginning with PR or is two words, the first leading with P and the second R. We may like to----"

Elizabeth suddenly cried out. "Stop. I've got something - maybe. Is that the diameter of a krugerrand? Piet, you know that? It has to be pretty close."

Piet shot a look at Jonny. "You fed it in when this all started. Remember, you wanted the detail for Hercules."

Jonny moved quickly down to the computer. It took all of a minute. "Not the same I'm afraid. Exact kruger size is 32.6. But really close I have to say, Elizabeth."

Silence all round as we digested her idea. But it was a pregnant silence. The jungle drums were really beginning to beat. Someone simply *had* to come up with something. Inevitably it was Elizabeth. This time she shouted!

"No, it's right, right, bloody right!! They're hiding them in something round. When you hide a lot of round things in, say, a pipe, the pipe must allow room for insertion. It is the internal diameter of the pipe!" She glared all around daring each one of us in turn to challenge her.

I added, as knowledgeably as I could: "And to avoid detection you must not allow too much room for movement. One point four millimetres is almost certainly about right. Gentlemen, I think the lady has a breakthrough. If this is wrong it is still brilliant thinking. If it is right---"

Piet broke in. He had been measuring and scribbling for some time. "The top corner figures are definitely not thirteen over eight. They are one and three-eighths and this more or less equals the thirty-four millimetre internal pipe size. He was old enough to want to check what the size looked like in feet and inches - an in build which had stayed with him from his youth - maybe too he had a cross check on his mobile if at that time he had one."

He sat back smiling. The cat with the cream. Maybe.

"That's *brilliant* and proves it!" Elizabeth looked at her watch. "We should stop there. I have just received a large cheque from my former employers and I would like to take you all out to an early tea in the docks. We've already missed lunch. Clear your minds. Think about sparkling wine, dancing women or rude songs. Anything but gold! We have yet to resolve what PR means - but you are not to think about that now!"

I guessed she was playing out something academic to do with her psychology, but tea seemed great. I turned to Piet and said quietly, "Any chance of a get-together later tomorrow? Something to discuss."

"Not going anywhere just now and I am totally free tomorrow. Where and at what time?"

"Coffee shop opposite Green Park tube station? I think you know it. Big place. I suggest round about three o'clock?"

"I'll be there. But make it *afternoon tea*." He frequently did his joke imitation of what he thought was the English upper class way of communication.

I looked around. The old camaraderie was now fully back. It was time to depart.

"I suggest we go one at a time. Wrap up well, it's awful outside. And move slowly. We want no attention paid to us. Elizabeth has to go first. She's a lady but much more importantly she's ordering!"

TWENTY-EIGHT

Wednesday was another cold, blustery day with driving sleet. Normal for late February she reckoned, but at such times as this Marguerite hankered after the softer climes of St Tropez, Cannes or one of those less well known, smaller places she so loved. But she had made her choice and, despite the weather, was enjoying what she was doing. She had just received an open text from Haffenbecker.

> SNOWED IN. PLANES GROUNDED PROBABLY
> TWO TO THREE DAYS. SUGGEST YOU AWAIT
> MY ARRIVAL. ANY FURTHER ADVANCES AT
> YOUR END? SORRY ABOUT THE HOLD UP BUT
> COMPLETELY UNAVOIDABLE. HAFF.

She was elated about the one really big success she had had. In her bag was a picture of David Johnston. It had been small but had come up beautifully when transferred to her Acer. The printout gave her an amazingly clear picture sized almost 30 centimetres square. She replied.

> OK. WILL WAIT. DOING SMALL
> INVESTIGATIONS BUT PROMISE NO HEAD
> ABOVE PARAPET STUFF. M.

In one way his late arrival quite pleased her. She now had time to look around, see exactly where Geldenhuys was staying, and what sort of access there would be to the premises. She would locate a variety of surveillance positions and could, at the same time, undertake some of the detailed research which, at his insistence, always had to precede a Haffenbaker break-in. In this sort of situation he was a perfectionist.

Marguerite decided on a mini stake out. Her "husband" happily was not around again. She studied Google Earth and other pictures of the area in which Johnston lived. She would get as close to his apartment as possible and photograph any of the detail there which Haff might require. It would be enormously lucky if, while she was doing her survey, he happened to turn up with their target - another, this time suntanned, person.

TWENTY-NINE

SOUTH AFRICA

It was Bern de Villiers fiftieth birthday.

He had lived in Johannesburg for twenty years now, working as a lawyer in a city where corruption and violent crime were rife. He reckoned he had done his share over the years to contribute towards some semblance of order in a very disjointed society and, in so doing, had lived well.

He studied originally the Roman-Dutch civil law which had been the mainstay of the apartheid period, but had extended his learning into British common law and, over time, he picked up the rudiments of the varied laws of custom of various African tribes. The South African legal system was a tangle of its constituent parts. As an attorney he had become a major player in running the South African arm of the American international legal firm for which he had worked now for nine years. They paid him substantially and business was brisk. He would of course stay.

He had the day off and had left his wife in their gated community house to carry out a very pleasant task. His father, a couple of weeks before he died some fifteen years ago, had handed over to him forty-three krugerrands, which he presumed were a form of savings, with the express instruction that he should cash one every few months, preferably with different banks or other exchanges. He now had eighteen left. Very surprisingly father had made him promise not to cash them more frequently than that, and he had assumed this was to avoid drawing attention and attracting theft. A kruger was, of course, a very valuable asset.

The precise reasoning behind all of this was not clear to him but over the years he had kept fairly rigidly to father's instructions. He never became aware of exactly how, long ago, the golden coins were acquired. His old man was certainly not wealthy, but neither was he poor. He had for many years held a two day a week accounts position with the old Norwegian consul in Cape Town and the remainder of his time was spent managing the financial affairs of a small boat repair yard, which, as a sailing enthusiast, he did up to the time of his death.

Bern and his wife would occasionally holiday in Cape Town, where they had both been brought up, usually staying with their two children at the Mount Nelson. He once went back to see father's old yard, now very much renovated. Instead of repairing small to medium sized boats they were these days specialising in selling new ones. The staff were young, modern and, seemingly, very much with it! Gone was all the hard work with which his old man got himself involved when away from the accounts - overhauling boats could be arduous and not very remunerative. Father would sometimes arrive home in a state of anxiety, fretting about the state of boat repairs and maintenance problems. Now, with the new ranges of boat, he could see that life had become much simpler, cleaner and easier.

He entered the opulent looking exchange section of the bank, whose layout he had reconnoitred last week, and made for the private interview room, where he pushed the button. An attractive olive coloured female member of staff appeared almost immediately.

"I would like to cash in a krugerrand please."

He made it sound an every-day event, as he always did on these occasions.

"Yes, sir, we can do that."

She ushered him in to a seat and closed the door. He handed her the golden treasure. She looked at it, weighed it and then went in to her computer. She fed in the usual personal details, studied it for quite a long time and then looked up.

"Currency?"

"Oh, dollars please, in cash."

"That will be one thousand and fifty-three U.S. dollars."

She looked at him for confirmation before opening the safe and carefully counting out the bills twice before handing them across to him.

Bern smiled. "That will do nicely. It'll pay for them all at our next braaivleis. We're due a party next week. And, I suspect, there will quite a bit of cash left over."

The cashier smiled. "A lot I would hope."

He departed, the burgeoning wallet giving him a good feeling. Yet again, as always on these occasions, he could not help wondering about father. Would that he could reappear, even for a few minutes, to have that discussion he had always skirted around.

THIRTY

"Daddy, I have a puzzle to solve. And you are the world's best at these things."

Elizabeth dumped another heavy log on to the fire burning in the huge old fireplace which she had loved since way back in her childhood days. She had left her London flat and driven home the day after their boat deliberations, jubilant and frustrated, both at the same time. She reckoned she had half resolved their impasse - certainly a pipe was an ingenious way of keeping krugers hidden for an indefinite period. She knew her father loved solving problems which would baffle most people. The more awkward they were the more he loved it.

"What is it?"

She walked across the comfortable lounge and put on the arm of his chair a picture she had reproduced showing all the detailed scribbles which they had seen on the boat.

He studied it carefully.

"Precisely what is it you want to know?"

"What does PR stand for? It could be English or Afrikaans!"

"There's something South African about it?"

"Yes."

She knew him so well. His razor-sharp brain was already at work seeking a solution.

"I don't speak Afrikaans."

"That makes it all the more difficult to solve."

She left quickly to join her mother who was doing things in the kitchen. He would sink into his crossword solving mode and could well come up with something, in this case probably later rather than sooner. This problem was a major one.

"Have you got a man in your life yet?" Mother was getting desperate for grand-children. She was one of those.

"No. Well, maybe, longer term."

"What on earth does that mean? Most men do not usually mess about. Your father was an exception of course - I had to marry him! But the others--. You *would* know Mr Right when he came along wouldn't you, after all you went through with Mr Wrong? Tell me you have not given up like some of them do."

"Mother, there is someone I like very much. These things are not straightforward, particularly right now. It may take a little time but I am working on it."

"That sounds good. I promise not to pry but just remember the male of the species is not very clever about planning his life. They spend their time all over the place. Doing this. Doing that. Nothing really positive. In my experience you have to guide things along carefully without appearing to do so. I know that sounds awful, but it's usually true." She shook herself free of the subject, and manoeuvred a change in the conversation. "And how are things at AandA. Your father was a bit upset when you left Harley Street you know. He thought you might be losing your way a bit. It might have been the wrong thing to do."

"Things are ok." She *couldn't* yet tell the story about what was going on. "Still investigating, researching and travelling. I am finding everything very interesting."

"Got it!"

A loud shout came from the lounge.

Elizabeth broke away and went rushing back.

"Those figures – one is inches, the other metric. But they are the same!"

"Well done father. And PR?"

"Probably Pro-Rata."

"Meaning?"

"Well if one halves the other does likewise, sort of thing."

Elizabeth nodded her head slowly from side to side. "That's not quite right is it?" Her head teacher style for use only with her father!

"No. I'm being too ambitious."

The rest of the evening passed with much sighing and grunting. Try as he might he could not get any sensible meaning from the puzzle she had set. Over cocoa before bed he suggested that a little more information was needed. Context? People connected? Occupations? Something to which to relate.

Elizabeth groaned inwardly to herself. He was not getting anywhere. The time had come for the last piece of information.

"Well, the only clues like that are a guy who worked part-time with the Norwegian consulate in South Africa and in a boatyard the rest of his time. That is all. There is nothing else."

He set to again, wrestling with what turned out to be an intractable problem. After a huge effort he had to admit that could not solve it.

The following day she drove back to her flat in London, slightly disappointed in her Dad's limited progress but really delighted with another piece of information she had come across which was most important for her friends to know.

THIRTY-ONE

At three in the afternoon the "opposite Green Park tube station" Caffè Nero was almost empty. I ordered tea for Piet and coffee for me, found a corner seat, and waited.

He arrived promptly as usual, tore off his coat and sat down quickly, breathing heavily. He quite clearly had something on his mind. Which made two of us.

"I just wanted to tell you about my meeting with Eisenbauer -somebody was asking after you---" My voice trailed off. Something was wrong. He was not listening. He was desperate to cut in.

"Dave, *I've just seen you!*"

"But, of course, old chap! Here I am! Sat here right in front of you. What the heck do you mean?"

"A woman. Downstairs in that restaurant, end of your Charles Street. She had *your* picture beside her. Right on the table where she was sitting. I stopped off for lunch there."

"You ate there?"

"Yes."

"We could have made this lunch."

"Dave. This is serious. I ate there simply because it is on the way here and I had time on my hands. She was sat downstairs in the window seat. Right beside her plate was your picture. I *bloody saw* it as I came down those stairs. At one point on the curve you are immediately above that table - you were looking up at me, clear as anything. I just managed to put on a poker face and move normally as I passed by her to go out. I was willing myself not to look. But it was *definitely you.*"

"Age of the woman?"

"Thirties, maybe a bit more. Smart. Blonde hair. Very attractive actually. And her view from that window was up the street looking right towards your apartment block."

In normal times I would have come up with something funny about my portrait, but given past events and the way things were looking, humour was now the farthest thing from my mind. His information was really serious stuff. I blurted out what I had to say.

"I arranged this get-together to tell you that while I was with Eisenbauer the other day he informed me a woman from the post office phoned and asked for *your* address. He told her you were staying with me!"

"He said that?"

"Yes, it seems he had it in the back of his mind. I don't recall mentioning the matter to him. He must have assumed it."

"Something is not right! Definitely! This bears all the hallmarks of those two thugs." He poured his tea with a slightly unsteady hand. "I saw what the bastards did to poor old Elias. They broke him both physically and mentally. Those guys are capable of absolutely anything."

"Apparently she had to deliver something. I was very surprised and thought long and hard about the whole thing afterwards. First, that is not the way the post people do their work and, secondly, I didn't think anybody would or could link you with AandA in this country. I decided not to bring it up with us all on the boat, but to discuss it with you here first."

"Looks like the two things are connected and the link is this woman. You can see the way this is going Dave?"

"Yes, I think so. Things might be beginning to look a tad dangerous."

"Those two guys who killed Elias have got some woman looking for us. A crazy thought but it really does look like that."

I had never seen Piet really so shaken up like that before. That picture had understandably worried the hell out of him.

"Hold it, Piet. Before we go too far. We're not yet *completely* certain of any of this. There may just be a way of checking. That woman, who might easily have found me on the old AandA website, could be looking for me because she thinks you are staying with me. If that is the case then why would she be after you?"

"Because she must know all, or at least something, about the Elias story. I wonder now if they have some idea of the cases we have and their contents? Probably feel they will reveal some sort of answer to their long-standing problem. Hell, they've tried everything else."

"OK. Let's put it to the test. I 'll go back and wander slowly past that shop and then cross the road. I will never look anywhere near the restaurant but you will be well behind waiting to see if she emerges, assuming she is still there - which she will be if she is searching for us. Probably drinking one glass of wine after another. Or worse, staying stone cold sober!"

"And what do I do?"

"Keep away from her at all costs. Simply see if she follows me. You could call me at some convenient point. I will not call you."

"Right!"

He drained his remaining tea. His worries had given way to a sense of urgency. I departed half a minute before him. My own increasing fear of things had returned, feelings which I hoped I had not transmitted to Piet - god knows he was having enough horrors of his own to deal with just now.

My mobile quacked. Much too soon for Piet. This was the worst possible time for it. I flicked it open. It was Elizabeth.

"Hello there."

She didn't stand on ceremony. What she had to say was important.

"I read some of father's South African law reports which he had left out. He gets global details of legal situations everywhere. *Guess what!* Those two thugs have been picked up and are likely to be given life sentences. Will give you a photo of it all some time."

"Thanks Elizabeth. That's huge news for us right now. Sorry, I must go. Something else going on. We have a lot to discuss. Can you fix everybody for the boat tomorrow morning at eight? And go carefully. Things may be getting nasty."

"Really how---"

"No time, see you tomorrow."

"Oh *David* ---"

I killed the phone as I turned down into the Haymarket and a minute later passed the window. Glancing in was tempting but I looked steadily ahead. Then I negotiated my way across the road through the ever present dense traffic and headed slowly straight along Charles the Second street for home."

It was all of an hour later when my mobile quacked again. It was Piet.

"I'm on the train from King's Cross. She followed you and took pictures of you going in to your place. I want to see where she goes and if she meets up with those two thugs---"

I stopped him.

"They are to be banged up for life, Piet. Elizabeth has seen details in legal reports held by her father. Absolutely genuine. We are now definitely dealing with someone else."

"Wow! *Very* interesting! Ok, I will find out where this woman goes!"

"Piet, make sure you in no way get caught or even seen! We are meeting on the boat at eight tomorrow morning. Make certain you are back. Essential we put all the bits and pieces together and see what sort of picture we get."

"Yes, see you there. Boy, is this whole thing getting hellish hot!"

THIRTY-TWO

We all arrived on time the next morning. Piet had returned to the boat late and, despite having only a short night's sleep, he was clearly ready for the day and anything it may bring.

Elizabeth looked accusingly at me. "Tell me all about yesterday when you cut me off!"

She and Jonny listened with increasing amazement as I related detail of everything Piet and I had done and learned the day before. When I had completed the story she said almost inaudibly, "Sorry, forgive me. I had no idea about what was going on. What an incredible experience."

I turned my gaze to Piet.

"Well I followed the lady to Cambridge and then trailed her car by taxi to her home---"

"Just like those movies where the villain is chased---"

"Shush Elizabeth, this is pretty dramatic stuff!" Jonny, very aware of the implications, was actually perched on the edge of his seat, eager to learn more.

"---I took great care not to be seen, dismissed the taxi a bit farther on, walked back and strolled around outside the entrance drive leading up to this whopping great manor house. I then wandered down the road a few hundred metres to the most ancient looking village pub I have ever seen. It took me a couple of hours and quite a few beers before I could get a useful conversation going. I was a stranger, you see, and in a place like that they are very wary of such people. But---the woman is Lady Banforth, married to the Lord Banforth. The wedding took place a few years ago. She has never had much to do with the locals and, according to gossip, she wasn't and isn't at all close to him. And there seems to be no information around other than an anaemic looking entry about their marriage on the internet. Lots about the Lord himself of course. He seems to have a finger in all sorts of pies, business and other."

All four of us went quiet. He was describing what seemed to be leading to a dead end as far as the lady was concerned.

"But she was watching you, Dave, in order to find Piet? It seems pretty clear to me that she almost certainly has to be Eisenbauer's post woman. The big question, I think, is how she got involved in the first place. I would guess that it would *have* to be something to do with Piet in South Africa--"

Elizabeth stopped abruptly as her *oranges and lemons* tune rang out. After a short time spent listening intently her face lit up and she indicated to us all to listen as she switched to speakerphone so that we could all hear the message clearly.

"Would you repeat that, father?"

"Yes, my dear. Quite simple really. PR stands for Pulpit Rail. You mentioned connection might be to the Norwegian consulate - well I went through everything possible and there was simply no spark there at all - but after a few trying hours it was your word *"boatyard"* which led me all over the show and eventually to *Pulpit Rail.*"

"But at the time I remember saying that it was most likely to be in Afrikaans."

"Ha, you see that's the beauty of it. In Afrikaans the word for Pulpit Rail is Preekstoel, and that *begins* with PR! Either way it *must* be right. Anyway, why on earth do you want to know all this?"

"Just a very tricky puzzle. You are certainly filling in a big gap. Thanks very, very much for all the hard work. I'll explain with a bit more detail when I visit again. Love you. 'Bye."

"Goodbye love. See you soon."

She clicked off and pocketed the phone. Then she looked quickly around eager to see the reaction.

But there was simply nothing! Each one of us was frantically trying to adjust to this extraordinary revelation. A south-westerly was still blowing, gently rocking us to and fro and we could just hear a couple of nearby engines starting up, their skippers aiming to catch the tide. There are moments in life when a totally unexpected piece of news completely blocks out all else. Time stood still for three whole minutes while our minds simply raced around all over the place!

Elizabeth, wanting to be absolutely sure, broke the silence. "Piet, is that a correct interpretation that father has made?"

"It's good enough. The Afrikaans actually can have the word "spoor" on the end of it but that takes away nothing from this absolutely terrific revelation."

"Then father's right! It's not a bloody pipe! Of course not. Far from it. You can't carry that sort of thing around without attracting questions from all sorts of people. And also of course when loaded up it would be quite heavy. The Rail is a very important part of a boat." She looked scathingly around at us non-seafaring types. "The pulpit rail goes all the way around the bows. If you are on the front end of the boat and the sea is a bit rough you can hang on to it. If it's *really* rough you shouldn't of course be out there but if your harness is clipped on to a jack line, you can also hold on to the rail if you are about to be washed overboard. Lesson over."

I noticed that, since hearing the solution words *pulpit rail* Jonny had been paying not the slightest attention. The end of Elizabeth's explanation jerked him back from his mental travels to the here and now. Something had really come up and he blurted it all out.

"Those measurements, then, look as though they have to be for the internal diameter of a pulpit rail and the kruger will then just fit inside. My god, Elizabeth, your Pa is a genius."

"He always was with things like this. Drives mother mad. He has a mind which does not give up. He can never let go and has occasionally gone into puzzle fatigue when he cannot solve something. I knew he would come up with the solution if I set the challenge. There can be no doubt. Pulpit Rail is the answer."

I was trying hard to piece everything together in a measured way so that we could be very clear about the situation and the implications for us. The broader picture. How that had changed in the last few minutes! I chose my words carefully.

"This is the tiny bit of information which may turn out to be enormous. The bit of grit which becomes a pearl. Half the world seems to be looking for it. It could be putting us many steps ahead of any competitors we may have but, that apart, I think this knowledge now leads us into very dangerous waters! Excuse the pun. We have red hot information which has the real potential to attract killers. I feel we must, at this stage, ask if anybody feels he or she wants out? There would be no shame in it. Probably a lot of sense. Stay in and you could end up like poor old Elias."

Piet shot back with an instant response.

"Dave, we go ahead. Certainly, as far as I am concerned. We've got so far along the road we can't stop now. I, for one, am prepared to take my chances." The other two nodded vehemently in agreement. "We could get hurt so we must be very careful. Your place is being watched because they think I'm there! Keep away from it. Come here. Share the boat. This place so far is safe." Piet's reaction to it all was quite clearly to go ahead with all guns blazing.

I carried on. "In that case we must keep assiduously to the careful bit. We already have rules. They must be even more closely followed. Anyone arriving or leaving here must check very carefully that there is no suspicious onlooker. Better still, I think we should now *only* come and go in the dark!"

"What is the thickness of a kruger?"

Elizabeth, now herself in another world, had been drawing pictures of the bows of a boat.

Jonny beamed. This was his territory. He knew all the measurements and had been putting it all together in what must have been a labour of love.

"Two point seven four millimetres."

She scribbled again, pulled a small calculator from her pocket and studied it closely.

"A twelve to fifteen metre, or if you prefer it, forty to fifty foot boat, say, could have a total pulpit rail length of up to something like fifteen metres. Could be more, could be less, depending on the type of boat. But that length would certainly take, well, at least a couple of thousand. We are, I think, looking at that sort of quantity. Maybe less because of the weight."

Jonny nodded. "This is *really* taking on some shape. Supposing somebody planned it all in great detail and very carefully loaded a boat with the loot. What would he, or they, then do with it?"

"Simple! The boat would have to be big enough for international waters. You put together a passage plan to wherever you like - say to the Netherlands, Madagascar or Madeira. A very lengthy journey would need frequent refuelling and top-notch seamanship, but, once there, no customs official is going to saw open your pulpit rails! - unless you are very unlucky and they have been forewarned or are themselves unusually gifted in the detection arts. You are home, dry and very rich! But then, if that had already happened, why does everybody still seem to be looking everywhere and with such aggressive intent?"

Elizabeth was glowing with excitement again. I thought I too was now getting a slight glimmer of light on the whole picture, and tried to answer the question.

"Because Maghiel would have made sure he, and probably his cohorts, were the beneficiaries - and he died at the very worst possible time! But there are one or two points we are missing here. For example, would that hypothetical boat crew have to know anything about their cargo? They would certainly be aware of its destination."

Elizabeth knew the answers to this. "Of course not. The boat could float around for years if necessary. All Maghiel had to do was monitor its whereabouts and, when appropriate, take it over in one of many possible ways. Think back to those heavy meals with the Norwegian consul officials - wasn't ---"

Piet shut her up with a loud shout.

"De Villiers! Bloody de Villiers! Remember Dave. I texted you. The old guy I saw in the Norwegian embassy spoke of their accountant who used to take

Grobelaar fishing in his boat in Cape Town. *There is a very, very large boat connection here!"*

"Bingo, you've got it. Whoopee!" Elizabeth now had no doubts. "You have to go back to your Norwegian contact, Piet, and ask how you find de Villiers these days. You are an historian putting together some Cape Town history. You have the right accent. Ask de Villiers about the old Norwegian consulate, people involved there, outside activities etc. Something will have to come out."

"Hold it. Hold it. Slow down." I was, after all, the boss of this outfit, wasn't I? "You are all roaring ahead. We must think it through. Piet goes back to the Norwegian embassy, speaks with his contact there, gets the de Villiers address if he can, finds the man, maybe finds the yard and asks the questions about what happened twenty-something years ago. That is an incredibly tall order and could be impossible to accomplish. There are all sorts of dead ends that might come up."

"OK so what do we do?"

Elizabeth was pushing for action and pouting at me a bit at the same time.

It came off my lips very quietly. "I think it is very clear. I should go with him!"

The rising tension dissipated very fast. Lanced like a painful boil. I wasn't for once being the boring old killjoy they expected.

"That would be great, Dave. Means we can be in two places at once if necessary." Piet was now really all fired up.

"One thing though. What about my flat? I need to do a visit to pack and I don't want to be jumped on while I'm doing it!"

"Late tonight. Unlikely there will be anybody there then. After that, back to the boat. I'll come along and keep watch with you while go into your place, just to be sure."

Piet was right but Jonny stopped the whole idea in its tracks.

"No, *I'll* do the watching. You are their target, Piet."

"And while the two of us are away looking at boatyards and hopefully talking with old men could you, Jonny and Elizabeth, work out some sort of very discreet surveillance on my place. Things could well be happening there and it would be good to know more about this Lady Banforth."

"It's in hand, Dave. We'll fix it. Worry not." He was already, in his own way, arranging the whole thing.

I felt the time had come to ease up a bit.

"Lunch time. Piet has a few more croissants and I have seen a couple of tins of beans. And there's unlimited coffee. We stay here planning it all and go quietly after dark about seven o'clock. Anybody any problem with this?"

They all said no.

As planned I left bang on time. Jonny followed ten minutes later. We would not meet. He was to give me half an hour in the flat to pack enough things to take and sort out passport and anything else which I might need prior to a week's absence. He would simply watch and call me if there was anything untoward. Once at home I put together a small bag with clothing, toiletries, and all other essentials. I then checked and tested the miniature security camera I had always had but never used, before positioning it in a hidden position in the ceiling from which it viewed the whole room.

Who were they? I felt it likely there had to be more than one. And how had they got on to us? I was inclined to go with Elizabeth's feeling that they had sussed out Piet. But how? Were they as violent as Kokot and Van der Merwe? Or were they under South African government or Mint control? If the latter the danger to us would probably be much lower. But we really had no idea about any of that. Then I retrieved an old suitcase and set about doctoring and leaving in it a few scraps of paper and cardboard, looking for all the world that they were left behind from the rest of Maghiel's life's history. That was what they may be seeking! A couple of Afrikaner words, design of a coin which could have been a kruger, and a quickly made rough sketch of the plan of the Mint as I knew it. I threw the case back into the cupboard and locked it. Something for any intruder to be going on with.

I then went to my desk and wrote a note to myself signed ostensibly by Piet talking about where the bulk case contents had been hidden in my chest of drawers. I placed this in the small safe drawer and locked it. Any would-be thief would tear apart the locked drawers and find nothing, but we would at least know they had been there. Shades of Elias. I glanced quickly at the clock. It was already time to go.

I grabbed the pack, walked quickly out, locked the door behind me and departed back to the boat, saying goodbye to my home for I knew not how long.

Mission accomplished. On time.

THIRTY-THREE

SOUTH AFRICA

The next night we left for Johannesburg.

After a ten-hour uneventful flight we hired a small Toyota and booked in to the airport Protea hotel from where, over a substantial breakfast, Piet called his Norwegian Embassy contact. There was a long wait. Then, happily, an answer. Shuter was in and Piet was immediately put through to him.

"Hello there Jan. Piet Geldenhuys. I called in to see you recently?"

"Yes Piet. Remember it well. How goes it?"

"Fine thanks. You recall you introduced me to one of your colleagues who knew about your Cape Town consul in the old days."

"Yeah, Web Potgieter. He only comes in very occasionally to see us. Doesn't work here at all though. He's been retired a pretty long time."

Piet gave me the thumbs up. "I wonder if I could contact him. Doing some research into the Cape Town of the old days. You know, recalling the way things used to be.

"Huh, you mean the *good* old days!"

"Yeah. Well, possibly. Do you think he could help - throw some light, even in a small way? Maybe even give us some direction about where else to go for information?"

"No problem. He's definitely your man. Knows all of that stuff. Jolly well ought to, he's been around long enough. Hold one minute. Just looking him up----yes, I have his number."

Piet scribbled it down and repeated it back to be sure. "Thanks very much Jan. A beer or two on me the next time we meet. Adios."

"Great. Goodbye Piet. I hope it works out for you. Come in and see us the next time you're passing. 'Bye." He rang off.

"So far so good. Now for the big one."

He dialled the numbers for the target. The answer took over half a minute to reply. Piet was getting to look nervous until a weak Afrikaner voice came across very, very slowly.

"Web speaking."

"Good morning Mr Potgieter. Sorry to disturb you. My name is Piet Geldenhuys. We met recently in the Norwegian embassy when we were together with Jan Shuter."

"Yes----I remember. You work with a Brit company. Back and forward all of the time."

"Yes. I recall that long ago you knew quite a bit about the consulate in Cape Town. What it did. How it went about its work. All those sorts of things."

"Yeah. A guy called Stig Ericsson was the big beast in charge."

"And you mentioned the accountant there, whose name I think was de Villiers."

"Yes, knew him well. Always in a hurry to do things. One of those sorts. Never wanted to miss a trick. Didn't do him any good though."

"Oh?"

"He died years ago. Had a heart problem for a long time and it suddenly became serious."

Piet looked downcast. "I am sorry to hear that. I was hoping to get some information on the old Cape Town, the fishing and boatbuilding that went on. Maybe put it all together in a book one of these days."

"Sorry I cannot help." There was a long pause. "He did have a son who might know something."

"Do you have any contact?"

"His first name was Bern. That's all I can remember."

"Is he still in Cape Town or has he gone somewhere else?"

"Oh no. He's not down there." A long dormant memory was slowly triggered. "He came here to Jo'burg. Some sort of lawyer I think. His father was very proud of that."

"Well many thanks, Web, for all your help."

"Sorry I cannot recall any more. Memory fades a bit with age you know. Best of luck. Send me a copy of the book if you ever complete it."

"Yes, I will. You have been a great help. Goodbye."

There was still a chance although by now I was sceptical. "Do you think the son will know anything?"

"We must try." Piet answered positively through a mouthful of what was now cold scrambled egg. As soon as he had finished his meal we went quickly up to our room where Piet had assembled his laptop. He muttered the words as he worked.

"Johannesburg. Lawyers. Bern de Villiers."

And up it came! Just like that.

Bern de Villiers. Attorney. Deacon Dadge Anderson. International Law Consultants.

Piet immediately phoned the number. It rang three times. They were already in.

"Deacon Dadge. May I help you?"

"May I please speak with Mr Bern de Villiers?"

There was a slight pause. "Sorry, he is off today. It is his holiday. Please call back tomorrow."

Before the phone went down Piet said very quickly, "The matter is urgent. I would be grateful for his contact number."

"We cannot give out home details, sir, I hope you will understand that."

My mind flew into overdrive while they spoke. Huge South African crime figures most likely had brought this about over the years. We had it a bit in London too. I quickly scribbled a note and placed it in front of him.

"You do not want home, just his mobile for business reasons."

Piet repeated this to her. There was a long wait while some conversation took place at the other end. Eventually she grudgingly gave over the number and didn't say goodbye.

Piet again wasted no time at all and called.

"Bern de Villiers."

"Good morning, Mr de Villiers. My name is Piet Geldenhuys. I am resident in Pretoria but am doing some research into the history of Cape Town."

He laughed. "I was brought up there but I regret I know very little about the place as it was. Been gone a long time."

"Your father's name has come up in our researches and we wondered if we could ask you a few questions related to him? It would only take a few minutes."

There was a short delay while he thought and we hoped.

"Ok, no problem. It's my day off and I am at home. Drive over if you wish this afternoon. But I really do

not know much. Childhood days are a long way off."
He gave his address.

"Excellent. Thank you. See you then. About two o'clock."

Piet pocketed his phone. "That part of Bryanston is quite up-market. He is doing well."

I smiled. "He's a lawyer for goodness sake. How many poor ones have *you* ever met?"

"Yeah. Good call though. He thinks we are coming from Pretoria. We won't disillusion him."

"Sleep for say three hours. Then visit?"

"Great idea Dave. I'm shattered."

We set the alarm.

THIRTY-FOUR

Haffenbacker landed at Gatwick on a cold but bright near - spring day. Marguerite met him at Arrivals and led him straight to the airport lounge.

"Sorry about the hold-up. They still have some snow but the runways are now more or less clear. Jacobi is following me later. So, where do we go from here?"

"This is David Johnston. I know exactly where he lives and Geldenhuys has based himself there during his stay in London." Marguerite handed over the pictures.

He gave her one of his approving looks which she so appreciated. "You *have* been busy! Those cases could be kept in there?" He studied the entranceway leading to the lifts for the upper level flats. "Which one is it?"

She pointed. "Second one along on the left. I can only guess at what is there, but very likely, yes, they may well be hidden somewhere. Any problem with getting in to a place like that?"

He studied the locking mechanism picture which she had enlarged, looked at it all ways round, and smiled. "Modern, neat and efficient but penetrable. When do we start?"

"Well, now for the bad part. After doing a recce of the place I was trailed all the way home. At first it was a feeling - the sort of thing us types are aware of but still unsure. I became certain when a taxi followed my car at a distance, but not very cleverly if he wished not to be noticed. I took the registration number but unfortunately at no time could I fully see the passenger.

I later sought out the taxi driver and told him all sorts of horror stories about this man - how he had terrorised me - that sort of thing. He described him as white, but someone who had seen a lot of sun. My guess is it was Geldenhuys - but how, how, how--?"

"What a fine old pickle to get yourself into!" Haff was almost smiling and she could have kicked him.

"---but, Breck Haffenbecker, I could not leave it there."

He wasn't a bit surprised at that.

"I donned my old woman kit - something I keep for special occasions - and went straight back the following day. It was cold and I hung around in doorways looking totally destitute 'till late. To cut a very long story short both men came, Johnston went in and Geldenhuys kept a look out well away from the scene."

"My God you are incredible. I'm really glad you're on our side! Hold everything for a moment." He slipped quickly away, collected a couple of coffees, and hurried back.

"It took half an hour. Johnston came out carrying a bag and as soon as that happened Geldenhuys disappeared."

"And you followed Johnston."

"Yes, with extreme caution, of course."

There was a long silence. He wanted to ask but held back. She wanted his appreciation and was not going to spill the beans immediately. The girls were on top. But he wasn't the weak stereotypic male she so loathed. He simply remained silent, wondering just how long it would be before she came up with the details. Time passed by but it was seconds rather than minutes before she came out with it.

"Their HQ seems to be a less than smart boat moored in St Katharine Dock which is just off the Thames at Tower Bridge. Her name is Marianne."

THIRTY-FIVE

Elizabeth arrived at St Katharines as dawn was breaking. She was following their new stricter security rules and would not be departing until after dark. The plan was that someone would always now be on the boat during daylight hours, mainly to access computer details if necessary, and to be available in case of any urgent situation arising. Jonny had done the last two days and had become bored he told her last night on the phone.

She fed in the numbers and passed through the gate into the Boat Owners Only area. Nobody was around. She walked across to Marianne and boarded quietly, carefully closing the door after her, and then push-buttoned the heating.

She then made herself coffee and unwrapped the baguette she had just bought. Breakfast on anything afloat was wonderful. She could hear the gently throbbing engines of newly arriving boats which were still being locked in from the river and moved a curtain just enough to study them as they motored towards their assigned moorings. Each was different, some sailing yachts, some power boats, several having spent the night crossing the channel. The crews aboard those would be desperate to moor and get some sleep. She envied them. Quite unlike Jonny she had things nautical wrapped in her DNA.

After breakfast she washed up and then set about cleaning the place. Her male colleagues were not bad but that was the highest accolade she could give. She pulled out the cloths and cleaning fluids she had brought in her small bag and set to work.

Half an hour later she unlocked the door down in to the lower cabin and had the shock of her life! The cases were not there – anywhere! She went hurriedly down, felt through the bed, looked underneath, and inspected every other nook and cranny. They were big and there simply was nothing anywhere. She returned quickly back up above and searched all over. Jonny---he might have taken them? Unlikely though, it would be contrary to his own planning. But he might just. She called him.

"Morning Elizabeth. How's the boat?"

"Jonny, did you take the Grobelaar papers?"

"No of course not. My rules. Leave them where----"

"They've gone. All cases and contents---

"Whaat—gone, are you sure?"

"Yes, just went down below. Nothing. I scoured around up top. Nothing. Nothing anywhere. What on earth are we going to do?"

"Computers?"

She looked over into the far dark corner.

"No, they're both there."

Her voice tone was rising to a higher note. She was almost sobbing, completely overwhelmed by what she had found.

"Mm, probably realised they couldn't break in to them. Passwords too good. Cool it Liz. Stay right there. Do not do anything. Will be with you in twenty minutes or a bit more. Right?"

"Ok, Jonny. Make it quick."

She sat down and tried to think rationally but her emotions had taken such control she couldn't focus. The bottom had just dropped out of the most exciting thing in which she had ever been involved. All the papers stolen! They had been outwitted – completely and utterly. She stared blindly into space. Somebody had been in here very recently. The mere thought of that alone horrified her. She let go and wept.

In record time Jonny arrived, breathing heavily. He almost fell in to the boat. She showed him the empty spaces where the cases had been.

"Was the door locked when you arrived?"

"Yes, all normal. Nothing else was touched."

"Let's sit down and talk it through. Second thoughts - the coffee shop is just open. Will maybe calm us both."

She followed him out, all thoughts of security gone. With no papers on board there was nothing to hide anyway. Jonny bought and they moved quickly up the winding staircase. Although there was nobody up top this early in the morning, they kept their voices down. He wanted to assess very carefully the damage done, having hatched an idea during his stomach churning tube trip here. When they were settled, he came straight to the point.

"Your drawings of pulpit rails and all that. Where are they?"

"Here in my pocket."

"Well by pure chance I kept all my measurement details with me too. Tell me if I am wrong but I think nothing about pulpit rails and all that will be found in the stolen stuff. If that is correct, then we are still completely in pole position.

Elizabeth brightened a little, her natural optimism trying hard to surface. She realised, somewhat ruefully, that through all this Jonny himself had managed to keep his cool while she had simply gone completely to pieces.

"I have also retained the Maghiel notes from which we extrapolated everything attached to my papers. Here they are." She pulled out several ragged sheets of paper from an inner pocket and gave them to him.

"Elizabeth, I think between us we may quite unintentionally have saved the day." The beginnings of a smile touched the corners of his mouth. He spent a long time carefully examining everything. "Yes. Almost certainly we're in the clear. All they will know about is what we had before your Pa's call."

"But what about the computers?"

"Probably nothing on there. They would have found nothing modern. If you remember our breakthrough comprised your father's call, our conversations and these sketches and notes. And, anyway, the computers are all pretty secure as only Dave knows how. Very unlikely any outside agency could get in."

They went silent, both buried in thought. Elizabeth at last was calm enough to explore the situation carefully as she sipped her hot coffee. She could not fault his logic. By sheer chance---. Whoever had done this dastardly thing would, as Jonny said, reach the dead end they themselves were at before father's revelations came through. They would find nothing. But it was now highly possible that that would cause them come back. She shuddered at such a horrible thought.

Jonny was thinking along the same lines. If those who had so expertly found and robbed them could still not get anywhere they would not be stop in their efforts to extract more information in one way or another. He recalled the murderous approach to the problem of the now imprisoned Kokot and Van der Merwe. No reason to suppose these new people would be any less aggressive, whoever their paymaster happened to be. They had to take maximum precautions.

"We've got to go to ground."

"Agreed." It mirrored exactly her conclusions. "And tell Dave and Piet."

"Yes, I'll do that. We must all keep clear of Marianne and Dave's place. Suggest when we leave here, we take round the houses ways home just in case we are being followed. You happy with that?"

"Yes of course, but how on earth did they find Marianne?"

"They followed somebody here. They are top class at what they are doing. We won't waste time going into it now. The damage is done. Keep in close touch with me all the time."

Elizabeth pocketed her paperwork and went off first.

A troubled Jonny followed slowly a few minutes later.

THIRTY-SIX

SOUTH AFRICA

We arrived on time.

De Villiers greeted us. He was a short stocky South African casually dressed in a vivid orange polo shirt and lightweight grey slacks. He pointed the way in to his study and followed us in and sat us down. He seemed to be in the house on his own.

"A cool drink of some kind?"

"No thanks very much. We've just had lunch."

I wanted to get down to whatever business there was to be had as quickly as possible. But almost immediately something in me froze. On his desk, made up as a paperweight, was a real, gold, perfect in all respects, krugerrand. It was unmistakeable - we had studied numerous pictures of them. I gave a guarded sideways glance at Piet. He had seen it too and looked to be struggling hard to keep his eyes off.

"Well now what can I do for you gentlemen concerning my father?"

Piet had rehearsed in the car. "We're doing a survey of "through the ages" boatbuilding in the Cape and his name was mentioned by a friend of mine in the Norwegian embassy. What sort of part did he play? Was he in any way involved in that industry as it was developing?"

"Well, he helped out on maintenance sometimes - it gave him a break from constantly poring over peoples' books - but he could in no way be called a shipbuilder! My father was a jack of many trades. Most people were, certainly in his earlier days. He basically earned his keep through accountancy but he loved dealing with anything which floated and sometimes got involved helping out with small boat maintenance in one of the minor yards down there."

"Is that yard still around?"

"Yes. But it is quite modernised now. It still goes by the name of Bezzy's Boats. The owner at the time was known as Bloody Bezuidenhout, but he is no longer around. I think that title they gave him was a reflection of his pricing policy. His particular skills were needed widely around the coast and he knew it. Still, that's the wicked way of the world I'm afraid."

"And presumably there are very few who remember those old days and what went on?"

"One old guy who came from Botswana, I think. But that's probably all. It is a bit late now for you to get much detail about how things were then. A long time has gone by and everything has changed dramatically over those years."

Piet then muttered in as casual a voice as he could manage. "Well I suppose we could look him up in case he remembers anything?"

"Name of Kashita. I hope he hasn't gone into full retirement yet. He's way over age. Mention me to him as I visited there some years ago. He may remember. We had quite a chat about father and the old days."

I was grappling with the problem of talking about the kruger lying innocently in front of him. We really ought to know a little more about it. Such an item on show would normally attract some comment from a visitor. I decided to be blunt.

"Is that a krugerrand you have there?"

"Yes, my father gave it to me - a form of encouraging me to save, I think. I was always short of money at the time and he told me to use it as a last resort if things ever took a downturn. I hang on to it in his memory. Unusual to have one on one's desk!"

"They're quite valuable." Piet also was trying to keep it low key.

He frowned and immediately changed the subject. He had decided our time was up. "Yes, the gold price constantly fluctuates of course. Now, is there anything else I can do for you both?"

I guessed we had gone as far as we could. "No. Thank you for your time. We are very grateful. When we are down there we will look up Kashita and will certainly give him your good wishes."

We stood up, shook hands and followed him to the way out.

Luck was with us and we knew it! We booked out of the hotel and drove frantically overnight all the way to Cape Town. One slept while the other drove. Two hours on, two hours off. At around mid-day we found Bezzy's Boats. It was by no means still a small set-up. We followed the drive in, left the car and were soon speaking with the only person we could find. He was working hard polishing an already gleaming motor cruiser.

"We are looking for Kashita. Any chance he is here?"

"That's me, but I only work here a couple of days a week. I do all the cleaning jobs. I think you want the management?" He pointed further into the yard, past several posh new boats on huge trailers, gleaming in the sun.

Piet took over. "No, we were actually given your name. We are doing some research on the old Cape Town. Bygone days and how things were then."

"I'm old enough for all that." His white teeth gleamed as his black face was suddenly wreathed in smiles. "I've been here for ever. I reckon I go back as far as almost any person in the boat world who is alive today. They tell me I'm the one they cannot put out to pasture. I know too much! So much that my knowledge is valuable!"

Piet took his cue from that and handed over a couple of notes from his wallet. "Do you recall a man called de Villiers?"

"Oh yes. Very much so." He carefully pocketed the money. "He called in here about three years ago. I hadn't seen him since he was young! Very different now. Wife and kids. A smart lawyer - of all things!"

Piet responded quickly. "No, it's not the son we are talking about. It's the father."

He thought that over for a minute, wiped the sweat from his forehead, and then motioned us to a nearby bench seat shaded by several overhanging tree branches.

"Only just. It was a real long time ago. He aided Mr Bezuidenhout with the books and did a bit of boat servicing to help us out when things were tough. He was always a part-timer. I think he did the jobs for the hell of it rather than just the money."

I joined in. We had to go fast. Somebody might come and break this up and we'd wait a long time for another chance to be right at the coal face. "What sort of servicing?"

"He liked repairing damage like on boats that had hit something. Or putting right something done badly.

He could see things. Liked the old wooden boats best but he did tinker around with the new plastic ones too. Always steady. Never rushed anything. He knew what held a boat together. That was what made him so valuable to the boss."

"Didn't he work with the old Norwegian consulate?"

"Yeah. He looked after the old man's boat as well as their books - he was quite useful to them. The only time he really got a move on with anything was when he was dealing with that boat! About the only clear thing I really remember."

"Oh why?" I bit my tongue. It was the wrong thing to ask.

He looked at me very sharply. "Is this still your investigation on old Cape Town?"

I replied very slowly and carefully, thinking hard as I spoke. "Yes, we're keen to know what people did. How they got on before all this modern machinery came in."

"Well the consul was returning to Norway and he wanted the upgrade done here as we were much cheaper. Then to have the boat shipped on after him. Must have cost a bomb but the man was loaded. He was one of those. I'll never forget de Villiers working like a dog to complete it. Not like him at all. New fittings in the wheelhouse, complete servicing of the engines and new fire extinguishers. When it was all completed they craned her on to a large cargo ship which was due to call in to Scandinavia somewhere."

Piet took over, very gently. "Did you help with all this?"

"Of course. I helped all the time. We worked harder in those days. Slave labour almost. All we do is new boats now." He actually sounded regretful.

"All you worked on in this boat was below decks. Never anything above?"

"Well, only the rails. Had to be strengthened. I remember Mr de Villiers swearing at having to work all night to get that finished. The boat was sent off for loading the next day."

Piet showed no emotion. "Rails. What are they?"

Kashita looked sadly at the hopeless white man. "They go around the boat. They had to be replaced with larger, stronger rails. He did it all in one night, which is an incredible speed, especially for him." He smiled at the memory of it all.

I ignored the buzz I felt from my mobile. "And the boat was then transported back to his place in Norway?"

"Yep. Think so."

"Do you know where?" I flinched at Piet's question which was almost certainly a step too far.

"Look here, mister, I have no idea. It was years ago. This is a funny way to find out about old Cape Town. All I know is he lived in a place called Flam - that word sticks in the mind."

The fur was about to fly so I challenged him quickly. "I'll bet you can't remember the boat's name."

"Odin."

I had noticed a movement through the distant office window. It was definitely time to turn the conversation back to the official reason for our visit. We had achieved most of what we came for.

"Were there any other shipyards around here at the time."

"No, just us." A figure emerged and moved slowly towards us. Kashita rose at once to move off.

"The boss. Have to go. Best of luck with your survey." He moved across the hard, back to his polishing and we returned with some haste to the car.

Piet drove off. He was on a high.

"Flam, Norway."

"Odin." I responded.

"PR was right."

"Yes." I pulled out the phone. "Message from Jonny. He wants a call asap." I pushed the button. There was a twenty second wait.

"Dave."

"Jonny, all ok?"

"No---and yes. Just listen. All the cases have been pinched from the boat. Our friends are highly competent at robbery. We have lost everything. But not to despair. The good news is that nothing of our final breakthrough is in their hands - PR and all that. Elizabeth kept all her scribblings and I have mine. Seems to me we are in the clear there."

My lack of sleep was now totally forgotten. I forced myself to concentrate and come to terms quickly with what he was saying. I flew through the other unrelated stuff on Hercules. No problem there. Nobody would fathom my passwords.

"They will work through all the paperwork and eventually come to a dead end then? I suggested knowledgeably.

"Yes. All is ok I think. Bloody lucky."

"If they haven't found enough they are very likely to come back for more."

"Yes. Marianne as well as your home have now to be no-go places."

"Agreed. We have big news and are on our way home. Can you research a boat called Odin in a place called Flam in Norway. The rails were upgraded and boat shipped home when the Consul returned there."

Piet shouted across. "Consul's name was Stig Ericsson."

"Phew! Yes, of course, we will go into all that. But I'll bet it has changed hands in the past twenty years. Dave, you and Piet have nowhere to stay. We have a spare room for Piet and you go to Elizabeth's place. And call us when you know arrival airport and time."

I looked at Piet. "Both say yes and very grateful. See you soon. We hope to get on the next plane back."

"Cheerio. Have a good trip."

THIRTY-SEVEN

No two people have ever reacted to anything more quickly! We dropped off the hired car in Cape Town and managed to get seats on the twelve-hour direct flight to London Gatwick, arriving in the early morning chill. Jonny and Elizabeth were there to meet us and whisked us off to her ground floor Pimlico flat. Soon we were sat around the kitchen table munching a magnificent bacon and egg breakfast.

"No talking about anything to do with what we have all been up to while we eat. Jonny and I have lots to say and you two have as well. Everything covering what we have done is on that other table ready for us to discuss after we have eaten. Meantime we chat sweet nothings. I reckon the speed at which all these events are happening risks getting us all far too steamed up."

Elizabeth had abruptly stamped her supremacy as the boss - it was her home - and maybe she was endeavouring to bring some down to earth common sense to bear on the situation. I had frequently noticed she did this calming down thing at work when we happened to be exceptionally busy. And just now things were getting frenetic.

I looked around the very small flat. She had put me into her visitor room, a tiny bedroom just capable of taking a single bed. I was thankful for it. The kitchen was really an extension of the living room. Elizabeth had the main bedroom and there was a tiny bathroom.

Jonny gazed at us, crunching happily away at his fried bread. "You know, us Brits just do not eat really good breakfasts these days. Usually at home we have a bit of cereal possibly followed by toast and marmalade if we are lucky."

"Dammit, I don't even get that!" They laughed. My bachelor breakfast habits were widely known.

"Well, while you're here, Dave, you will be fed." Elizabeth sounded almost matronly. "Poor starved creature!" She eyed me up and down. "You know I think you have lost a bit of weight since I last saw you. Rushing around in aeroplanes and cars does that, you know."

Piet then got involved in detail about the sort of South African food to which he was accustomed, leading to a full-scale discussion about the varieties of fruits produced in South Africa. Then he got on to wines and, following a comment from Elizabeth, we had a dissertation on snakes with some pretty lurid stories of how these venomous creatures kill. We kept trying but it was obvious to us all that, behind the small talk, there was an enormous desire to get on with things. Too much was happening in our lives which we could not disregard for very long. Quite suddenly all the dishes were magically whisked away and we moved as one across to the other smaller table. On it was one sole sheet of paper which I had failed to manage to read upside down from a distance. The black printed words there read

FLAAM
BERGEN
STAVANGER
ODIN
LARS ERIKSSON (SON OF STIG)

Whilst we assumed it was our activities in South Africa were of paramount importance it was now Jonny who started the ball rolling.

"Ok everyone. You know the boat was skilfully raided and so well was it done that Elizabeth was there for half an hour before realising anything was wrong. You could call it a top criminal professional job. Significantly they took only items relevant to our own investigations. In no way could it have been a normal robbery simply aimed at carrying out a theft of anything that happened to be around. But I'm delighted to say that whoever they, and perhaps their masters, are, we can, for purposes of this meeting, not be too worried about what they took. All they have got will be leading them nowhere because due to incredibly good fortune they are way behind the curve. At best their investigation will take them to where we were before Elizabeth's father's revelations changed the landscape. That was where, you will recall, we had decided we were at a dead end! None of the PR detail can be found by them as Elizabeth and I both kept all our scribbles in our pockets, in order to copy out more clearly later and then to file with the main stuff."

I added my thoughts. "Really well done. But they are obviously top-notch investigators or criminals. They will certainly be looking to get more out of us. We have deduced they are somehow aware of the link with AandA and Eisenbauer. They will now wonder why we are going on with the investigation if we have no further information to guide us. You two were absolutely right to keep us away from Marianne. Things could get nasty from here on in." Of the four of us I had always been the most boringly cautious, but now I could see they were catching up fast.

Jonny steered us back on track to the here and now. "Yes, of course, we must be very careful. As soon as we fully appreciated what had taken place with you Elizabeth started working day and night. She will tell you why. Please listen very carefully." He gave her the slightest of nods.

She stood up, teacher-style, and looked down at her carefully selected prompt words staring provocatively up from the table.

"I have used the web, the phone and book references non-stop since you called from Cape Town with those names and we have learned a lot. Stig Ericcson passed away five years ago in Flaam, which you should pronounce Flum, a small place situated at the head of Sognefjord in Norway. Population there is only a few hundred, if that, so they probably nearly all know each other. I had a long and very interesting conversation with Stig's wife about their time spent overseas in Cape Town and, amongst many other items of interest, I learned that Odin was taken over by her son Lars. He spent his leisure time exploring the fjords and surrounding waters but his work was actually with a Swedish company based in Stavanger where he would normally keep the boat."

"So, he would----"

"Piet, I suggest you let Elizabeth finish!" The stinging tone of Jonny's voice made me sit up. It was a rebuke. We had worked together a long time and I knew that way of speaking. Something big was coming - that was for sure.

"Well, he married his long-time partner about two years ago when he learned he was to be sent by his Swedish masters to England to help open more of their furniture stores here!!"

Piet simply could not hold back.

"He's here now?"

"Yes!"

Nor could I. I was stunned.

"What about the boat?"

"The nearest I could get was that they motored it over across the North Sea - mother said she was extremely concerned about this at the time - and they keep it somewhere on the Thames. She did not know where." Elizabeth pointed at her printed words. "There you are. All points covered. Yet again we have a completely new situation." She sat down to a huge round of applause.

"Elizabeth has been bloody brilliant. She did it all. I just sat here looking on, cracking jokes and providing the snacks while she went at researching it for hours on end." Jonny, too, was clearly rapturous at the results. "They carried on a very lengthy conversation and, rather like you two, Elizabeth was taking the line that she was looking at the history of Cape Town. From what I heard it was clear to me listening in to most of the conversations that took place that Mrs Eriksson would find it impossible to pinpoint to the real reason for the call."

"Fantastic, Elizabeth, really well done. What next? Where do we go from here?"

"Well, Dave, there are one or two more clues. There are only three headquarters of largish Swedish companies selling the type of products she described. One is in Doncaster, which we can probably forget, one is in Walton and the other south of Oxford. Those last two are within easy reach of the Thames. It is likely, but not certain, that Odin is within seventy miles of us and not too far from one or other of those two places. Maybe we could speak to all likely long-stay marinas, but that has to be a joint decision made by us all I think."

"We can't do that. We would draw attention to ourselves from the marina staff and maybe then from Ericsson himself. I think that has in it the seeds of major problems."

I was sure Piet was right and that Elizabeth was simply trying to get us thinking. "Well, how do we proceed from here on in? The essential thing is to find the boat and ascertain if, after all these years, the stuff is still holed up in the pulpit rails, if indeed it ever was there. If we do discover the boat, cut through a pulpit rail and find nothing do we pay for the repair? And how on earth do we even begin to explain what we were doing? If we find something, do we simply then take it and do a runner? I am getting a bit perturbed about procedure."

I looked around at their expressions. We had a very tricky situation on our hands the length and breadth if it all was beginning to show.

"Maybe we could buy the boat?" Jonny had a solution but one that hit the buffers straight away.

Elizabeth shook her head. "Even at its age I would guess the going price would be a hundred and fifty thousand pounds. Twin diesel huge horse powered engines need to have a very substantial, and therefore expensive, boat around them. And, anyway, I would think he must be wedded to it given the history and his present-day usage. People can get very close to their boats you know. Treat them as they would a close friend. And, anyway, why would he want to sell?"

"Why not seek out Ericsson, explain everything, and give him a good percentage? Coming out of the blue he would probably join us rather than oppose." Piet shook his head as soon as he had uttered the words. The moment he spoke he realised it was possible we could lose everything and that could in no way now be right. "No, I withdraw that. It is not the answer."

I tried to give things a positive touch. "I think we should first find the boat. We do not know exactly where she is, whether the mooring is open to public view, or if she is tucked away in some isolated place. Worst scenario, the boat may not be in this country at all. Once found we can then deliberate further on what to do."

There was general agreement to this. We had reached some sort of next stage. The atmosphere became less tense. It was break time. Jonny looked at his watch and quickly stood up. "Have to go. I promised to be back. Home and family need me for the next couple of hours. And I suspect Piet needs a bit of shut-eye."

It dawned on me that details of our Cape Town visit had not even been requested, such was the significance of all we had heard. Elizabeth had the next move already planned.

"Right then, everybody back here tomorrow sharp at 0800 hours to plan the hunt!"

Her flat had become our new HQ.

THIRTY-EIGHT

Then they had gone and we were alone. Elizabeth gave me a guided tour which took all of two minutes. I was not really listening but managed a few yesses and noes. I had always seen her first and foremost as a psychologist, not a member of the opposite sex. Or maybe as a human being whom I was simply using to enhance my own AandA career. I was now getting a whole new view of her as a real woman in real life outside the confines of a company environment. She simply wasn't just capable, which was my business view of her, she was exquisite.

"So, there you have it. Two small bedrooms, one bathroom and a kitchen-cum-living room. And very cosy it is for me living in the middle of Town."

"Yes, close to where you worked too. Quite convenient. You know, Elizabeth, I can't thank you enough. It was either this or yet another of those ghastly characterless hotels."

"Cooking might have been better there." She made a face. "But I will do my best. It's never been my top subject. And the whole world knows of your culinary deficiencies, so we won't be relying on you for a range of cooked delicacies!"

I put on a show of complete dismay. "Don't you be too sure, young lady. I do a good omelette, beans on toast, ratatouille and spaghetti bolognaise, which could be useful given the right circumstances."

We sat down in her two comfortable chairs. I knew her well enough to sense things were brewing in that agile mind. She was holding back on something and my guess was that it had to do with the river. An extension to our discussion on Odin perhaps.

"David, you must be exhausted after that flight and all the South African shenanigans."

"Not too tired to listen. We did get a wee bit of shut eye on the plane."

"Well---ok. Unlike you, I've been living with this local situation for many hours. And I know the river much better than anyone in our team. The people on it, generally speaking, form a very enclosed society, although you wouldn't think so looking in from the outside. Many know each other and are certainly familiar with a lot of the boats which ply up and down. I agree that it would be very unwise simply to ask the staff in each marina if they knew of Odin. The question on every lip would be--- Why? And we don't want that at all. So there has to be a better way."

"What about driving a car from one marina to the next? An easy thing to do and unlikely to arouse any interest anywhere. We can wander around at our leisure checking on all the boats and be completely at our ease."

"Up to a point. That is until one realises that there are probably more boats moored on river banks than in all the marinas put together, many of which would be invisible from the road. There are very many landowners like farmers, house residents, Thames Water lettings etc., all the way along who have the right to moor on their particular river frontages."

"Then why not go by boat? That way one covers shorelines and marinas."

She smiled. I felt that maybe we had arrived at what she had already planned. "Two boats. Jonny and Piet should hire an out of season one in Oxford to move from there down river as far as Wargrave, and you and I will take father's boat from my home near there down to London. Not really very clever as it seems we could be getting some snow tonight. But we can deal with that situation if it occurs. Each boat will examine every nook and cranny in the river as well as all marinas and other mooring places. Whoever finds Odin immediately informs the other."

It was clear that she already had had it all worked out. "Great idea but I don't think that either Piet or Jonny are knowledgeable boat handlers, and that's putting it mildly. May be a problem there?"

"No, it's all right. Honest. Jonny learned a lot helping me with Marianne who, incidentally, I've now put up for sale. We should get our money back if we hang on long enough, or, what's more probable in my view, make a sizeable profit. And, of course, these hire boats in non-tidal waters are easy to control. It's not a bit like being at sea. The two of them should be ok."

"How long will it take each boat to travel its own half of the river?"

"Two to three days if we really go at it. A boat the size of Odin is too high to get under the Oxford Osney bridge, so that cuts down the length of river which we have to consider."

Inadvertently I let a yawn slip out. I hadn't really slept that much flying back from Cape Town and I was really beginning to feel fatigue setting in.

Elizabeth, seeing how things were with me, started getting her forthright mode on again. "I really think you should sleep. You are looking worn out. The bed is made up. Go!"

"Yes, thanks Elizabeth. I really do need to get some shuteye." I got up and made my way to my room.

"Well I am off shopping and our next get together will be tea at four o'clock. You have five whole hours to catch up!"

And sleep I did.

The moment my head hit the pillow a rush of thoughts sped through my brain. Who were these people who had so expertly stolen the Mubanga papers? How were we to handle the Odin situation if we found her? When would I get back to my flat? Relief came quickly with the anaesthetising effect of her immaculately prepared bed. I slept the sleep of the gods. No thoughts. No dreams. Just total oblivion.

It was actually dark when I awoke to the sound of a voice. Elizabeth poked her head around the door and switched on the light. "Dinner in a quarter of an hour. Tea time was long ago. I let you sleep on."

"Aah, thanks. Overslept. I'll be there." Reluctantly, I returned to the real world.

The small table was beautifully set and the lamb chops were quite out of this world. The red wine was rather special and the woman looked ravishing. "You know I don't deserve all this. You were just giving me a bed. Remember?"

"Well I don't often get a man around the place. It's a nice experience, even in these rather mad times. Besides you're my boss! I'm honour bound to look after you."

"Not so now. They've paid me off. I'm a free man! You know, I'm only now appreciating your full contribution at AandA. Your input to the whole thing there was huge. It's no wonder Eisenbauer wanted to hang on to you."

Behind the smile she gave was a look that fleetingly revealed some inner thought which I could in no way fathom. The sweet was a marvellous Pavlova. She must have worked hard at it all. Replete after the sumptuous meal we moved from the table and slithered down into the settee. It was a long time since I had felt so completely relaxed.

"What happened to your partner, David?"

"Well she left. My fault. Job and general way of life. She couldn't stand it. Looking back, I can see that for her I wasn't the most gleaming car in the multi-storey."

"Maybe she had her eye elsewhere?"

"Possibly. She's now married somebody more suited to her chosen way of life. Works in a bank, I think. I was a mess for quite some time after she dumped me. Things went from bad to worse and then slowly righted again. I gave up the booze and concentrated on work. What about you?"

"I was taken for a ride by a real thug four years ago. Father had warned me off him - he can size up anybody with just a glance. I suppose his work helps with that - and, silly me, I took no notice. I've been a bit careful about Mr Male ever since."

I changed the subject. "Snow or no snow you know we really ought to get moving in the next couple of days?"

"Yes, we must. I know one of the hire companies in Oxford. They keep a small pleasure boat in commission, I think for their own use, all winter. I'm pretty sure we could hire it. And Father's boat is always ready to go. He keeps it that way and I help."

"That three days. Do we sleep aboard?"

"Of course."

"Are you ok with that Elizabeth?"

She laughed. "*You're* not a problem. Remember I've been able to vet you for a long time." She stood up. "Stay there. I'm clearing these things away. I need ten minutes and then, Sir, drinks will be served."

I was entering uncharted territory. Something deep down was stirring. Women for me had been taboo ever since Sally had stormed out. I didn't even look at them as most men do. They were poison personified and I had kept well clear. But this one was something else - pleasant, beautiful and highly intelligent with it. During those years with her at AandA I had rarely noticed the hair, blue eyes, shapely body and the challenging aura that she unwittingly carried around. That siren voice was sounding again from deep within me - "*forget it, chum, you'll get yourself real bloody hurt again!*"

Coffee came and was accompanied by two brandies. She poured while I luxuriated in the moment. "If we find Odin I think we have to work out a way of looking first and, if no krugers fall from the pulpits, apologising and compensating afterwards."

I had been working on this myself. For the first time since the beginning of this venture I realised that Elizabeth was, like me, an *overall picture* person. She was as concerned as I was about where all this was going, the potential for us being criminalised, and the eventual overall cost to us if it all went wrong. "Like planning some sort of accident? Our boat mistakenly hit yours---very sorry about that, Mr Ericsson, we'll of course pay up for any damage done?"

She smiled. "There in one. Unless you have a better idea?"

"Nope. But what, just what, if we were to find those things *are* still tucked away in Odin's PRs where they were so carefully stored decades ago?"

"I've thought about that too. The world is a funny place. The owner might well claim it all. There could be legal reports all over the papers. Everyone from prisoners Van der Merwe and Kokot to the South African government and the unknowns who are chasing us will all become aware. It would be a nightmare we would have to ride out---but at least if we had taken say, one half, and left the rest we would have enough, each hiding his own share. Elias Mubanga could rest easy. Cheers." She raised her glass.

A large swig of the brandy spread a pleasant warmth through my body. She had answered one of the major questions which had been bugging me. Of course! Why not. Keep only about half! Pacify the owner with the rest. "You really are *marvellous*. I've been tying myself in knots about rights and wrongs. The need to avoid publicity too. I have a feeling in the circumstances that the boat owner could claim full ownership if he were to know the other half existed. He may have to answer questions about all that gold, of course. All of that."

"Praise like that demands a refill. I haven't been called marvellous all these years." She went across the room and came back with the bottle.

"But here's one for you David. Just *who* is on to us? Your flat, our boat, the picture of you - they seem to know an awful lot about our project. Must have spent a huge amount of time investigating us."

She had touched a sensitive nerve. I'd been worrying over this too for some time. "They have had high level training of some kind. They're just *that* good. Seem to turn up when least expected. But I'm sure they can know nothing of Odin or our hidey-hole here. We're free of them for a while."

"Skill like that usually comes from official training. Military intelligence. Police Special Branch. Something set up to monitor money or valuables like gold and diamonds? Maybe some or all of this could be linked to the South African government? Hey, now there's an idea!" She slid back down beside me and took a sip from her glass.

"But would the authorities really be able to keep going for over twenty years and through a complete regime change?" My view was that they would have to drop it in that enormous length of time. People within organisations all have their limits.

"Yes of course they would. Systems like that, once in place, stick around. And it really was an awful lot of money to lose!"

"We just have to be vigilant." I put my hand on her arm to emphasise the point - we were conveniently close! "You know this could get really messy and maybe worse. They know a lot about the whole situation and god knows how they have tracked us down. Time and money must be being spent lavishly. We must be quick as well as careful. We have your father to thank for that massive breakthrough. He was brilliant."

"Yes, Daddy is all crosswords and quizzes in his spare time. There are not many minds like that around." She snuggled down more deeply but did not remove her arm.

"You know he---" She stopped abruptly as the doorbell rang. We both jumped up staring at each other for a couple of seconds, thoughts whizzing around wildly.

"Who on earth?" She looked a little scared. "At this time of night?"

I did some rapid thinking. If *they* were on to her, and I really could not believe they were, it was likely they would not expect to find a second resident in the place.

"You answer it. I'll hide."

The bell went again, this time for a demanding twenty seconds. I hid one glass behind some books and smoothed things out a bit before disappearing quickly and very quietly into the darkness of my room.

"Who is it?"

Elizabeth then screamed as the sturdy front door was smashed open with a loud noise of the safety chain and lock breaking apart under huge force. It was them! Had to be! They had found the right place and were here at the best time to tackle Elizabeth on her own.

She shouted. "What do you want?" And then, "Please don't hurt me!"

A gutteral male voice shouted out. "South African Security. We have reason to believe that you have stolen valuable items belonging to the Republic of South Africa and we are here to get them back."

THIRTY-NINE

It was very dark in my room, just a small shaft of light being allowed through by the partly opened door. My mind was racing madly around. What to do? What in the name of all that is bad were *they* intent on doing? I must find some sort of weapon. Anything! My brain quickly zeroed in on one thing I had earlier seen by the far wall.

A hockey stick!

I edged my way across the small room and felt around in the space I recalled having noticed beside the small cupboard. In very quick time my fingers closed firmly around the handle. Looking back I could just see out through the gap where the door hinged on to its frame.

"Where are those krugerrands?" The second person was a woman who sounded very British upper class. Except for a slight something----

"What on *earth* are you talking about?" Elizabeth, extraordinarily in such circumstances, had become ice cool indignant.

"I'm sorry my dear. We do not have much time. We are not prepared to engage in nonsenses. We need to know right now. We will get it out of you - and quickly! I hope pain, disfigurement or something else will not be necessary. Now, once again, and these are my last words on the subject - the hiding place please?"

Elizabeth became scornful, spitting out the words at the woman. "I thought you said you were part of the South African government? Would *they* agree to the beating up a woman in a foreign country? Do you spend your life going around doing this sort of thing? I really don't think so."

The man moved in on her, grabbed her arm and twisted it hard around behind her back. "Talk, or this gets worse." He jerked her arm slightly to emphasise his point.

"You bloody bullying bastard!"

In any other circumstances I reckoned her alliteration would have sounded quite good. But, right now, it scared the hell out of me. These people seriously meant business. All the warning noises we had made to each other in the past days were now coming to fruition.

"Talk!" He increased the pain.

"No. I've nothing to say to you! Just you let me alone!" Then she screamed out in agony as he wrenched her arm a third time with a savage jerk, clearly intended really to hurt her.

I was ready. His legs were four feet away the other side of my door and Elizabeth's aggressive attitude was holding his total concentration. I again strengthened my hold on the weapon. Surprise was my great advantage factor. Three quick paces and a huge swing of my anger-driven hockey stick felled the man to the floor, where he lay gasping and groaning in terrible agony. I may well have broken his leg, and at that moment hoped I had done so. I had to hit with all my might in order to put him out of action. Elizabeth and I then both moved forwards together to secure the woman, but were stopped in our tracks. She had whipped out a small revolver.

"Stay back or I shoot!"

She clearly meant it and we held off.

"Haff, get up!"

The poleaxed man rose, pulling himself up with the aid of a chair, slowly, so slowly, and painfully. But he was physically strong and motivated. The determination in his face said it all.

She waved the pistol at me. "Drop that stick to the floor and kick it away from you."

I hadn't had much thought about using it against her but, given the situation, I did precisely what she demanded. The hockey stick slid slowly away to the skirting board. I decided I had to try and take some sort of initiative. Our situation was dire.

"Now, those krugers. Where are they?"

"I really quite seriously do not know what you are talking about." The weapon was now pointing at my chest. "And if you insist on shooting us I would not advise it. The police will be here any time now."

Haff, despite his pain, cut in very quickly.

"What the hell do you mean?"

"I just called them." I nodded backwards. "My mobile's in there. Better for you, maybe, that they didn't walk in on a murder case. The penalty for that can be quite nasty." I sounded much bolder than I was feeling.

To my dismay the woman was made of very strong stuff. In another time and place she would have looked attractive, not just fierce. What I presently saw in front of me was controlled aggression with its finger on the trigger. The two of them were obviously quite ruthless, wanted those krugers, and would do whatever it took to get them. Shades of two other people we knew.

"Haff, check it."

He staggered painfully into my room and turned on the light. I cast around forlornly for some solution. The light switch was too far away and there was no sort of missile close by which I could use. The gun was unwavering and I had to think of Elizabeth. It took all of three minutes for him to shout out the result of his checks on a phone with which he was not familiar.

"Nothing on his cell."

"That's because nine nine nine doesn't show up." I really had no idea about that but played for time. It would have been a good move had I called the emergency services. I simply hadn't thought of it in the heat of the moment.

He limped back in with us, bent down very slowly and recovered the hockey stick. I fully understood the ferocious look he gave me. Retribution would be coming, one way or another. And it would be soon.

She waved the gun and said calmly, "There was no call. We start again. And this time we *will* make some progress. Where, exactly where, are those krugers?"

My mind was now racing ahead. Everything was leading to disaster and pain. But I felt, rather than saw, a sharp look from Elizabeth. She was demanding continued total denial. The woman detected it at the same time as I came out with the required response.

"I do not know what on earth you are talking about."

She studied Elizabeth, a handsome tyrant surveying a beautiful younger woman, and then looked me straight in the eye as she instructed tonelessly, "Haff, you *have* to go to work on the face. We have no time."

He pulled a wicked looking knife from a slotting arrangement he had in his trouser pocket area, then staggered a couple of steps forward and slashed Elizabeth's left cheek. Blood immediately ran copiously down her face.

She cried out very loudly. "Stop it! You cannot do that. You wicked, awful man!"

He did not put away the knife, instead turning towards me, a look of pure hatred clouding his face. His leg would be giving him considerable pain for weeks to come and I was the one who had caused it. I knew they could and would continue relentlessly. These two were set to do anything to get the information they so desperately wanted. I was simply unable to let that happen. Elizabeth would hate me for it but I had no choice. I would have to tell everything we knew. Except, of course, the bit about us having found out who she herself was. That could very possibly get us killed.

"I ask again. Where are those---" She stopped short as my mobile quacked out loudly from my room. Haff limped the same journey again as quickly as he could, brought it out and handed it firmly to me.

"Answer it! Everything here is normal. One word out of place and it's the other cheek or far, far worse! Whoever is calling must learn nothing." He raised his knife menacingly in the air facing towards Elizabeth, and with the other hand pushed the speaker button as I held the phone. Inwardly I curled up at the name I saw. It was a call that had come in at precisely the wrong time.

"Hullo."

"Dave, we've found the boat!" Jonny was very excited.

"Well Jonny I----"

The woman came threateningly towards me while the man shuffled slowly over to recover the hockey stick.

"---thing is when we left you Piet and I decided to try and cut short the search and we visited three big marinas. We found Odin in the third one. She is moored in Shepperton, tucked away in a far distant corner. But easy to get at. Maybe we should all go tomorrow and have a look? I have to say the pulpit rails looked in good shape, untouched it seems."

The man held up in front of me a quickly scribbled note. His writing speed far surpassed his walking pace. "Tell him NOT TOMORROW." He raised his knife again.

"Jonny, not tomorrow. I paused a second and thought frantically. "It's the weekend. Too many people. We have to be careful. Leave it until Monday."

"Ok, we'll do some thinking and pick you both up early Monday morning, snow or no snow. Great, don't you think?"

"Oh absolutely."

"You sound a bit unenthusiastic?"

"Just woken up."

"Right, well maybe when you've thought a bit you will appreciate what a fantastic job we have done! Cut out all the legwork, as it were. Cheers for now. Go back and get your head down."

"Bye." I flicked off the phone.

Haff was re-energised. Turned on. Really with it! Leg all but forgotten. They too had now had a lot of their investigation work cut out. Jonny had given them all the answers. They had no more questions to ask. He smiled at his fellow gangster.

"So, it's Odin, lying in Shepperton marina and our gold is housed in her pulpit rails. That does make a lot of sense. Pretoria will be very grateful."

The woman's face hardened, yet again. "But Haff we cannot expect these two idiots to leave us alone?"

"No, they come with us. I have it all planned." He was now the one back in control.

"What?" Elizabeth exploded at him. She was holding a tissue to her cheek which was still bleeding.

"Shut up! " That woman was not mincing her words. I still could not place that very slight voice intonation. Maybe the south of France somewhere?

I shouted at them. "You *cannot* take us prisoner like that. This is a free bloody country. We wish to stay here. We will not come!"

That prompted the woman to fire a bullet into the floor beside me. There was little noise but a nasty looking hole in the carpet had appeared.

"We can take you with us unless you would prefer to have the alternative." Her features now were like carved stone, and she spoke even more icily. "Make sure you follow our instruction in every move you make and every word you say - or else---" *Her instructors back home would have appreciated the calm resolve of their pupil right now.* She was not to be denied.

Haffenbacker had also produced his own pocket pistol. He waved it at me saying very calmly, "You both are to come with me." And in a strange moment of concern for his captives, "You had better get warm coats, you will need them."

I moved across the room and unhooked my overcoat. Where the hell were they taking us? Some form of incarceration while they raided Odin, no doubt. In a way I was thankful that Jonny's call had saved that beautiful face from becoming any more disfigured. The present wound would heal. Additional slashing would have left permanent scars across the cheekbone. By whatever means, they had fully intended extracting from us whatever information we had. Now they had obtained all we knew from Jonny I reckoned they would simply keep us confined. His eyes never left me as he flung my mobile back into my room.

Elizabeth was already in her thick coat. He beckoned us both outside and into a six seater van whose door was partially open. Lady Banforth (I should not even *think* that name) sat in the rear still holding the weapon. We struggled in to the centre two seats as Haff slammed the door on us. It was very dark all around and a light snow was falling. There was simply nobody about who could witness what was going on. He hobbled around to sit in the driver's seat, slammed shut the door and then started to fiddle with the car phone.

"J. Everything ok. The holding option please. I trust you have it all prepared."

"Ready as planned."

"Good. All is going well. See you soon."

There was a slight Piet-like twang in the other man's voice. Clearly a South African connection, but I was now certain these two crooks had nothing to do with that country's normal official policing.

Beside me I could feel Elizabeth quivering. The awful predicament we were in was hitting home. I held her hand, down below, out of sight of the nasty woman sitting behind us, and kept holding on until we arrived at our destination somewhere in the East End about half an hour later. They walked us down a side alleyway and we were pushed unceremoniously through an open door beside which stood a man whom I presumed to be "J". This led straight into what appeared to be a store room. The man slammed the door shut and locked it.

FORTY

I looked around examining the hole into which they had imprisoned us. There was one small window up high which was strongly barred. A low wattage bulb shone out weakly from the ceiling, its light revealing an old settee, one small table, and absolutely nothing else around the room. It was all horrible and we were bitterly cold. I tried to fight against those depressed feelings surfacing again. We had failed miserably. Our fate was now totally in the hands of others. They were going to let nothing get in the way. And I was responsible for dragging Elizabeth and the others into this whole godforsaken mess. For her sake I must try and keep hope alive. Funnily enough she seemed to be doing the same for me!

"We'll be out soon!" Elizabeth seemed quite sprightly in the circumstances.

"How come?"

"A hunch. I just have an idea. But maybe you shouldn't put big money on it. I've never been good at the races."

I doubted her forecast. "We do seem to have gone from top to bottom in double quick time."

"Yes, I suppose so. But we're not right out of the running yet you know. Don't be too downcast. Things do change."

"Well a couple of months ago we had decent jobs and relatively steady lives. Now look at us. Nothing really to get out of here for!!"

So much for my comforting her!

She was trying out the ancient couch.

"David Johnston, come and sit down. It is still night time. What do you do at night? You count sheep. And sleep. Wrap that coat tightly around you, pull up the collar right over your ears, and sit close. We'll keep as warm as we can. We must be ready for whatever this predicament we are in throws up in the morning."

I meekly obeyed and was soon in the designated position. It was cold, but, as time passed, not that cold. She rested her head on my shoulder and fell instantly into a deep sleep.

Light was showing through the small window when I came to. I must have slept quite a bit, pushed into it by her firm instructions. I stretched my aching limbs and tried to get back some feeling into my wretched body. My shifting around returned her to the here and now.

"Still cold?" It was the best greeting I could manage.

"Yes, but not *very* cold." Elizabeth still seemed to know something that I didn't. She stood up, stretched, and walked straight over to the door. I could not believe my eyes as she opened it, gave it a further push, and we were looking out and slightly upwards to what was now a relatively busy street.

"What on earth---?"

She stopped me in mid-sentence, index finger to her lips.

"I will explain. I hinted last night but you were not in listening mode, to put it mildly. If they have found what they wanted, why keep us? If they did not find anything the same thinking would almost certainly apply. They've gone. Probably on a plane to somewhere far distant by now. Perhaps back to their South African haunts or maybe somewhere more exotic."

"In my book they must have found the krugers. Otherwise they would be back to beat any residue of information out of us, just like Kokot and Van did to poor old Elias."

"No! Because they know now for sure that we have no further angles to pursue. They have already established that beyond any doubt. Jonny gave them our complete up to date progress report. So why invite massive police activity by leaving us locked up, possibly even to die if we could find no way out. We cannot take any action against them, even if we were to establish where they are now - they know we are too implicated ourselves for that. They will either have everything, or at the other end of the scale, nothing."

She looked around our present accommodation, the grim ceiling and paint-flaking walls, and shuddered.

"Thank goodness we are out. I wonder who actually owns this place? Let's get to that small hotel up the road a bit on the other side that I noticed as we arrived last night. I'm desperate for hot water, a bath, some food and lots and lots of hot coffee."

It had more or less stopped snowing. We staggered out, trying to smarten ourselves up as we went, and hurried across the road to the modest hotel. Given the condition we were in it seemed to us like a palace. Above all it was warm. Elizabeth, ignoring the quizzical "where's the luggage" gaze at reception, casually booked us in to a double room. A coffee croissant breakfast would follow us up. She thanked the lady for the key and led me up one flight of stairs. Once we were in she straightway took over the bathroom and was soon splashing away, happy in her new found freedom.

My top priority was the room phone. At the third attempt I managed successfully to force my memory to tease out Jonny's number.

"Hello."

"Jonny it's Dave."

"Sleep well?"

The strong, steady voice would not be like that for long.

"Just listen. We were attacked last night by you know who - well we know the woman anyway." There was a gasp at the other end. "They had us at gunpoint while you spoke. Can you pick us up - the Sunrise hotel somewhere in the East End?" I gave him the telephone number. "And I suggest Piet goes straight now, if he can, to the marina to see what has happened to the boat. Very carefully in case they are still there."

"God, Dave, are you both ok? I thought you sounded a bit strange last night. Should have followed it up." He sounded very alarmed.

"Yes fine. We're both free people now with a big story to tell. Please move fast. Can you make it in an hour or so? Oh, and could you bring a card or something with which to pay the hotel bill. We have no money on us."

"Yes, to both, no problem. Piet's already shot out and is on his way to the boat. Jenny is driving him in her car. I'll come straight to you. Don't worry about a thing. I'll be there. Out."

There was a tap on the door. I collected breakfast and immediately killed a croissant. The coffee was good. I tried to imagine the upheaval that must now be going on in that well-ordered household. I hoped Piet would come up with something in Shepperton, and, at the same time, keep himself well out of the limelight. We must not be connected in any way with what investigation might already be going on there.

"It's all yours." Elizabeth came quickly out of the bathroom covered in a huge towel and carrying her clothes. "Wonderful to get clean again. Go on, get in there. There's lots of hot water!"

I pointed her towards the food tray. Then wandered in and ran the bath. I wondered at the change in this woman. Usually of a modest, though somewhat strong-willed, disposition she was showing real guts in the face of all our adversity. She almost seemed to be welcoming the shocking things that had happened, apart from the bloodletting bit. I noticed that the scar on her cheek was beginning to heal over.

My hot bath in these circumstances was a complete luxury. I wondered where our project went from here. Probably a wrecked boat and a furious owner. Not our problem - we didn't do it and they didn't know us. Very possibly the damage would be limited to the pulpit rail and maybe a small part of the boat's fabric. Though who knows what those people would do if they found nothing. My friends - I simply could not help feeling deeply guilty about them. Perhaps I would find some way of helping their getting back into the normal work environment. Piet, I knew, had an offer or two in South Africa and Elizabeth was financially all right, though returning to the Harley Street hub or something similar might be difficult. But Jonny was shortly to be pushed out of AandA/Global, and I hoped I could help him to find some sort of employment elsewhere. Of the four of us he had the most to lose.

My left foot crept upwards to the hot tap. I wanted to continue this luxury for as long as possible and more heat had become necessary. I could feel the aches and joint pains sustained in last night's sleeping positions slowly easing. Elizabeth did not seem to have any such problem - well, she was not letting on, anyway.

What was I myself going to do? The idea of setting up my own small company became increasingly appealing the more I thought about it. I certainly had a service to offer but I couldn't expect any help from my previous employers. I could target small companies who were seeking to grow, and that could well be the cornerstone of a business. Maybe, maybe----my body was shutting down and I almost fell asleep. Dangerous! My foot went back up to the tap and wriggled it around until it was firmly off. Then I let go and must have slept for about ten minutes until the cooling bath water dragged me out of my slumbers.

I needed money to start up. One could get a business loan, the banks and others were always pushing their wares. I didn't like the idea of borrowing but that was now the only way to secure adequate finance. Marketing my own skills was more difficult - I was more of a boffin than a sales type at heart.

I pulled myself out, dried off and moved gingerly back into my clothes. Then I wandered out and had the shock of my life! Elizabeth had not dressed and had been sleeping flat out on the double bed covered only by the towel. She leaped up, somehow managed to keep her modest covering in place, ran across and threw her arms around me giving me a huge and long-lasting kiss. And even after that she would not let go.

"You know we slept together last night and you took absolutely no notice of me. Am I *that* awful?"

"I—I think you are wonderful----" I was in a major state of confusion as I had in no way expected this. Realisation was hitting me about where things might be going next and I pulled myself together fast. She was definitely not her normal self. Events had affected her. I was about to fold my arms around her when, unbelievably, the room phone rang. I *had* to answer it.

"Hello."

"Jonny. I've arrived. Downstairs."

I somehow managed to keep a sort of normality to my voice though it was difficult. "Great to hear you Jonny. Wait there. Down in a few minutes. We've some things to put together."

"Ok. Don't be long."

Slowly, carefully and thoughtfully I replaced the receiver.

"Oh my god!" Elizabeth, still managing to keep the towel in place, ran off and started feverishly donning her clothes. "You must think I'm a really scarlet woman."

I moved over quickly and put my arms around her.

"You are incredibly special and lovely and beautiful. Especially when hiding away in such a lovely big towel." I held her quietly for all of a minute.

Her muffled words came out very slowly. "I've sort of been a bit soft on you ever since you talked me out of Harley Street." Then more loudly, "And you've always ignored me - treated me as some sort of clever employee, almost a robot. Certainly not a woman!"

I held her close for about a further two minutes. Then we split apart hurriedly, finished dressing and went quickly out to the lift. We met Jonny down in Reception and guided him in to the adjacent small room where there were several comfortable chairs. There was nobody around.

I said automatically, "Sorry we're late."

"It's ok. Took the chance to settle your bill. Well you two look all right---"

He stopped abruptly when he saw Elizabeth's scar.

"It's fine. Nearly healed now. But it would have been a much bigger mess if you hadn't grabbed their full attention giving them all those details on the phone."

"Hell, of course! I'm so sorry, Elizabeth. They were holding you at gunpoint! I'm glad I stopped them from going any further. Suppose I do have my uses sometimes."

"Well knifepoint as well actually!"

I saw his eyes wobble a bit as her words sank in. At the same time he slid his buzzing phone from his pocket. When he saw the caller name he put it straight on to speakerphone.

"Jonny!!" Piet had some real news that he blurted out instantly. "They've made a hell of a mess of the poor old boat. Torn out the rails all around, not just up front, and wrecked a large part of the decking. One side of the boat is holed. It's going to cost someone a small fortune for a lot of expensive repair work to be done. I hope they are fully insured."

"Any evidence of the loot - was it there or not? They presumably will have made off with it?"

"I don't know, Jonny. I have my own internal war going on about this. It's stringing me out something awful. I've a strong feeling that you may all have the answer to the problem lying quietly in those dark recesses of your minds."

"What the heck do you mean Piet?" Jonny looked at us and shrugged. I think he felt the pressure of events was causing Piet to lose his marbles.

"Does anybody right now recall the diameter of a kruger? It is very important that I get confirmation."

That one was etched on my brain and I called out, "Thirty-two point six millimetres exactly."

"Thanks Dave. That confirms the figure I was working on."

Where on earth was he going now?

"So what?"

"Well, I thought the pulpit rails looked a bit smallish in diameter so, on the pretext of helping out, I took a couple of measurements. They were both about twenty-eight millimetres across! Maybe twenty-nine but certainly no more."

"Did you have a ruler, tape measure or what?" I was very surprised at what he said.

"No, thumbnail. I have biggish thumbs so know the measurement. It's been a joke over the years. Distance across mine is just over twenty millimetres. There was definitely not much more than that. I'll swear it on anything you like. So, on that basis, krugers would not have fitted in to those rails. Our friends would have found absolutely nothing!"

I was puzzled. "Piet, are you *sure* about those diameters?"

"Yes, to within a millimetre. I'm certain I'm correct."

"That brings the whole exercise to a grinding halt." I looked at the other two. "We need to examine things once more to see where, and how, it all went wrong. Let's all get together on Marianne this evening at, say, seven for a chat?" They both nodded positively. I couldn't think of a better way of dealing with the situation for Piet, who must have been feeling devastated at his own findings.

"I'll be there." He still sounded surprisingly keen.

As was Jonny. "I'll lift you two to Elizabeth's place and see you on the boat for a sort out later."

"Hot soup and lots of it." Elizabeth was on the ball yet again.

FORTY-ONE

She was as good as her word.

Four large bowls of piping hot tomato and chili soup together with a couple of fresh baguettes were delivered to the small boat table exactly on time. It was great to be back. We now had little fear that our adversaries would reappear. And strangely the atmosphere felt upbeat and not at all what I would have expected in the circumstances.

"There is some cheese and a few biscuits. This, and the soup, is all you get but, despite that, you will need it to up your concentration levels because I have something important to say. She lowered the tray to a minor hum of anticipation and waited for a short time to be sure she had our undivided attention.

"It may not be that this is all over."

My reaction was instant. She would not be messing about. "You mean you know something big that we don't?" I was caught somewhere between being aggravated that she had not told me whatever she now had and being full of questioning about how it might fit in with recent events.

When we had arrived back at her place earlier any thought of intimacy was utterly forgotten. She had seen right through me.

"You said seven tonight because you wanted to give yourself time to get out there, see Odin, and check on that diameter. Right?"

"Well----yes."

"We'll both go in my car." It wasn't a question.

"Ok. But I was hoping to do it quietly. I don't really doubt Piet's knowledge about the width of his thumb nail but, yes, I really do feel that a double check should be done. After all a thumbnail is curved but the diameter is a straight line. He could just have been mistaken."

An hour later we came to a halt in Shepperton marina parking and exited quickly from her car.

"Piet said she was tucked away. Must be over on the far side." I pointed to a distant line of moored boats.

We walked past two parked marina trucks, a couple of offices and the small boat sales area. Then around the huge crane they used for hauling out. And there, across the next bank, we saw a small huddle of warmly dressed people all staring at one large white boat. She was Odin! The name on the bow stood out like a beacon. A serious looking policeman was taking statements and was accompanied by a couple of marina staff. We joined in, eager to inspect the damage.

Elizabeth whispered to me, "Look, most bits of the torn off pulpit rail have been thrown across over on to the bank. They've also wrecked quite a bit of the decking area."

She had pulled out her digital callipers, used, I knew not how, in her former occupation, and was edging her way over.

I eyed the distance. About twenty metres. I hissed at her. "The best way is for us to go fast over there, measure accurately and depart. We must take no notice of anybody and look neither to left nor right until we have that reading."

I felt rather than saw one or two of the onlookers already staring in our direction. We walked quickly across. She straightway bent down and measured the diameter of the chromed rails in a couple of randomly chosen places, while I found a broken end and made a mental note of the metal thickness itself. At that very critical moment one of the marina staff shouted authoritatively at us.

"Don't touch please. Police investigation. Nobody to go anywhere near!"

"Very sorry!"

Both of us shouted it out, knowing that in those seconds we had obtained all that was wanted. We stood up, turned and walked slowly away, speeding up slightly as we neared the car. Elizabeth dropped her very useful callipers into my lap and drove off. I read off the measurements. They confirmed everything Piet had said. Lady Banforth, Haff and maybe the other guy, having done enormous damage to the boat, would have found nothing.

"It's been a bloody hoax chase all along."

Piet was staring emptily into cabin space. Everyone understood why. He himself had started it all and was now convinced that Elias had misunderstood or misjudged the entire situation.

Elizabeth produced a large coffee pot and mugs. Dammit, I could not understand just why she seemed to be savouring the moment so much, even basking in it!

"You've more for us Elizabeth?"

"Well, yes, I do, David. Had you been awake in the last couple of hours before we drove here you would have been fully in the know."

"Good heavens! You mean he's been sleeping all the time?" Jonny thought that was funny!

"Elizabeth, for goodness sake get going. What on earth is it?" Piet was desperate to hear anything.

"Well, gentlemen, for once I did some very deep thinking. The Mubanga story really, really rings true.

First Kokot and Van der Merwe were prepared to kill. Secondly the lady and "Haff", who seemed to have some on/off official link in South Africa, were happy to use violence which could have become extreme if circumstances had evolved differently. Not one of these four people would really spend years chasing golden krugers for the benefit of their health. Well, we all know that. But to me, just at that one moment, I felt I was going mad. There had to be *something*. What on earth had we missed? The Maghiel links in Cape Town were well proven. Detail from the shipyard about changes made to Odin's pulpits had to be spot on. That's not the sort of thing a man thinks up - even if it had happened many years before. It was an unusual event which stuck with him. The more I thought the more convinced I became. The problem then was what to do next? We had exhausted all lines of enquiry."

"Exactly. We all *know* that!" Piet put the empty soup plates back on to the tray. "I'm off to the galley to wash up."

"Piet, just wait please!! I'm getting all this off my chest because it sort of leads me to the crux of the matter."

"Which is?"

Piet arched his eyebrows, still being petulant. Jonny and I looked on hopefully.

"I phoned my friend again. *She* told *me* that Odin had been smashed up. News like that travels fast, and of course she would have been concerned, because it was family. We chatted for a while about boats - Odin was made in Gothenburg as was a similar boat owned by Arvid, older brother to Lars."

"A similar boat? They are not usually purchased in pairs by a small family. An awful lot of money." Piet held back on his desire to go off and clean dishes.

"Not similar. Virtually identical."

"What did Arvid call her?"

"Thor."

Jonny's classical education came bursting out of him.

"Thor and Odin are Nordic gods. Thor goes together with thunder, lightning and storms. Odin is one-eyed, long bearded and is associated with knowledge and wisdom. Just thought it's the sort of thing you all ought to know."

"Anyone like to guess what happened then?"

Elizabeth looked at us expectantly. Important detail was coming. I could feel it in my bones.

"They might have called them Odin 1 and Odin 2?"

Piet was returning rapidly to normal. He came back and sat down. Our interest in what she was saying had changed from polite to positive.

"No, not at all. But that's not a bad try. They simply swapped titles. According to mother they swapped the boat *names* after father died as each preferred the other god. Seems crazy but that is very simple and is what happened. And, of course, with two identical boats you can do that - unless of course one day someone in authority checks the engine and hull numbers." The words were purred out as from a very contented cat and she viewed the audience like a mother instructing her incredibly inexperienced offspring.

Silence reigned for all of five seconds.

"Then the boat in this country is not the one. It's the *wrong bloody boat!*" I yelled it out, restraint gone to the dogs.

"We've been looking in completely the wrong place! It's not Odin that was smashed up, *it was sodding Thor!*" Piet had become delirious, smacking Jonny hard across the shoulder. "And that's why those pulpit rails were the wrong size. Poor old Lars has had his boat rubbished and it was all in error. Hell, what a mistake! This means we are really back in business. When do we start?" Piet very clearly felt vindicated.

"I haven't finished."

We froze. There was even more?

"Thor will soon be up for sale."

My spirits began to soar. "My god, Elizabeth, where?"

"Not yet decided but as the summer approaches she will go off to a sales place, or even back to Gothenburg where she came from originally."

While all this had been going on something more sinister was nagging away, trying to surface in my brain. Like Elizabeth I, too, had been thinking, but in a different way. She was right. Those two had been highly skilled and had carried out the assault on us in a very professionally trained way. They certainly put the frighteners on Elizabeth, and me, by slashing her cheek and threatening more. Not nice but very effective when pushed for time. Thugs who will do that do not easily give up.

So, what would they do?

Hang around somewhere spying on our every move? No, they were aware that we knew nothing more. And yet-----

Find us and bug us of course.

Probably wrong but these sorts of people leave nothing to chance. We might just have some other angle at play. I quickly scribbled a note and passed it around.

"Sudden thought. We may have a listening audience. Talk gibberish."

Jonny and Elizabeth looked shocked. Both had not thought about the possibility of the boat being bugged after her theft discoveries. Things had just been too traumatic. Elizabeth stylishly, almost regally, led the way, recalling instantly all she had, and had not, said.

"I will contact Mrs Erlander in Copenhagen again soon reporting that I called in to see Odin and it was a mess but repairable."

"Great. For the time being we will let sleeping dogs lie and try to work out something." I hoped that if there were any listeners-in they would buy that.

We broke up abruptly. Elizabeth went off to get her car and the other two went the other way to find theirs.

I moved quickly around the boat, pulling, lifting and feeling, particularly in the more remote places. I reckoned if there was anything it had to be somewhere in the main cabin where it would catch and convey most of the conversation. Cinema films tend to show bugs positioned in lighting systems or flowers, but these are not necessarily the most effective places. I examined in some detail the cooker, fridge and sink areas, and then the hot air entry system. I went through each drawer with a fine toothcomb. Also, the miniature drinks cupboard and everywhere beneath the revolving table.

I was about to give up and assume all was well. There was nothing as far as I could tell. Then, with a final peek into the darkened underneath of the bench seat in the far corner where human hands rarely go, I *found* it. I left the small rectangular matchbox-looking item well alone, climbed out of the boat, locked up and went off to join Elizabeth in her car.

FORTY-TWO

"What on earth now?"

Elizabeth had barely started the car before her anxiety about our situation started showing. After explaining that in the boat there really was a listening device I had insisted on checking that her car was clean before we left. I knew something about these things having been on some pretty exacting courses on the subject at AandA. In that case it was foreign competitors trying to add to their, usually unsuccessful, computer hacking.

"They now know quite a bit about all the latest that has been going on. But, if you recall what was said, I think they will still not have enough detail. We must go to Norway and buy the boat as or before it goes to market. Should be easy." Despite deep doubts I tried to make it sound simple.

"That's fraught with problems. And we would have to find a way of checking the pulpit rails - or even searching everywhere in the whole boat - before we make an offer?"

"Yes, difficult." I nodded.

"If rails *look* ok is that enough to make us buy the boat and bring her home?"

"I suppose so. We could always re-sell to avoid a complete loss."

"Have you *any* idea what us bringing her entails? A small boat, with whose handling we are totally inexperienced, brought across the North Sea in cold weather and down into the Thames or some other haven. It would be a bit foolhardy. You probably only want one medium sized storm and you could easily sink. I'm the only one of us with that sort of boat experience and I say No. Possible, but difficult and maybe dangerous."

"Right." I had assumed this would be the case. "We definitely get her transported?"

"Yes, that would, of course, have to be by a large cargo boat sea crossing. But it will be expensive." She made a face out at the darkness all around us. "And the documentation for it all will be horrendous."

I was more concerned about the boat's arrival in the UK.

"If we were found to be importing stolen krugerrands in volume I would think we would be up for having committed some sort of crime?"

"Yes, but Maghiel Grobelaar was a great planner. That hiding place is unique. No-one would ever think about carving open a pulpit rail to have a look-see. Especially since this robbery took place so long ago and is forgotten - even if it ever was truly in the public domain, which I doubt."

"Right. Then we stash the cash. Where?"

"We divide it up and, over the years, we visit exchanges in differing countries, cashing in one or two at a time. Personally, I am going to hang one around my neck!"

"Sounds good. We would all have to conform to a discipline. No going off at a tangent and cashing the whole lot together!"

"Of course. That must be made clear to everybody - that is if we ever get that far."

The rain was now driving hard against the windscreen. It was being blown at us by a strong, gusting wind. I tried to imagine what a night spent sailing across the North Sea in these conditions would be like. Fighting wind, rain, cold and swell, however experienced the crew, would be very hard. I shuddered at the whole idea.

"I'll have a look around your place when we arrive before we do any speaking. It may well also have been bugged by our friends. They're thorough to the point of perfection."

"Why? We can transmit more dud info. I'm really good at talking rubbish!"

I smiled. "Of course. I'd forgotten about your speciality. Good idea."

Despite the foul weather we were moving swiftly over the wet roads. At this time of night there was a minimal amount of London traffic and we arrived at the car parking space in just over half an hour. We inspected the damaged front door which she had somehow managed to make open and shut more or less securely, and moved quickly inside out of the rain.

Elizabeth, as usual, went straight to the point.

"I suggest cocoa and bed. Tomorrow we can decide how we go about things." Then for any would-be listeners she added, "And I will talk to Copenhagen some more."

I played along. "Yes, fine. After that I'll move back in to my place and we'll all try to resume a normal life!"

We moved a heavy table across the front door. Then drank a very welcome mug of cocoa, chatted at some length about our days with A&A and where our future careers might lie, and then retired to our beds.

It must have been about three in the morning when I felt a movement and jumped up, dazed and thinking those ghastly people had reappeared. I was ill-equipped for another confrontation, particularly in view of the weapons arsenal which they carried around with them. I listened carefully but all around was silent. Suddenly an arm grabbed my shoulder and pulled me firmly back down on to the warmth of a very female body. A finger was placed over my lips and she whispered two words into my right ear.

"No noise!"

FORTY-THREE

The following morning, unsurprisingly, I woke rather late and found myself alone. Household noises were being made outside so I quickly washed, shaved, dressed and went to join her. My greeting consisted of a cursory peck on the cheek followed by a note being held up before me which read,

"Pub down road - that is definitely not bugged!"

The rain had stopped and the sun was trying to shine through some thin cloud. It felt a very pleasant, fresh day as we strolled to the local friendly hostelry and had prepared for us two very welcome omelettes. And two very large mugs of tea. We sat in a secluded corner, as far away as possible from the main restaurant area.

"Last night-----"

"I'd rather not talk about that now please! We have crucial plans to make. You laid down most of the basics yesterday when you were in my car if you remember. We have to get on with things and pretty quickly too."

She was right, I thought, and forced myself back into work mode. "Then I suppose the first move to take is for you yet again to contact your friend Mrs Eriksson?"

"Already done. She was up and about this morning when I went out to the car and called from my mobile. The latest is that Arvid's boat is lying in Bergen yacht haven and was going to be put on the market in a couple of months so that it would be about right to catch the season. But, by some extraordinary intervention - her words not mine - it has already been purchased by a broker intermediary over there called

Johansson. Her son is very happy to have sold off Thor so quickly and easily outside the normal selling season. She and I are now like old friends. We talked about all sorts of things and she likes me calling. I feel slightly guilty at misleading her when we speak. I suspect she sometimes feels a bit cut off in tiny Flaam after the life she has led. Very understandable when you look at its position on the map."

She smiled at me. At that moment it must have been obvious that I was much more interested in her than in some bloody boat! But she was hell-bent on getting on with the day so I again swallowed my feelings and joined in with her planning. I had a few ideas.

"There is only one best way of dealing with all this. I will get the plane up there, buy the boat and get her shipped across to---well, where do you suggest?"

"I've been thinking about that. Our bug spies have only ever heard us talk of Scandinavia, which is a big area, and Copenhagen, which is not only the wrong place but is in the wrong country. By sheer chance I never mentioned either Mrs Eriksson or Norway when I was speaking openly to everybody before we ever thought about Marianne being bugged. Anyone listening in will not be aware of either name. I suppose we should call those awful people *the buggers!* Very appropriate really. Well that is what they do isn't it? In answer to your question - right up north somewhere away from everything, as far as you can go I would think. Looking at the map I'd say that would be Wick."

We both smiled. She obviously had worked on the answer but now awaited the inevitable questions.

"Where on earth is that?"

"North-east coast of Scotland - right at the top. Nearest point to Norway. Not far from John o' Groats.

They have very adequate cranes and all the other facilities you need for lifting a small boat from a large ship. But to get a cargo ship to call in there will really cost. I have to say there is not a hint on the internet of any suitable carrier going in that direction - we might have some difficulty there. We will have to be careful with our resources. I hope soon to have the money from the sale of Marianne added to our total. She may actually be sold but we may have to wait a few days for the whole thing to finalise. That plus our settlements from AandA - I got fifteen thousand - should pay for Thor and hire some sort carrier ship."

I balked a bit at this line of thinking. Everyone's hard earned savings! And, of course, some of us had a bit more than others. We would have to handle things carefully but I accepted her reasoning without a quibble and led from the front.

"You're right. I will transfer my take of about fifty thousand over to you right now. You be ready to send electronically whatever amounts I agree with the present boat dealer and then with the carrier. Keep Piet and Jonny in the loop but out of the cost of this unless things get grossly expensive - then they can chip in. We should move fast. I think this is right up my street. Get the whole matter over quickly. I can leave almost at once." I finished breakfast and swallowed down the remaining tea.

"But I was hoping to come with you."

"No, Elizabeth. That will not be right at this stage of things. I need you here. We must keep in constant touch on everything as it comes up. No doubt some or all of us will meet the boat on arrival in Scotland. But above all else you have, almost unwittingly, now become the exchequer. And I suggest you tell Piet and

Jonny what I am doing after I have left. Explain the sudden urgency which called me away!"

We walked from the pub back to her place. Using her computer, I transferred the money across. Then I checked that my passport was in the small travel case I always kept with me and collected my warmest things together in another larger bag which she gave me. In it I found a thick Shetland sweater she had bought for her father's birthday. Very thoughtful. It would be seriously cold up there.

While I was making my arrangements she booked me on to the Norwegian Air Shuttle flight from Gatwick to Bergen, again outside the flat on her phone. Very conveniently the plane would depart in three hours. Without further ado I loaded in my luggage and settled down in to her car for the slow stop-start trip to the airport.

FORTY-FOUR

NORWAY

Bergen, still emerging from deepest winter, was frozen under a clear blue sky. A tepid-looking sun was making the ice particles glint.

I changed a couple of hundred pounds into Norwegian krone at the airport, booked in to the Magic hotel, and shortly after that found a taxi to take me straight to the attractive moorings. I was quite surprised to see such a large number of boats there and immediately began the long hike around to find Thor.

It was about twenty minutes later that I spied a boat tied way out on one of the farthest pontoons which looked identical to the Odin I knew. My heart leapt as I came closer, my eyes instantly zeroing in on to the pulpit rails. They were considerably more substantial than those that had been smashed off the bows of Odin and were pretty obviously the size we sought. My head swung round to the bows just in case. And at once I saw the boat's name was Thor!

I walked the ice-crunching way back to the harbour offices. Despite my shoes being of quite a solid style I still slithered around a bit. Once I had made the return journey I asked around for Mr Johansson. Very fortunately he was nearby dealing with another boat owner. I waited. It was warm inside and I served myself a hot chocolate from a machine which I recognised! He arrived back in a quarter of an hour and I introduced myself. Like most Norwegians he spoke good English. He was in his early fifties, well-built and, I guessed from the look of the man, more broker businessman than sailor.

"I'm aiming to purchase one of the older style Storeberon boats? We Brits have a passion for them."

He looked me up and down. Then closely eye to eye. This time of the year was not at all the best time for him to achieve sales. Was I serious? Would I pay? The examination seemed to prove positive, probably in some way due to the expensive looking pullover just peeping out from beneath my thick outer coat.

"I've two of those on the books. A Storeberon Royal Cruiser 34 and a 38. Immaculate condition, and both fully serviced and winterised. And, of course, we do hold very satisfactory inspection reports. Would you like to come and have a look now? Or perhaps later?"

"Yes please, now will do nicely. The 38?"

He walked me the long way back to where I had seen her moored and explained how all his newly acquired boats were always thoroughly overhauled before being put up for sale.

"We had an American after this sort of boat. But it wasn't big enough for him!" We both laughed. "Come aboard. See the beauty. Twin diesels. Fly bridge. Fridge. Cooker. Radio. All mod cons."

We moved slowly through the boat inspecting the Volvo engines, the galley and the very attractive satin varnished mahogany interior. She looked to be in top condition and had obviously been well maintained over the years. Many thanks, Arvid. I went through the motions of how I guessed a normal buyer would act and question.

"Fuel and water?"

"One thousand litres and four hundred litres."

"Navigation?"

"All there including upgraded GPS." He knew all about boats. I didn't and was already beginning to feel it.

"What about price?"

"I've already worked that out in sterling. If you can take delivery now on quick sale the boat will cost ninety-five thousand pounds."

I winced. "Any give on that? It seems a lot of money."

"No, truly sorry. That's very much at the low end. The price will rise by twenty-five per cent in the season."

"If we were to purchase, I would have a small problem. I'd like the boat road transported across to England." I tried to speak casually as if this was all in a day's work. "How would I do that?"

"Sorry, sir, most carriers do not go there, particularly at this time of year. It is a huge journey. Just look at the map. Nobody invites that sort of work. So much better to drive the boat across the water don't you think? Hugely lower distance. No ice and snow blockages. No lifting on and off transporter ships. No hassle."

"Would a road haulier do a special job? I realise it might be a bit expensive."

"I am sure we could find *someone* if you would pay a *premium* price but it would still be difficult at this time of year. And tricky for local hauliers to come up with any sort of satisfactory solution."

I spent some time walking over the deck, outwardly inspecting everywhere but really looking all over the pulpit rails. Thor's looked much more solid than Odin's. And the diameter was good. I did a casual fingernail check - mine was twenty millimetres. The total looked to be about thirty-five millimetres and that was precisely what was needed. We could still be barking up the wrong tree but the odds were rapidly diminishing. I moved my eyes quickly away from the rails and down towards the deck as he came up to join me.

"Are you interested then?"

I thought fast. "Yes, possibly, but I must make a couple of calls home to check with my partners. Can't do this without a joint decision!"

"Ok, stay here if you like. It is a lot less cold inside the boat. Come back and see me when you have decided or call me if you need more information." He gave me his card, climbed down and left to return to the warmth of his office.

I descended into the main cabin and hurriedly phoned Elizabeth. I got an answer, delayed a little. She would have had to move outside. She asked me how I was.

"Fine. I'm on the boat."

"Wonderful. Are you cold up there? And what's she like?"

"Great. No, not too chilly. I'm down below. It's not exactly freezing in here. But problems. What we are looking for appears to be in place. But getting the boat moved will be expensive. There will be very considerable expenditure on top of the boat's ninety-five thousand pounds cost, and very few carriers are likely to want the job at this time of year. In fact, I fear the whole exercise could cause a lot of haulage interest - maybe, I feel, with press attention - which we certainly do not want."

"I know and I agree about that. While you've been over there I've done a lot of work studying the land and sea distances involved. It really does look crazy to haul the boat by road through all those countries. What sort of condition is she in?"

"First class. I'm not the expert though."

"Has she been serviced?"

"Yes, and winterised of course." I began to feel nautically competent.

"Do you know how much fuel she holds?"

"One thousand litres. Twin diesels."

"And all the usual navigation stuff?"

"Elizabeth, why all these questions?"

"*Because we can bring her across the sea ourselves.* I've been doing all the chart work. Presumably she has a fully functional GPS and all the navigational bits and pieces?"

"Yes, upgraded. He was proud of the fact. But you said no to us doing this! Only yesterday. It is crazy and dangerous! Remember?"

"Yes, I know. But women can change their minds in a flash. Did you not know that? It's inbuilt. Nothing we can do about it. I'm coming over. If the boat is in good nick and the pulpits ok we can get Jonny to transfer the money - we have enough in the kitty, everybody's actually insisted on chipping in - and we will bring her back across to Wick."

"What?! Where? Just you and me! Across the North Sea? We agreed that's completely mad. And I know *nothing* about boats. Elizabeth, you are aware of all this. What on earth are you thinking about?"

"But I do know. I *am* a fully qualified yacht master which is really necessary. Please find out the likely distance she will go without refuelling - and assume all the worst scenarios. You are supposed always to have one quarter still in the tank when you arrive anywhere.

I'm on my way and will text plane details so that you can collect me - that is if you wouldn't mind?"

Living lifelong with this woman was really going to have its problems. "Right. I give in and goodness knows how we do it. Remember your passport. And heavy clothing, it is very cold. And please be careful."

"I'm bringing much more than that and it's all packed. Oh yes, most important of all, keep a close eye on the shipping weather forecasts." She laughed.

"I love you."

"I wouldn't settle for less!" And she ended the call.

It was about one hour later that the text arrived. I was deep into wondering how she could have changed so much and so quickly. I had settled into my small hotel room, had a shower and was gradually managing to relax a bit, when the mobile shuddered.

Arriving Bergen tomorrow 1130 hours ready to depart for Wick at say 1500 hours. Imperative I see boat immediately after arrival to check everything. Jonny will transfer money on our ok. Should take fourteen to eighteen hours to cross depending on weather. But it could take quite a bit longer. Suggest you equip yourself with more warm clothing, non-slip boat shoes, waterproofs and snack food and drink - will all be available where you are. Jonny and Piet will meet us with tools etc on arrival Scotland. Elizabeth x

FORTY-FIVE

Early the following morning I settled the hotel bill, packed my bag and went off to the local chandlery which I had checked would be open despite the time of year. I guessed warmth and waterproofing were the most important things on a voyage of this kind so I took their advice and purchased accordingly. Then I hunted around for some ground coffee, two tins of a hot chocolate drink and a variety of instant foods. A call to an ebullient Mr Johannson fixed a meeting at approximately midday in order for my colleague to complete a further, more thorough, boat inspection.

I arrived at the airport as the plane was coming in to land and found my way to the sparse waiting area. Elizabeth appeared shortly with a huge case on wheels which she had hauled heroically through the customs area. I was incredibly pleased to see her. After a big hug we took a taxi to the marina where I introduced her to Mr Johannson - it was now "call me Marius!"- then I followed meekly behind them both, managing two heavy bags, as he led us back to the boat. He produced some boat manufacturer booklets and, once we had heaved ourselves aboard, the two of them settled down to the real business. If we were leaving today this had to be done quickly. Her first question to him summed up her firm intentions for me right away.

"Assuming we buy can you fill up the water tank and refuel fairly fast?"

"No problem. We can do that straight away. Half an hour to do the job."

"Servicing record?"

He showed her and she studied it intently, noting each year's entry in the register. Then they moved to the stern of the vessel for a detailed look at the engines.

"Batteries?"

"They were newly replaced with the service."

"Heating?"

"Eberspacher as normal, serviced and working well." That was a name I had come to know.

"Dual control?"

He showed her. "Bit chilly up there though. Not to be recommended at this time of year."

They went up on to the fly bridge to inspect those controls and returned back down out of the cold within a couple of minutes in order to study the wheelhouse. Then they got immersed in a wide range of detail and it was at least an hour before she was fully satisfied. Johannson, I could see, was in his element. A sale seemed to be coming up at this very difficult time of year! It had literally put a spring in his step. She checked on gas and refrigeration and then got around to battery keys, radio and start up. No problem there and the engines, coming out of their winter service and shut-down, purred like soothing music. I noticed from time to time that she would cast an eye in the direction of the pulpit rails. Once she intercepted my look and nodded happily.

"Very important, Marius, we must check on the weather. Straight line across to northern Scotland. It's the quickest way to go but we must at all costs avoid even a hint of a storm."

I had checked all the detail. As had he. It would be calm seas, some little wind and even a bit of sunshine during the next twenty-four hours. Not totally guaranteed of course, but very likely as these days the forecasters had become pretty accurate.

Elizabeth looked at me. "David, what do we think about purchasing right now? Any difficulties you have with this?"

"Why not? We both don't have return air tickets! But only if you yourself are satisfied the boat is completely sound, of course."

She turned to Johannson. "If you give us your bank payment details, we can arrange for a special and immediate transfer of the money. Once that arrives we would, no doubt, have your permission to take the boat?"

"No problem at all there. I will go off and get all the necessary arrangements moving right now." He knew a sale when he saw one.

She smiled and turned to me. "Looks like I have a bit of unpacking to do. Can you take over managing it all with Marius from now on?"

I was only too keen to become a part of the action. Inevitably she had had to handle boat things. Johannson gave me his bank numbers and departed with some speed saying he would shortly produce the necessary sales paperwork. I texted Jonny, gave him the information, and asked him to settle the bill for ninety-five thousand pounds with Johannson's account. Shortly afterwards he called back to confirm he had actually visited the bank to ensure there were no hold ups with the money transfer. All had been done to facilitate a smooth transaction and it would be a question of minutes.

"Fingers crossed, Dave. See you in Wick. Never been there, looking forward to seeing the place. Have a good trip. Weather looks good. We've been checking."

"Thanks Jonny. I'm bloody nervous about all this as you can imagine!" Deep down inside I was actually petrified and tried all I could not to think about the dreaded North Sea.

"You're in jolly good hands. Elizabeth knows boats." He laughed. "Just be a good boy now and do exactly what she says." He suddenly recalled something. "Oh, one interesting thing you should know. Piet went back to do a bit more spying on his lady friend and he swears she was not around. He stuck it out for a full day but there was no sign of her or the noble Lord. We've been wondering if she and her mates have hopped it? I hope they have done exactly that! Cheers for now."

I wandered in to see what Elizabeth was doing. Her clothing had been put neatly into the small cabin to one side. She was sat at a table covered with a mass of charts and other paperwork which she had brought with her.

"When we are out at sea we follow what the GPS is telling us, but it is very important that we also keep the chart work going. That way we double check our position. There will be a good tide advantage if we are able to leave on time today." She was totally engrossed as if her life depended on it, and, truth to tell, I supposed it absolutely did.

"We're going to be crossing all night?"

"Yes, and we are booked in to Wick. Oh, that reminds me. I've programmed the GPS but we must check the navigation lights." She stepped around to the wheelhouse and nodded at me to go out. "Have a look."

I went on deck and looked up. Green and red lights were shining out at cabin level and a white light showed above us. I thumbs-upped through the windscreen and went rapidly back in out of the cold. Elizabeth was looking purposefully at her watch. "Time flies when you don't want it to. We haven't got long to departure time!"

As if on cue Marius Johannson arrived back.

"Money received. Many thanks. Here is all the invoicing and receipt, boat instruction books plus a lot of unimportant paperwork for you. And bits and pieces for the boat - spare keys and all that. We'll take her across for fuel and water."

Elizabeth started up and we were very soon off under Marius's watchful eye. Refuelling and water took just on half an hour.

"I know you want to catch the tide. My advice would be to get well out before dark. May I thank you both very much and wish you a very safe journey. Contact me from Scotland if you have *any* problem at all." He pointed. "Open sea that way and clearly marked. You cannot go wrong. Let me know when you have arrived safely. I will be thinking of you."

He shook our hands, gave a final almost wistful look around, descended from the boat, cast off the ropes for us and stood watching our departure.

Elizabeth gently revved up the engines and we moved slowly away from the refuelling bay. She was getting the feel of an unknown boat. We went out, turned into the main channel and very steadily started making our way towards the sea. After about twenty minutes she began to talk to me, explaining the radio and how to do a Mayday. I pencilled some notes, knowing I would not remember everything. Then the emergency life raft on deck and how that worked. We moved up a few knots and the engines really came into their own, sounding much more workmanlike. Elizabeth was visibly becoming a lot happier.

"Now - clothing. It's warm in here and we only go outside if there is a real emergency. Heavy clothing and life jackets must be on before leaving the cabin at any time. Can you lay it out for us both? Yours one side, mine the other - on that seat. And one life jacket each."

I did just as she had indicated, arranging things to be as speedily accessible as possible. Serious organisation was now taking place and I was more than happy to be told what to do!

"Food. We've had nothing for some time - you know how to work the gas cooker---I suggest two hot chocolates and some of those lovely Danish pastries that I know you bought."

I spent some time working it all out and was able to deliver just as the boat started bouncing around more in a widening channel. Surprisingly the movement affected me very little.

"Going up to ten knots and setting course." Elisabeth was fully engaged and was keeping me informed at the same time. I looked out behind and very soon I was watching the shoreline stretching farther away from us on either side of the boat. We were getting near to the open sea. Then suddenly the boat really started to roll and I hung on grimly to a nearby handle. Only after that when we were well out did she get around to eating.

"Oh, that's really good. I'm famished. Now, see here. This small screen. If the boat follows that line all the way we eventually finish up in Wick. When you take over the wheel all you have to do is to keep following that course but shout like hell at me if you see any other lights around, or indeed anything that seems unusual." She increased speed again and things became less bouncy. "We will go to fifteen knots. We are already up on to the plane. More fuel efficient like this and a much smoother ride. Skimming over rather than driving through. We will try to keep it that way all the time."

I had not really given much thought to the idea of my taking over the helm from her but it was dawning on me really seriously for the first time that she could not go on solidly for eighteen hours or more. I was going to have to do my bit. I found myself paying ever closer attention.

"Would you like me to have a go now before it is really dark?"

"Yes! A really good idea. No ships in sight and as far as I know there are no hazards out there. The navigation lights are already on. Waves and weather perfect."

She moved away and I slid in to her seat. It was a strangely exhilarating feeling to be moving steadily over the sea's long gentle waves. The daylight was changing to dusk and it was not that long before darkness closed in all around us. The bright navigation system became my friendly guide. Over the next hour I saw the lights of a couple of distant ships. They were far enough away to avoid having to consult the skipper. She seemed still to be deeply immersed in her charts, but then disappeared for a few minutes.

"Supper up. Hot pizza with all sorts in it. I suggest I take over control and we rotate now every two hours."

That night will for ever be etched in my mind. I could not sleep in my down times and during sessions at the wheel I was acutely aware of the very cold black sea beneath us and its constantly changing wave motions. The idea that we might suffer engine failure or some other equally disastrous problem haunted me. Only once on my watch did I call on Elizabeth's services when a massive container ship passed in front of us crossing from port to starboard. She took us the long way around behind it. I kept up the coffee intake thinking that would keep me awake. I noticed that each time when she took over from me Elizabeth would slightly increase the speed and reduce back down at the end of her two-hour stint. Strangely the very last thing on my mind at that time was the valuable cargo we hoped we were carrying. I had actually forgotten all about it!

It was at about four in the morning, a short time after I had taken over from her, that Elizabeth, instead of getting some sleep, came back and glided her body down into the seat beside me. She was about to drop an absolute bombshell - a complete nightmare.

"Those pulpit rail diameters are still just too small to hold the krugers."

I sat rigidly upright at the wheel, momentarily seeing nothing due to a buzzing noise that started going right around my head. Shock was too mild a word to describe it. Sheer bloody incredulity was a better description, but still not strong enough.

"They looked ok to me," was all I could manage to blurt out.

She explained, "And me too. I measured with great precision. Like you, I thought they looked right. One naturally assumes that as it fits with what we are doing.

They are just on thirty-five millimetres in diameter, more than the size of a kruger. But we have to deduct the thickness of the rail which we know is about two millimetres----- times two for both sides of the circle-----to arrive at the internal diameter of thirty-one millimetres. The kruger itself is thirty-two point six. *It will simply not fit!!*"

"When did you find this out?"

"I've just taken some of my very careful, absolutely accurate, measurements. There is no mistake."

"Hell, but I finger-nailed it very carefully. That seemed to be all right - well within limits I suppose."

To say I was totally gutted about our situation would be to put it mildly. We were jinxed. If she was right, and she always was on things like this, we had wasted huge amounts of money and expended enormous energy and time to no avail. Days chasing around the world. Weeks doing strange things on Marianne. Let alone being held up at gunpoint and all that went on that horrible evening. And it was my fault.

She went on, "But I think it's another of Grobelaar's hoaxes. I feel the man built them in purposely to fox any would-be adventurers like us. Either that, or a mistake was made when the new rails were installed. They, too, could also have got it slightly wrong."

"You mean you think the stuff could be hidden somewhere else yet again?"

"No - well maybe, I'm not sure. I had another idea. Those vertical posts around the stern. That is not how it happens on all normal Storeberons of this size and date of manufacture. I ran off these pictures at home. Have a look."

I clung to the wheel, mesmerised by the luminous froth of waves shooting past the boat and traumatised by her revelation, all at the same time. What a fool! I should have measured much more accurately. At the time I had simply been relieved to see that the forward pulpit rail was so much more substantial relative to the sister boat we had seen in Shepperton marina. Everything seemed to confirm our thoughts!

I studied what she had thrust in front of me. "Yes, you're correct. Nothing like. This boat obviously had a complete re-vamp, not just the rails."

"But there's more. If you think about what Piet told us and what you both discovered during your visit, Maghiel, if he hadn't died, was probably using his Norwegian consul friend without, of course, telling him. At a future date, maybe a month or two later, he would arrange to be visiting Norway on business. His friend would automatically invite him to visit. Then, one way or another, he would recover the stash."

"But he couldn't smash up his friend's boat----"

"Mm no, that's a bit of a problem. But maybe not insurmountable. Needs thinking about."

That observation went unerringly to the heart of the matter. We fell silent. I could feel that optimistic, extrovert, wonderful woman beside me deflate like a cycle tyre losing all its air. I tried words of comfort. After all we had been through we were simply out of luck. Smile and carry on. I felt we should be good at that by now.

I suggested brightly, "We should make a good profit on the re-sale of this boat. Buy in the low season in Norway and sell in the summer in Britain."

That was not really any help, and in the limited cabin light I could just make out a little dampness on her eyelid. I leant across and held her hand. It was awful - she, like me, had vested so much mental as well as physical energy into this venture. It wasn't simply about krugers. It had become an idea. A target to meet. Almost a crusade.

"Go off and get some rest. We'll talk a bit more when dawn comes. Won't seem so bad then."

It would! It really would!

She staggered away, holding on to various strategically placed handles to keep her balance in the rolling boat. I hoped she would get a little shut-eye and went back to concentrating on my job, making sure that we were keeping on course.

What a mad enterprise! We had chased half way around the world, been pilloried and near tortured by a gang of crooks, lost good job-hunting time and spent a small fortune. All for nothing. I sank into defence mechanism mode, or, in other words, a non-thinking brain. Follow the bright line. Watch out for any lights. The stuff had been taken and had so far not been found. Maghiel Grobelaar had carried out a perfect job. Wherever he had hidden everything was still a complete mystery. And there now existed a mighty long trail strewn with failed hunters who had paid a high price. The man was an evil genius and we were yet four more bodies who had been cleverly and horribly hoodwinked.

The boat ploughed on through the dark, oily sea and into the black night.

FORTY-SIX

Light was just beginning to show on the far distant horizon. I was drooping and had well overrun my shift to give Elizabeth some quiet time, shattered as she was by the discovery she had made. There was no reason to call her and I could never in this situation allow sleep to take me.

My mind kept repeating the same mantra. *Rails wrong! Rails wrong!* Feelings wander all over the place in a situation like this. An awful lot of money, let alone emotion and time, had been wasted on the project. The only thing on the credit side was that jobs hadn't really been lost as everyone at AandA anyway was for the high-jump within a few weeks or months. But the whole thing had turned out to be galling, humbling and bloody devastating. I should have checked much more closely.

I tried again and again not to concentrate on our failure. Clearly Elizabeth's thinking on the larger stern verticals was a last gasp attempt to prove we were still in with a chance. She must have felt it a possibility - otherwise why say anything? I tried to push the whole thing away and concentrate on my present task. Another big boat, probably a tanker, was running parallel to us a long way off the port side. Thank goodness I hadn't had to face something like that head on. Crossing the North Sea fortunately was not anywhere near as congested as the English Channel.

"Coffee?"

Manna from heaven! Elizabeth was back and lowered my mug down to its usual place beside the wheel. Then she sat closely beside me.

"Thanks. Marvellous. Just what I need. You know that providing the sea stays moderate, the wind does not increase and I have a spot-on navigator at work, I reckon I could do this as a living!"

"Yes, massa' yerr reely doin' well. I'm impressed." She giggled. "Jus mind you donna getta gail a-blowin' though."

I smiled at her. "Just you listen to me young lady, I have a suggestion."

"I wasn't really thinking of listening to anyone else." She looked cheekily around the boat.

"My brain keeps dragging me back to your idea of the larger stern verticals being used. Why on earth so large and no doubt above standard sizes by far for a boat like this?"

But she was hardly listening, having already come to terms with everything in her own way.

"We must cut our losses. We'll sell the boat, settle all debts and form Johnston Associates Forward Marketing Limited or something like that. Jonny and Piet will almost certainly join in and we will *succeed*. Is that what you were going to say?"

"No. But it's not such a bad idea. Needs a shedload more capital than we have though. You remember that the wooden handrail around the stern is bolted down on to a sort of steel plate running around underneath it?"

"Yes. You can lean on it and contemplate the disappearing world behind you. When the weather's ok of course."

"Well that wooden rail must fairly easily pull off the verticals which hold it in place, or would have done had the large screws holding it only been there for a few months rather than years."

I could still see no land, though I had been peering ahead for some time. A distant flashing light seemed to be moving towards us and in quick time a helicopter swooped low overhead, circled around a couple of times and then returned the way it had come. We said nothing. Silence sometimes speaks volumes. *Was somebody monitoring us?* Sorting ourselves out from this mess would be challenging for a long way ahead.

"Another forty minutes and we should see a lighthouse. That is if I have things about right on the chart. Go on with what you were saying."

"Well if we unscrew and remove the wooden rail ----"

"You might be able to lift off the top bit, look inside, or at least stick something down the rails and see if there is anything there. You know I have a really bad sinking feeling about all this."

"Worth a try though wouldn't you say? Do we have any screwdrivers, hammers and that sort of thing aboard?"

She went quickly away and came back with the boat tool bag. I glanced at the range of items on show and nodded. Those would probably do the job.

She shuffled me out of my seat and took over.

"You go and check. Ship's torch over there. Put on something very warm and cover your head. It'll be freezing out there on the back end of the boat. But at least with the canopy up you can't go overboard. Try, if you can, to walk but it may be safer to crawl across the deck. She is rolling quite a bit. I shall soon be contacting the Harbourmaster."

I got into my thick jacket and woolly hat, grabbed the torch and tools and went carefully up the steps and through the sliding door. Immediately the wind and wave noise hit me despite the protection offered by the canopy. Things shrieked all around and I straightway suffered a landlubber's lapse into panic. All alone in the middle of nowhere fighting wind and wave - "For those in peril on the sea" were words that now had real meaning.

Having made certain the door was firmly shut I lowered myself to the floor and crawled slowly towards the stern. Once there I held on firmly to one of the posts, but still the boat insisted on rolling me from side to side. I wedged my leg against the small secure table base which was to my right side and immediately revised my assessment. I really was *not* in any way suited to this sort of life!

I flicked on the torch. There was no screw head to be seen lower down on any of the posts themselves. I heaved myself upwards, holding firmly on to the wooden rail, and then pulled out the largest screwdriver and set about unscrewing the rail's fittings. It was very hard work on a moving boat, with unstable torch lighting and in the freezing cold. Slowly, very slowly, I managed it. Fourteen screws and twenty minutes later the wooden rail slid off, pivoting on the one remaining screw. I shone a light down inside the first vertical bar but could see nothing. I unhooked the long thin rod held across the stern which, in sunnier times, would have been used to hold up a sunshade, itself now presumably stowed somewhere down below. The rod slid into the first vertical and, depressingly, went right to the bottom. I examined all eight of them and desperately disappointingly found nothing, nix, zilch! I was becoming seriously cold and replaced everything in double quick time, but not before Elizabeth had broken all the rules and was at the open door, screaming at the top of her voice for me to come in.

I completed the job, lowered myself to the floor, and crawled back as fast as I could. Once I was inside she slammed the door across and hurried back to the wheelhouse, shouting back furiously at me as she went.

"Get that coat off. You will warm up more quickly that way. You should *not* have stayed out there so long."

I slowly acclimatised, my hands becoming agonisingly numb as they adjusted to the cabin warmth and then, after a couple of minutes, I went over to sit beside her.

"You told me *never* to leave the wheel. That you said was an absolute."

"I had no idea you would be so long. You can seriously damage mind and body when you become very cold." She glanced ahead and quickly changed subjects. "Look, I think that's the lighthouse way ahead."

A distant, tiny light shone out for a short time, disappeared and then came back again. We were almost across that massive stretch of water. I felt my inner sea fright easing. But not abating altogether.

"You do care about me then?"

She gave me that look that came very rarely, the one I could never quite fathom.

"Well I suppose so. How else am I going to get the four kids I promised father? Anyway, how did you get on out there? Sorry I was so aggressive but you were stretching things. I am guessing at, and can live with, a big negative."

I simply was unable to conjure up any suitable response to that remark about her projected family!

"You're right. There wasn't anything. The whole damned erection out there has nothing to do with the real boat structure. It was added after the boat was built, perhaps for extra safety, but certainly not as a repository for stolen goods. If anything was ever hidden in there it has gone now."

We lapsed into silence after that, each thrashing out what should be the next move. There was really nothing more to be done. The project had failed. But this woman beside me had yet again jolted my whole being with that small, incidental, remark about children! I wondered if Father would want her married---and immediately cursed my stupidity. He would be firmly rooted in tradition about that sort of thing. The idea of having a large family with her filled me with an incredible sense of awe, wonder and self-doubt. Unquestionably Father would expect to be asked for daughter's hand. Equally certain was that daughter would lay down to him exactly how he would respond. But would I come up to scratch with her in the longer run?

I was interrupted by an irritation on my chest. My phone was vibrating. We were within signal range. I extracted it from beneath several layers of garment and read,

DAVE. DO NOT COME TO WICK. PIET RECOGNISED LADY BANFORTH WITH TWO MEN PACING THE MOORINGS YESTERDAY. WE HAVE HIRED A SUBSTANTIAL BOAT AND WILL BE COMING OUT - MAYBE COLLECT PRODUCT AND RETURN TO ANOTHER PLACE IF THIS

HELPS. CONTACT US WITH POSITION AS SOON
AS YOU RECEIVE. JONNY.

I read it out to Elizabeth. She took it calmly, cutting the power and letting the waves take us.

"Those thugs must have had my flat bugged in several places. Or was it my car? Something you missed? Doesn't matter now, it's time for damage limitation. Can you take over here and give me the phone? I will send them our position and ETA but tell them no point in coming out. Mission aborted."

I took over the wheel. We were wallowing in a bumpy sea. I went up to ten knots as we were now battling more than modest waves which were becoming challenging and, occasionally, really angry. Funny how I now felt able to cope!

She fed in the details, explained there was no need for them to come out and that the mission was a failure, pressed Send and turned to look at me just as a largish wave hit us sideways on.

"Elizabeth. Just say we *had* found a couple of thousand krugers. How would we have handled them? I reckon that at thirty-four grams each their total weight would have been something over five stones in old currency."

She shook her head. "No need to worry now. If there is a reception party waiting for us I imagine they will behave themselves in the mooring area. We don't want this boat smashed up like the other one. And I wonder if those two will come anywhere near to us - for all they know we could call in the police. And they certainly would not welcome that. Just going to put a few things together. Shout if you need me." She went quickly off.

I suddenly remembered something and shouted after her.

"No you weren't bugged."

She turned around.

"How come?"

"While I was chatting with Maurius he remarked that an American had shown interest in this boat."

"And?"

"Well I reckon it was a probably muffled South African voice whose owner had heard from our bugged Marianne that she was for sale. We never said where but Scandinavia was mentioned. Recall it?"

"I remember."

"Well I reckon they phoned all main Scandinavian boat sales places checking on the name. From that they established Bergen to be the place. Check with UK marinas, particularly within range of Bergen, and bingo - you had told the harbourmaster there to expect us."

She went off, full of thought.

Five minutes later my mobile vibrated again. I read the blurb.

DAVE. NOW TWO MORE OFFICIALS FROM SOUTH AFRICA HERE. ACCOMPANIED BY SCOTTISH POLICE OFFICER WHO SAYS LOOKING FOR MAN CALLED GELDENHUYS! THEY ARE DEEP IN CONVERSATION WITH LADY BANFORTH. SEEM FRIENDLY. PIET KEEPING WELL HIDDEN. THEY KNOW YOU ARE OUT THERE. GO VERY CAREFULLY. J.

I was wondering how to respond when Elizabeth came rushing back throwing off her weatherproofs.

"I think I may have found everything!!"

"Wh-aat do you mean?"

"I've been outside doing a final search. Round handholds running the length of the engine room but hidden beneath a ledge. Cannot be seen unless you get right down there, bend down, and look up from underneath. They act as grab handles but are long cylindrical bars - easy to hang on to in rough weather, but I have not seen that sort of thing on other boats. Largish diameter and almost *certainly* the size we want." She was shaking with excitement.

"But the newly installed pulpits? Why?" I was no longer steering anywhere and the boat had started circling. I decided it was the wrong time to admonish her for going outside.

"Another hoax - or maybe they simply replaced them for some reason and used different sizes. I really feel I may be right this time. What do we do - we are something like half an hour out and they all know we're coming?"

I left the wheel and grabbed the toolkit and my coat which was near to me. "I'll go check. Probably nothing there at all if our experience so far is anything to go by. Suggest you circle a bit or maybe just hold her steady."

As I was departing she shouted, "I left one half of the floor above the engines up. Be careful! These waves could easily tip you in."

I went quickly out, using every grab handle within reach, then pulled up the other half of the floor to reveal both engines and looked down around each side to port and to starboard. It wasn't really an engine room as such, just space sufficient to accommodate the two huge engines which were now becoming quieter as Elizabeth eased back on speed. I lowered myself down to engine level and saw immediately what she meant. Two cylindrical bars, diameter at least forty millimetres, one port and one starboard, running along each side of the boat. Very useful to hang on to in a rough sea when dealing with some engine emergency but unusual to boat expert Elizabeth. And, most importantly from the Maghiel viewpoint, not visible from above.

The torch gave enough light for me to see the way the bars were fixed. Four brackets equidistantly spaced held them firmly to both sides of the boat. Heart in mouth and using my full strength I just managed to turn the first bracket screws and then pulled the released bar end slightly downwards.

Nothing!

I unscrewed two more brackets. Depressingly there still was nothing. Her hunch was wrong. I hauled myself out and went back in to the warmth to tell her. To her great credit skipper Elizabeth went into auto pilot, checked all around and only then turned to me and screamed at the top of her voice,

"But they have to be somewhere - it simply makes no sense. This whole thing is insane!!"

FORTY-SEVEN

SCOTLAND

She then went momentarily silent, staring at me in disbelief, aghast that this final possibility was as negative as everything else.

"Pulpits, vertical stern rails and now the engine room. I *still* think we've missed something. David, I am sure we have overlooked something *really big*."

"Maybe, but we now have to be practical. See this thing through and carry on. Life goes on. We go on. We come to terms with it!"

"Yes."

In no way did she mean it. Our speed increased. I carried on the coming to terms with the situation bit.

"We purchased this boat in Scandinavia and hope to make a profit by selling her here in the summer. That has to be at least something to the good."

"Yes. Now, how do we deal with Haff and that awful woman? We should tell the police about their raid on my place, guns, our imprisonment and all the things they get up to!"

"Don't think so Liz---"

"Do not call me that please. I hate it!"

"Sorry. I doubt they will be there. My guess is they've now informed the Johannesburg authorities in order to get a thank you payment should anything ever turn up. They won't want to see us any more than we want to see them. That feeling has to be mutual."

"Yes, agreed. They should move away fairly soon." She looked hopeful. "I really do not want to come up against them again."

"Well, let's hope they disappear. I suspect we will be very thoroughly searched by someone in authority and whoever does it will finish up with egg on his face. I wonder who sent the helicopter?"

"You'd better reverse all you have been doing down below or they will certainly be suspicious of what they see."

I'd forgotten. I shot back out and down to the engine room, positioned and re-bracketed the handrails, retrieved all the tools, levered myself out and lowered the floor back into place. I looked all around the decks. Nothing out of place. Little time left to think, we were getting close now.

Land was peeping through a morning coastal mist. A beautiful sight. How many people at any time in their lives cross the North Sea at night, see oil rigs, fishing vessels and ocean liners and arrive on a beautiful crisp morning such as this? Would that we had time and peace of mind to enjoy our arrival in Scotland. I hurried back to join the skipper.

"I've just spoken to Jonny. Confirmed to him we are totally without cargo. He was very disappointed but is concerned to get us through all this unscathed. He says there are not a large number of boats in the harbour. The two of them will keep a look out but not join us when we arrive. They will be of more use to us by remaining out of sight right now and watching to see how events evolve."

Elizabeth was now being guided by buoys, strategically positioned to take us in. I sat beside her and felt a slight tremble as I held her spare hand. In a few minutes we had land appearing on both sides of the boat and the speed came slowly downwards. We passed several large vessels and soon were entering the marina where we saw a number of small motor and sail boats. We found our correct mooring slot and glided carefully in. I did the ropes. She cut the engines. There was an eerie stillness all around us. And absolutely nobody to be seen.

"I'd better walk over report our arrival. I radioed in to confirm but we should let them know we are here. There is a formality about this which is important."

"I wouldn't. I have a strong suspicion they will be here before you get to the harbour office." I was revisiting the estimated value of our non-existent haul. "Go and put your feet up and try very hard to forget it all, even for a short time. I'll hang around out here for a bit and we'll see what happens."

She went off.

I tidied up. Mugs, plates, charts and all sorts of clothing. Binoculars and a bleeping GPS. I was thinking about putting together some sort of breakfast when, sure enough, there was a tap – tap – tap on the port side window. I looked across to see who was there. I could just make out an expressionless, rigid looking, smartly uniformed Scottish policeman.

"May we come aboard. Routine check-up?"

"Of course, officer." I slid back the door and in he came followed by a stocky man with a red face and an air of constant activity.

"What can I do for you gentlemen? I'm David Johnston."

"Constable McBride and this is harbourmaster, Andy Feathers. We'd like a short chat. Sorry it's so early in the day."

I pointed to the bunk seat and had just sat myself down opposite them when Elizabeth appeared. She slid herself quietly on to a fly bridge step and said brightly,

"Can we offer you both a coffee, or tea or something else?"

McBride looked tempted but his mission made him nod his head without even looking at Feathers.

"No thanks. Just a few questions." He turned to me. "Where have you come from?"

"Bergen. We left yesterday. Came right across. Departed in the afternoon and just kept going through the night. We were lucky. The good weather they forecast actually happened and we had an easy crossing."

Feathers chipped in. "We did have forward notification of your arrival." He seemed to be mildly disgruntled.

"Yes, I thought we would come over to your office a little later. At this time of the year we didn't think things would be too busy." Elizabeth knew the score and I guessed did just enough to settle the harbourmaster.

McBride stared at me again, this time very positively.

"I'll come straight to the point. It has been suggested to us that you may have acquired large amounts of gold coin which maybe is not your property. Is that correct?"

"Good heavens, No! I wish we had *any* gold coin on board. Might pay for the slap-up breakfast which I could do with right now to say the least. Where on earth would you get such an idea as that?"

Feathers took over. He did not want any upset on his watch but had no choice.

"We have two very senior South African government officials here who claim that their intelligence has zeroed in on your boat as a carrier of stolen goods. As harbourmaster I have to check it out. You are probably aware of the law on this sort of thing. May we have a look around?"

"You cannot search this boat without a warrant." Elizabeth sounded as if she knew something on the subject, and, I slowly realised, she should, given the father she had.

"Warrant herewith."

McBride had one!

"No point in even asking us really then?" I tried to sound and look annoyed.

"No sir. We really do *need* to look."

"In that case, since we cannot sleep and recover from a very hardworking night, we will go and have breakfast somewhere ashore. Is that permitted, or do we have to stay here while you search?"

"Yes, of course you can go. All your belongings will be safe. And, again, I do apologise for the upset."

I looked around. "Come on Elizabeth."

"I need a few things." She rushed off and was back in one minute carrying a smallish shopping bag in which there appeared to be very little.

"Open please."

There was a protracted silence as the contents were checked over by McBride. Nothing "significant" was found and he handed it back looking slightly apologetic. We put on our heavy coats expecting them to be inspected too. But strangely they were not interested in doing that. We then stepped down off the boat, walked quickly away, and left them to it.

FORTY-EIGHT

"Good trip then?"

As soon as we were away from the marina Piet closed in on us, followed closely by Jonny. It seemed to have been a long time and everyone had been through a lot. Once out of sight of Wick harbour we had a four-way greetings hug.

"Yes thanks. Everything went as planned by the skipper. A huge new experience for me, of course. And I, for one, am famished. We desperately need food. Anywhere around here open?" I felt a raw coldness in the morning air. The bright early start to the day was changing and the skies were already clouding over. It was beginning to look as if we could be in for a thoroughly wet and windy time.

"All fixed. Hotel Mack's place. We checked it out yesterday in case this sort of thing happened. Seafood is a speciality but bacon and eggs can be had if preferred. When the cavalry moved in we were pretty sure you would leave them to get on with searching the boat, since there would be nothing to find."

In very quick time we arrived. The outside of the hotel had that sort of dour Scottish defying-the-weather look about it but once we had passed inside through two massive doors the warmth was very welcoming. The large dining room looked attractive and several tables were already occupied. One lone waiter agreed we could have the most isolated distant corner table where we had an intensive discussion about the menu. Unsurprisingly we ordered the "English" breakfast all round.

"From what I glean from the phone texting and conversation it really is all over now?" Piet having started the whole thing had more reason than the rest of us to be upset, though he seemed to be speaking more in sorrow than anger.

I tried to be as informative as I could, though what we had been working towards was now no more. "Yes 'fraid so. Aboard the boat we thought we were sitting on a fortune but we searched everywhere and it simply was not to be. Pulpit rail size just a wee bit too small. The enlarged back end of the boat rails proved completely empty and a new engine room handrail of the correct size, which Elizabeth found, was dismantled by me, searched and also proved negative. On the brighter side we have a boat which should sell for thousands more in the summer months than we paid for it coming out of winter. But, very regrettably, all our activity has come to nothing. Incidentally, you said something about our two, or three, friends still being around?"

"They disappeared the moment the police and South African inspectors started taking an interest. I wasn't a bit surprised. I reckon they've done their informing and have probably gone." Jonny's conclusions mirrored my own.

I tried to keep positive.

"In which case we can deal with the boat import situation and whatever else the harbourmaster requires, and then freight her southwards for us to have a bit of fun with before the selling season in about four months' time."

"I suggest we sail her back ourselves. At a guess it would take about three days? Fantastic skipper. And *fun*. We need something radical like that to cheer things up." Piet was just about smiling - which in these circumstances was quite something!

Elizabeth's face was a picture. "So far we've been lucky. We may well be subject to some pretty awful seasonal weather at some time during the trip. There are difficult navigation areas down this coast and when you get near to the Thames you are in the busiest shipping lanes in the world. You guys have no idea what we would be going into."

Jonny said quietly, "But it could be rather good for us all. And we would keep the boat near to us down south and be ready to sell when the time comes. No overland haulage costs. I think it's a really good idea. I have a few holiday days left. But I think maybe that is asking too much of Elizabeth? Without her input we are nothing!" *Breathtaking sweet talk!*

"Well, all right, maybe. If you all *really* want this. I'll do it if I can have one day to sleep, refuel, purchase the relevant charts, and generally check everything. But don't say I didn't warn you. I know what things can be like farther south. I can do it but it will not be a picnic."

At that moment breakfast arrived and took priority over all else. While we mourned our failure and examined with each other what might be some sort of future, our hunger was slowly eased. I was in the middle of demolishing a second hash brown when my eye caught a movement in the distant dining room entrance. I sat bolt upright and my full attention was riveted, unbelieving, at what was there right before my eyes.

Haffenbacker was slowly guiding the other two to a table beside a window. They did not look our way and seemed very preoccupied, chatting quietly to each other all the time as they sat down.

I gathered my wits together and whispered to the others. "Heads down everybody. Guess what! Our three captors have just arrived and are now seated at the table way over to the left by the large window. They must have been staying here."

"Oh my, oh my. The Lady Banforth! They *haven't* fled the scene after all." Piet took a quick look over his shoulder and managed a rueful smile. "What on earth to do now? They can hardly pull out a sodding gun here in front of all these people."

"Think quick. They'll see us before long. We could have some sort of a punch-up but I'm not sure where that will get any of us?"

I was sure Jonny was right. Any form of nastiness would be totally out of place and they certainly would not welcome any publicity.

Elizabeth had been very quiet, her hand moving involuntarily across her nearly healed cheek. "I think we should go over, surround their table and give them a huge greeting. Treat them as long-lost friends. Then let us see what happens!"

I came in sharply. "No! Just before they arrived in the restaurant I'm pretty sure I saw them deposit a couple of bags at the desk outside. They're in the process of pushing off. Haff carried his briefcase in and dropped it down on the floor beside him when he sat down. Wouldn't it be great to get hold of it! What's inside might be illuminating, particularly for those South African visitors we've heard so much about, and maybe, of course, the police."

"Golly, yes. What a *wonderful* idea. I would really love to know exactly what's in there. He must be a mine of information. But how?" Elizabeth very quickly cottoned on to my drift.

Things started happening to Jonny at that moment. His eyes lit up and the whole body tensed. Something in him had been triggered by our remarks and he came straight out with it.

"I reckon I could get it done! Charades is my great thing - particularly at Christmas. I get accolades for my performances and even though I say it myself I really can turn on a good show. Deception, that's the big game plan, and that's what is needed here. I can really deceive well!"

I had heard something of his acting prowess. "Come on - how on earth *can* you get hold of it?" We were still talking in hushed tones despite being at such a distance from them.

"Piet and I will leave. They do not really know us. In *exactly* five minutes' time, Dave, you and Elizabeth must be very bold by going over and engaging them in conversation - any damned subject you like to build the tension and hold their interest. Do not ease up on it for one second. Just keep them talking. During that period of time I will ensure that his bag does a runner. But I say again you must be absolutely sure to keep them occupied one way or another or it will not work and will end up in total disaster." He looked at his watch. The action had already commenced.

"But how---?" I did not understand.

"No time Dave. They will be off soon and then it will be too late. *Just do as I say!!* We meet up when this is all over near to, or in, the harbourmaster's office."

Piet and Jonny rose slowly and walked casually out, carrying their bags with them. During the time that we had been talking I noticed that Elizabeth had carefully been tying a scarf around her head. Haff was continuing to engage the others in deep conversation, their backs still more or less towards us. I glanced at the time. Already there were just three minutes to go.

"Any idea about what he's going to do?" Elizabeth looked a little uneasy and with so little let on from Jonny I felt the same.

"Not a clue. But I know Jonny. He said we must keep their attention. That's easily done. We talk, listen when they talk, and then we talk again. The actual subject matter does not seem to be matter. He just wants them all kept occupied."

"They are going to get really horrible with us."

"Probably not here. Just think of the unwanted publicity and time behind bars they'd get." I didn't feel as confident as I sounded. "Anyway, it's time. We must appear calm, confident and, above all, *we have to keep them engaged!*"

I left enough notes on the table to cover the meals and waited for a couple who were just leaving to pass by. We both rose, picked up our coats, and strolled, much more casually than we felt, across the room to their table. At heightened times like this the mind - well, mine anyway - can do strange things. Digesting the impact of our presence on each one of them as we stood looking down at their table was difficult. Astonishment was not the word. Neither was Horrified. Aghast, Stunned, Stupefaction---my mind filtered them all in a nano-second. I settled on *Incredulity.*

"Good morning!" Elizabeth had become crisp and clear Harley Street clinical.

There was no reply. All three remained rooted to their seats. They were clearly shattered to see us. Eventually the woman replied. "What on earth are you two doing in here?"

"Just wanted to show you that my face had healed nicely." She pulled her scarf slowly to one side whilst turning her head ever so slightly to ensure that they could get a clear view. "See, only a small mark left. Am I not a very lucky girl? Could have been much worse couldn't it?"

"Well that's good. Now will you *please* go away." Haff in his accustomed manner was issuing a very gruff positive order to us both, rather than a request. It was my cue to continue the exchange of words.

"Certainly not! You cannot go around breaking into houses, holding people at gunpoint, knifing them, imprisoning them, shooting them even, and expect to get away with it. That's the law of the jungle which simply does not exist in these parts."

My voice was gradually rising in tempo as I warmed to the task and I could sense other heads in the restaurant turning our way.

Jacobi had been completely silent. He stood up, a little man setting out to solve a big problem.

"Can we discuss this outside please? We are disturbing all the people around us who are simply trying to enjoy their food. It is not at all fair to upset everyone like this."

"No, certainly not. And you are as culpable as these two." I stared at him as one about to go mad.

Haff tried reverting to what for him was normality. "Sit down Albert! We have a situation here. Either you two go away and leave us alone or we will start big trouble for you. Right here! Right now!"

I laughed and stood aside as a waiter's trolley delivered their cafetiere and slowly moved on.

"Do you really think we won't report all of your criminal acts against us to the police?"

"You can't!" Marguerite spat it out.

"Oh, and why not?" I hissed back even more sharply.

Her eyes became slits. "Because you are thieves. *We* are the ones tracking *you* down. You know that----"

"That is not true. We haven't stolen anything! Trying to carry out the request of someone who died some time ago nowhere near equals the foul acts you people are prepared to get engaged in to line your pockets. Knifing Elizabeth like that is a really major crime and----"

"David, we *must* go!" Elizabeth wanted out.

"Not yet, I haven't finished----" But I knew I was getting short on words with which to continue the onslaught.

"Yes, *right now*. We can deal with these criminals later." She grabbed me forcibly by the arm and tugged me away, much to the amusement of our breakfasting audience who were now switched in to the aggressive exchanges and really beginning to enjoy the fireworks.

I gave up and stormed out after her. "We were supposed to wait for Jonny?"

"You idiot! The coffee!"

"What coffee?"

"That was him with the trolley?"

"*What? That* was Jonny? Doing the coffee delivery?"

"Yes. He had on a hat and waiter's jacket. So good he certainly took you in."

"Did he get the briefcase?"

"Think so. I didn't dare watch. Just kept my eyes looking straight ahead. We must get out of here very fast. They will be after us when they discover---"

"God, yes." We pulled on our coats as we flew through the doors, then slowed to a very fast walk. "Jonny was right. The harbourmaster's office is our safest place. They're probably still going through the boat check but nice to know that the law is not far away. Those three will really be after us with a vengeance when they discover---"

I ran out of puff. We arrived in very quick time, still breathing heavily. I looked through the window. It was empty inside the main office so we entered and shut the door. Three minutes later Jonny and Piet staggered in and collapsed into two of the harbourmaster's chairs.

"His briefcase is safely hidden in there." Jonny pointed with pride to the large plastic bag he was carrying.

"What the hell are we going to do with it? They'll murder to get it back. A really superb disguise, by the way." That was the very least I could say. His execution of the event had been absolutely perfect.

"In all likelihood they do not yet know we have it. In due course they will realise that you and Elizabeth could not possibly have pinched it - you were both on your feet facing them the whole time." He stopped and drew in a few quick breaths. "To them I was just the waiter. Shortly after coffee was delivered by me their breakfast was brought in by two others. And I know that the toast went in separately too. All of that will keep them eating and drinking for a while. Plenty of alternatives for them to think about when they then discover the theft. We have probably an hour plus a bit while they panic together, try to work out exactly who did the job, and then remonstrate with the hotel management."

. "How did you get the hat and jacket?" I was keen to know exactly how he had achieved such a great success in so short a time.

"Money. It cost me twenty quid. The guy was very happy. A further thirty after the bag theft had him swearing secrecy as he took back the uniform. Nobody else there saw anything. Only the two of us will ever know. Well, three really, if you include Piet."

"Very well done, Jonny. Clean as a whistle." Praise from Elizabeth was really worth having! "What happens now?" She looked at me, presumably hoping for some sort of guidance.

"We look into that briefcase? Is it locked?"

"No." Jonny pulled it from the bag, opened it up and removed a heap of papers which he lay across the table. "Piet, keep a look out."

I studied my watch. "Let's do this methodically." We all looked at the top sheet. It was a plan of Wick. "I suggest anything to do with us comes out. Anything which incriminates them or is neutral stays in."

"Picture of you Dave. That is the exact same one that I saw in the shop."

"Stays in. Nothing incriminating." But after five seconds of reflection, "No, on second thoughts, let's take it out." I wasn't at all happy to have my picture associated with this gang.

"Woops, a big find. A list of their organisation. Looks like it was called the "Diamond and Gold Resolution Society" -that's then crossed through and the word "Daggers" inserted. Yes, of course, the latter name is an abbreviation. They seem to have a widespread range of members. Addresses in many countries. Attachment to this is headed "Current Projects – Resultant values. Gosh, they've got projects everywhere." Piet was in his element. "And it includes *Mint South Africa - up to two million dollars.*"

"Leave all of that in."

Jonny had something else. "Transcript of what went on in St Kats - the very words we spoke!!"

"That all definitely comes out." I had become the arbiter. I don't think anyone else wanted the job!

"And several pictures of Marianne?"

"Out."

It took about fifteen minutes of rapid reading and sorting to pull out everything which had any association with us. We left the copious details of other operations in which they were involved. I folded and very carefully pocketed what we had removed. Jonny pushed the remaining papers neatly back in and shut the briefcase.

Piet suddenly called out, "Long way off but I can see two guys near to the boat - probably finished their searching."

"What do we do with Haff's case?" Elizabeth wanted to be off quickly to do boat things which had now become more pressing.

"We leave it here." I grabbed the case and walked quickly into the harbourmaster's inner sanctum. We had to deposit it somewhere where it would appear simply to have been forgotten. I eliminated the drawers in his desk and a space beneath a distant table. Then I saw the place - just behind some bookshelves. I thought that would be about right. But then no, it was far too remote. In the end I left it resting against the inside leg of the table, where it was not immediately in view but would be found fairly soon.

"They're walking away from the boat, probably coming here. We have two minutes to be out."

"Right. We're away. They must not see us departing." I could now not get us out soon enough. We definitely did not want in any way to be associated with that briefcase.

The rain was still coming down but we only fully became aware of it when we were safely a good distance away. I spoke quietly to Elizabeth.

"How quickly could we be off?"

"Fuel will take an hour or so. Relevant charts are all for sale here. Will take minutes. I must do a passage plan. We could be off in a couple of hours. Bang goes my lovely rest!"

"Very sorry. Can you work on all of that right away?"

"Yes. I will go back to the chandlery for the charts and a check on the weather. There is just enough food aboard. I'll settle the bill for one night's moorings. When we are all on board we will motor over for fuel and water. Then we're off, no matter what!" She scampered quickly away, pulling up her hood as she went.

We trudged slowly onwards and stopped as the harbourmaster and policeman came close. McBride looked at me.

"All yours now, Sir. We've completely finished and everything is returned back to normal. You wouldn't know we'd been around." A good police officer being as diplomatic as he could in what for him had to be awkward circumstances.

"Thanks very much. Nothing of any value then?"

"No, sorry. False intelligence."

"That's ok officer. These things happen. And we did have an excellent breakfast. We will be off soon, going southwards."

Andy Feathers knew all about the possible problems into which we might be moving.

"Awful in the rain but the sea is fairly calm. There is no rough weather likely, although that can change. But you want to watch out. March can be very cold out there."

Constable McBride was abject in his contrition.

"I'm very sorry again about the disruption. I will put in a report. I am sure everything on the boat is back in place. Any problems just let us know."

"I'm certain there won't be, constable. It is a pity you found no gold though. We could have done with some of that!"

I shook hands with them both and they moved away, eager to get to some shelter away from the wretched weather.

FORTY-NINE

The journey southwards went smoothly for the first twenty-four hours. Elizabeth, having herself overseen everything for the departure from Wick, and then set me on course, had departed to put her feet up with the proviso that we get her up instantly if any difficulties were to arise.

Over the next four days we passed wind farms and oil rigs and ships of all sizes ranging from huge cruisers down to tiny fishing craft. Our chores sorted themselves. Piet did most of the cooking whilst Jonny tried his hand at the basics of navigation. I spent a large amount of time at the wheel, but throughout I really only felt comfortable in the job when Elizabeth was nearby. We refuelled twice and over three nights stayed in Newcastle, Whitby and King's Lynn. On the final run along the Essex coast we ran into an unexpected violent storm which scared the hell out of the three males aboard. Elizabeth brought us safely into Bradwell Marina where all collapsed for the day.

The following morning was bright and calm and, following a busy day negotiating the Thames, we locked in to St Katharine's that evening and moored in Marianne's old berth, the buyers having recently taken her away. The week's activities had completely shattered us all. Jonny understandably needed to go home. He took Piet with him to stay the night, collect his bags, and then later to return back in to my place.

Elizabeth and I went to the local Indian for dinner which seemed like heaven after the incessant boat and sea challenges we had endured. Piet's cooking had certainly contrasted rather unfavourably with this place. We returned to the boat elated after such a long, successful voyage, but extremely tired. She went to her small cabin and I to mine.

It must have been about three in the morning when I awoke from a deep sleep. Someone was on the boat. In the darkness I began to imagine that Haff and company were back. Then through the silence I felt a small movement beside me. She was slowly squeezing into my very limited sleeping space. I moved right up against the side of the boat in order to give her room. This time there was nothing said about "No noise."

The following morning the weather had changed, the sun was out and the smell of coffee and toast came wafting through the boat.

"Coffee and not much else in five minutes." Last night's events were obviously forgotten and life was back to normal. "And I have something quite important to discuss."

"Oh, and what's that?"

I suspected she would be on about forming a company despite our shortage of funds. I was only too aware of the full range of costs involved, from enormous London office rentals, computers and other software, to the whole process of setting up anything, let alone a complex business like ours. I rolled gingerly out of my bunk bed.

"It's not anything to do with business." She put that one to rest straight away! It took me all of ten minutes to arrive at the table.

"This is the last remaining food on the boat. Two eggs, a small part of a loaf of bread, a nearly empty marmalade pot and the last few grains of coffee."

Elizabeth must have been up and about doing things for some time. I could happily have slept on for another hour or two more. The cabin was warm and the coffee very welcome. I could not resist asking for an explanation.

"So, if it is nothing to do with business what did you want to discuss?"

She poured herself a weak coffee, cleared her throat and was quiet for a while. Then out it came.

"I have strong feelings and I should be very careful what I say. I have led us up the garden path throughout our whole investigation and really do not want to do the same again."

"But----"

"Well I thought I would confide in you and not arouse hope in Jonny and Piet. They have been subjected to all sorts of pressures - Jonny has a family and a very short-term job and Piet has been chasing around the world for nothing. Both have lost money despite the future sale of Thor - I know as I now seriously keep the books in so far as one can in these circumstances."

"Right. Understood. Therefore, you can confide in me. Definitely safe."

She looked gorgeous. We should have been talking other things. I crunched on my remaining toast, which helped!

"Well, all right, but just between us for now-----"

"Elizabeth, what is this? *Of course* I will keep whatever it is to myself if that's what you want. We are pretty close you know. Couldn't really be much closer could we? I can be trusted."

"Yes, I guess I know that. I just feel such an idiot. Right, so here goes. I phoned Mr Johannson in Bergen yesterday to let him know how it went and that we had arrived safely. If you remember he did ask us to do that."

"Yes, Well done. Good old Marius. I never thought--"

"Well, he told me that Mrs Eriksson, on learning of the sale presumably from one of her other relatives, had called him and thanked him on her son's behalf. He told me they had a long conversation during which she kept referring to Odin as having been sold. He thought that strange and corrected her saying he had sold a boat called Thor."

"Easy mistake for an elderly lady to make."

"Yes, but she then said that she had always been unsure *if they had switched names or not*. He wasn't at all certain just what that was all about so he says he just let it hang in space."

"Wow, so we could have been working on the wrong boat all the time. *Elizabeth, that cannot be true!! After all we've been through.*" My mind was beginning to take off in all directions. "Odin, therefore, could still be bloody Odin. Which means the loot could still be moored in Shepperton marina." A moment's pause to think. "No, but it couldn't, they've pulled that boat to bits looking for it and found nothing."

She had already been over this, of course.

"Yes, they tore apart all pulpits, pushpits and everything on deck but did they ever think to look below decks? You never know it is just possible----"

"Are you really suggesting that we go back to Odin, and we now think possibly that she is the original Odin, break in to the boat, ascertain whether or not stainless steel tubes are built into the small engine room, remove them if we find them there, and check as we did on this boat?"

"Yes---or no. I really don't know any more." Her voice had gone very faint. I had that desperate feeling that it was time for *me* to man up.

"Right, first things first. We both now have cold coffee. Any more in the pot?" She walked our mugs to the galley, emptied out any remaining cold drink, somehow found enough grains to do a refill and brought them back to the table. She raised hers.

"Cheers."

We both drank. Mine tasted extraordinarily, but nicely, different. She explained what it was.

"I keep a tiny bottle of brandy for boat emergencies. I reckon this is one!"

"Excellent idea." I drank some more and felt greatly encouraged for what was to come. "We can't now just leave this alone. We also cannot alert Piet and Jonny to it in case we have another false alarm - which I think we both know from experience is a racing certainty."

"What then do we do?" She really had passed the buck and, for once, seemed happy to be getting out from under.

"I think the first thing is for you to call your friend Mrs Eriksson. Speak only to her. It's a "sorry wrong number" if she doesn't herself answer. Let her know, if you are driven to it, that after your chats with her you went to have a look at the boat in Bergen, and so liked it that you bought it. Alternatively, and better if possible, simply get into a conversation and see if you can swing it around to boat names - by any means you can use. If it's still a goer maybe we'll plan exactly how, where and when we do something."

Out came her phone. She found the name and upped the volume. Within seconds a voice answered.

"Eriksson."

"Mrs Eriksson. It's Elizabeth phoning from London."

"Oh, good morning my dear. How are you today?"

"Very well thank you. I just wanted you to know that we found the boat we wanted - like we talked about."

"You did. I'm very pleased to hear it. I hope you like it. It's always very nice to buy a new boat. We have sold our boat in Bergen. I spoke to the man who sold it. He was delighted."

We exchanged glances. "That was Thor wasn't it?" I sat there holding my breath as she spoke. The conversation was following exactly the path we wanted.

"No, Odin." There was a long pause. "No, sorry, it was Thor. I think I remember telling you the names were changed but at the end of their long discussions I seem to recall that they did not do it. I don't know why. It's all so long ago." She uttered a long sigh. Nobody ever told her anything. "Thor was the boat that was sold."

Elizabeth did not bat an eyelid and stuck strictly to the job in hand. "And how are your sons Lars and Arvid."

"They are both very well thank you. And your dear father, how is he?"

"Oh fine. He enjoys his house so much these days. I think he will like it today. The sun is out, which is good for March."

"It is here too. When the sun shines down into the fjord there is nothing more beautiful. You must come up here one day and see it."

"I might just do that at some time. Everybody talks about the beauty of your fjords."

"Well, yes, they are right. But it can be very cold too. For an old lady winter can be bad. But we do keep very warm inside."

"Well look after yourself and enjoy the sunshine. I will say goodbye now."

"Goodbye my dear, look after your new boat, and thank you so much for ringing. Please make sure we speak again soon."

She shut down the mobile and gave me a penetrating look. Decision made! We do something! "That conversation to me indicates that another Shepperton trip has become absolutely essential."

"Yes, I was thinking while you were talking. We need to ask to see the engine in order to check if there is any tubing down there. The boat may already have been done up but I think that's unlikely in the short time that has passed. A lot of work was needed. Somehow getting down below is all that matters."

"Right. Let's clear up here, go home and take your car to Odin to see how things are."

"Agreed."

FIFTY

Shepperton Marina that bright, but fresh, March afternoon was an absolute picture. Bluish skies with the occasional cloud and a gentle breeze blowing. Spring had truly arrived. We found a convenient parking space and set off on the long trek around the whole area to check that Odin was still in her berth. She was not. It took ten minutes to find her, one of forty or so boats tied up alongside the pontoons which were reserved solely for boat sales!

Surprisingly she had already been completely overhauled and looked immaculate. The price was formidable, and, for us, prohibitive, at one hundred and fifty thousand pounds. The pulpits had been restored and the damage done to the boat's fabric totally repaired.

"She looks brand new. They've done a fantastic job on her." Elizabeth was impressed with the transformation and for a moment seemed to have forgotten the reason for our visit. "I can understand the reason for selling. They must feel the boat is tainted. Can we just go aboard and look around?"

On this matter I was close to being brutishly single-minded. Have a look. Find nothing there. Walk away and get on with life.

"No! See the notice. You have to request access from Reception. So, we'll go and do just that!"

We made our way off the pontoon, moving deftly around a couple of other visitors who were studying various boats. It was that sort of bright and busy day. The offices were not far off and we joined a small queue.

Within a couple of minutes we were picked up by an eager young man who, in response to our request, led us out to inspect Odin. A sale would do him no end of good. He told us his name was Godwin. He showed us over the boat from top to bottom. The fly bridge, the cabins, all safety equipment, storage areas and electronics. Frustratingly propulsion seemed forgotten until Elizabeth said carefully, "And the engines?"

"Oh yes, madam. Down here. He opened up the floor and, after asking his permission, I lowered myself down to have a look, ostensibly at the massive diesels, but really to inspect any handrails which might be in the area. As I looked warily around my heart gave a leap. They were all there, identically positioned as in Thor! Those tubes looked to be an integral part of this particular make of boat! Eventually after some talk with the young man about engine performance, servicing, fuel consumption and the rest I heaved myself back up on deck to find a smiling Elizabeth. She had obviously bent down and seen. We thanked our guide, promised that we would be back soon, and departed in something just less than indecent haste. There was a frantic need to talk and we made our way quickly back to the car.

"First things first. I noticed a lovely hotel over there - she pointed down river - and it is tea time. You can spoil me with some Earl Grey. Do you like it?"

"Yes, very much."

Well, I did now.

We drove the short distance over and once we were past some overhanging trees the place came into full view. We parked, entered the attractive building whose lounge looked out across the river, and found seats where we could talk. I ordered tea for two and the toasted teacakes I knew she liked.

"It's simple really." She damned well knew it wasn't. "We just need to have a look. You're pretty much *the* expert at that by now!"

"Agreed, but how the devil do we do set about doing that all over again?"

"We have to get aboard when nobody is around."

"That will simply not be possible. The boat will be all locked up. She's a valuable commodity. Especially after all the renovation work that's been done."

We sat quietly for a while concentrating on the problem. Then she came up with a suggested plan.

"Ok. We could come again, say tomorrow, for another look. I keep him talking while you tell him you want to do a serious engine inspection. I'm sure I could engage him for fifteen minutes or so."

I was quite certain she could easily do that. Tea and teacakes arrived and she poured. Earl Grey had not been a problem to the management. I wanted to pursue her argument.

"You're pretty close to some sort of solution. But I see a major problem. Inevitably I would make some noise which Godwin, understandably, would want to investigate immediately. If, on the other hand, we asked for a trial trip and looked serious about eventually acquiring the boat, he would take us out for a run on the river. I'm sure they do that as a matter of course. I could then, some way from home, ask to listen to the engines - a very reasonable request by potential owners - and he would be unable to leave the wheel. I guess he would offer no objection to that."

"It might be dangerous for you down there with the engines running?"

"No, mechanics do that sort of thing all the time. Just noisy. We could assure him that I would not put fingers near to moving parts. And I could check very quickly providing those end screws are not encrusted in. Actually one could apply some WD40 before we set off if we were adept enough."

"Tomorrow then, we arrive with your tool kit and a couple of large, strong bags? You never know."

"Tomorrow, yes. Tool kit, no. Simply a good range of screwdrivers, lubricant and, I agree, bags for the product!" I had a thought. "We'd better check on Marina opening times. We could book in for a river run early. I'll go over and fix it now. Stay here in the car and I'll be back in a few minutes." I stopped in mid-track. "I'd better settle the bill first."

"No, don't worry. I'll do it. What's yours is mine, what's mine is yours. Remember?" I seemed to recall something being said like that when she was in my bed, although I also recalled that money management was not exactly the most pressing issue on my mind at the time.

"Yes, there was something. Right. You pay."

I walked off back across to the Marina. It was now late afternoon. The crowds of boat worshippers had reduced to a trickle. I could not see the young man anywhere so went straight into the office. There was now no queueing and in control sat just one tiny lady wearing a huge pair of spectacles. She was almost totally hidden behind large computer. Behind her on the wall was a large plan laying out the entire mooring areas. She turned her owl-like gaze in my direction.

"Can I help you?"

"Please, yes. I am interested in the boat Odin which is for sale, just out there."

As I pointed casually through the window I was, for the second time in my life, completely stopped in my tracks! Urgently! Something really badly wrong! There was Godwin on Odin's deck showing someone around. But it wasn't that. That was normal-----

"Sir, you wanted to see Odin?" She was petite but, as is often the case with tiny people, sharp with it.

"Yes, er, er, well no! I made a superhuman effort and forced myself to get a grip. "I'll leave it for just now. Speak tomorrow. Sorry-----"

I lunged my way outside taking care to keep myself totally concealed from Odin. I had seen and recognised Godwin at once but what followed on from that was one of those horrific - unbelievable - instant recognition - events which occur maybe only once, or maybe, not at all, in a lifetime. The man he was showing around was the taller of the two South African officials whom we had last seen walking around Wick!!!

I could not believe it and looked closely again. It was for sure. He had one feature I knew well - a jutting chin. There it was. He was definitely that man. And, as I was taking it all in, he was joined by his shorter colleague whose skin was an off-white colour - probably mixed race. Those were the same two people. What on earth to make of it? I pulled out my phone and noticed my hand was slightly shaking. The answer was immediate.

"Yes Dave?"

"Remember those two South Africans in Wick?"

"Yes, of course."

"They're aboard Odin right now. No mistake. I'm sure."

"Don't let them see you!"

Her instant reaction had been the same as mine.

"It's OK, I've moved out behind the building. What the hell are they doing here?"

"They *must* have followed us."

"But they're doing just what Haff's lot did. Are we bugged again?"

"No. Constable McBride swore that definitely nobody would be allowed aboard Thor except the one marina workman - and he himself stayed there the whole time to enforce it. But they did know we were coming to St Kats. I recall telling that to the harbourmaster while they were present. They're stalking us just like the other lot. They must be. Oh my god!"

She was getting scared and that made two of us. The situation was very frightening.

"Come on back but keep out of their sight. David be very, very careful!"

I moved from the protection of the building very gradually. They were quite immersed in what they were doing and seemed to have no eyes for anything else. Once outside in the road the high hedge shielded me completely but I did not relax in any way. I just made for the car as fast as my legs would carry me and collapsed into the seat gasping for breath. Elizabeth was on her phone and finished off quickly. "Yes, thanks. Come back asap." She shut down and turned to me. "This is really awful. No, it's not, it is *horrendous*."

I gasped. "The last thing we wanted. Question is are they goodies or baddies? Are they here on their government's business or maybe their own? What the hell conceivable work can they be carrying out down here on that boat?"

"I was just talking to Jonny. Told him everything that was going on. He's right away going to have a chat with Andy Feathers, the harbourmaster, to see what he can establish. We both reckoned Andy would be helpful rather than restrained on the issue. He has no reason to be otherwise."

"Great. Was Jonny a bit miffed at our doing this alone?"

"Not a bit. He wasn't at all surprised at our action given the new state of play. Very worried by the immediate turn of events though. Not one of us has the slightest clue about those two."

"What now?" I was pretty sure she would come up with an idea or two.

"Well, we must find out about them. Jonny is getting their names and any other available detail and then will get Piet to use his Pretoria police friend to try to establish, in his own way, exactly who they are and what they are truly up to. They will come back to us as quickly as they can. He said fifteen minutes, but I reckon it will take quite a bit longer than that."

I tried to relax a little from my enormous shock, as she continued with her appreciation of what was going on.

"Then we must establish exactly what they spoke about to our young friend, Godwin. They will leave at some time - we must watch out for that now. Immediately they've gone we can collar Godwin and, one way or another, establish the gist of the conversation he had with them."

She was absolutely right. I nodded and pointed. "I will go and hide myself in those bushes and will call you the moment they move away from the marina and towards the car park. They must have a car. I doubt they could have come any other way."

"Right. I will wait here and note the car make, registration number, colour - all of that - when they get into it."

"I then will go straight on to question Godwin before he makes his way home. It must be near to their closing down time now." As I went off I noticed she was fixing that scarf firmly over her head again. That act seemed to have become a sort of war symbol.

It was just ten long minutes later when the two South Africans left the boat and, as we had surmised, moved off in the direction of the car park. A couple of minutes after that Elizabeth called me to declare the coast clear - they had driven off - and I went in search of Godwin. I almost bumped into him just as he was hurrying off, his day over.

"Hi there Godwin, you've finished a busy day? Presumably you are now on your way home?"

"Oh, hello. Yes, I am. I thought you had left us some time ago."

There was no point in beating about the bush. "As we were leaving we happened to notice you were showing two men over the boat just now. We were quite concerned about it. I hope they didn't buy?"

"No, not at all. Funny really. They looked around but all they seemed to want to know was why the boat had been vandalised when she was moored in our Marina. I said I didn't know, well maybe somebody just hated the look of the boat or something. I wasn't there at the time so I had no full details of exactly what happened and why it was done. The owner was pretty miffed though, I can tell you that! He was, understandably, driven right up the wall. And his insurers wouldn't cover the cost!"

"But they weren't in the buying mood?"

"No. I would say they were not really interested right from the beginning. Strange people - Aussies maybe. They just seemed to be looking for something, sort of feeling their way around the history of the boat. They certainly were not potential buyers. I know every one of those when I see them. I've got to go now. We have a rock concert tonight!"

"Right Godwin. I won't keep you. Thanks for that. Oh, one more thing. Just so that we know. Are they likely to be coming back?"

"No, the boat is yours if you want it. Cheerio."

Bye for now, and thanks. That's very good to know."

I did a relaxed stroll back to the car, rather pleased at what he had said, but still deeply perplexed. It seemed quite possible we had not been followed but that they were doing their own independent investigation. Elizabeth was alive with information when I arrived back.

"Piet phoned. Those two are probably *both* top security people working for, but not employed by, the South African Mint. Piet's police friend didn't know them but said the Mint took on such people for their investigations. Rumours are rife over there that the theft of krugers which happened long ago was about to be resolved. How, when or why - he had no idea, except that the top South African police people had started things off a while ago by picking up two suspects who quickly spilt the beans by telling all they knew in order to save their own skins."

"Mm, those would be our old friends Johannes Kokot and Elan Van der Merwe. I really would not like to be in their shoes just now!"

"The two you have just seen are are Hansie Botha and Jabulani Mosemola. Jonny says the harbourmaster spoke highly of them both. There had been a meeting in his office between them and two other men and a lady but he had no idea what was discussed. Our policeman friend was apparently under instructions from above to facilitate their investigations, whatever that may mean."

I tried to put together a scenario which fitted. "Haff must have seen the light with them around and probably tried to lay claim to some sort of fee from the two men for putting them on to the track of the krugers. I wonder---"

"Oh, and he said Constable McBride took away a brief case left behind by one of them." Elizabeth's recall of her conversation was fired up again. "Let's see if we can get Piet and Jonny to dinner on Thor tonight. We all need to examine everything that is happening very closely. I'll fix the food. There are things happening here---"

"Agreed. I think we should go. You drive. I'll phone and fix with the other two."

I, too, felt that a reappraisal of the whole situation had become very necessary.

FIFTY-ONE

Dining aboard Thor was easy when compared with confines of Marianne. We could stretch out more. The galley arrangement had greater space and, of course, we were no longer constrained by worries about Haff and his fearsome friends.

Elizabeth had dropped me off at my place where I had a quick bath and change of clothes. I checked all IT equipment and camera and spent awhile looking over my work papers and then took some time checking all around. If anyone had been in nothing seemed to have been removed or even touched. My pad seemed to be the one place where there had been no interference - well, as far as I could see. Then I took the now familiar journey out to St Kats.

Once aboard Thor I found Jonny and Piet waiting to be updated. It went without saying that Elizabeth had somehow found time to bring fish and chips for all, which she now pulled from the oven. I passed around some of the lagers which I had remembered to bring.

Piet stared at me long and hard. "These guys on Odin. Could *they in any way* have known that you were in the same place at the same time?"

"Been thinking about that. I'm quite sure now that they could not have been aware of me. It must all have been an extraordinary coincidence. The strangest thing was that they did not seem to be looking for their lost krugers. They simply wanted a look around. No particular part of the boat, just somehow getting the feel of it. But, of course, I suppose that is about how we would approach the problem too!"

"That's mad, Dave! All the way down from the northernmost tip of Scotland to Shepperton marina just to have a look! Why? Why? They must have had a kruger reason."

"Piet, I have no explanation. Logic doesn't seem to apply any more. It is just possible that Haff let on about the boat. Maybe he and his friends told them everything. After all they had little to lose - having smashed the place up they knew nothing was there so they could tell the two South African officials the whole story - as they saw it of course."

Just then Elizabeth shouted for a carrier. Jonny was nearest. Worries and questions were put to one side for a short time while we ate, but the calm couldn't last for long. It was Piet who broke the silence.

"Of course, there is no point to anything if what we seek is not there, and I strongly suspect it damn well isn't." That sentiment brought the whole thing quickly into perspective.

Elizabeth looked up.

"Agreed! Therefore, we should be planning how we find out without having to buy that prohibitively expensive boat. All other casting around is irrelevant right now. If the cache did in fact happen to be tucked away inside we would then have enormous things to think about. If not, we can simply shrug our shoulders and walk away. Personally, deep down, I suspect quite strongly that Odin holds the key but, of course, I have been way out with my ideas all along. I just have this feeling right down inside that I cannot shake off."

"We have to work quickly. Like tomorrow. Despite the price I'm sure that beautiful boat will soon sell to someone." As Jonny removed our paper plates I pulled out a couple of charts of the Thames I had brought with me and spread them across the table.

"Shepperton Marina is there and Odin here." I used a pen as a pointer. "We need twenty minutes aboard her without company."

"And afterwards some privacy to remove very quickly a couple of horrendously heavy bags on some sort of wheels if the investigation proves positive." Piet was right back in the hunt after his dark days. "We wheel or carry from boat to car, load up, refix those handrails, and get the hell out!!" He made it sound like a piece of cake but everyone knew that it simply wasn't.

Our lagers were quickly finished. Elizabeth, wanting to get on with things, collected the empty bottles. She then called out from the galley that coffee was on the way.

Jonny had been silent for some time and was now looking a bit strange, almost as if he had just arrived back from a trip to another planet.

"I have an idea."

He looked at Piet as if seeking inspiration.

"Better be good."

"Why do we not get ourselves taken for an Odin trial run. During the course of this we somehow lose what's his name - Godwin. Maybe if we moor up waiting for one of those locks to open and then cannot start up when it does, he might go off to get help. He might lose the ignition key, for example."

Piet half liked the idea.

"Not bad. But we need a slightly different scenario to that. He'd simply phone for a replacement key. He would not leave the boat just for that so I think on that basis the whole thing would be impossible to carry out."

Elizabeth arrived back with the coffees, lowered the tray to the table and handed them around.

"There has to be an element of shaming him if he gets found out. Boat people generally are very touchy about correct procedures, safety on the river, knowledge of knots, security at sea - all of those sorts of things. Just look at the RNLI. They must appear to be excessively efficient to attract trust from others and also to be highly competent in order to do the job, particularly in a rough sea or driving cold wind and rain. Something should happen so that Godwin, who, at his age must be pretty new in the job, would wish to put right without his masters and peers knowing. What on earth could we instigate that would lower his esteem in their eyes?"

She sat down. We sipped the coffee in silence. Nobody seemed to have a clue. We kept looking around waiting for some bright comment to emerge. A happy party was taking place way over in the vicinity of the Dickens Inn and peals of joyful laughter came floating across the water to us. We hardly noticed it. The paucity of ideas was distressing. There just *had* to be something.

"Knots, you mentioned knots." I muttered it almost unwillingly and without really knowing why.

"Yes, so what?" Elizabeth wanted more.

"Ropes----- ropes." Something was pushing at my brain but I was still simply exuding hot air.

"What about them? Come on. Out with it." She knew a bit about my strange way of resolving situations. "David, do not stop now!"

That got me there and I stammered it out.

"Lose the bloody ropes. He couldn't tell that to his masters."

"Yes! Yes! He'd go get some more rather than be a laughing stock. You simply do not lose the ropes on the river! What if they were to disappear before we came to a lock. We cannot tie up to the shore but we ourselves help by attaching the one smaller rope that we happen to have remaining and offer to look after the boat until he returns. He goes a short distance across country - the river bends a lot - straight back to the marina to find a new rope or two. He would hope none of the staff would be around. Anyway, he would avoid them if he could. That would just give us the time we need." She, the expert, reckoned somehow this would work.

I tried to expand on the idea.

"We would anyway handle the ropes while he drove. That would be normal. There should be four ropes, two stern and two forward. But there weren't. I particularly noticed she had only one rope on the bows attached to a centre cleat so that it could go port or starboard, whichever side was tying up. Stern, I didn't notice. But if there was only rope there we could cast off by leaving it at the marina mooring! If two ropes, which I would expect, we could manage to lose the other. Not overboard though!"

"Could we not carry on through the lock in question using just the one small rope." Jonny was not a river sailor.

I knew the answers to that one. "Definitely not. A lock's a dangerous place. Water enters fast and a boat like Odin must be firmly held with two long ropes. You vary the length of rope depending on the boat's movement in the lock - up or down. He will have been taught that in no uncertain fashion."

"What if the---"

Jonny stopped short as Elizabeth's mobile rang out. She pulled it from her jacket pocket, looked to see if she knew the caller, shrugged her shoulders, pushed the button and spoke.

"Hello. Good evening."

"Is that Elizabeth Nye?"

We could all just make out the voice. It had a strongly South African accent. I strained to hear. She put the speakerphone on, one finger to her lips while she turned around to face us all, demanding silence.

"Yes, who is this?"

"I am sorry to call you so late in the evening. My name is Hansie Botha and I was in Wick harbour when you arrived there. We were not introduced. I *obbtaained* your telephone number from the *harbourmasster*. I'm in London now."

I didn't know at that moment how the others were feeling. I just knew my legs seemed to be turning to some sort of jelly! Those two South Africans! Phoning Elizabeth! Out of the blue! It seemed impossible. Hell really was beginning to freeze over.

"What can I do for you Mr Botha?"

The icy calm which she seemed to be able to turn on for this sort of occasion was back in place.

"Well, you probably realised we, that is myself and my deputy, Mr Mosemola, were behind the search which took place on your boat in Wick - for which we owe you our most sincere apologies. It was a totally unnecessary *introosion*. But, despite all that *weent* on, we do still have a problem."

"Can I help you with that?"

"Well, we think so. We wondered if you and your colleagues *maaht* be interested in coming along for friendly discussion with us. That would be all. We simply are seeking an *exchaange* of views. You see on matters relating to volumes of money there are often deep *complexitees*, so much so that countries often help each other. In this case the building of the Bank of England would be the venue for our meeting."

She looked around pleadingly at us all. I rapidly wrote YES very large across one of the maps on the table. She nodded.

"Well, happy to help. I'm not sure we can assist you in any way, Mr Botha. But I, for one, have never been into the Bank building and that would be a great experience."

"Right, my dear, shall we say tomorrow, Wednesday, at say *teen* o'clock?"

All three of us at once violently did a thumbs down. We would be taking Odin out!!

"Sorry Mr Botha. It will take a day or two to get everyone together. We all live in different places."

"Thursday then - at *teen*?"

"Yes, I could arrange that I'm sure."

"Right. You have to go to Threadneedle Street. The main entrance. Oh, and when you arrive could you make sure to ask for Sir *Jeremee* Trumperton. He is the Bank's *assowciate* who is guiding us in this matter. *Specialisses* in that sort of thing. Thank you so much. I look forward to our *meeteeng* there. Goodbye for now."

FIFTY-TWO

We were all utterly stunned!

I leaned back helplessly against the side of the boat trying hard to get some sense out of that conversation. Lights came and went in my head. That call was simply unreal! But no! It happened! What to make of it? Where to start?

Piet probably had the right idea by trying to give the impression of being laid back about it all.

"I thought you did really well with the way you handled him, Elizabeth. One could never have made this up. It was like a massive bomb arriving out of the blue and without any warning."

"Well I could hardly have told the man to go away could I? Besides it is all very interesting. He actually seemed friendly and that's the last thing I would have expected. If you wanted any further confirmation that the two of us were not seen at Shepperton I think that was it."

The whole thing was bizarre. I could still not get any sense at all out of what was happening.

"The Bank of England bit. There can't seriously be much skulduggery in that hallowed place can there? If so, then what is the link between the South African Mint and the Bank of England?"

"Money."

"Gold."

"Krugerrands, of course."

We were all singing from the same hymn sheet but I could not imagine what sort of ideas those two South Africans had put together before coming up with the idea to call us.

"The two organisations - the Bank of England and the South African Reserve Bank - probably have arrangements in place to help each other. Gold, other valuable minerals, Anglo-American, platinum and the rest. That's vast. And here there is Hatton Garden, the City and all of that. These international connections must be going on the whole time. But I know that doesn't get us very far----"

Elizabeth nodded with vigour at Jonny to keep going with his assessment of the situation and he obliged.

"----and sometimes unstraightforward situations will inevitably occur so----they help each other, often unofficially, which is another way of saying "privately scratching one another's backs." Pretty clear I think." Jonny thought he had brought some clarity, some clue, about what they were up to. "We have to remember it is millions of pounds worth if anything at all. They've ground all the information they can out of Haff and Co. and we are all that's left in the whole sorry saga."

I still didn't understand. Nothing was making any real sense. "Yes ok. But---- the Bank of England. Sir Jeremy what's his name. What's that all about?"

Piet tried very hard to be positive.

"What if we did have the krugers stashed away somewhere? It's illegal. The goods have been stolen. And we would be very likely eventually to cash in too many at once and get caught. Or give ourselves away in some other way. Therefore, sensible people that we are, we would try to avoid doing that. It follows that if we did have them in our cupboards at home we are rather stuck. The Bank of England can securely collect and hold. Dammit, did you know that they have massive bullion holdings, not only British, but global,

297

beneath the bank, way underground. One or two million pounds worth would be easily and safely handled by them and kept or transferred back to Gauteng or elsewhere. Hence the cooperation. We are small beer. They just want to quiz us in case we are in on something like that---which now could be the case of course."

"And we then say to them--?"

"Heavens, Dave, how the hell can I tell you? As yet we don't even know if we do have anything or not."

His petulance combined with that attempt at logic in a completely illogical situation broke the tension and we all burst out laughing.

It was getting very late. Time to break it up. Everything so far was hypothetical.

Tomorrow it was all going to happen.

FIFTY-THREE

"Good morning. Bright and early? You must be really interested in that boat. I hope?"

We had wasted no time in getting there the following day. I replied to him in what I thought was a potential buyer's voice.

"We would be grateful for a run in her if that's possible please, Godwin. Nothing dramatic - we just would like to see how she goes."

"Yes, no problem. Just a minute." He popped his head around the office door. "Taking out Odin, Lily. Would you mind unhooking the keys and passing them over please?"

We followed him across the hard and down to the pontoon where we boarded. He really was in his element. Godwin sensed a good sale was in prospect. He went through all checking formalities, spoke shortly about boat safety, and then positioned us to handle the ropes before he started up. Things then happened quickly. Elizabeth made sure she was already beside the forward deck cleat. Jonny and Piet each took a stern rope. I managed a covert drop off of a small bag containing screwdrivers and WD40 on to the deck beneath the seat.

"Cast off stern ropes."

Piet did as he was told - Godwin was looking straight at him. Meantime, as were about to depart, Jonny, unseen by Godwin, managed somehow quickly to release his rope from the boat and then drop it carefully down on to the pontoon as near as he could to the stern.

"Cast off forrard."

Godwin shouted this as he was looking at surrounding boats. Elizabeth took full advantage and unhooked the rope from her cleat, wound it neatly and dropped it firmly out beneath the pulpit rail and also down on to the pontoon. Godwin hadn't noticed her totally incorrect procedure. We then moved slowly past numerous moored boats and five minutes later were out into the river, turning to starboard upstream.

"We'll go up to the lock and then turn back." He shouted this out to us all. That gave us our first awkward moment.

"But surely we must go through to see how she performs in the lock?" Piet shouted at Godwin.

"Well---maybe---but that does take a long time."

I wondered why he seemed so doubtful. Probably wanted a short trip.

"We *must*, Godwin." I was standing close and I meant it.

"Right, Sir, we will of course do that." He certainly was not going to hazard this sale.

It took all of fifteen minutes for us to arrive at the lock gate. Fortunately, there were a couple of boats inside waiting to descend to our level so Godwin took us neatly in to the mooring area to tie up and wait for the lock water to come out.

"Secure boat."

"I've no rope."

Elizabeth's voice was panicky. She was good. It sounded truly genuine.

Godwin stared down at the place where the rope should be. "Where is it?"

"Back in the Marina. I undid it as you said. It's on the pontoon. I'm so sorry. Must have handled things the wrong way around." She looked as ashen faced as she could.

Godwin was visibly concerned. He "trod water" desperately now keeping the boat out away from the bank. One could sense that his whole body was crying out, *"How on earth could she do that?"*

"Stern ropes?"

"Only one, Godwin. Not sure there was another. You really must think we are idiots." Piet's face, downcast at this series of mistakes, said it all.

Godwin looked crestfallen. And pretty obviously cursed us beneath his breath for being such incompetent landlubbers. But he was quite ready and able to deal quickly with the situation.

"We need one more rope to get us through the lock. We keep a spare in the anchor box in front of you, Elizabeth. Please get it out and attach to your cleat. It is quite easy. I'll show you how."

Two other boats came up behind us to moor. Godwin executed a smart looped turn in the water to get us away from the lock area while Elizabeth performed the operation satisfactorily, without his help, after several tries. With a rope now at each end of the boat we moved safely back in behind the new arrivals and slotted each one through mooring rings.

We were secured and my plan hadn't worked. I had not thought of the boat carrying a spare rope! It was a bad idea anyway and might well have landed us in trouble in a variety of other ways, I was sure. We were unlucky and were now precisely where we did not wish to be - simply waiting for the lock to empty so that we could enter.

"Aaah. Ooo."

Piet shouted out in pain. We all rushed to the stern of the boat where he was lying across the seat with his hand held to his chest. He looked awful.

"Heart problem? Can you manage to get off the boat and up to the lock keeper?" Godwin had gone white, and was very uncertain about what to do.

"Ye-es. Help me."

Godwin took most of his weight as we all helped lift him gently off the boat and down on to the river bank. I lost my concern as it dawned on me, far too slowly, just what Piet was up to.

"Elizabeth, help Godwin."

"Right." The penny had just dropped with her too.

As they made their way slowly up to the towpath I went quickly across the boat with Jonny, grabbed the tools and moved to the engine area where, together, we lifted the floor to reveal the two large engines. I literally threw myself down first. He followed. No time to waste now. Move fast. We both knew it. They would arrive at their destination in minutes.

"Jonny, we are only going to check if there is anything here. Cannot carry away." There could not be any time in the circumstances to do anything more but at least we would *know* once and for all!

"Yes, I totally agree. Brilliant idea on the spur of the moment from Piet! Big screwdriver?" He passed it over. There was a problem. I could not move the bracket screws.

"WD40."

"Right. Here."

I soaked several brackets and the screws which held them with the magic liquid.

"That stuff takes minutes, sometimes hours, to be effective." He was worried. This was our one chance.

"I know. But this *has* to turn right now." I gave a whole series of very fierce wrenches. There was no movement and my hand was beginning to bruise.

"Let me try!"

Jonny pulled out from a pocket a pair of thin leather gloves which he had not had to use when handling the ropes. I moved out of the way as he changed places and grabbed the screwdriver. He went for the lower screw holding the bracket and gave it everything. Absolutely all he had. His muscles were rippling and he was doing himself no good at all.

But it slowly turned!!

Immediately he moved to the second screw above. He did the same there. It eventually turned too. Together we quickly removed the first bracket and end piece. I poked inside and felt nothing. There was that sinking feeling again. Jonny, using superhuman force once more, unscrewed the second bracket so that we could incline the longer handrail slightly downwards. If anything was there gravity must make it move. We looked and waited. I was now certain this again was a no no situation.

Then the unbelievable happened before my unbelieving eyes. *Krugerrands started sliding out and dropping to the floor.* In my idle hours, usually as I awoke in the morning, I had frequently wondered what one's feelings in this situation would be like.

I now knew! They were a sort of---nothing. We had no time! Right away this huge thing had simply to be a fact to be stored and nurtured for future planning. We righted the rail and stopped the slide immediately. Then Jonny pulled himself up on deck to check on the whereabouts of the others. His reaction was instantaneous.

"Blimey. Godwin's coming back!!!"

My body froze. My brain went into overkill. I shouted up at him. "Get out there and *stop* him. Any way you can. I need three minutes."

He leapt off the boat.

I loosely screwed back the second bracket. The first had to be firmer to hold the end cover plate strongly in place. Already I could hear Jonny remonstrating with Godwin. They were *that* close.

"We *must* stay up there with him, Godwin."

"He's in good hands with the lock keeper and the lady. They both know how to handle it. I really have to get back on to the boat. My orders are always to stay aboard and it's more than my life's worth to be away for long."

"No! You come back with me! You cannot just leave him like that. The man is seriously ill. *You're* the one who knows how things work on the river. How to get help and all that. I don't."

Seconds later I had nearly finished the final bracket. Two strong turns and it was in place. I dropped the screwdrivers and WD40 back into the small toolkit bag and threw it above on to the deck, then hauled myself up out of the engine room and quickly lowered the floor, at the same time my foot shoving the bag back beneath the seat.

Jonny, trying to stand his ground, was now being pushed hard backwards and had just arrived at the side of the boat. Godwin was clearly becoming suspicious about his strange behaviour and was straining to see what was going on.

"What's your problem Jonny?" I called out loudly in as steady a voice as I could muster.

He looked around, realised I was up from the bowels of the boat and must have finished, and said immediately, "Godwin will not stay with Piet while we assess his condition. I think he should." It sounded awfully lame reasoning but the pretext had held the young man back for just long enough.

"Oh, I would leave him alone. Let's get Piet off to a doctor straight away. Or would you think he is able to be moved back on board and returned to our car in the marina?"

"They were just asking the lock keeper to come up from down below where he is dealing with the lock gates, but we'll see if it's at all possible to collect Piet now."

I joined Jonny and we walked quickly up the bank and along the towpath into the small lock hut to find Piet talking to Elizabeth and Michael, the lock keeper, who, unfortunately, had just arrived. On seeing me Piet started saying he reckoned he was a bit less uncomfortable and with our help he could return back to Odin.

"You can't do that, not at all, we must phone an ambulance. For heart pain we have always to do a 999. It is the fastest way." Michael was fumbling to get his mobile out and cursing. The one time he really had to do a call---

"No, I'm ok and I will go under my own steam. Thanks very much for the offer." Gently he rose up and walked slowly out, aided by a very caring and attentive Elizabeth.

"Well, call me if you have a problem." Michael pocketed his phone, mumbling inaudibly to himself.

Elizabeth, now outside, shouted back, "Thanks Michael. We'll do that."

A contrite Godwin helped Piet on to the boat after he had staggered all the way back. "Sorry - I was wrong. They tell us always to remain with the boat when we are out for trials. Nobody ever talked about ill-health. How are you now?" He guided Piet to a seat in the warm cabin.

"A little better thanks. Could do with a cup of tea."

"Right, we'll go quickly back to the marina." He started up. "Ropes off everywhere. There's tea making stuff in the galley."

Godwin was back doing the job he knew best and in full command. We hauled in the ropes in double quick time, our techniques suddenly improving a lot. He quickly turned the boat around and proceeded at an illegally high speed back to the marina.

I came up and stood beside him at the wheel.

"A really nice boat, Godwin. I'm very impressed."

"Yes, glad you like the performance."

"We are very drawn to her. Maybe we would like to buy. Would it be possible to secure her with a small deposit?"

"You want to buy?"

That really was joyous music to his ears.

"Yes. We'll deal with Piet first - Elizabeth and Jonny can drive him off, but I'll stay and complete the transaction if that would be acceptable."

"Right now? Today? You'll have to see Lily about the money." He became advisory and lowered his voice. "She'll ask for a large deposit but I know she will actually accept a smaller amount if you insist on it, Sir." He was desperate to be sure of the sale.

Back in the Marina we all helped Piet off the boat and out in to Elizabeth's car. Godwin then left to prime Lily.

I muttered quietly to everyone, "Get together half an hour in the hotel." I pointed across the way. "You go too Jonny. I'll tell you all over there. No time to explain things right now."

I hurried back to the office to find Godwin deep in conversation with Lily. He withdrew quickly as I arrived. A somewhat obsequious lady welcomed me!

"Do have a seat, Mr Johnston. I understand you may wish to buy Odin."

"Yes please, we all like her very much. Is there any give on the price? It's an awful lot of money."

"No, very sorry. This boat will sell very easily. We normally ask for a five per cent deposit if you wish to secure her." She put on her hard business lady look. Her years of experience told her clearly that this man really wanted the boat.

"But that's seven thousand five hundred pounds. I need time to release money like that." I reckoned I still had about four thousand in my current account.

Lily appeared to think long and hard. "Well, we could accept half that amount if you pay the total fairly promptly."

"We will settle up within a week of formalities being finalised."

I pulled out my wallet in which I always carried a couple of blank cheques while she typed the invoice which incorporated the guarantee of sale. I read it through carefully and fast, signed everything she wanted, wrote the cheque, shook hands and made my way out. Godwin was now nowhere to be seen so I hurried to my car and drove out of the Marina and across to the hotel.

FIFTY-FOUR

I caught up with them in the lounge. They were listening to an animated Jonny confirming all that had gone on in that very short time we had down below Odin's deck.

"We truly, honestly, really had found the krugers!! Yes, we had! We had! No ifs, no buts! Do not question it. I was there. I saw. I swear to you that the krugers were there! And in some quantity!"

The other two were trying hard to digest the words and actually believe what was coming out of him. They couldn't fully deal with it after the litany of failures we had become almost immune to experiencing. The joy began to build in Elizabeth. She became ecstatic as realisation sank in. Her scepticism at last could be jettisoned.

"We really did it? I simply cannot believe it!! All that time! Those journeys! Thor and Odin - the mix up! And it has all come right and now we have only to think about how to handle the new situation!"

The sounds of delight being emitted by the three of them would soon be noticed. I looked around, half expecting to see someone we knew. Forever cautious these days. We were certainly not alone. There were three other groups of people eating, drinking and conversing. Nobody was openly interested in us yet, but it was not a chance I was prepared to take. I spoke quietly but with meaning.

"Back to my car if you don't mind. I think we should talk in a less public place. This whole thing is now dynamite."

They were in absolute agreement and simply had been too gobsmacked to be aware. We trooped out, walked across the parking area and climbed into my Jaguar. The rain was back again, slow and misty rather than heavy driving and cold, but not even that could even slightly dampen our soaring spirits.

"One each." I passed over three krugers and left the fourth in my pocket.

"We *really really* did it! This one is going to be a medallion around my neck and I'll keep it for ever. Very, very special." Elizabeth was giggling at it and singing to it all at the same time.

"There were many more in there - we could feel some of the weight. If both sides of those long rails down below are stuffed with krugers there could be hundreds if not thousands." Jonny was answering the questions before they were asked.

"Incredible. It was not all in vain after all. Yippee!" Piet had recovered quickly from his weeks of doubt. Elias had been right after all and his efforts were paying dividends.

"Thanks to your inventiveness Piet, yes. You did a superb job at being ill. Without that spark of on the spot genius the whole thing would have fallen flat as a pancake." I was full of admiration for that act he had concocted just in the nick of time.

A sudden cry came from Elizabeth who was inevitably questioning our next moves. "We really do not want anyone else buying her now! There were several people admiring the boat yesterday. Remember?"

Sometimes, very rarely in life, one feels one is at the peak of one's powers.

"It's ok. I've bought Odin!!"

Eyebrows shot up all round, especially Elizabeth's who knew all about me. "What, right now? You haven't got that sort of money!" Her eyes were popping.

"Yes, well, a deposit anyway. She is legally reserved. Nobody else can buy her, certainly for the near future. We have a week or more to come up with the full amount." I changed tack, regrettably but necessarily. "Don't want to put a damper on things but I feel we should forget all the celebrations right now. I really hate to wreck everything but we have an immediate problem. Our meeting tomorrow! Remember we are due in to the Bank of England to be quizzed, or at least to listen to, whatever else those guys are after. Events have now made whatever happens there a thousand times more complex. We cannot go anywhere near telling the truth. Neither do we really want to tell downright lies to such an auspicious bunch of people. We're stuck! We really do now have a very tricky time ahead of us."

"Can we plan any sort of strategy in advance? Oh, also, I hope you can manage this without me. It is a work day and I've already pushed things a bit. I would like to keep the job going a little longer."

It was easy for us to forget that Jonny was still employed. "No strategy. We don't know enough. It simply has to be played by ear. We've no idea what will come up or what course the meeting will take. We do, I think, need to appoint a spokesperson, or we might as a group start saying contradictory things, which would certainly not look good and could, in fact, land us in real trouble. Conflicting statements and all that. And, yes, of course three of us can manage. You must keep that job going, Jonny."

Piet then said quite firmly, "You, Dave, you're the boss and the one least likely to put your foot right in it with them. We'll sit round and listen. Maybe chip in, but only if appropriate." He looked around hoping for their agreement. Everyone nodded.

I was greatly relieved. It was probably the best solution although I was not daft enough to believe too deeply in my own talents. But we simply did not know what would be put before us tomorrow and could not afford to go off in all directions.

"Right I'm happy to do that. May I suggest we now all go home. Calm down after all the excitement. Feed well. Sleep well. Don't think about things too much. And three of us meet tomorrow outside the Bank's main entrance at ten o'clock sharp. Can you believe it? I cannot! I'm actually going to be wearing a bloody suit!"

Piet and Jonny drove off first. Elizabeth drove up alongside me and I lowered a window. "I'm doing shepherd's pie. The best there's ever been. Come back to my place if you'd like some."

She drove off at speed.

FIFTY-FIVE

I came out of Bank tube station at half past nine and made my way across Threadneedle Street. Although just past normal rush hour time there were still, inevitably, hordes of people on the move, all thrusting their way around as is the norm in early morning London. The sky was overcast but at least it was not yet raining. The forecast had been a bit ambiguous.

The previous evening's meal had been excellent and the wine perfect as usual. We had recalled our North Sea trip with something approaching nostalgia, chatting away like an old married couple. The highs and lows of it all were somehow quickly becoming history but we did not want to let the memories fade. We wondered about Haff & Co and speculated, at times wildly, about the two South Africans and Sir Jeremy. True to form Elizabeth had looked him up but, despite googling far and wide, had found no references. I, too, had had a go, but with the same negative results.

I told her how good she looked - well, quite a bit more than that really. She smiled and said it must be due to the resolution of our krugerrand problem, but even so she confessed she was still churning over inside in regard to the Bank meeting in the morning. Nothing about it was making much sense to her and the more she thought about it the more puzzled she became. I had to agree with her. We were walking blindly into yet another situation. Eventually, hating the idea very much, I said it was time for me to go. She was adamant that I should not. I should stay with her and then the following morning I could drive across to my place. There would still be plenty of time to put on my glad rags and get to the Bank. I took her in my arms and told her not to worry about tomorrow, things would definitely look after themselves as the discussions took place. Well, in love and war exaggerations do occur all the time! She whispered something like, "I controlled the boat at sea. The events coming up at the Bank are now down to you." I could feel the high drama of the past few days pulsing through her. I lifted her up and carried her into my small room. She told me to go and turn off all the lights. That took a matter of seconds. When I returned, slowly feeling my way, it took me a very short time to discover that she was simply standing there in the dark, waiting---

I was jolted unwillingly back to the here and now as I spied Piet standing to one side of the pavement near to the Bank's grand entrance. I worked my way around the back end of a huge red bus and went over to join him. Elizabeth joined us shortly afterwards. She and I just said "Hello" to each other and turned our attentions quickly elsewhere.

"Excellent suit, Dave."

"Not so bad yourself!"

I don't think Piet had worn a tie for months but he was fully kitted out now. Elizabeth simply looked a million dollars, but then she always did.

It was time.

We strolled as casually as we could in to the world-renowned building where we were received by a colourful gentleman in a very up market top hat who asked for our names. He then pointed us through a smart security area where we were asked to wait. Almost immediately a short thin wiry man who was balding on top appeared as from nowhere, came into the waiting area, and asked us to follow him across the design covered marbled floor.

Sir Jeremy had a smallish office situated at the distant end of the main building. He was seated at a modest desk behind which was a well filled bookcase. A small pile of files rested on the lowest level shelf. The man looked to be in his mid-fifties, tallish build, with a typically English aristocratic style about him, and a Royal Air Force moustache. His dark navy made to measure suit was set off against a flamboyant tie.

He stood as we arrived, shook us all warmly by the hand, and introduced Botha and Mosemola who rose from their seats which were situated on either side of his desk. They too held our hands and smiled warmly at us. Chairs were already in place and coffee was brought in very promptly with some panache by the same thin man. They had clearly gone out of their way to make us welcome.

Back in his seat Sir Jeremy shuffled a couple of papers around before looking intently at Elizabeth. It was pretty clear that there were to be no preliminaries and he got straight down to business.

"Good of you all to come at such short notice." He cleared his throat. "We have a suspicion that you may be able to help us - that is our two South African friends here - with a problem that goes back over many years."

"And how might that be?"

I attracted his gaze away from Elizabeth and, by so doing, hoped to lay down a marker that I was to be the main spokesman.

Botha himself also wanted to waste no time and cut in right away with a continuation of Trumperton's diatribe.

"Many years ago there was a theft of golden *krugerrandss* from the Mint in South *Afrikaa*. We have known for a very long time who did it. He is long *deed* and his two would-be *accompliccess* are now in prison. They killed at least one person in their *massiff* efforts to find the gold. But *despaate* all of that to date nobody seems to have *fahnd* it. Every lead goes, how do you say, right up the garden path."

"Which is presumably why our boat was done over in Wick?" I was careful not to say too much, but it was difficult to remain completely silent. Their faces were giving nothing away and if we were innocent beings then I felt a little mild aggression would not be out of place.

Sir Jeremy Trumperton took over again. "There seems to be an uncanny link with Norway and Norwegian boats. That is where your boat Thor came from wasn't it?"

I had boned up for that one. "Yes, Elizabeth, who is an experienced and seasoned yacht master, with me as crew, went over and bought out of season in order to get a good price in the summer in this country. We sailed her over as the cost of freighting would have been prohibitive - just one look at the map shows the scale of the problem. A truck would have to travel through half of Europe. We decided to come back across to Wick which is, as the crow flies, about the nearest point in the UK."

I waited for an observation of some kind, maybe even a funny one about birds, but nothing was forthcoming. Humour was definitely not on the agenda. Just three stern faces which never changed.

"Do you know a man called Haffenbacker or a lady going by the name of Jessica Morgan?" Mosemola now wanted to add to Trumperton's line of questioning.

I shot a look across at Elizabeth. Jessica Morgan was not the name we knew her by. But we knew them all right! Fortunately, with some very quick thinking she was able to come up with some sort of relevant answer whilst I remained tongue tied.

"Yes, I think it was those two who came to my flat one evening asking questions about krugerrands. They were pretty abrupt about it all. This presumably ties up with that theft you were talking about?"

Sir Jeremy bristled in a way that only his type of man can and I sensed something of real substance might now be coming out. He was, no doubt, at the centre of whatever was going on and we might be about to learn the status and exact purpose of all their investigations.

I certainly wasn't wrong!

"I must explain about me and what I do in this place. I am not on the staff of the bank and have absolutely nothing to do with its day to day running. That work is organised, bullion and cash are meticulously stored and the country's financial wellbeing well cared for. However, there come times when situations arise that concern wealth but which cannot readily be dealt with by any bank because the problem is neither straightforward, transparent nor legal. Sometimes, when you are dealing with big money, whether cash, valuable metals or electronic transfers, something goes wrong. Wealth goes astray. It can be by human error, which does not concern me, or it can be by theft, and that does. Situations can become difficult, often impossible, to resolve by any of the known and trusted normal methods. So abnormal ways have to be found. Officially, in the Bank's eyes, we do not exist. And yet here we are with a perch on which to operate from inside this great institution."

I concentrated hard on drinking my coffee. We now knew why he could not be easily traced. I could see pretty clearly where this would be leading and started to mull over what our response should be.

He coughed, looked around at each of us, and continued in the same head teacher style. "If a friendly foreign power has such a problem we are here to help. Likewise, in a reverse situation they would help us. We are all here today to help the Mint in South Africa recover what was stolen all that time ago."

We remained silent. There really was nothing that we *could* say. I was sure there was a lot more to come out of him. Piet had stayed quiet throughout and it suddenly registered with me that his accent, though quite mild, would certainly not prove helpful to us at this juncture. I guessed he had become aware of the problem soon after our arrival. It was something we should have thought of much sooner.

"Mr Botha has asked for our help in settling this situation. Long ago, as we all know, they lost a lot of wealth from the Mint and, despite the length of time that has elapsed, they want it back. Nothing too unusual there is there?"

I broke in, "Do we know the volume of the loss?"

"*Abaht* three thousand krugers we think. We do not know exactly, but somewhere *arand* that *amant*." Mossemola had a close interest in the figures.

317

"That's enormous!" Elizabeth gave off an air of incredulity.

Sir Jeremy suddenly rose up and marched across to the wall opposite where there was a huge hanging map which he uncovered. He picked up a pointer stick and started wielding it like a conductor's baton. Looking at his global chart I was not at all happy at the way things were moving. They really did seem to have been closely monitoring us.

"This is what I call the kruger footprint."

He followed a marked route from Cape Town across the seas to Bergen, thence to Wick or London - the line from Bergen was split in two and went to both places. He looked solemnly around at us all giving time for his revelations to sink in.

"We are just not sure about the last bit - that is, where it all finished up."

He put down the pointer and returned to his seat, still staring around at us to gauge reaction. But what he saw there had to be completely negative. Truth to tell we did not know what to say in these strangely unfolding circumstances. It was scary. They were on to us but were unable to tease out exactly where their damned krugers were to be found. Until yesterday we, too, were in exactly that much more comfortable position of not knowing.

Botha said authoritatively, "That was why your boat was searched. We had heard that it may be carrying the cargo we were looking for and we had the support of the Scottish police."

"Why on earth would you think that? You must have travelled all the way up to the north of Scotland and back for no reason?" Elizabeth made a good effort at sounding scornful, at the same time again giving me precious thinking time.

"We were tipped off. Soon after the theft had occurred all those years ago a company called the Diamond and Gold *Ressoluttion* Society was commissioned to find the missing krugers. They specialised in that sort of thing. For the *parst* ten years they were thought to have *seesed* trading. We simply had no contact with Mr Jacobi, their man in Johannesburg, who seemed to have disappeared. Suddenly, very *reecently* actually, we were contacted and informed they were on to something."

"Oh, so they directed you towards our boat. They presumably must have been on some sort of commission arrangement to encourage them do that? What an awful waste of time for everyone." I was getting to understand their picture of the whole thing. For us bluff and lying now had to be the only way.

"*Teen* per cent had always been the going rate. But nothing was found in either boat."

I sounded surprised. "Either boat?"

"*Yess*, they put us on to two boats. The other was in a Marina near London."

"And you found nothing there either?"

Masemola butted in. "No. But there is *sometthing* else."

"I don't think we need to discuss that here!" Botha jumped on him. Then, realising he had been very abrupt added lamely, "One of the D and G people left hees briefcase with the *harrbormasster* in Wick. We learned there that they had been involved *criminnally* internationally in any number of cases other than this one."

"So, all they told you about krugers may have been off centre then?"

Sir Jeremy had been listening intently, looking from the ceiling to the walls and back again, no doubt trying to fill in the missing part of the narrative. He remained silent.

Botha continued, "They would have *keppt* the krugers themselves had they found them. But they didn't so they pointed the finger in the hope that the British *authorittiess* would do the dirty work and they would be the *teen* per cent *beneficciariess*."

Something then happened quite abruptly. The atmosphere mellowed. We had reached a crunch point. This was exactly what Sir Jeremy was all about and he became almost paternal.

"Occasionally people can become enmeshed in a situation. Holding stolen goods of this kind is a lifelong drudge. It is there for ever and one is stuck with it. Unravelling that type of thing is what this department tries to do. We have the facilities of the Bank available for secure collecting, transporting and delivering bullion, notes and securities. And we are able to settle commissions amicably and in cash. To some, over the years, we have appeared too good to be true. But we resolve the unresolvable!"

"And in *thees* case the fee will rise from *teen* to *fifteen* per cent, paid tax-free in your country or to any other destination and in any currency."

I got the distinct feeling that Botha had made that decision on the spot in that instant. I was right in the firing line. I had been nominated as spokesperson. What happened now was down to me. I knew what we should do and hoped the others agreed. Fifteen per cent was a lot. And holding stolen goods, I had to agree, could be a problem.

"It is possible, gentlemen, that we could help if we think over all our past movements. But we do need to work it through. From all you have said, and from our own experiences, we can carry out our own investigations, which may, or may not, lead somewhere." I did not dare to look at the other two, who must at that moment have been wishing they were not here but somewhere far, far away.

Sir Jeremy took over in almost regal style. He must have seen this sort of thing many times before. It was, as he had been so keen to point out, what he did.

"Fifteen per cent paid by the Mint. Collection and insured transportation from anywhere. Safekeeping in the bank here with a transfer transaction later arranged with the authorities in Pretoria. Anyone presently outside the law can in this way be brought back to legality without fuss, awkward questions or police interference."

Piet and Elizabeth had already almost imperceptibly nodded their agreement. Our inquisitors had not noticed but I had.

"I would like a few clarifications if I may. We do not, of course, wish to be followed or monitored in any way."

Sir Jeremy replied instantly. "Agreed. That simply is not our style."

I believed that. He was just so true blue Brit! "If we are successful, just how is the pay out to be made?"

"Straight in to your bank account, immediate transfer, no questions asked. Your bank details would be useful, in case we have to deposit anything. You will never be questioned about such a payment originating from here. Oh, and please keep closely in touch with my mobile at all stages and any time, day or night." He handed me his card which I carefully pocketed. He looked to be in his element. Very few parts of government could be run in that unaccountable way. He seemed to be proud of it. I looked at the other two. Both nodded. I removed a similar card from my wallet, carefully wrote down my Lloyds Bank details, and handed it to him.

"We do possibly have some ideas. We will follow them up and would hope to be asking for transportation of the product within a week if we are successful. If we do not come across anything at all we will let you know immediately." I had a last-minute thought. "As a matter of interest do you know where Mr Haffenbacker and the lady are now?"

Botha came in surprisingly quickly. "They left Wick before we did and we are not sure of their *whereabaatts*. I *giss* they will now be on to their next job somewhere. But I can assure you they will no longer have *eny* interest in this affair."

We rose, shook hands all round, and the thin man, who seemed to inhabit a small annexe, was summoned. He led us back through that magnificent building, nodded to Security, and guided us out into the mighty roar of London's traffic. This time we really did have an awful lot to mull over.

FIFTY-SIX

"Phew."

Piet's first word uttered since going in to the Bank summed things up. We were all suffering from pent-up tension. At Elizabeth's suggestion we took a taxi the short distance to the Tower of London, which was situated very close to the St Katharine Docks. From there we would be near to Thor at her moorings, we hoped happily isolated with no human beings anywhere in the vicinity.

I said it quickly before anyone suggested otherwise.

"No going aboard."

"Safety first? She might be bugged again. You just never know. Some nasty people we know seem able to get in anywhere."

"Right first go, Piet. With those three at large anything can happen. They may still be around, probably getting desperate. We must not now go anywhere near the boat if we want to talk. And we certainly do need to discuss what the hell is going on and what the devil we do about it!" I bit my tongue to avoid following this up instead with the business term "going forwards" which was so popular in AandA. Synonymous in my mind with that other daft term "low hanging fruit."

I strolled around towards the entrance to the Tower Hotel. Together we entered that rather splendid place, walked upstairs to the bar and took our seats looking out across the river back towards Tower Bridge. Piet ordered three lagers which arrived almost immediately.

"First thing, call Jonny?" Piet pulled out his phone.

"Make it gobbledygook."

He nodded at me in agreement and was through immediately.

"Hello Piet. How did things go?"

"Hi, just to let you know all well and we are on track for fifteen hundredths." He said it slowly. "All very much above board."

There was a short pause.

"Think I understand. That actually sounds quite good. That would answer some of my perceived fault lines in our situation. Sorry, this is awful, but I've got to go. Things a bit desperate here. See you tonight?"

"Yes, ok. Will do."

"Oh, one thing. Tell Dave that Eisenbauer has gone. Really and truly fired! Complete upheaval. Apparently thrown out, reason unclear. All sorts going on. People standing on their heads. You know how these things go sometimes!"

And that was that. I was amazed to hear that my successor was no longer in position. He certainly always seemed to be a major operator in the Global system. I wondered how that would play out with the company. He really wasn't that bad at the job. Not, I suppose, that anyone is for ever.

"Right, master, what is the plan now." Elizabeth purposely ignored Jonny's comments and, keen to know our next course of action, was looking expectantly at me.

"If you really want it spelled out we have to get on to that boat, carry out what is now a manoeuvre at which we are highly proficient, and transport whatever goodies we may find to a waiting car. Master does have a sort of plan but it is, as yet, full of holes and he needs a lot of help."

"The Marina people are not going to let us do that before we've bought the damned thing." Piet had little reverence for boats or for the people who sell them and I was sure he was right.

Elizabeth said quietly, "I agree. And peace of mind for us all has now become essential. We have been buffeted about by too much bad stuff. We do not have anywhere near enough money but we can take out a loan from a number of specialist boat loan sharks. I can fix all that. I know nearly all of them. We simply must do this and then later we can sell two boats in the summer season at a good profit."

I had that slightly anxious feeling again. She was more engaged with the boat business than with what we were doing. I gulped my lager and looked across to the Tower. One last heave and we could be there. She was right. We were constantly now in a state of high alert. Without any prompting we watched everything. The three of us were understandably twitchy throughout our visit to the Bank. We thought all the time, trying to understand---and now, at last, we had arrived at the point where we had to act. At a distance, highlighted in the watery looking sunshine, the iconic bridge looked peaceful, almost kind. It had been around a long time and seen many things. But I knew just what a nightmarish battle would be going on amongst the cars, buses, lorries and taxis passing over it. We ourselves were now in that situation, just about to drive on to the bridge. Enough of that! I forced myself back to the here and now. In my own mind, for once, I was almost happy about events but I wanted their confirmation.

"Do we trust everything which went on in the Bank?"

"Yes." Elizabeth was positive enough.

"Yes. And No!!"

Piet stood up spilling the drink he was holding and looking for all the world as if he had seen a ghost. A realisation. Some sort of out of world experience. He had suddenly gone very strange. I wondered just what the devil was bothering him now.

What is it Piet?" The look of him really concerned me. "Sit down. Relax. Take things easy. Slowly. Talk about it."

"Heels. Heels!!"

"What?" Elizabeth spoke gently to him. This was more her line of country than mine. "Heels, Piet? What does that mean?"

He slowly seated himself down, still looking haunted. I detected beads of perspiration on his forehead.

"I trust everything that went on in the Bank. But not *outside*."

She kept going. "Ok Piet, what happened there? I don't think there is anything on the outside of that place to be worried about is there?"

"Cast your mind back to our meeting in that coffee shop when I told you, Dave, about your picture and where I had seen it?"

"Yes, of course. Remember it well. Quite some time ago now."

"Well, at the time I was a bit taken by the ankles of the woman sat there in the restaurant. I've always been a women's ankle admiring freak. It's just one of those things." He looked momentarily embarrassed.

Neither Elizabeth nor I said anything. We were waiting for some sort of punch line but knew not what. I couldn't fathom what on earth he was talking about.

He'd been touchy about things for a long time but this was something else.

"You remember, Dave, you met me at the Bank first thing this morning?"

"Yes. Some way from the entrance."

"I was standing there looking out."

"Yes."

"Well I've been feeling something since then but could not place what it was. An idea stirring me up inside making me constantly uncomfortable but which I was unable to place. Now I recall. There was a woman across the road standing still as that massive, heaving crowd passed her by. She was looking at me. She sort of came and went, people surrounding or passing by her most of the time. But through it all she just stayed. She would probably have seen you two arrive."

"So?"

"Her ankles and heels. I only got glimpses. They were the sleek ankles of a woman much younger than she seemed to be. And now I'm getting focussed I think it is possible she was the same woman who had your picture that time - and we know all about her!"

That had to be a real stretch of the imagination but I knew and half accepted what he was getting at, and what must have been unwinding in his mind all morning. If he really was an ankle freak it was quite possible his brain would put those two sightings together and, over a period of time, zero in on a conclusion.

"She may be one of *them* and somehow they may still be on our track. They use her to shadow us. A spy dressed up as an older woman? Who on earth knows what they learned from those two South Africans in

Wick and any bugging that may still be going on in our cars, houses, bags or other places. Just as well you stopped us from returning to the boat Dave. It may well be that they knew we would visit the Bank."

Deep down I was sure his anguished mind had taken one jump too far and said so.

"I doubt that. Any chance they will revisit Odin then? Just why would we be calling in at the Bank of England at the same time as the two men from the Mint? Something big? Considerable amounts of money? They won't damned well give up, no matter what. I feel that deep down in my bones, as you do Piet. We've been crossed too many times. They've vested too much time and money in Project Kruger to come away with nothing. They want that loot before they go to ground. But young ankles on an old woman and viewed from afar? I really don't think so!"

Piet was calming down but I knew his mind would keep on trying to puzzle things out. They were both looking at me again. We had to act fast and right now, Piet's fantasies notwithstanding.

"Elizabeth please get the loan arranged. That must be done today. We go and pick up the boat first thing tomorrow. We drive her somewhere where a road passes by very close to the river---"

Elizabeth knew where. "Chertsey's the place. Only a couple of miles upstream from the marina. Few if any people and the road itself runs along almost parallel to the river and is only feet away from it."

"Right. Chertsey it is. I suggest we all go to Shepperton to be in on the purchase. Elizabeth and Jonny, providing he can get away tomorrow, both board the boat and drive her to Chertsey. Piet, you and I take my car there. It's big enough for the heavyish cargo we hope to find. Once unloaded safely into the car I reckon we drive to some suitable urban meeting place, at the same time phoning for the promised security van from the Bank. Whilst we wait for it to get to us we count the krugers. Things must really go very fast. No messing about from now on!"

FIFTY- SEVEN

The following day dawned bright and cold. Jonny somehow got the time off and drove Piet. I collected Elizabeth for the trip back to Shepperton where we all met more or less on time at ten o'clock. Jonny and Elizabeth went off to look at the boat. Piet and I slipped in to the offices. There were a couple of cleaning ladies there and an overworked Lily, surrounded by a variety of bits and pieces of paperwork.

"Good morning. We have come to finalise the purchase of Odin." I looked around outside through the windows. There really was no elderly lady with young looking ankles staring at us. Indeed, there were very few people in sight at all!

"Good morning. That's really great. You would like to complete the purchase straight away?"

She came off the computer and took Elizabeth's prepared paperwork from me together with a cheque interim payment of ten thousand pounds and the insurance papers. I crossed my fingers while she studied everything. We really, really wanted nothing to stall now.

"That looks fine. I'll just have to pass it through my director, Mike Evans. He's in tomorrow." She looked contented at having finalised the sale.

"Well actually we've come all the way out today specially to do a short run to check that everything is in place and works - ropes, fenders, vhf, safety equipment - all of that. I wonder if we could please have the keys?" I stared knowingly, perhaps longingly, at the board of boat ignition keys hanging on the wall behind her.

"Well, I don't really know---"

"Just a run around the marina area and maybe a bit outside? We simply want to check if there is anything we need to purchase for the boat before we take her away."

She was troubled but after a little thought said, "Well, ok, you are covered by our insurance until the sale is actually completed, but please not too far or too long." She looked again at all the documents and the cheque, leant over backwards and hooked off the relevant keys, passing them to Piet quickly, as if to do the deed before her mind changed.

"Thanks Lily. Thanks very much. We will not be long. See you soon." We turned and walked away, more quickly than normal. At the mooring Piet gave the keys to Elizabeth. She looked at me for confirmation.

"Chertsey river bank next stop. We'll be there with the car, parked as near in as we can. Get the boat out of here fast, there's a strong possibility that Lily could change her mind. I don't think she should yet have let the boat go. She was very hesitant about the limits of her authority and may well be on the line to the boss man right now."

Piet and I then went quickly off to my Jag. There were just one or two people around and the parking area was still pretty empty. The car GPS got confused at the words "Chertsey river bank" so Piet took over as navigator using the maps I always carried. He was good. It took all of fifteen minutes for us to arrive at the spot which Elizabeth must have had in mind. We found our way around the small bar barrier and parked off the road on the bank situated just above the slow flowing river, and waited.

They arrived half an hour later. Elizabeth brought the boat in perfectly and we tied the bow rope to a tree and the stern one we pegged into the ground. Piet loaded on to the boat the tough leather bags we had brought and in which we would carry away the krugers and I followed up with the exact tools we needed to do the job.

Jonny had the floor up and was first down below. I passed him the right sized screwdriver and he was instantly at work with a vengeance. Elizabeth stayed up top on the fly bridge keeping watch and Piet stood on deck ready, hopefully, to carry bullion loaded bags from the boat to the car. A chug-chug river maintenance boat passed and they did the accustomed wave but, apart from the occasional passing car, whose drivers had eyes only for the narrow winding road, we had the world to ourselves.

It didn't take Jonny long. The very intensity of the moment spurred him on. He soon had the golden coins sliding easily into the first bag. Before it became too heavy to lift he heaved it up to me. As one we left our appointed stations and gathered round excitedly to take a quick peek at what we had. The first viewing was very moving. I had a fleeting glimpse of Elizabeth wiping away a tear. We really had been through a lot to get to this point. But the very vulnerability of our situation was soon felt and we went very quickly back to work.

Jonny confirmed that all handrails were more or less full of product and Piet, in all, managed to carry seven moderately heavy bags up across the sloping grass bank and in to the car. When he had finished I went below and helped him to get everything back into its original position. In a very short space of time the place had been returned to complete innocence after all those years of its monumental deception. Elizabeth went over to the car to help arrange the bags where, shortly afterwards, we all joined in the count. I had brought a number of specially strengthened box files in the car boot. We all knew things had now become dangerous. To have so much gold inside the car was somehow very likely to attract interest! Hidden in the boot things seemed marginally safer. That is, anyway, how it felt to me. In a short while Jonny elected to stand watch just outside the car in a position where he could have a clear view of river and road. We steadily counted the medallions into rows which fitted snugly into the boxes. Gradually we filled seventeen which were then stacked in to the boot where they fitted snugly. As each box was filled Elizabeth noted down the total. It took us just under two whole hours to do the job thoroughly. At the end she was marvelling at what her figures showed. "We have two thousand seven hundred and ten if everything has been counted accurately, and I think it has."

This statement was greeted with silence. Each of us was doing a mental calculation as to the value. My mind automatically added three zeros to that number, although I knew that gold prices were notoriously volatile. The total value was a staggering amount, probably on a good day well over two and a half million pounds but infinitely variable. I pulled myself away from any more contemplation and called Lily.

"Sorry we got held up. We're on our way back now. With you in ten minutes or so."

"Oh, thanks for phoning in. I was getting worried. Godwin is here and was coming out to look. No problem now. He will await your arrival." There was relief in her voice.

"Not to worry Lily. All going well. Perhaps Godwin could help us tie up when we arrive back if he's free? We're not good on the ropes as he knows."

"I'll make sure he's around. 'Bye." I turned off and shouted the order, "We'd better get Odin back right now!"

Elizabeth looked at Jonny. "Ready to go, sailor?"

"Yep." He wasn't keen to lose touch with our new found wealth but knew he had no choice. Before they departed, however, Piet went into his now familiar negative mode and put into words what I had dared not even contemplate.

"Do we *really* totally trust those guys at the Bank. I know we agreed with all they said but it's a bloody huge amount of money. People do strange things when large sums are involved, you know."

We all knew! Piet was right to doubt. But I did wonder what else we could do? And his judgement did seem to be doing strange things just lately. Agreements made in the Bank of England had to be pretty sound. To me the content of our meeting there was now making complete sense.

Elizabeth came up with a pragmatic solution to help calm everybody's woes. "We'll keep one box with us on the boat, transfer it to Jonny's car in the marina and take it home. Then we'll see what happens. If anything does go wrong at least we will have something. But if all goes well, as I suspect it will, we can then find a few more of the goodies to declare to them. Well, that, or maybe we might not!"

No problem there. We all agreed with alacrity. It was an excellent idea. Hedging our bets did help settle the nerves.

"Now, about phoning Sir Jeremy. We don't want to be anywhere near the river or boat when they collect. It would probably not be wise to give them even a clue about where we found the stuff after all everybody's been through. Any ideas on a place which might make a good collection place for them?"

Jonny came up with the answer with no hesitation.

"M25 Cobham service station. Well away from all river and boat things. Not too far from here - say half an hour - and bags of parking space. Phone for the security vehicle to be there when you are on the M25 approaching the place. We can do a handover in just a few minutes."

I was keen to get moving. "Right, sounds good. Let's go. And all keep in close touch on even the minutest thing that may come up."

Elizabeth and Jonny walked quickly to the boat. Piet and I, in very short order, managed to feed in the detail of our motorway destination, this time successfully.

FIFTY-EIGHT

Cobham Services is reached by following a short winding road leading off the M25 motorway. We eventually arrived at the crowded car area and nosed out a parking place some way from the large main building. We locked up carefully and strolled in to the main hall in order to purchase a sandwich lunch. The ground floor was heaving with people so we found a seat upstairs from which we could look out across the whole crowded parking area and right back to the motorway. We reckoned it would be useful to scan across the widest area possible.

"Time to phone Sir Jeremy." I pulled out the mobile and called him. The answer was immediate.

"Trumperton."

"Sir Jeremy. David Johnston here."

He wasted not a moment and went straight for the jugular. "Have you anything?"

"Yes, quite a lot."

Piet quickly shoved across a paper napkin on which he had scrawled, "Well over one thousand."

"Any ideas yet as to how much?" His voice remained steady enough but I knew this figure would be of critical importance to him and, particularly, to his associates from Pretoria - or was it Johannesburg?

"We think well over one thousand and still counting." I was keen to offer him as little further explanatory information as possible. I need not have worried. He was transfixed on monetary volume.

"I thought the total would be considerably higher than that?"

"Oh, don't worry. We're pretty sure there are many hundreds more. I'm not actually working on the totting up of the totals."

"Excellent. Well done. You must have worked hard. That is a very commendable result. Whereabouts are you, and where and when do you want us?"

"Cobham Services station. M25. Near junction nine. We're upstairs above the coffee shop. Most parking areas are pretty well taken. Probably better to find a place over to one side, where we can meet, rather than centre stage. Packing up the product should be complete in the next half hour."

"Thanks. We'll have lock up transport there in between forty-five minutes and one hour, depending on traffic, David. They will pick up from you. We will phone every quarter of an hour just to check all is still in place. I hope you are watching out for product security?"

"Yes, no problem there. Look forward to their arrival."

We shut down. No further conversation was necessary in this business transaction.

"Why only a thousand Piet?"

"Just impulse. Sorry to cut across your conversation with him like that. It was probably the wrong thing to do, but at least you said we were still counting."

"You're *still* having doubts about all this. Surely, we really cannot get anything more reliable than what comes out of the Bank of England? That scenario there just had to be genuine and yet it is pretty obvious to me that you still have bloody reservations about the whole thing."

"You're completely right Dave. It will be great to get this whole business over and done. Easy to imagine dragons where there are none. I admit I'm guilty of having done it all the way through this mad exercise - which I started - and unfortunately most of the time I was right. Not really on this occasion though. I certainly don't now have quite the same negative vibes."

I mulled over the words "really" and "quite" for a few seconds.

"On my reckoning we should each come away with something over ninety thousand pounds - good compensation for all the effort. Great shame your Elias is not around to benefit."

"Yeah, he would have loved it. It wasn't just the money with him, he was a devil for thinking things through and unravelling challenges. It's unfortunate he had no wife or kids to whom we could donate something."

We munched the not too bad sandwiches and sipped the lemonade beverage Piet had found. He reckoned we should drink nothing at all alcoholic when driving on motorways, or indeed when anywhere near a car you would be driving, and who am I to carpe at that. But also, maybe, he wanted to keep a very cool head just now and I had to agree.

"Do you still have those binoculars in your car?"

"Yes. Always kept in the side pocket. Why?"

Piet overdid the effort to sound casual.

"I think we should have them here. We could probably see the security truck arriving and maybe go and meet it. They'll need help with finding somewhere to park and load up. If you like I'll wander over and fetch them."

I smiled and handed over the car keys. "Make sure you lock up properly behind you. Rather important right now!"

I was quite attached to my miniature binocs. They were of Austrian manufacture, originally very expensive, and at least ten years old, but the magnification and clarity were still perfect. They could bring up a tiny bird several hundred feet away and show the minutest detail.

Piet was back in ten minutes or so despite having to push and shove his way through one of the crowded entrances to the building.

"There we are. I found them straight away." He lowered the binocs to the table, returned to me my keys and sat down. He was puffing a bit after the exertion.

"Something continues to bug you Piet. I can tell. You're still being a bit of a fidget. You implied that whatever might be germinating in that dark soul of yours is nothing of any importance - indeed, is not really there any more - so what is it that to you is so insignificant?

Just then my mobile quacked, much to the amusement of a couple of businessmen sitting adjacent to us.

"Johnston."

"Trumperton here. Is all well?"

Up market Englishman speak.

"Yes, Sir Jeremy, no problems, thanks.

"Great."

I pocketed the phone and waited for Piet's response. He was very hesitant.

"I don't really think anything's wrong. You know sometimes one can go into a sort of anguish over nothing. Things were nagging away at me much more before our Bank visit, but you are correct in feeling I cannot fully put things to sleep."

"I know all about that sort of thing. Jonny and I call it a wiggle. And you've been there on and off for a mighty long time. What's really behind that word anguish? "A sort of anguish" is very different from simply saying that absolutely nothing is wrong. So, come on, out with it?"

He went into a minor trance, unsure about making a fool of himself, but still racked by doubt. I was reading him line by line. Then he stiffened up.

"Well ok, let's just trouble shoot for a bit of fun. Elizabeth tried hard but failed to trace the name Sir Jeremy Trumperton. She's usually pretty thorough. We've seen that often enough. I thought all Sirs in this country were traceable somewhere. Barons and Lords certainly are!"

He was back on the British aristocracy bit again.

"Yes, agreed. A bit strange. But he was strongly entrenched in the Bank. You saw his position there and what he said seemed to me to be utterly credible." I couldn't myself fault those credentials and, because of our experiences, I was being very strict with myself on the interpretation of evidence these days.

"Right. So why in the middle of the day from here did you call him on his personal mobile?"

"Easy. Because it's on the card he gave me. You were there when he passed it over."

"And what about his address?"

I extracted my wallet from my deep, safe pocket and pulled out the visiting card.

"Name, mobile number and email. No address."

"That's not at all good, Dave. That's quite unusual, you know. Any businessman who has no address on his card is immediately downgraded in his client's mind until an address can be found and validated. He could not use the Bank's address because, in his own words, they gave him space but no real legitimacy. Of all people you yourself ooze that sort of address thing!"

Very, very gradually he was beginning to make me less resolute, getting under my skin without really seeming to do so. His mind was still right now affected by past events. After all, we had lots of bad things to look back on. And I was maybe in some small danger of being pulled subtly in to his orbit. No, no I was *not* going there!

"Well he did explain the underhand, almost sinister, nature of his business. The Bank would never wish to be openly associated with that! He is therefore probably required to work only from a mobile - and certainly not have the Bank as an address! That makes complete sense to me."

In spite of myself I brought up Bank of England on the mobile's small screen. There was a main telephone number but my eye caught a second smaller number against the words Fraud and Cyber. I called it.

"Bank of England – Fraud section."

"A small question if I may. Do you know of a Sir Jeremy Trumperton in the bank please?"

"I'm sorry sir. We can only deal with fraud and cyber questions. Please contact the Bank general enquiries. They deal with all that sort of thing."

I called the other number.

"Bank of England. Your name please?"

"Ignatius Smith. May I speak with Sir Jeremy Trumperton?"

"One second."

There was a pause of at least half a minute.

"I'm sorry sir. There is nobody of that name here."

"Do you hold the complete list of all people working there?"

"Yes sir. We do and he is not on it."

I re-pocketed the phone and muttered defensively to Piet, "Of course! He said he was not part of the Bank. They would obviously not wish to know even of his existence. Someone at the top might sanction an office for him but that would be all."

"Well, everything must be all right then." Piet picked up the binoculars for the fourth or fifth time and panned out across the access roads and all the parking areas. "No security vehicle yet. It's going to be difficult anyway to pick it out amongst that mass of cars. Any ideas on what colour it might be?"

"I should have asked him. I wonder just what we are looking out for? I would think some sort of unmarked---"

"Good god!"

Piet cut me off in half-sentence. He was struggling to get the words out. I don't think he was exactly shaking but he was at that instant in a total state of panic, just like before but much more so. His breathing seemed difficult and he looked quite ill. He whispered very faintly.

"The old woman. The one I told you about. She's coming through the entrance door down below. Definitely her! Same dress! Same everything! Then I got a quick flash of those ankles. It's *her! Again! Dave you've got to believe me!!*"

I quickly followed his gaze, looking from one person to another. There were many older women to choose from and it was quite impossible for me to see any ankles. I simply did not possess his skills in that area and the whole place was packed.

"Immediately behind that very tall bloke with the black hair, right now shoving his way through the swing door."

I spotted her. An elderly lady with greyish hair showing out beneath a small flat hat, limping slightly but nonetheless keeping her place in the flow of people. She kept in line and made her way slowly to the far distant seating area downstairs where she found a place and gently eased herself down into it. She began slowly to look around. Piet's ideas were now beginning to burn their way into my soul too!

"Look away Piet! You mustn't let her know that you have seen her."

He was staring into space, frozen in time, but turned away at once reacting to the timbre of my voice. He muttered repeatedly to himself, now almost sounding like a mad man.

"Who *is* that bloody woman?" I managed to get out that warning to him just before my whole being started churning around too, upside down and then correcting, movement sidewise and then severe dizziness. I felt as if I was being hit constantly in the midriff by the world champ. My senses were leaving me. One part of me was trying to right the ship, in a boiling sea, the other was totally out of control. We were in desperately dire straits but I could do nothing whilst I tried to deal with this enormous shock. *Piet was right.* My head lowered itself slowly down on to the table. I *had* to get myself back together. Struggle and push. Those dark recesses of the brain. Who knows how all of that gets to work. The most complex computer ever. We still did not really have the remotest idea about these things. I think I had now gone to some sort of stage of total reliance on natural recovery. That constituted all that was available at the moment. Sheer bloody tenacity to return to the real world. It was that or die, such was the enormity of the shock. I had never ever been here before.

Slowly, very slowly, I began to regain some control.

"Dave, Dave. Come back! Come back!" Piet tried to fill me with some of his nasty lemonade. That did, in some small way, help me slowly to return to the present.

"I know who she is." I gasped it out. I had recognised the cut of the face and nose, despite all the disguise. And the general curvaceous body build she could not fully hide behind her purposely crumpled old woman's clothing. But above all it was the ears. Not ankles. Ears!! They form the parts of the body you cannot disguise without completely covering them or having surgery. Those lobes I would know anywhere, even from this distance. I had read somewhere that in some societies long lobes like that are themselves one of the main components of female beauty.

That woman, my friend, is Lady Banforth and we are in one hell of a situation!"

"Dave. She looks nothing like her but I know what you mean. I can't yet get a good look at her legs!?"

"You saw her ankles but I saw the ears. That is definitely Lady Banforth!! The woman who had me at the point of a gun!! What it has to mean, Piet, is that Haff and his lot are working *with* Trumperton. We have been totally, absolutely, utterly taken in. This is a bastard of a sting of gigantic proportions. And it is going on *right now*. Main thing to concentrate on is to get ourselves out alive. These people have no limits when it comes to treachery. We are in one hell of a lot of trouble."

Piet took another very careful look, his eyes moving slowly from her head to toe and back again.

"Bloody hell, I think you're right! I'm an idiot! Of course, she is that damned Lady of the Manor! Now I *do* recognise her. The disguise is incredibly good and similar to the looks of the woman outside the Bank." He carried on quietly muttering at himself, his dragons in no way slain but growing by the second as original suspicion now became fact.

I continued slowly managing to drag myself back into the here and now. Things were steadying. The urgency helped. I could think more or less straight again. Everything had passed through my mind at one time and caused mayhem.

Very gently and slowly I lifted up my head and looked down and across at the woman. She was talking to someone on her phone. Who and what? Might it be Haff or the South Africans? Now that we had made that connection my best bet was that she was conversing with an incoming vehicle. She may well have seen us, having been told by Trumperton of our location, and most likely was currently confirming with them the position of my car, having checked it out, because that had to be their overwhelming interest. All that nonsense in Wick was total farce. It was not too late, metaphorically speaking, to kick myself. Piet's fears were soundly based. The South Africans were part of their team! Or at least they were working together to one end. The Bank? How on earth was that done? The thin man had to be key. I tried to think it through but soon left quickly alone. We had one overriding action to take and that was to consider the here and now and decide what the hell to do to get ourselves out in one piece.

I unnecessarily re-wound history.

"Piet, this is all horrendously dangerous. We know they are prepared to maim, maybe even kill, if they have to, to achieve their aim. Remember what they had started doing to Elizabeth. No compunction at all about slashing her face. And they had guns. If they get near we *must* simply yes and no them - complete agreement with everything they want. We have to act as if we are totally unaffected by any of their skulduggery. Remember it is all about the krugers, nothing else. All the way through it is simply the golden coins they have been after, not in any way was anyone trying to settling an international krugerrand problem. That was all complete eyewash."

I quickly pulled out my phone and called Elizabeth at home. She answered after three rings.

"Just listen. We're at Cobham Services. The same old lady Piet said he saw at the Bank has just walked in down below us. She is the Banforth woman. No doubts at all about it. Remember those large ear lobes? She and her lot have to be in league with Trumperton and the South Africans. They've been working together the whole time. We've been completely done over. The security truck is arriving at any minute to collect you know what."

"God! *Let me think! Let me think!* This is the most hellish thing. I wish we had never got involved. They'll do something really awful if you try and stand up to them. Just go along with it all, Dave. Hand it over to them and have no further interest in the project. I love you!!"

"Ok Elizabeth. Piet and I have already agreed that we've lost all ends up. His suspicions were right all along. We will play dumb. See you soon."

Woomp---- there was a huge explosion sound from far over to the right side in the area of the distant parkings. The background hum of conversation inside the building ceased for all of ten seconds and then crescendoed as if to a huge question mark. It had to be an attack of some kind and people these days were hooked on the idea of terrorism. Fear of it was never far from the surface. All were instantly wary, some already looking for cover.

"Here comes the cavalry!" Piet, ignoring the explosion, was studying the entrance road through the binocs. "Black and big four by four has turned into the same parking lane as us. All other traffic has come to a halt to stare at the smoking car on the far side, but this one has not stopped. Hell, he's already pulled up right behind your car. Absolutely spot on. Obviously knew precisely where to find it."

"Lady bloody Banforth has been busy directing them there. No doubt about that now!"

I grabbed the binocs from him. Three men jumped out and started to work on the boot. One was holding some sort of crowbar but the back opened up instantly without it being needed.

"This is it Dave. They're going to take everything. Every damned thing!! What to do?! How the heck do we stop them?"

I had very firmly to repeat myself to him.

"Nothing! Stay here! Sit tight! If we try and take any action we know they are quite prepared to use violence in a big way. It could be they won't come anywhere near us. Come to think of it why should they? They have all they want."

"But we'll lose it all. Every single kruger!"

He made as if to rush downstairs. I stood in front of him. There would be no way down. One thing I knew for sure. My friend was simply not going to get past me.

"Let me go, Dave. All we've been through. It *can't* possibly damned well end like this."

"Sorry. I will not let you get yourself killed. They will do that if we get in the way." I tried to change his mind set. "Take a look down there. The Banforth woman is edging her way out. Watch her nubile body movement in the crowd. There's little evidence of her age showing up now. I'm staying here. So are you. Do what you like. But you'll have to completely finish me off before you can get past!"

We saw her wrestling her way through the crowded exit. After a minute or so of pushing and shoving she rammed her way out and ran across to a modest looking black Renault. Her work was done. We watched her quickly slide down into the seat and drive at a very normal speed towards the perimeter exit road which would lead her out on to the motorway.

"I can't see the thin man, the one who led us into the Bank." Piet was staring through the binocs again. "Snakes alive there's Trumperton. I reckon they've already completely emptied the car boot. Clever 'cos hardly anybody standing around there can look past their vehicle and see what they are doing to ours. All nicely shielded. And, anyway, Joe public is still engrossed with that explosion. Very, very clever!"

I relaxed my efforts to stop Piet. He seemed at last to have grasped and accepted the full dynamic of the situation. I looked across at the fast disappearing plume of black smoke. A fire engine had arrived and they seemed to have the situation under control. How had those crooks actually managed the timing for all of that? And with such precision, arriving in their vehicle at exactly the same time as the car was blown up?

It didn't take long for that penny to drop. Of course! The woman would have positioned the explosive on some poor bastard's car, moved over to check on us, or maybe not - we were really irrelevant providing we could not interfere - and at the right time detonated the device from where she had sat below us in order to divert everybody's attention away from what was going to be happening between their vehicle and my car. At the same time she would have directed them straight to our car, having already established its parked position. Ingenious, quick, effective and incredibly well planned.

"They're off. Slowly. Not causing any upset. Nobody would know they've been up to anything. Smooth as clockwork. They're now as rich as Croesus. We're the church mice." Piet was morbidly counting our losses and no doubt regretting he had ever instigated the whole thing.

I knew I had to keep him active though I was not really in a fit state to do so. "I suggest we tell the others. We've nothing to watch out for now. Funny, really, they were not a bit interested in us. You do Jonny, I'll call Elizabeth."

Most people had moved quickly away at the time of the explosion, no doubt thinking the restaurant might be next. Coffee mugs and snacks were left lying around in their panic to get out. We now had the upstairs to ourselves. I could hear Piet muttering hell fire things to Jonny. All his warnings had been right and he was not taking it lightly.

With Elizabeth it was a bit different.

"You both ok?"

"Yes. And they have all gone. Went as quickly as they came and have taken everything with them."

"Thank God for that. I've been worried sick. Not like me. But there seemed to be nothing I could do to help. Get back quickly. There will be a better dinner even than you have ever had before!"

"Right. I may have a smashed up rear end to the car but I'm sure it will still go." She did not even mention the krugers that had now found a new home for all time.

Minutes later, when Piet had finished with Jonny, we made our way down below and out and across to my car. The huge crowds were beginning to move on slowly. The smoke had ceased but the firemen were still checking everything. They would never be able to work out the full story - and we were the last people who would want to lay it out for them! My rear boot was hardly damaged and somehow the alarm had not gone off. Haff, I sensed, was *the* expert! While I was examining the car all round to see how much damage we had suffered, Piet sat in, threw his coat over on to the back seat, and went silent. I guessed he was now descending into the depths of despair.

I drove off slowly and carefully, in that way somehow trying to deal with our still jangling nerves and shattered egos.

We'd travelled a few miles along the M4 motorway heading into London. We hadn't spoken, each of us trying hard to get back to normality in his own personal way.

Piet broke the ice. "We'd better have some sort of get-together to sort everything out."

"Yes. Selling off remaining boats, repaying cash to everybody. And the rest."

There was another Services Area a mile ahead. Surprisingly, in the circumstances, Piet asked if we could stop there.

"Of course. Coffee, a leak or a sleep?"

My main object in life was to get back to Elizabeth. For me it was now only hard cash -well gold, anyway - that we'd lost. And somehow that sort of wealth had lost its attraction.

"Just something I want to check."

We pulled in to the car park where, unlike the other place, we found considerable unoccupied space.

"Park somewhere where there is nothing nearby that can hear us or see what we are doing?"

I wondered almost angrily just what he was up to now, made for an isolated area in the far corner and turned off. Piet got out of the car and pulled that something slowly from beneath his seat, lifted it up and then lowered it steadily down on to the place where he had just been sitting. He opened it up and---we were looking at one of my box files full of krugers! I knew that to be about one hundred and seventy pieces in all.

"You see, Dave, it was my inherent distrust of something---so I took the precaution of moving a box when I collected your binoculars."

There was an infuriatingly self-righteous look in his eye, but he truly deserved the moment. He closed down the lid, returned the box whence it had come, sat back in and quietly closed the door.

"You cunning old dog!" I was finding mere words difficult. I had been alarmingly and wholly wrong in my aggression towards him about his instinctive feelings. "You've been right all along. I apologise for baiting you. You want to tell the others?"

"No. You tell Elizabeth where we are. I wouldn't say anything about krugers just yet."

I put on Speaker phone and called her.

"Where are you?"

"M4. I'm dropping Piet off and will then come to you. Should be about an hour."

"That's really good." I detected a minor hesitancy in her voice. "I've arranged a get-together if we can all make it in five days' time - Sunday morning, my home - well my family home actually. Mummy and Dad will do the lunch. They're really good at that, except sometimes when he gets it wrong! The weather forecast is fine and the garden there will be just right. We have an awful lot to sort out and I do have some ideas - money, jobs, Piet and his next moves. Is that all right? Jonny has already said he will be there."

Piet rolled his eyes when he heard her talking about his future but we both said "yes thanks." It was a good suggestion and it did seem the logical thing to do.

FIFTY-NINE

Elizabeth wined and dined me when I arrived back at her place after dropping off Piet. She seemed very emotional about all we had been through and I had to explain to her in minute detail the happenings at Cobham Services. The timing of everything, all the participants with particular reference to Lady Banforth and, of course, the well-timed explosion. She wanted to know it all. I took little persuading to stay over with her and left the following morning as she had fixed to go and see her family. Little did I know her real reason for that visit.

Elizabeth's car took her speedily to the place which she still regarded as home. She needed to see her parents, particularly her father. She was burdened with mounting problems and he was the one person in the world whom she felt could help her. But it would not be easy and for several days she had been practising the words she would use when explaining her whole hang-up to him. How to get his opinion without giving him the full story. The trouble was he was so damned astute. She had to handle things very carefully or he would piece together everything in a very quick time and she wasn't quite ready for that yet.

Her arrival at the beautiful house immediately caused her anguish to subside. Here lay the peace and common sense she had known all her young life. She badly needed to bounce her problems off her father, at the same time prising him away from mother who, with the best will in the world, did not possess his cerebral depth for dealing with matters like this.

After exchanging the usual greetings with them both she waited for about half an hour until she was alone with him. Then she pounced.

"I wonder if I could get your advice please father?"

Sir Edward Brady Nye pricked up his ears at that! It was usually "dad." Something special was afoot. He was aware that she was involved in some major activity outside her normal work. She had already used him in it to some extent but had offered no further explanation of what the devil was going on. The experience had left him a little anxious about the well-being of all involved, Elizabeth in particular.

"Yes, my dear. Of course, I'm at your disposal. Anything I can help you with I most certainly will. But I am getting a little out of things these days."

"Shall we sit outside? Warm sunshine for once and I love looking across at the river. This place gets more attractive each time I see it. The boat is looking great."

"It keeps me fit I can tell you. The stern is positioned under that willow tree which has grown enormously since you were younger. Cleaning that hood year after year is a real pain. She is getting a new one this summer. Now what was it you wanted?"

They sat side by side on the lengthy lawn seat. Her first words confirmed to him that something of substance had come to fruition. The cake was cooked but, as so often happens in life, perhaps it had sunk down a bit in the middle.

"Can we keep everything hypothetical? I do not want to talk positives. Too many people involved and a lot of obscure situations."

"Of course. Go ahead. I suppose this has something to do with your goings on with that South African situation we talked about?" Behind the friendly façade he felt a mild worry for her that he could not quell. But none of this showed.

"Yes and no. Yes, it does involve South Africa but there are many additional factors which have occurred outside that country. Question. If you found something valuable which was not yours but had been lost for many years would you be legally entitled to keep it or would the law say it should be given back? I know that is an almost impossible question to answer but I have to start somewhere."

"Am I to be the father who solved the meaning of PR for you or legal adviser to you in all this? It's rather important to know. They are two completely separate people and their advice could just be one hundred per cent different."

"Both please."

"Well if it has to include the latter I need to know all the facts. "Hypothetical" would not give me enough of them to arrive at some sort of reasoned decision. It is not in any way a word normally acceptable to the law, particularly when conclusions have to be reached. That's pretty obvious."

She cut in quickly. "All right, make it Father then. You see the whole matter comes down to something like this. We were given a challenging situation which, using an awful lot of time and effort, we followed up, and eventually stumbled on a mass of gold coins."

"In a ship or a shipyard in Cape Town?"

"Well yes but there is a no again. It all started there but finished up in Norway and then here in the UK."

"I really had better stick very rigidly to being Father. Gold of any kind has deep legal implications to all countries of the world! I don't think we really want to go into all that do we? Incidentally you should know that I am in the throes of taking early retirement - unusual for the job I was doing. Those guys normally go on until they drop but I really did not want to follow their traditions."

"I'm very pleased to hear that, Daddy. You can spend your time here now with all this."

Elizabeth looked around the green grass slopes, the blue sky and the lazy Thames running slowly by. The four of them had to avoid the legal consequences of possessing some of the Mint's gold, although their holding was now very much reduced. Life was so simple and straightforward here. She had to get back to that simplicity and at the same time save her friends, particularly Dave, who seemed oblivious about where their exciting actions had led them. She had lived with an increasing sense of guilt all the way along but it had now become much enlarged and in danger of ruining her daily life.

"Does that gold legal situation apply if it goes back twenty odd years and everyone has forgotten about the original theft to acquire it that had been undertaken then?"

At that inopportune moment mother arrived with tea. She placed the tray on the seat between them. "I could join you but I get the feeling that you need each other at the moment. I do hope all is well, Elizabeth?"

Mum's vibes were nearly always spot on target. She withdrew quickly back into the house, not wanting to wait for an answer.

Elizabeth poured while father pondered. She knew very well what he was thinking and more or less what he was going to say, and very quickly out it came.

"My dear, I think you had better tell me everything. Promise to listen to it all as father though, nothing else.

I wonder if you are not getting into something a little bit complex? I can only really help you if I hear the full story."

It was what she had expected but she had suddenly lost her dread of the idea. She knew he was right and her firm resolve became less firm. In her boots she had felt that would happen too. In doubly quick time the words came tumbling out. She told him nearly the whole story, omitting some of the events that were not relevant to this conversation, but that was all.

"Well, you *really* have been places. The North Sea! That was brave but it was also incredibly foolhardy. You know you should never have attempted a crossing like that, particularly without a seasoned crew. All those lessons I gave you---"

"You're telling me off already!"

"No, Elizabeth, just being a worried father. Anyway, you navigated across to Wick all right. That was jolly well done. For my sake just do not do it that way again please! Now, as for the position that you are all in---"

"Yes, what on earth do you make of it?"

"Tricky. But an absolute legal minefield which as father I will not go in to. It is very clear that the vast bulk of the heist is held by those who wrested it from you. The Mint search goes on and it is those people they will be targeting if they can ever establish who they are. The two Mint employees involved will have disappeared with a share of the loot. They really are for the high jump if they are ever found."

"But do I have to live with all of this knowing that one day there might be a knock on the door. It will affect not just me but maybe bring unwanted publicity for yourself possibly and Da---"

"David! Tell me more. Are you planning to marry the man? And is that largely what this is all about?"

She avoided that one - for now.

"Well I am really concerned for all four of us actually. The others do not seem to see a problem. I know we do not now have the large cache of gold coins but I still feel some deep-seated guilt. Well, that is a bit strong. It is fear really that one day this will come back and hit hard just when the whole thing had been forgotten."

The newly retiring High Court judge stared down to the river. Two boats were passing. Most of the crew were sunning themselves, and it was only early spring. This daughter of his---

"I think I had better give you my thoughts. As a father of course. You reacted to the murder of a man in South Africa who himself, after many years, was trying to trace the product whereabouts of a theft carried out by the past head of the department in which he worked. You all spent huge amounts of time, money and effort in carrying on his work. At the end of it all a group of others who, according to the contents of that briefcase were seen to be a highly organised bunch of crooks, wrested the krugerrands from you in an extremely strong and violent way. At that time no decision had been made about what you would do with what you had found. It seems to me from your reaction here today that some or all could well have been returned by you to the original owner - the Mint. The true answer to that of course can never be established by anybody, anywhere, at any time."

"Well, there would have been a pretty fierce talk about it, particularly with Piet who started the whole matter rolling. But I suspect that when all was said and done we may well have returned quite a bit of the loot. As the crooked man in the Bank said it is difficult to know what to do with huge numbers of gold medallions when you actually possess them."

Edward Nye looked all around hoping for some sort guidance.

"Let's walk about a bit. We're a little in the shade here." This was getting too much like a court case.

They rose and began to follow the path down towards the river. "You know you haven't yet done anything really wrong, Elizabeth. The bulk of the cache, or call it stockpile if you like, is no longer with you so it is simply not known what you would have done with it. A small amount was retained by you. I do not think any court anywhere would find that situation one where it would want to take any action against you all. It has cost you a lot of time, money and effort actually to find out and follow up what had happened." He took a deep breath. "The answer to the problem is simply to do nothing. Any action taken by you will exacerbate things everywhere. Those who sought to steal may well be found and eventually punished as holding on to that sort of thing would be deemed a massive theft. That bit is legal speak. As a father - well, nobody knows you have *anything*. So, forget the hang-ups and get on with life!"

Elizabeth turned and faced her father, stopping him in his tracks. Tears were appearing on her cheeks. She threw her arms around him, sobbing more than she had at any time since childhood.

"You are right. I have been too strung up with it. I never understood when this whole thing began how sensitive I would become about it. I am still worried but now a lot less. I just lack the huge enthusiasm of the others."

He turned her gently around to face down to the river.

"See out there and all the way across. Old Father Thames. He knows how to live. Just keeps rolling along - well, most of the time anyway. Only very occasionally does he get rough and floods. But he always returns back to normal. You must try to do that. Now tell me all about David."

SIXTY

The following Sunday, as arranged, I pulled into the very attractive walled parking area at midday. The house was situated just outside Wargrave and was old, large and beautiful and offered a view over grassy slopes right down to the banks of the river Thames. It must have been that way for hundreds of years and the whole area looked indestructible.

Elizabeth introduced me to her parents. Mother was an older version of her daughter, impeccably yet modestly dressed. Father was a fairly lean, tall, fit looking man who was clearly used to wielding authority, but who also seemed very much a home lover. In my judgment everything both inside the house and outside seemed to be in the right place.

He latched on to me immediately I arrived, diverted me away from the entrance hall and led me out to see the spacious gardens. There were a few beautifully kept flowerbeds, a couple of well stocked fishponds and several lengthy hedges. He admitted to having to bring in outside help to keep them and the large expanses of green lawns in good order. Then he steered me down to the little boathouse on the river's edge. Moored alongside was his immaculate forty or so foot long boat facing up river and gently bobbing about in the slow stream. Two all-weather seats looked out across to the other bank. He motioned me to one of them and sat himself down in the other. A number of ducks swam straight towards us and a few birds circled. The noise they were all making left me with the strong impression that they often were fed something!

"Your two friends are being shown around inside, David. I thought we should have a chat before you all four get together for your meeting which Elizabeth tells me you are having after lunch."

There was a fairly lengthy silence and I began to feel a little nervous. He had sought me out. I thought something was coming and it sure did!

"It's about Elizabeth."

"Yes sir, I----"

"Edward. Please!"

"Thank you, Edward."

My feelings quickly turned from nervous to desperately nervous. What on earth had she been saying? How much had she told him about me, or us? I was not only scared but now decidedly wary. Dealing for the first time in your life with the father of the woman you love is an alarming position to find yourself in!

"Exactly what about Elizabeth?" The duck quacking ceased as I breathed out the words.

"She seemed to think you would know. I suspect she is playing "Elizabeth" games. All her life she has been skilled at leading me up the garden path. But this situation seems rather more serious than usual. There has been a man in her life for some time. Her mother, of course, knows most of the detail about that, or thinks she does. Her sister knows of something too. Those three are aware of everything that I am not. I have to say that is not unusual! The poor old male of the species is often left out in the cold." He looked up into the distant blue sky behind me and then lowered his gaze to look me straight in the eye.

"It's you, isn't it?"

He then turned almost in embarrassment to study the far distant trees, and I realised with some surprise that I was not the only one of us who was feeling decidedly uncomfortable. I managed what I hoped were a few appropriate words to suit a situation such as this. "Yes, it is, and at some time I was going to ask you what you thought about that situation. Maybe now?"

He looked even more uneasy. This great man had been put under considerable tension by his own near and dear. Oil on troubled waters was called for and, that, even in the present tricky situation, he was certainly good at despite his inner turmoil.

"You know I think we have both been shunted into this situation. She does that sort of thing. Gets it from her mother. They can sometimes paint one in to a pretty tight corner." He was giving off signs of mild exasperation.

I knew exactly what he meant. What woman lacked in shoulder width she more than made up for in all sorts of obfuscation to obtain her objective, leaving the poor man frequently in a state of cloudy indecision, and, occasionally, even torment. I decided that this was the moment to take the bull by the horns and breathed in heavily.

"Edward, may I marry your daughter?"

He relaxed and beamed all at the same time, turned and shook me strongly by the hand. The overcast skies had cleared.

Of course, old boy. If she wants to marry you who am I not to agree? More than my life's worth! That is really excellent. I think we've dealt with the matter. That's put that one to sleep! I was quite worried about the whole thing. It turns out we really do understand each other. Now perhaps we can go back to behaving normally like a couple of blokes."

We both exploded into peals of laughter and chatted for a while about nothing in particular. Then we stood up and made our way slowly back up to the house to join the others. I reckoned that in that short time he had sold himself to me for life and I hoped I had achieved the same. Half way back he stopped and looked as if he wanted to confide something to me, but then I realised it was the other way around.

"One thing you may be able to help me with. I've been concerned about Elizabeth's worries about her activities in the last few weeks. She's always been completely open about what she does but until very recently that door has been tight shut, even locked."

"Yes, we all agreed to keep quiet about the project we were involved in."

Edward thought about this for a minute or two. He seemed to be putting what I had said together with what he knew from elsewhere.

"But is she ok?"

"Yes, it's all over. It was a bit risky but all is well now. You will know everything fairly soon - but I think Elizabeth might be the best one to tell you all about it."

"That's good. She has confided something already which doesn't actually make a whole lot of sense. Thanks so much. I'm grateful to know that all is more or less settled."

Edward's leg of lamb lunch was a splendid affair. He was rightly proud of his culinary achievements and inbuilt was the patter to go with it. Mother's sweet, too, was delicious. And the wine? Totally above my pay grade! It was a wonderful meal eaten in a very homely place. The whole experience seemed to be bringing us all back to some sort of relaxed equilibrium after the extraordinary lives we had been leading. The lively conversation was actually about real things, important and unimportant - it didn't matter and it was fun and seemed to go on for ever. The price of oil. Avocado pears from the supermarket. Nail parlours to the new fashions in the design of mens shirts. This was reality and it was all over far too soon.

At three-thirty the meal ended and Elizabeth guided us out to Dad's den for our much-heralded meeting. Inside were some very comfortable chairs which had been placed around a small table. Boating pictures adorned the walls and, again, I was very aware of that sense of permanence. Elizabeth, somewhat dauntingly, was now carrying a pad and pen, all held together in a smart leather holder. I realised she had been carefully preparing for this moment. The message was indeed very clear. We did not take long to seat ourselves down and then instinctively looked at her to set the ball rolling, which she did in no uncertain fashion!

"Dave, this is your meeting. You're the boss. I'll be taking any necessary notes."

Jonny and Piet were immediately both convulsed. Near to collapse, shaking and trying to hold back what might have been very inappropriate outbursts of hysterical laughter! Talk about me being shoe-horned into a situation! I mentally filed away an anecdote that I was sure her father would appreciate. Thankfully, knowing her as well as I now did, I had half suspected something like this might be dropped into my lap at short notice and had managed to jot down a few details myself last night. Gone was the idea of the friendly chat I hoped it might be! And, to be fair to Elizabeth, we did have an awful lot to sort out. Everything administratively was in a state of flux and the future for us all was, to put it mildly, unclear. I slid a very small notebook from my shirt pocket, eyed my single word notes, and really had no choice other than to go straight in to battle.

"Right. Thank you so much, Elizabeth. Order everybody." Almost immediately they ceased choking and paid me some sort of attention.

"Item one. Krugerrands. The happy news is that we now have three hundred and thirty-nine. It would have been a more rounded figure but Elizabeth stole one!"

"No, half that!" Elizabeth was adamant. She had counted!

"Ah, this is the great surprise. Didn't tell you both but Piet, following through on his very appropriate scepticism, hid a second box file under the passenger seat of my car. Those thugs never gave a minute's thought about looking down there! Why would they? So, we are quite a bit better off than we thought. Still relative peanuts of course compared with the massive value that has been lost."

I watched Elizabeth closely. She was upset. She seemed to be struggling coming to terms with the news rather than rejoicing at it. I thought of Edward and what might have passed between them and then of my occasional mild suspicions about her reticence to run with the money. I carried on regardless.

"I suggest one hundred for Piet, who started this whole thing, and eighty each for the rest of us."

That was instantly unanimously agreed and Elizabeth very quietly muttered that she would arrange to put the correct quantities into boxes for each of us.

"Something up Elizabeth?" Piet had noticed her lack of enthusiasm. "Sorry it isn't more?"

"No Piet. Just really worried that one day we will be sought out by one authority or another looking for stolen money."

I carried on, assiduously following my notes.

"Now, how to exchange a krugerrand for cash. I am sure this will be a major priority with us all, so I have put together some considered guidance. Disagree if you have a better idea. No more than one a month to be cashed each time by a different dealer, bank or whoever handles these products. Ascertain details first and keep each other informed. We must in no way draw attention to ourselves. If you wish to exceed that amount, tell everybody in this room and visit several different exchanges."

I waited and looked around for any disagreement. There was none.

"I shall leave mine in a safe deposit box in this country and cash in a bit each time when I'm over. I do not want to be done over by some enthusiastic young customs official somewhere!" Piet had his solution already worked out.

"Item two. Boats. Elizabeth?" I very happily passed over the baton.

"Marianne is sold. We managed to get the same price that we gave for her. I already have an offer for Thor which is just above the price we paid in Bergen, which I have accepted. I hope you all agree with that. It was a premature sale but there is a really sizeable hole in our finances. Odin, we are in the process of buying on terms. Suggest we sell in May or June, probably at a considerably enhanced price. We then pay off the loan and share out any profit."

"Thanks Elizabeth. I think we are all happy with that?"

I looked around. Again, there was no dissent, simply murmurs of thanks.

"Good. I can now immediately repay about one half of everything everybody put in. The remainder will follow after Odin's sale." There were cheers for her all around and, I noticed with a quick glance, some relief. I moved quickly on.

"Item three. Security. I think we are home and dry on this important matter. Our adversaries have all departed the country or have totally gone to ground. And, anyway, they have no further financial reason to be interested in us."

That was about all I had to say and I hoped it covered most of the queries that may have been in anyone's mind. Elizabeth was still continuing to avoid having any eye contact with me.

Piet had something very much on his mind.

"I carried out a small investigation of my own and spent yesterday in the countryside checking on Lady Banforth. She has disappeared completely from the manor. I took the bull by the horns and went in saying I was an old friend. Their estate's manager was there and explained very guardedly that she had, for no apparent reason, disappeared. He didn't know why and seemed totally unfazed by her departure. The noble Lord was nowhere to be seen. My conclusion from all this, knowing what we knew, was that she had bolted rather quickly.

Just then there was a tap on the window. Edward opened the door. "I wonder if I could interrupt proceedings? I think I may have some information which could be of interest. And, probably more importantly, I was instructed to bring in tea and a cake that Mary has made for the occasion."

He lowered the large tray down on to the table. The huge Victoria sponge looked magnificent.

"Gosh am I glad I came!" Piet seemed to have a thing about sponge cakes as well as female ankles. I found myself musing about what other things he held in his repertoire.

Elizabeth found a fifth chair and made her father sit down with us. She was very obviously keen to hear what he had to say. An intrusion like this was not in his nature. Something was afoot.

He spoke slowly, almost as if from the bench.

"I think I have a bit of interesting information which may well affect you all and could possibly influence your meeting here. The early evening news, which I have just heard, tells of a man and a woman yesterday being stopped at the airport in Lusaka, the capital of Zambia. They were found to be carrying a huge number of krugerrands in their baggage."

"Mwa---poleni!! That has to be Haff and the Lady!" Piet had come alive. "They've been caught! Walked right into it."

Jonny, a word man at heart, looked quizzically at him, then couldn't resist despite the new situation.

"What's that word mean?"

"*Good day* in Chibemba. I only know a few Zambian words and that is one of them. Sorry all, just showing off. Maybe I---"

"Piet! I think we should let Daddy continue."

Elizabeth just knew there was something still had to come. She could read him better than anyone.

But then Edward started to tease her.

"Elizabeth you know I love to hear all these strange words in foreign languages. I spend much of my time these days-----"

"Daddy stop it!"

Only I noticed the wicked little smile as he looked across at me. It said lots of nice things in a nano-second.

"Ok, I'll continue. That's not the end of it for sure. No, not by any means. The next bit of information to come out is that two gentlemen were apprehended in Botswana at the airport on the same day and they were also loaded down with krugers."

This time Piet exploded. I could feel all his bottled-up pessimisms and indeed fear being expunged from his system.

"The two from the Mint! Oh my god they really are in *real* trouble!"

Edward smiled at us all. He had us well and truly hooked on his line.

"There is more. Very rapidly the South African authorities have laid claim to all of the loot. They indicated that they had been given some detail by the Scottish police and customs people in many countries had been alerted. The two parties concerned are likely to be extradited for trial in South Africa. The Mint has already claimed that the total amount of krugers found more or less equals the loss suffered by them so long ago. Apparently, their figures are a little obscure after so much time has elapsed. I could hardly believe my ears when I heard all this coming out of the television set."

"That briefcase must have set McBride and his masters alight. Justice is in the process of being done!" Jonny immediately bit his tongue, as it quickly came to him that he was in the presence of one of the leading lights on the subject.

Edward, mission accomplished, rose to go.

"Just thought you should know what is going on. I had a feeling that the information might be of use."

He walked out, smiling, and closed the door behind him.

SIXTY-ONE

We were stunned into a short-lived silence which was broken in hushed tones by Piet.

"Elias would be a happy man. We seem to have come through unscathed and better off. That would have been good enough for him. Organised crime has been seen to fail and his ideas have borne fruit. It's feels like magic."

Jonny, the deep thinker as always, was a little more inquisitive.

"What about Sir Jeremy and the small skinny man who you tell me gave you all coffee during your Bank visit? Where have they disappeared in all this? They have to be around somewhere. Are they back at work or in hiding?"

I thought I had some of the answers, having spent much of my daylight hours pondering the uphill and down dale sort of life we had experienced.

"Trumperton was not a Sir. I have checked everywhere and that is also confirmed from Elizabeth's researches. I think he was brought in to do a job, or it could just be that he was associated with their criminal organisation. There once was a Sir Jeremy Trumperton. He died forty-five years ago. They may well have looked for a powerful sounding name and pinched that one for the man's use. It certainly sounds the part and went together well with his groomed moustache, no nonsense manner, and that incredible way of speech."

"Well, how on earth did *he* get into the Bank?"

"I think, Piet, that the small man was probably a bank employee. Fairly low level and therefore not on the high take home salary of most of them in there. A guy who would welcome what, to him, would appear a substantial sum to carry out such a very unsavoury job. He probably arranged to "have a visitor in" for some specific requirement of his own. In comes Trumperton or whatever his real name is, takes over that small "office" which they then fit out for the occasion. It was a surprisingly tiny place if you remember. Probably a maintenance area or something like that. A person of his supposed stature would have occupied somewhere a little more up market would they not? I seem to recall that at the Bank entrance the small man was on the spot to receive us visitors for Sir Jeremy Trumperton, probably having previously briefed security that the man was coming in for a meeting with god knows who. An internal employee would have the trust of everybody in a place like that."

"Where is he now then? Back at his job?"

"My guess is that he would disappear the moment the news of his activities became public - if it ever did. He probably has been given quite a few thousand to add to his bank account. But he will certainly not now be reappearing in the Bank. Though, on second thoughts, will he? There is no obvious connection between him and the krugers - well, not yet, anyway. It does give credence to Piet's assertion of the presence of a woman with ankles being outside the Bank watching us!"

"I thought we were supposed to be having Mum's sponge cake!"

Elizabeth was ever the one to break something up when it was getting too speculative. She picked up a large knife, cut four huge slices and then set about pouring the tea.

"Now *that* really is a cake to die for!" Piet was in some sort of heaven and munching happily away. "My bachelor existence doesn't stretch to making something like this."

"Well you should learn. Are you aware that men are supposed to make the best chefs! You ought to get some lessons. She changed tack abruptly. "Funny that those four should end up in two different African countries?"

Elizabeth put down the teapot and sat back in her seat. "Surely they would not be resident there?"

Piet spoke with his mouth full. She had hit on his subject. He had been working things out.

"It seems obvious to me. All four of them must have been South Africa bound. They could drive or fly to Johannesburg from each of those two countries, or, if they were worried about being caught when using normal communication routes, there are ways through the bush which no customs officer would ever be able to check out. Imagine the scenario if they had not been caught out. The two Mint employees would return to their jobs. Their official mission in the UK to seek out the loot had failed but their work at home continues as normal and they are free to cash in a krugerrand each at varied intervals of time as we ourselves have discussed. As for Lady Banforth and Haff, well his base is in South Africa and she is part of his team. Settle her down there, return to what his briefcase revealed as his HQ in Geneva, and each of them can cash one in every so often for the rest of their lives. Lord Banforth's man could not have been less interested in her disappearance when I saw him, no doubt reflecting his master's feelings. That also closely aligns itself with what I learned in the local pub. She did not fit into that community. That leaves only one missing person. The third guy who held you two imprisoned in the East End. What about him?"

This dragged to the fore recent memories which were burned in to the depths of Elizabeth's mind and which I knew she would never forget.

"I heard him speak on the phone to Haff when we were shunted into their car that evening. There was definitely a South African accent. He probably has taken an uneventful plane trip back home and will be the only one who will not serve a prison sentence. And almost certainly he will not yet have been given share of the krugers! Now of course just a dream. How he must be cursing just everything!"

There was a pause while she collected her thoughts. Then out came what I had been dreading.

"I suppose everybody is happy with the krugers we have ourselves managed to hang on to. They are not really *ours* are they?"

Piet turned on her.

"Not ours? Most certainly they are. It was all planned that we should take risks, dangerous ones, to help to achieve the dreams of Elias. In a limited way that is what we have done!"

"But can you live with that situation Piet? I know I'm as bad an offender as anyone here. It is not truly *our* money, it really belongs to the South African Mint."

"Of course it is bloody well ours! Without our investigations there would be nothing. Those krugers would still be floating around aimlessly in that boat and nobody would have anything. And, ironically enough, that includes the South African Mint."

Piet was understandably getting all wound up. The mere possibility of losing the remaining tranche of plunder we still had was worrying the hell out of him. We had to nip this in the bud. My search for peace might not succeed but we had to try. I had been aware in recent times that all was not well with the way she saw things. Her worries about what we had achieved had to be resolved and her doubts put to rest. I was prepared to lose every single kruger if it settled her down. But my priorities now differed markedly from those of Jonny and Piet. We had to try another tack.

"Let's put it to Edward. Ask his advice. He is a complete outsider but knows quite a lot about what we have been up to. Indeed, he has been an extremely useful part of it. And his legal standing is second to none. That might be useful. What do you think Elizabeth? Could his views help and would it be politic to talk to him about the situation we find ourselves in?"

She thought long and hard. She had told her father about nearly all of the exploits undertaken over the past few weeks. Eventually she said quietly, "I think that would be great but I would only agree to it if Jonny and Piet accept the idea."

"Jonny agrees."

"Piet agrees, but wants to keep his hard-earned share whatever Edward comes up with."

That certainly did not take long. Elizabeth smiled, seemed to make some internal calculations of her own, and went out to fetch her father.

"Edward may well not want to get involved. You can hardly say we have been acting totally within the law ourselves. I hope we will not put him in an embarrassing situation." Piet looked concerned.

"I don't think so. He is a man who can well look after himself---" I stopped abruptly as Edward's figure appeared showing through the glazed part of the door. He arrived inside looking a little dishevelled and sat himself down. Elizabeth followed him in.

"Just doing things to the lawn borders outside. Sorry I'm a mess. You simply have to keep at it around this time of the year. Things are beginning to grow so damned fast! Now what can I do for you all?"

I kicked off.

"Edward, good of you to spare us the time. We need clarity on our position. We have---"

Edward broke in. I think I am aware of your positions regarding those krugerrands and I know Elizabeth is a little unhappy, not, I may add at being in possession of some of them, but at being found out at some time in the future. She thinks that would wreck her life, certainly for a lengthy period of time, and maybe permanently. As a man of the world I am not sure I see things in such stark terms. Are my thoughts going along the right track?"

"Absolutely bang on. You are instantly in the groove. Would you be willing to give us some sort of legal opinion?"

"Difficult, David. You see there are so many possible facets to this situation. Different countries have been involved at varying times. Different legal systems. Many people have been seeking the lost product - let us call it that, they are such down to earth words - over a long period. Some are already in prison. Some maybe going there soon. The whole thing, certainly as seen from the viewpoint of any legal enforcement body, is a nightmare. Just where would you begin to clarify exactly what had been going on in order to enable you to form any sort of legal opinion?"

I replied, in a way that I hoped would encourage him on. "They must be sure about those they have in custody now. Caught with their hands in the till."

"Exactly. Any movement from that point, and I am pretty sure there won't be one, will involve different jurisdictions and will lead nowhere because the Mint has just said it thinks it has recovered all its losses. Elizabeth and I spoke about this strictly as father and daughter, nothing legal involved. From every point of view, speaking as Father, the matter now has to be left well alone. Speaking as a man of the law I simply would not know where one would begin if someone suggested that somewhere in the world there could be more krugerrands. I really think you should consider your new found wealth to be the cost of recovering the Mint's gold and righting that wrong!"

He spoke eloquently and sensibly. Without the shadow of doubt the matter should be left to rest. Edward, for me anyway, had summed things up admirably. I could see Elizabeth unwinding a little and perhaps beginning to get over her worries about the future. She wanted to believe.

"Yes Daddy. I really do get the point. I think I agree that we should be thankful for what we have and make it work for something positive." She looked around at us all. "And I think that aspect still has to be worked on."

"I can certainly help out there. Great things to reveal." Jonny's face was deadpan.

Elizabeth was actually smiling. "Me too. I have ideas. But everything depends on how things move on from here."

Edward looked at his daughter and then towards me.

"Job done then! Have I your permission to return back to my simple weeding? I presume you will all want to get on with your meeting."

We thanked him profusely as he rose to go. A great man who was able to get to the core of a matter in words of succinct logic, understood by everyone. He rose, smiled at us all, and returned back outside to continue with his horticultural endeavours.

I did some quick thinking.

"I think we were on Item four. The next thing we have to discuss is where we go from here. I have no job. Piet, I think, has a few possibles lined up back in South Africa. Jonny has a part time arrangement with Global which comes to an end before long and Elizabeth removed herself from them to concentrate on what we were doing. So, as I see it, our lives are in a bit of a mess. Anyone want to talk about all this?"

Jonny was first. "I'm on to something very interesting but I need a day or two to clarify things so another get together would be useful."

"Me too. I have things back in Pretoria to which I have to reply. Basically, I've been offered a couple of jobs in the wine industry. I am not keen on either of them."

I thought this rather strange of Piet who was always very work conscious. Elizabeth clarified things a little.

"David, we three have been talking and we have a couple of moderately mad ideas. May I suggest we all meet again in Shepperton in, say, two days' time.

Early - say nine o'clock. There will be one subject on the agenda which will simply be "Where things go from here." And if the weather is at all good we can take out the boat later."

SIXTY-TWO

That night was a bad one for me. I simply could not sleep. And I could not fathom why. At one in the morning I pushed on the light and did what I rarely ever do - went out and made myself a cup of tea.

Something was wrong. It had to be. I would have to unravel things before I could get to sleep again. This sort of thing would happen in AandA times when Jonny and I were challenging the known limits of computer science. I would be aware that something was going astray. We were missing a part of the advanced marketing narrative.

I put a spoonful of sugar into the tea I had poured, sat on a hard chair and stared fixedly at the shiny table in front of me. Elizabeth was still unhappy, though less so after her father's soothing words but, surprisingly, I was sure it was not that which was bugging my sleep.

So, what was? It had to be something in the day's exchanges between us which had registered with me and made my mind metaphorically sit up and question. Before the get together things were as clear as a bell. Uncluttered by doubts. Right here and now that seemed to have changed but I really did not know why.

I sipped the tea. It was hot. I knew everything with Edward was pleasant and straight. We understood each other despite coming at life from different ends of the spectrum. There was nothing there to be even slightly concerned about. And very naturally Piet seemed to be looking forward to getting a return on his endeavours. His extraordinarily accurate and confrontational input all along had been critical to our final outcome. He was a reasonably happy man whose hang ups had finally been laid to rest. And Jonny - well he was just the same person I had known for years. Anything troubling him would be shared with me. No question. We had been real mates right from the beginning. There would never be misunderstandings there. We both would simply not allow it.

So, was *anything* wrong? Was I imagining a hornets nest where there wasn't one? I stirred the tea. The sugar was not getting through to me. Not that I really believed the old wives tale about the mental and physical strength it gives. Oh god, just why could I not sleep? There was always a reason. Think of other things and the penny will drop.

There was no heating on in my flat as that is how I prefer to sleep. But right now it was getting damned cold. Dressing gown from the back of my bedroom door. Then I sank back down into the only comfortable armchair in the place. If I was going to be miserable and stay awake it was better to do so comfortably. Thoughts turned to a whisky ginger. At this time of night? My dear mother would be horrified but I fixed it for myself nonetheless. As the libation touched my lips something clicked ever so gently at the base of my mind. Well I thought it did. I took another sip. Then a large gulp. In no time at all it was finished. My eyes closed, not to go to sleep but to luxuriate in the short afterglow of the alcohol. And short it was. My mind started to rewind some of Jonny's words that were seemingly moving upwards from my feet to my head. I sensed that the feeling was no longer confined exclusively to the brain. My whole body was trying to grab on to an idea which was moving around the flat like constantly flashing lightning. Unable to stop. Frantically calling out to me.

Calm down you idiot! Either get back to your warm bed or have another whisky, this time a neat one. I fixed the latter and sat down again. What on earth was it that Jonny had said? Something about that small guy in the Bank. *"What about the small skinny man who gave you all coffee?"* That was it. But what, just what, could possibly be getting to me about that? I swigged at the now much stronger drink and thought again. There was simply nothing there for me. The skinny man, the skinny man?? What about him? ---no, he was simply the conduit they had used to achieve their foul purpose. He had escorted us in to the bank and had laid on the coffee. Nothing else.

Then it hit me. *Skinny man had played no part in the subsequent robbery.* The theft from my car was carried out by the others but he was not one of them. *But he was not one of them!!* That meant *something*. It had to be significant. Before I finished off the drink, realisation quietly and very slowly dawned. If he was not present at the motorway services, and he wasn't, he would no doubt have remained in his job. He would still be there. Well, maybe. *A criminal like that in the heart of the Bank of England!* He could be carrying on all sorts of things right under their very noses. I came over all patriotic and then staggered back to bed, fell in and went quickly to sleep.

Job done!!

The following morning I leapt out as the alarm went off. Tired still, but alert, I washed, shaved, dressed and breakfasted in record time. I then put on my balaclava which I had not worn for years and positioned an eye patch last used in a stage play years ago. In a daft way I felt disguised.

Looking like something out of Treasure Island I took the tube to Threadneedle street. I had no idea what to expect there but was now a person with firm objectives. I needed to learn more about this man and somehow to warn the Bank of what had been, and maybe still was, active in their midst.

On arrival I decided to take the bull by the horns and marched straight in. The same all-round security that we had seen before was in operation. There was no skinny man to be seen anywhere.

"Good morning Sir. Just what can we do for you?" He was a large, tough character, not to be messed with.

"I would like to talk to the head of security please." My voice sounded rather pathetic in that large arena. Another man glided slowly towards the first. Backup!

"Sorry Sir. Do you have a pass?" He could see that I did not. "We are not permitted to let you through without some form of identification."

"No, I'm afraid I don't have one. But I *must* see him. It is a very important matter."

He smiled weakly. This one looked and was a real nutter. The two men closed in to escort me out of the Bank. Shut things down before they start.

"Sorry, but I'm staying right here and if you lay one hand on me I shall fight and shout. You would not want that would you? All these people around. And in the Bank of England of all places! You'll be well and truly written and pictured across every newspaper in the land by the time I've finished!"

I felt strong. My cause was just.

That unnerved the big fellow a bit. He looked around to ascertain how many people were within earshot.

"You can talk to me. I'm security."

"Are you the boss?"

"Well no, of course not."

"I must speak to the chief. It really is important!"

They say that fortune favours the brave. I now truly believe it. At that moment there was a stir in the background. Surrounding staff suddenly began to give off mildly servile vibes as a figure, whose car had pulled up outside, surprisingly used the public entrance to the Bank and was gestured hurriedly through. Occasional perusal of the business section of my daily newspaper enabled me to recognise the new Governor of the Bank of England! As he was passing me my strange dress caught his eye. You rarely, if ever, see that sort of dress in any bank let alone this one!

I seized the opportunity.

"Good morning Sir. May I please speak with you?" I ripped off the balaclava and eye shield in one movement.

The two security guards moved in. This time I was to be escorted out of the building - fast.

The Governor held up his hand.

"Not so fast. What do you want?"

His eyes sought some explanation. This sort of situation was as new to him as it was to me.

"Simply a word with you, Sir, but on a matter of considerable importance. I can be brief."

He stood for a couple of seconds studying the situation. Perhaps I was not the crazy man he had first seen. Then, decision made, he nodded towards me.

"Come through this way."

Big security man frisked me thoroughly and accompanied me very closely as I followed the boss. We passed through a small office in which were sat a couple of women engrossed in their computers and then entered another smaller room. It had only one occupant in it.

"Thank you, Jackson. You can go back to your duties now."

"Yessir."

My heavyweight guard departed with a grunt. The Governor turned to me.

"This is James Marchant. He controls everything around here. Just what did you want to tell me?" Marchant came over to join us.

"Well Sir, it's all about what I think is a massive breach of security in your Bank. Linked to the recent recovery by the South African Mint of its lost krugerrands."

The two men exchanged glances and Marchant ushered us both to a couple of seats. He pushed a button.

"Coffee for three right away please Sarah."

SIXTY-THREE

I was the first to arrive, for once even earlier than the skipper. The story I had to tell! We thought things were all over! They weren't then but they were now. No more worries. Elizabeth need wrestle with any of her doubts no more. She slipped into the boat just five minutes later. I gave her a huge hug and then launched into the spiel I had rehearsed all the way during the now familiar drive here.

"I've got a lot to tell you before anyone else comes. I'm sworn to secrecy - so you are the same. Is that ok?"

She looked at me as if I was mad.

"Yes, of course, if that's how you really want it. But you will have to be quick. Piet will be here any time soon. Is it *that* urgent?"

I smiled weakly. "Just listen and give me your deepest attention. When he arrives I will do an instant full stop."

"But I thought---"

I knew what she was going to say and quickly put my finger to my lips.

"Just between us for now. A lot to tell in a short time. I had an amazing day."

Elizabeth managed to continue looking thoughtfully engaged with me, but beneath the façade I reckoned she too had things to say. Thoughts buzzing around everywhere. Anyway, I pushed right ahead, confident that my story was paramount. Nothing could be more important at the moment. So I thought!

"I went back to the Bank yesterday to check on the skinny man. Remember, we hadn't accounted for him. By a massive stroke of good fortune, which I will explain at another time, I ran into the Governor of the Bank."

"The real top man?"

"Yes! He actually gave me the chance to speak privately with him. I told him some of the things that had taken place with us, and emphasised the role of Mr Skinny. He and one of his senior officials, in whose office we met, were instantly on springs. Well, wouldn't anybody in that position be leaping up and down at such a revelation! They straightway put out a security check and, you wouldn't believe it, found some other skulduggery actually in progress right there and then in that very same Sir Jeremy room!! Apparently Skinny plus someone else, having made their victim feel all was above board due to the hallowed place they were in, were in there talking some wealthy character right out of his money - he was to invest in something, lose it all, and, the Bank security people told me, this time the thin guy would depart altogether. The sums being discussed were definitely big enough to finance his early retirement to some distant sunny shore. Smithers - that is Skinny man's name - was arrested on the spot together with his new partner in crime. I didn't stay around long enough to discover his name as well."

Elizabeth's eyes were by now willing every word out of me and at the same time scanning the marina entrance gate for any sign of Piet's car. It did not take her long to understand the enormity of what I had been through. Her own priorities were shelved.

"What on earth did the Governor have to say to you after all that was over?"

"Massive thanks. I later was given a second coffee in style while explaining our krugerrand position to him and how we had come across this man. They already were fully aware of the find by the South African Mint and, without even being asked, told me that a full recovery of that theft made so long ago had been achieved and the Mint people were absolutely delighted! The Governor was extremely thankful for me lowering the boom on the Skinny operation and asked me to keep the whole story under wraps. I said I would and trusted he would reciprocate with us! There was no problem there. Of course, I did not mention that we had made a few bucks out of the situation."

"Piet's just arriving - right now!"

She smiled a greeting as he clambered aboard.

"Good morning. Hope I'm not late. Quite a bit of traffic."

My confidante smiled, managing to cover her frustration at his choice of arrival time.

"No Piet. Just right. You can help me do some breakfast! Your in-boat cooking skills have become top class after all the experience you have had and are now recognised fully on this boat for what they are."

He raised an eyebrow at me. How sincere was that! But then together they cooked up a scrambled egg breakfast for three.

"Jonny had to turn up at work but said he would join us later. He suggested we reverse things a bit. If we were to take out the boat now, he said he would be here by early afternoon. He reckoned there was no point in discussing things without him as he would probably have a few items of importance to throw in to our discussions."

Strangely, Elizabeth already had some inkling of this and had our trip all planned. There was a wonderful fresh feel to the weather with sun showing through as only it can on a beautiful English spring morning. As soon as breakfast had ended we motored out of the marina and turned into the slow river flow. Old Father Thames was truly living up to his name.

"We'll go as far as Hampton Court, have a quick look around, and then turn around. All being well we should arrive back here about lunch time."

Piet and I, to our great surprise, then found ourselves facing strong, disciplined tuition. No easy ride down the river which I had anticipated. We very soon became experts on handling the ropes and fenders and also on navigating the boat safely and correctly through several of those difficult Thames locks. By the time we had arrived at our destination, somewhat exhausted and needing a break, we found we had to turn the boat quickly around to get back in time for Jonny.

Several times during the trip I attempted in various ways to extract ideas from Elizabeth about how she felt today's get together would go, but she was not yet ready to pursue the matter. Piet, too, was saying nothing. I began to wonder if they, as well as I, had been up to something since we last met. There seemed to be a conspiracy of silence which I was at a loss to understand.

Surely enough, as we motored slowly back into Shepperton marina, there was Jonny offering us a helping hand with mooring the boat. Elizabeth cut engines as he came aboard. He moved to the chart table and somewhat unceremoniously lowered down a package. A twinkle in his eye indicated to us he thought he had done something brilliant!

"Sandwiches! I have a lot to discuss and don't want to be stuck preparing lunch for you blinking lot." We opened up the pack and took two each.

"Well we'd better get into things because we all seem to want to say a few words and we are already late." Elizabeth, good skipper that she is, first checked that we were safely tied up and then sat down, looked quickly around to ensure that she had our undivided attention, and started the ball rolling.

"I had a chat yesterday with Andy, the harbourmaster at Wick. He said the police had been unhappy about the status of the two South Africans and some very senior Scottish fraud officers were in close touch with Pretoria, particularly as they had unravelled some interesting information found in a briefcase left behind by someone. He told me that four people had now been arrested. It all ties up completely with what father was saying. Anyway, we know the detail now and I thanked Andy for all his help."

That's really good to know, Elizabeth. We are totally at peace with all authority in Scotland. There seem to be no rough edges remaining." Piet was back to being a happy man and he too wanted to get on with things. "Which leads us nicely in to the main purpose of our meeting here today I think."

He nodded knowingly at her.

"Yes, Piet, it does. This concerns the future. Our futures. Where we go from here on in." I only just detected a hidden, slow, stifled snigger, emanating from Jonny. "We three have talked at great length. The unanimous conclusion was that we very strongly want to form a company with you, Dave, at its head. Doing what we did the way we did it and maybe even employing some of the old staff who were thrown out of AandA. All we need is your agreement, Hercules, all the know-how you and Jonny have squirreled away, and of course an office. It is really a fairly simple thing to set up."

They were all looking earnestly at me trying to gauge the reaction. What they didn't know was that I had walked all over this ground and had found the idea wanting. I rose up, Nelson style but with two eyes and two arms, and paced the space. Then turned and faced them all.

"You must be bloody mad, all of you. Have you any idea what it costs to set up even a small company in London? Yes, we have money in krugers but we cannot cash in much of that for the foreseeable future, and anyway we all have expenses to deal with which have mounted while we have been playing pirates. Sorry, nice idea, but it simply cannot be done."

I sat down and fiercely chewed off a large part of my second sandwich.

"My turn to speak. And this is important to come out before Dave digs himself into a hole that's too big for him to emerge from." Jonny was very keen to be heard and it took me awhile to realise that what he was saying was linked to his recent endeavours.

"We three agree that we could commit say thirty each of our krugers to this project. We cannot pay in all at once as Dave pointed out but we could gradually exchange them and get the company off the ground in that way and -"

I interrupted rudely.

"Jonny. Office premises. Salaries. Auditors. Marketing. And staff! We have no clients. The whole idea is horrendous."

"- if you will let me continue. The reason I arrived late today was because I had a date with the Global directors. They want to talk about renewing the relationship with us. They've been moving that way for a couple of weeks but I held my peace in case nothing actually came of it. This morning I was summoned to a meeting where, to cut a long story short, I took it upon myself to say we would prefer to work *with* them rather than *for* them. They agreed and suggested therefore that they pass over a range of marketing investigations on a contract basis initially for three years to see how it worked. They really want us! I told you Eisenbauer had been fired. As far as I could make out all but one board member could not stand his overbearing pomposity."

They were all looking at me. Studying my posture. Reaction? Retreat? Apology even? I remained as poker-faced as I was able while he continued.

"It was more than that too. Eisenbauer could neither fully understand nor unravel the crunch part of our methods and seems totally to have failed to get into the loop. They have run into some pretty immediate problems." He looked innocently around at us all. "I agreed that you and I could be there first thing tomorrow morning to discuss!! Hope that was not overstepping the mark? Old chap?"

The other two applauded him with gusto. My momentary dose of what I thought was realism had been demolished. He had been brilliant. I had absolutely no reason to question anything he had done. It was exactly what was required to get us off the ground. Business is littered with the corpses of companies who started with insufficient backing. This offered an independent company with income from the start. I joined the applause and could not hold back a massive smile.

"I owe you a huge apology. Jonny, you've been superb. I can, of course, make it tomorrow."

A bottle of champagne and four glasses had miraculously appeared, pulled from the small fridge by Piet. We no sooner had toasted the new company when Elizabeth took centre stage. There was now to be no holding her back.

"Subject to our leader's approval I would like to assume the role of company secretary, in charge of human resources, and keeping the books, until we can afford a proper accountant. You, Dave, and Jonny can work as you did before - and Piet?"

She looked at him knowingly and I could now see they must have planned all this but had kept things quiet from me in case Jonny had failed to confirm that Global were still on side.

"I would like to remain as your man in Africa - the whole of it. Maybe with a visit to London every three months. A business trip but also to cash in some goodies. How does that work?"

"It sure does Piet. That would be really great!" I knew that Africa was at the fore of Global's expansion plans. "There is, however, the small item of share ownership in this new company. One quarter each."

"You're the boss. You should have much more." Jonny was coming on strong.

"Sorry Jonny, we're all in this together. We succeed or fail equally. My idea or nothing."

Elizabeth smoothed the moment.

"Right Dave, we all agree."

I nodded. "We had better start looking for some small office space *straight away*. We need a good address and *fast*."

"It could be on a boat."

For all of one second I wondered if Piet was in his right mind. Then dawned the realisation that they were laughing at me. The whole thing had been cooked up between them without my knowledge. I was the appointed leader and already I was being pushy!

"Well I thought I was supposed to be the bloody boss man. No, we definitely cannot work on a boat! From here on in boats for me exist for pleasure activities only, and not too much of the fenders and ropes either!"

Inevitably it was Elizabeth who led the meeting's final quarter. She stood erect and looked around. I wondered what on earth could be coming now.

"A couple of things. I have been unhappy about Odin."

"What now, Elizabeth?" Piet had thought that finally everything was all sorted.

"Well---Lars has lost his boat through no fault of his own. He was insured but not for that kind of vandalism and could not himself afford the massive cost of putting it right. Hence the sale of the boat."

Jonny cottoned on immediately.

"You'd like us to give it back."

"Well, er, yes." She looked awkwardly at Piet.

"Actually, I quite agree with you. I reckon you must have been talking to the lady of the fjords." His response surprised us all. "We could afford to tell him part of the story, give him back the boat, and pay off the loan by changing one kruger into cash every so often. I have actually agonised on this one a bit too, believe it or not."

"I could arrange everything if you all agree?"

She looked around hopefully.

"We are taking a chance. He could claim the whole---" I stopped quickly. "Sorry, that's nonsense, everything which it sought has been recovered by the Mint! I agree, we give back Odin to her owner."

"With some sort of explanation to Mrs Eriksson." It wasn't a question from Elizabeth.

"Well, since we are on the subject of getting things fully settled, I intend giving something reasonably substantial to Elias's brother who, at my request, has been tracked down by my sister. He is now back in South Africa."

"Central funding, not you personally! We have all benefited from what was accomplished by Elias. I'll see to it Piet. Let us talk together afterwards."

"Thanks, Elizabeth, very grateful."

I felt it was time to call a halt. We had to prepare for tomorrow.

"Well, all resolved. Things couldn't have turned out---"

Elizabeth cut very sharply right across me and beckoned to Jonny to refill our glasses. What on earth else was there to go into now? To my mind we had resolved everything. Preparing for tomorrow at Global was all that remained to be done.

"There is just one more item I think should be brought to everyone's notice. I would like you all to know that Dave and I are getting married - father recently told me - and for our honeymoon we are going up to the Norwegian fjords on a cruise ship which calls in at Flaam. There I will be giving one of my krugers, made up into a medallion necklace, to a certain Mrs Ericsson. That is, of course, unless my future husband disagrees."

-*-

ACKNOWLEDGEMENTS

I had help. My thanks go to:

My wife Rosemary who helped with everything.
Mandy Lovell who read, re-read and found
improvements.
Simon Garland who worked on format.
Nick Smith, my grandson, who designed the cover.
Saskia Osterloff and all at New Generation Publishing.

ABOUT THE AUTHOR

Donald Smith resides in Caterham, Surrey. He has two children and four grandchildren. He worked for six years in Southern Africa and has spent time in many parts of Europe.
Main hobby – floating his boat!

He has written two books:
Rhodesia the Problem
The Coming of the Rains